Remains to be Seen

a Groverton Hauntings novel

Also by the author

Groverton Hauntings
Weekends Can Be Murder
Remains To Be Seen

Sic Transit Stragon
The Stragori Deception

The Nash'terel
The Earthborn
The Bloodstone

Adventures in Godhood
Imaginary Friends
The Many-Storied Man (forthcoming)

Remains to be Seen

ARLENE F. MARKS

Milton, Ontario

First edition, July 2025
Published by Brain Lag
Milton, Ontario
https://www.brain-lag.com/

ISBN: 978-1-998795-24-6 (softcover)
ISBN: 978-1-998795-25-3 (ebook)

Cover design by Catherine Fitzsimmons

Library and Archives Canada Cataloguing in Publication

Title: Remains to be seen / Arlene F. Marks.
Names: Marks, Arlene F., 1947- author.
Identifiers: Canadiana (print) 20250178923 | Canadiana (ebook) 20250185040 | ISBN 9781998795246
  (softcover) | ISBN 9781998795253 (EPUB)
Subjects: LCGFT: Detective and mystery fiction. | LCGFT: Novels.
Classification: LCC PS8561.R2868 R46 2025 | DDC C813/.54—dc23

Content warnings: Death, sexual assault (referenced)

This book is dedicated, with affection, to anyone who can see themselves in its pages.

One

S ara Traynor's kitchen was spacious and sunlit. Generously equipped with storage cabinets and decorated in cheery yellows and airy greens, it reminded Selena Watt of the home where she'd grown up, on her parents' dairy farm, and she said so.

Sara set a brown ceramic teapot down on a trivet in the middle of the square wooden table. "Believe it or not, until I inherited this place seven years ago, the kitchen was in the basement, and this used to be two bedrooms and a sitting room. The original structure was built more than a century ago, by my great-great-grandfather. You saw the plaque beside the front door?"

Selena nodded yes.

"We've managed to keep it in the family," Sara continued, "and my name is on the deed, but because it's been designated as a heritage property, any major renovation plans have to be approved by the Groverton Historical Society." Lowering herself onto the seat across the table from Selena, she added, "It took us nearly as long to get the permits for moving and modernizing the kitchen as it did for the contractor's crew to complete the actual work. The place was a godawful mess for two solid months."

Selena gazed around the room again, trying to visualize what Sara had described. They would have had to knock down walls, upgrade and redirect the plumbing and wiring, possibly even relocate that broad, double-paned window to centre it over the stainless steel sink.

"Wow," she murmured. "All that done in only two months? I'm impressed."

"Well, as they say, many hands make the work go faster." Sara paused to fill both their glass mugs with orange ginger tea, then went on, "And I suspect it also helped that the Society sent someone out to monitor and record everything for their archives."

"Is that standard procedure?"

"For *our* Society? Oh, yes." She nudged a plate of homemade oatmeal cookies invitingly in Selena's direction. "They're very diligent about preserving local history. But enough about them. You said on the phone that you're looking for real estate here in town. Are you thinking of moving to Groverton?"

Peering at her hostess over the rim of her mug, Selena swallowed a mouthful of the fragrant herbal tea, then declared, "I am. Standerville is a nice little community, but it's never going to be more than that. If Watt's Greatest Travel and Leisure is to grow, it needs to be in a larger, busier town. Groverton is perfect for me. It's already a hub of tourism activity, with three different chain hotels and two major resorts in the area. There's also new housing development going on, which means the pool of potential clients is increasing. And it doesn't hurt that I've got friends here," she added with a grin. "So, I've been browsing the local listings online. Some of them look promising, but there's one in particular that may be just what I need. I have an appointment with a realtor this afternoon to view it in person. Wish me luck."

The realtor had texted Selena an address where they were to meet up, but it wasn't the location of the place she'd specifically asked to see. That was her first clue that something had gone awry. The second clue was that the tall, dark-haired woman who stood waiting for her on the sidewalk in front of the house was not the agent Selena had spoken with at the realtor's office the previous day.

The woman had evidently parked on the street, leaving the driveway empty. Opting for caution, Selena did the same. She drove past the house and pulled up at the curb two doors away. There was probably a very reasonable explanation for this unexpected change of plans. Nonetheless, it didn't feel right, and if the murder mystery weekend at Rafferty House the previous summer had taught Selena anything, it was to heed her instincts.

The walk from her car gave her a chance to size up this stranger. She was dressed all in green, right down to her shoes—a polished mannequin in a tailored pantsuit, with salon-sculpted hair, a picture-ready makeup job, and an imperious tilt to her head. The woman wore a smile that had probably been applied along with her lipstick. It was a perfect match for the coolly appraising stare that Selena could practically feel against her skin as her legs continued closing the distance between them.

Alarm bells now jangling like mad at the back of her brain, Selena halted an arm's length away and said in a higher-pitched voice than she intended, "I thought I was meeting Brenda."

"I thought you were too. I'm afraid Brenda has been… called away unexpectedly. Normally, we would simply have rescheduled your appointment for another day, but since you've come from out of town, I felt it was important not to waste any of your time. So, I'm filling in for her instead. I'm Tricia Vickery."

Selena recognized that name. She'd seen it displayed on a wall plaque in the reception area of Hearth and Home Realty. So, Brenda's boss was taking over this showing? Judging from the sharpness of her tone, she was no happier about the situation than Selena was.

Ah, well… Nodding stiffly in acknowledgement, Selena accepted the business card Vickery held out to her.

"Brenda was going to take me inside the house at Beech and Webber. She called it 'the castle'. Is it still available?"

Vickery frowned as though deliberating how best to deliver bad news. Selena braced herself to hear it. Then, to her surprise, the other woman replied, "It is, and we will be going there eventually. First, however, I've read Brenda's notes and selected two other properties that you might find suitable for your needs. To give you a basis for comparison, if nothing else."

"I gather this is one of them?" Selena gestured in the direction of the two-storey brick house beside them.

Vickery unzipped her skinny leather briefcase, pulled out an information sheet, and thrust it into Selena's hand. "The asking price is a little higher than the range you indicated, but as you can see, it has nearly everything you want, and it's been on the market long enough that the seller might accept a reduced offer."

Scanning the document, Selena knew without taking a step inside the building that this one would not do. "Nearly everything" wasn't good enough. The location was wrong, it was a single family dwelling instead of a duplex, and even if the purchase price ended up within her means, the cost of converting the top floor into a separate apartment and putting in the necessary upgrades—not to mention the rent she would have to pay on another place while the work was being done—would simply boost it beyond her reach again.

"I don't think so," Selena said. She tried to return the sheet, but Vickery wouldn't take it.

"Well, how about just going inside for a look around?" she coaxed, curving her lips into a practised smile. "Who knows? Maybe it will spark some decorating ideas."

Selena gave a mental shrug. Sure, why not? Vickery wouldn't want to waste her own time either after going to the trouble of setting up this showing, and it wasn't as if her client had somewhere else to rush off to.

Fifteen minutes later, Selena had seen nothing that could change her mind about this place. The tile work in the bathroom was pretty, but not worth diving into debt over.

The second house on their itinerary was only marginally better. It did have two separate apartments, but one was in the basement, where Selena refused to either live or work, and it wasn't walking distance to anything but a convenience store and a public elementary school.

Strike two.

Vickery's smile dimmed noticeably as she handed Selena the third information sheet.

At last. The castle.

"This one has everything on your wish list and is in the middle of your preferred price range."

Well, of course it was, Selena thought with some asperity. It was perfect. That was why she'd selected it to view in the first place. Still, the way Vickery's features were puckering gave her pause.

"But there's a reason the asking price is so low?"

Vickery drew a deep breath before replying. "The house has a history."

"From what I've heard, half the buildings in Groverton have a history," Selena countered. "I know it's not a heritage property, not yet, anyway." Not that it would have made a difference to her plans if it were. The interior had already been renovated, and she really liked what she'd seen of it in the photos on Brenda's computer screen.

"It's on the Historical Society's monitoring list, but it has… shall we say, certain worrisome features…?"

This woman's evasiveness was trying Selena's patience. "Features? Like what? A moat?" Then, as a more practical concern occurred to her, "Or is it something to do with the construction? A problem with the foundation, maybe?"

"No. The building has been thoroughly inspected and determined to be sound. But there is talk—just rumours, really, nothing that can be proven… Never mind," she decided, drawing herself up to her full height and giving off the air of a gladiator about to enter the arena. "We can discuss them later. You want to see the house, Ms. Watt? Follow me there."

The building nicknamed "the castle" occupied a large corner lot, one block away from both cross-streets of a major intersection. As Selena made the turn from Beech onto Webber and brought her car to a stop at the foot of the driveway, her jaw dropped.

The exterior photo on the realtor's web site did not do this place justice.

Stretching nearly the full width of the property and with hardly any front or back yard to speak of, the house looked for all the world like a red brick castle surrounded by a grassy green moat. A shaded veranda hugged the front and sides of the building, but instead of the standard gingerbread trim hanging down beneath the eaves, a shallow, crenellated barrier poked upward along the edges of the roof, creating the appearance of battlements.

"It really is a castle, isn't it?" Selena murmured wonderingly.

"Built by someone who felt he belonged in one," Vickery muttered in reply. She pulled a key out of her pocket. "Shall we go inside?" *...and get this over with?* said the tone of her voice.

"Sure."

The second Selena stepped onto the veranda, a strange tingling started up inside her. It resonated in her core, as if her internal organs were humming in harmony, then broadcasting the music to every other part of her body. For a moment, her nerves danced maddeningly to the tune. Then the sensation ceased, leaving a ghostly impression of longing and sadness clinging to her thoughts, emotions without memory that settled over her mind like a web of spider's silk.

If the sentience of Rafferty House hadn't taught her better, she might have thought she was imagining things... but she knew deep down that she wasn't. Selena Watt and this century-old building with the modernized interior were somehow on the same mysterious wavelength, just as Larry Holmes and Rafferty House had been nearly a year earlier, and what she had just experienced felt disturbingly like a cry for help.

Show me, she thought-called to the house.

There was no response.

Unsure whether to be relieved or disappointed, Selena tossed a final glance around the veranda and followed Vickery through the front door.

The images on Brenda's computer had clearly been recorded earlier, while the house was still being lived in. Now it was unfurnished and the windows were bare, letting in splashes of late afternoon sunshine upstairs and down. Selena strolled from one large, empty room to another, hearing the slight echo of her footsteps and noticing the workmanship evident in what had been left behind. There was much to admire about this place: polished hardwood floors, pristine walls, crown mouldings, marble countertops, artfully wrought chandeliers that collected the light and scattered shards of it in every direction...

When the two women met up again in the foyer, Selena remarked, "This is impressive." She nearly added, *I shouldn't even be able to afford it,* but stopped herself in time.

"Everything is new and upgraded," Vickery told her. "The current owner went all in on the renovations. Then he went away, instructing me to sell the property for whatever I could get for it. It's been vacant for about three months now."

"You're saying he bought it to flip it?"

Vickery frowned. "That wasn't the impression I got when we were finalizing his purchase of it a couple of years ago. It sounded as though he planned to live upstairs and host social events on the main level."

...which would explain the presence of two full kitchens, one per floor.

"So, what happened to make him change his mind?"

"No idea. His wife may have had something to do with it, though. Prue Davidson. Apparently, she's a well-known interior decorator in the Toronto area, although I must confess, I'd never heard of her before her husband bought the property. She stayed down there while he pretty much lived in town, clearing up some legalities and overseeing the renovations. When they were done, she came up to add the finishing touches. She was seen talking to some of our local artisans and home furnishing suppliers, giving the impression that she planned to turn part of the house into a showroom for their wares. However, a couple of weeks later, Mr. Davidson told me that she'd gone down to the city and wouldn't be coming back, and that I should put the house on the market again. A day or two after that, he'd left as well."

For Selena, this had a very familiar ring. Arthur Pyke's plans to turn Rafferty House into a dinner theatre venue had also been thwarted. And something Larry had said back then rose unbidden to the surface of her memory: *"Maybe the house is haunted. Or maybe any house with a history like this one's is going to behave the same way and we just don't realize it because there aren't that many of them around."*

"You said the house had a history…?"

Vickery's frown deepened into a scowl. "It's just rumour," she replied. "Some people believe that there may have been a murder committed on the property."

"Recently?"

"Heavens, no! But when a string of new owners keep customizing a house, moving into it, and then walking away from it with no warning and for no apparent reason, people like to speculate. Some of them have very active imaginations, and their stories have spread. So, Loch Ness may contain a monster, and the old McFadyen residence might be haunted. There, I've disclosed it, even though it's nothing but idle gossip," she said disgustedly.

"Well, I happen to like ghost stories," Selena informed her with a grin. "I also like everything else about this place, and I want to put in an offer, conditional on the sale of my current dwelling, a home inspection, of course, and the arrangement of financing. How soon can you have the paperwork ready?"

Vickery stared at her, surprise written all over her polished mannequin features. "You're certain? There are several more properties I was planning to show you—"

"That's not necessary," Selena assured her. "I've got a feeling about this house. I think I belong here."

There were four adults at Sara's dinner table that evening: Sara, her brother Larry Holmes, Selena, and a short, rather quiet man who kept nervously adjusting his eyeglasses, whom Sara introduced as her friend, Curt Wakefield. Sara's two boys had already eaten and were playing a video game in the rec room (formerly the kitchen, Selena recalled) downstairs. Apparently, teachers didn't assign homework this late in June.

"You're all guinea pigs tonight," Sara announced, setting a steaming hot baking dish down on a placemat in the middle of the table. "I found a recipe online and decided to try it out. No promises, and if it's a dud, we can always finish off the pizza that's in the fridge."

"Well, I'm sure it'll be terrific, whether it's edible or not," Larry assured her.

Selena shot him a look. Unless the smoke inhalation had destroyed his sense of smell, he had to know how rich and tantalizing the aroma was that wafted off their main course.

"It's moussaka," Sara told him in a *so there!* voice, "and I've made a Greek salad to go with it."

As she busied herself removing the clear wrap from the salad bowl, Curt cleared his throat, pushed his glasses back up the bridge of his nose, and ventured with a tentative smile, "Since there seems to be a theme to this meal, may I ask if there's ambrosia to wash it down?"

Sara laughed. "The wine of the gods? 'Fraid not," she carolled back to him, "but I did pick up a bottle of retsina from the LCBO. I've never had it myself, but the clerk described it as dry and a little spicy, so I guess we'll be finding out whether we like it. It's chilling in the fridge. Larry, if you wouldn't mind doing the honours...?"

"Sure," he replied, rising from his chair. "I'll be your sommelier for the evening."

Soon, all four of their goblets were charged with the golden-coloured wine.

"Sara's obviously done some research on this, so what's the Greek word for 'cheers', little sis?" Larry asked.

Her cheeks dimpled. "You know me so well, big brother. It's *yamas.*"

"*Yamas!*" he repeated loudly, raising his glass in a toast, and together, the others followed suit.

The moussaka and salad were both delicious. Evidently, Selena wasn't alone in thinking that—for several minutes, everyone ate in silence. However, she couldn't help noticing what was happening to Curt. Each additional sip of wine that he swallowed seemed to peel another layer of tension away from him, mellowing both his voice and his facial expression. By the time his glass was empty, he was leaning back in his chair, grinning and nodding as the conversation flowed around him.

Selena had also noticed the way Sara looked at him, and how quickly she blushed and looked away each time he met her gaze. Perhaps now was the time to ask the question that had immediately arisen in Selena's mind.

"So, Curt, how did you and Sara meet up?" she inquired brightly.

"We did some research together," came his reply. "For the past three years I've been the curator-slash-manager of the Groverton Historical Museum. Shortly after I got here, I went to the library to find out more about the train wreck of 1933, and Sara was the first person on staff who welcomed me and offered to help. After that, I looked for her whenever new artifacts arrived and I needed information about them for the catalogue. She's quite the history buff, as it turns out."

Actually, Selena suspected her friend was more of a Curt buff. And she had to admit, when he was loosened up like this, he was rather attractive. She could see what Sara saw in him—the sparkle of good humour in his blue eyes, the lock of sandy brown hair that fell so appealingly over his forehead…

Selena glanced automatically at Larry. *Oops!* He'd apparently noticed the byplay as well, and now his features were darkening. Best to change the subject before Sara's protective older brother could ask any follow-up questions.

"Speaking of history," Selena cut in, "I promised to tell you how my appointment with the realtor turned out."

Seated across from her, Sara leaned closer, grinning in anticipation. "And…?" she prompted.

"I'm putting in an offer on a house. It begged me to buy it, so that's what I'm doing."

"That's wonderful! Is it far from here? Where is it?"

"At the corner of Beech and Webber Streets. I'm buying the castle."

Sara's smile wilted. "No! Tell me you're joking."

"Listen, I know what I'm getting into—"

"No, you don't! Curt, tell her!"

"Yes, Sara," she countered patiently, "I do. Larry, tell her."

Larry's eyes widened with belated comprehension. "You meant that literally? The house spoke to you?"

"Not in words, but yes, it sent me a message. Just like when Rafferty House communicated with you. You were right about old houses with similar histories."

"That house on the island communicated with you? You never told me that," Sara said, giving her brother a reproving look.

He let out a sigh. "Because I knew you'd never believe me. You would dismiss it as a false memory, or as delirium resulting from not enough oxygen getting to my brain during the fire. And so would everyone else. But if we have a sentient house right here in Groverton—!"

"Not so fast, Mr. Fire Inspector," Sara scolded him. "First I want to know all about Rafferty House. Then Curt and I will tell you what we found out about the McFadyen place. Then Selena can decide whether she really wants to go through with this purchase. You haven't actually signed anything, have you?" she added, speaking rapidly to Selena.

"No. Vickery wants me to come into her office tomorrow so we can present the offer."

"Oh, good," said Sara. "You can still change your mind.

Now, talk to us, Larry."

"Okay, but there's not that much to tell," he replied, frowning. "The house had been in the Pyke family for generations, as a summer home. Then the family stopped going there. It sat vacant and neglected for about forty years, until Arthur Pyke inherited it and decided to restore it and turn it into a resort hotel."

"To prostitute it, you mean," Selena corrected him sharply. "And the poor thing must have hated the very idea of it. Rafferty House was aware of everything that went on inside it and was able to react to it. Don't forget that it saved your life, Larry."

"Technically that's not true," he countered. "Other humans were the ones who pulled me out of that fire. *They* saved my life."

"Well, I'm sure the house did everything it could to keep you alive until they were able to rescue you," said Selena, her chin rising. "Even Sergeant Brassard had to concede that you had a special connection with it, and she was a dyed-in-the-wool skeptic."

"Okay, I'll grant you that much. It did feel all along as if the house and I were in mental communication somehow."

"Wow," Sara murmured when they were done. "You're going to be a hard act to follow, but here goes: according to public and archival records, Hugh McFadyen arrived in Groverton in 1924 with bagfuls of American money. Where he'd come from and how he'd made his fortune, nobody knew for sure, although the local newspaper floated the theory that it might have been ill-gotten gains from smuggling liquor into the U.S. Whether that was true or not, McFadyen never denied the story. What he did was spread his largesse around. He supported local charities, invested in businesses that boosted the town's economy, sponsored cultural events… and the rumours eventually died down. Over the next few years, he became quite wealthy and influential."

And believed he belonged in a castle. Selena nodded to herself, finally understanding the ironical tone of Vickery's comment earlier that day.

"He had the home constructed in 1927, on what later became Beech Street," Curt said, picking up the narrative. "In late 1932, McFadyen returned from an extended business trip, bringing with him his new wife, Gertrude, and her live-in nurse, Lillian Friendly. Gertrude was said to be in delicate health due to a childhood illness, and so she hardly ever went outside. Her nurse was constantly with her, which explains why there are so few photographs of these women in the archives."

"It didn't help that Gertrude came down with influenza the very next day after her arrival here," said Sara. "A doctor was summoned. He ordered the house quarantined, and McFadyen was forced to lay off all his inside help until such time as the quarantine could be lifted. In her already-weakened state, it took months for Gertrude to make a full recovery, but she finally did, and she was given medical permission to travel. Evidently, that was what she and Hugh were about to do when a train jumped the tracks as it was pulling into Groverton Station on March 3rd, 1933. The derailed train demolished the boarding platform, killing nearly everyone on it, including both McFadyens."

"That's nice, but—"

"Surprisingly, Lillian wasn't with them at the time," she continued, talking over the rest of Larry's objection. Once Sara warmed to a subject, she was uninterruptible. "Perhaps she'd left on her own well-earned vacation. Or maybe she'd gone ahead of them and they were supposed to meet up later. Either way, there's no record of her ever returning here. Not that she would have had a reason to, of course, with Hugh and Gertrude dead."

"Which is all very interesting, I'm sure," Larry said impatiently, "but I thought you were telling Selena about the house...?"

"The house," Curt cut in. "McFadyen died without a will, so the town took ownership of the property. It sat vacant for almost a year while the council argued over what to do with it. Eventually, they came to an agreement. They were going to repurpose the building as a boarding house, hire people as live-in staff, and rent out the rest of the rooms to transient workers—but there was a problem. They couldn't keep a cook or building superintendent longer than a couple of days. People started saying that the place was haunted. Even after all their claims were disproven, they stuck to their stories."

"Which were...?" said Selena.

"That they'd experienced sudden random drops in air temperature, shadows that mysteriously appeared and disappeared, with no visible source... mainly, though, it was the sensation that they were not alone, that some invisible presence was in the building with them, making them feel deeply anxious, even depressed."

"At last, it was decided to knock the house down altogether and build something else on the site," said Sara. "A contractor was selected, plans and permits were filed, and everything was set for demolition."

"But...?" Selena prompted her.

"The contractor backed out. He let it be known that God had spoken to him, and God did not want that building destroyed. Well, this being a God-fearing town, his pronouncement apparently discouraged all the other contractors in the area from taking on the job. Tenders were put out, but no one would bid on them. The building sat for years. Eventually, the council was contacted by a wealthy gentleman in Toronto—obviously an atheist—who had heard about this 'haunted house' and offered to take it off their hands. The sale was finalized in 1949. Since then, the property has changed hands more times than anyone cares to count. The buyer moves in, lasts at most six months, and then packs up and leaves after putting it back on the market."

Selena met Larry's inquiring gaze. "Rafferty House was cursed," she mused. "Maybe the castle is too."

Sara uttered an exasperated syllable. "Maybe it *is* cursed. Or maybe it's haunted, or even alive. Or—who knows?— maybe it's all three. But for certain it's like a black hole swallowing up people's time and money, and that's not what I would wish for anyone, especially not a friend. Selena, *please* don't do this! I just know you're going to regret it."

Putting on her most patient smile, Selena reached across the table and took her hand. "When I was at Rafferty House with Larry, I could sense an emotion that pervaded the air inside that building. It was sadness. I felt exactly the same thing when I was standing on the castle's front porch. And what you said about all the times it's been abandoned…? That's a reason for *any* living thing to feel depressed. Maybe I can help it. Maybe I can't—but I won't know that until I try."

"But—"

"Listen, I'm not a first-time buyer, and this is not an overnight process. It could take days for the offer to be accepted, and weeks on top of that to meet its conditions. At a minimum, I'll need to find a buyer for my current property, arrange for financing for the new one, and have a thorough home inspection done. So, at any time during that period—"

"I can help you," Curt blurted out. "With the inspection. I can tell you whether the place is haunted."

Three pairs of eyes now turned to stare curiously into his face.

Clearing his throat and shifting uncomfortably on his chair, he went on, "There's a reason I've taken an interest in the

story of Gertrude McFadyen and her husband. I've met her—
or rather, her ghost—at the museum. It's housed in what
used to be the Groverton train station. Apparently, she's been
haunting it since the derailment in 1933… and she's madder
than hell."

Two

As he drove home that evening, Curt was plagued by uncertainty. He hadn't planned on outing himself like that, between courses of a Greek-themed meal with Sara and her brother and their friend. But the way they were talking had made him believe that they would understand. That it would be safe. Now he wasn't sure anymore. The conversation over dessert had been awkward, punctuated by uneasy silences. Had he made a huge mistake? Had the retsina clouded his judgment, causing him to drop his guard?

Did that mean he was impaired? Should he even be behind the wheel of his car right now?

Too late—he was nearly at his house.

But perhaps it would be best if he left the vehicle out in the driveway rather than trying to manoeuvre it into the garage.

Normally, a glass of wine at bedtime helped to calm his mind so he could sleep, but he doubted whether that trick would work for him tonight. He needed to talk to Ruth and Clara.

The museum was only a couple of blocks out of his way. Curt made the detour, steered into the parking lot, and pulled to a stop near the end of the building. He had no need to go inside—the people he was seeking could always be found on their bench, on what had formerly been the boarding platform.

It was his bench as well, for he'd earlier had it resurrected, incorporating all the parts of the original that still remained from the disaster—a former curator/manager had actually put them on display inside the building—into a faithful reproduction made of modern-day materials. This piece of furniture had been the finishing touch, replicating the train platform exactly as it had appeared just before the derailment. Turning it into an outdoors exhibit, in other words.

That was what he'd told the Historical Society to get them to approve the restoration. In fact, he'd had it done for himself, so that he could physically sit down with some of the ghosts who had been created on that terrible day and listen to their stories. He'd done the same with the ghosts he'd found inside the museum, attached to various items. Almost without exception, they were sad. They regretted the lives they'd led, or they had had unfinished business when they died. Curt had been doing his best to help them find peace. In his past three years as curator, he'd managed to "untether" half a dozen yearning spirits.

Ruth and Clara, however, were special. So were Len Paxton, the porter, and Orville Mead, the ticket seller. All four of them had had the misfortune of being on the platform when the train smashed into it. None of them had had regrets or unfinished business, however—they'd just had a deep love of trains and of being around the train station—and all of them had become his friends.

Curt had been seeing ghosts ever since he could remember, and what was more, the ones who'd realized they were dead had been able to see and communicate with him as well. For the most part, they'd been kind to him. He'd met some angry spirits too, of course, but even the ones who'd given him nightmares had never physically harmed him. It was always the living he'd had to fear, the ones who couldn't see what he saw and would surely judge him to be a freak, a fake, or mentally ill.

That was why he'd kept this side of himself a secret. When he was too young to realize how unusual his behaviour was, his parents had excused it—to themselves as well as to others—by saying that talking to imaginary friends was just a normal childhood phase, one that he would outgrow with time. Later on, if overheard, he would lie, saying that he'd been talking to himself.

Until now, no one had known the whole truth about him. Some had made guesses that were close to it. He'd managed to detour them away using logic. But now the genie was out of the bottle, so to speak, and Curt's mouth went dry at the thought of what the consequences might be.

As he rounded the corner of the building, Clara saw him first. She waved a cheerful hello and patted the seat beside her in invitation. Then she nudged Ruth to get her attention and pointed him out to her as he approached. Smiling, Ruth nodded and slid over so he could sit between them.

March had been a chilly month in 1933. Both women wore cloche hats and ankle-length overcoats, and Clara's hands were covered by soft leather gloves. He had no idea what colour any of these garments were. Ghosts appeared to him to be opaque and three-dimensional, but the image was always in shades of grey.

"It's a lovely day for train-watching," said Ruth's placid voice at the back of his mind.

Curt no longer looked to see whether a ghost's lips moved in sync with their words. They always did.

Never one to beat about the bush, Clara asked, *"And what has Mr. Wakefield been up to? Have you taken that young lady of yours for a romantic drive up the mountain yet? Or a picnic on the beach, under the stars?"*

"Neither, I'm afraid," he replied with a sigh.

Ruth half-turned to face him. Wagging a stern finger, she said, *"Don't you dare get cold feet about asking her out! I meant what I told you—you're a catch, Mister. You're smart and good-looking, and if I were thirty years younger I'd be setting my cap for you myself."*

Clara had been observing his face meanwhile. *"What's wrong, Curt?"* she said softly. *"Did she turn you down?"*

"No, but... I met a friend of hers this evening, and this lady is interested in buying the McFadyen place. You know that people think the house is haunted. Well, I'd had a bit of wine, and when she said she could sense how the house was feeling, I... told her about Gertrude's ghost, here in the station. And the looks I got from Sara and her brother...!" He shook his head.

"So, you told the truth and you're wishing you hadn't," Ruth summed up. *"Why? Because you don't think anyone believes it? Or is it because you think you've ruined your chances with your young lady?"*

"Trust me, Curt, if there's any substance to this girl at all, it'll take more than that to drive her away," Clara assured him.

The back of his hand felt suddenly cold. He glanced down and saw her patting it with her own.

"Listen to Miss Clara, Mr. Wakefield. She knows all about relationships," came Len's voice from behind him. (Indeed, she did. In her day, Clara had been a very successful match-maker—among other, less reputable things.)

Curt turned his head and saw the porter's ghost emerge through the closed metal door beside the bench. In the fading light, his facial features were hard to discern, but there was no mistaking that pillbox-shaped cap on his head. Soon it would be dark. Clara, Ruth, and Len would be all but invisible, making them imaginary friends, indeed.

"I'd better get home," he told them. "See you tomorrow."

"Sweet dreams, handsome," Clara called after him as he headed back toward his car.

Amy had already unlocked the museum's doors and taken up her post behind the gift shop counter when Curt arrived the following morning. As usual, she was shadowed by the grey-scale figure of Orville Mead. The antique cash register she was using had once been located behind his ticket sales window, and he went wherever it did.

He'd also apparently developed a crush on her. Curt could understand why. Amy was young and pretty and extremely personable. Orville was going to be disappointed when she left at the end of August to return to university. Unless she took the cash register with her. That wasn't likely, though, and not only because the machine was so large and unwieldy. The Historical Society had put security measures in place to make sure nothing went out the door that oughtn't to.

"Good morning, Mr. Wakefield," Amy said brightly.

He smiled at her in response, then met Orville's gaze and dipped his head in greeting.

"Nena called. She wanted me to tell you that she's running a bit late, but she'll be here in time to take the first school group scheduled for today. We've got two coming in," she continued, reading from the screen of the countertop computer. "An art class from Groverton High School will be coming in at half past one for a pencil sketching exercise. Twenty students and two teachers. And the grade three class should be arriving in about an hour, for a visit to the Indigenous Peoples exhibit, and a lesson on building a birch bark canoe. Apparently, they're going to be making model boats this afternoon and racing them in the pond."

"Canoe-building techniques," he echoed. "Well, I can think

of only one person with those qualifications—"

Amy's cheeks dimpled. "Nena's way ahead of you. She's arranged for Jack Little Fish to give the kids a practical lesson, but he says you'll owe him a dinner, and it better be inside a restaurant this time. His words."

"Fair enough. I'll be sure to take him out somewhere nice this evening."

Amy's attention shifted then to something over his shoulder, cueing Curt to turn around. When he saw who was standing just inside the museum's entrance with a querying look on her face, his thoughts began to whirl.

"Good morning," Selena said. "Are you too busy to talk?"

By sheer willpower he recovered his wits and replied, "No, of course not, but… after last night I wasn't sure any of you would want to speak to me again."

She gave a little shrug and adjusted the shoulder strap of her purse. "You did kind of blindside us. But now that I've had a chance to process what you said, I have some questions."

As Amy busied herself noisily behind him, Curt ushered his visitor out of the foyer and into the History of Groverton hall. It had taken him months to get this exhibit just right, and he was especially proud of it. Occupying the large space that had once been the waiting area of the station, it was a kaleidoscopic trove of paintings, artifacts, and sepia-toned photographs dating back to 1845, when the first settlers broke ground in what would later become the town. The centrepiece of the display was a tall, hexagonal glass case containing items found in the rubble after the train derailment. They included a lady's handbag with tortoiseshell trim, a miniature wooden rocking horse, a hat pin with a mother-of-pearl head, and several pieces of unclaimed costume jewellery, among other things.

Selena was clearly not here for a tour, however. She halted

several steps past the doorway and asked in a lowered voice, "Were you serious when you offered to help me inspect the castle for ghosts?"

"Yes," he replied, matching her tone.

"You really see them?" she persisted. "You don't just detect them with technology, like those ghost hunters on TV?"

"I see them as clearly as I'm seeing you, only not in colour," he assured her gravely, "and I can converse with the ones who know they're dead. And anyone capable of sensing the residual emotion inside an old house may be able to communicate with them too."

She looked troubled. "I don't understand."

He paused to choose his words, then said, "I can only speak from my own experience, of course. There's a lot about this that defies explanation. But here's how it seems to me: I think that a ghost is the memory of an emotion. We imprint ourselves on things that matter deeply to us—things that we love, but also and especially things that symbolize or make us feel strong negative emotions each time we encounter them."

"Or remember them? Like the sadness a person would feel looking at a calendar on the anniversary of a tragic loss?" she said in a sombre voice.

She was speaking from first-hand knowledge, he was certain. Was he about to reopen an old wound? Curt hesitated for a couple of heartbeats, then decided to push on. "Yes. When we're alive, just thinking about something we've imprinted can make us relive whatever emotion we've attached to it. When we die, the imprint remains behind, and depending on *how* we die, it can tether a part of us to it, producing a manifestation that only an individual tuned to a particular wavelength, as you put it last night, would be able to perceive."

"And you believe I'm that kind of individual?"

"I don't know. I suspect you are, but if you want to find

out for sure, let me know when you're ready to return inside the house, and I'll go with you."

As her lips curved in a smile, Curt felt a weight lift from his mind.

"I'm meeting with Tricia Vickery this morning to present the offer," she told him, "and we should know by tomorrow whether it's been accepted. Apparently, the current owner is anxious to be rid of the property, so she doesn't expect there will be any prolonged negotiation. How does tomorrow evening sound?"

He nodded thoughtfully. "I'll make myself available and wait to hear from you."

"Georgian Bay has worn many names, but it was first named by the indigenous peoples who lived on the land around it. To the Ojibwe it was always a very powerful and spiritual place. The Anishinaabe called it *Waaseyaagami-wiikwed*, and many of us still refer to it as *Manidoo gaming*, or Spirit Lake. Perhaps it was because the mist on the water in the early morning reminded people of the spirits of the dead rising into the air, or because it had a quick temper and could become suddenly angry.

"Yes, angry! The sky would darken and the wind would blow hard across the water, whipping it into mighty waves that would attack any boat that was trying to cross it. Large boat or small, the storm did not care. It only wanted to break that boat and sink it to the bottom of the lake.

"The Huron-Wendat called it Lake Attigouatan. They also told a story about a god named Kitchikewana, who had a violent temper and guarded the whole bay as his own…"

Nenokaasi "Nena" Cartier was a retired university professor and a gifted storyteller who'd joined the part-time staff of the museum a couple of years earlier. Besides setting up and managing the Indigenous History exhibit, she also conducted tours and presentations for school groups. This morning she had greeted Ms. Walters' class while wearing a mid-calf-length blue cotton skirt encircled by two brightly-coloured ribbons sewn onto it just above its hem, and hand-stitched leather moccasins. From the moment she'd told those children that she was Anishinaabe and her given name meant "hummingbird", they'd been enthralled.

Curt loved watching Nena work her magic on an audience. However, today he had some work of his own to do. So, he turned from the doorway and directed his steps toward the tower.

Groverton had already established itself as a trading port with the potential to be much more when it was added as a terminus to the railway line in 1858, necessitating the construction of a train station. Seeing an opportunity to attract even more wealth and commerce to the area, the governing council decided to make this the first all-brick building in town. It was designed to be enduring and impressive, a harbinger of future prosperity. Its waiting area therefore needed to accommodate large crowds of people. Its freight-handling facility had to be capacious. What was most important, it had to stand tall, to be visible from anywhere in the town and from points beyond it as well. And so, a massive tower was put in the middle of the structure, rising fully three storeys high, with an office and storage room on each of the first two floors for the station manager and his assistant, and a "crow's nest" lookout at the top.

Currently, the museum's curator/manager had the office and storage space on the first floor, and the Historical Society kept its office and archives on the second. As a de facto member of the Society, Curt had full access to these records. That was where he was headed now.

He climbed up two short flights of polished wooden stairs separated by a landing, past a series of portraits mounted at eye level on the walls. It was a chronological roll call of the distinguished Chairs of the Historical Society. Some of their images were painted, most were photographed, but all were stiffly posed and formidably sober-faced. At some point, one of them had made the decision not to formalize the place occupied in the town's history by the McFadyen residence. What the reason might have been for that was one of many questions that had been crowding Curt's mind of late.

On the second floor landing, he turned left and let himself into a room lined with floor-to-ceiling shelving containing labelled brown bankers' boxes. In the centre of this space sat a plain wooden table and chair, and on the table, a computer connected by cables to a freestanding server the size and shape of a refrigerator. To minimize the wear and tear on old, fragile documents, the Society had had them digitized.

Everything to be found in hard copy in this room had been scanned and saved on the server. At least, that was what Curt had been told when he arrived here. Whether it was the truth would take time to determine. Meanwhile, he'd chosen to focus on a mystery, and he had a feeling—reinforced by the previous evening's dinner table discussion—that Gertrude's angry ghost was at the centre of it, and that the house in which Hugh McFadyen had kept his wife while she was alive was somehow involved.

The Society's documentation regarding the construction of the castle was less than exhaustive, but that was to be expected. Fortunately, the newspaper morgue at the public library had been able to fill in many of the gaps—Hugh McFadyen had been rather a colourful figure in Groverton back in the day, eminently reportable. However, learning more about him did nothing to clear up the mystery.

Curt decided to approach it from a different angle.

He logged onto the computer and called up the records for 1932, then searched them for any mention of Gertrude

McFadyen's name. It was a short list of references: a newspaper item about leading citizen Hugh McFadyen "finding love" while in the U.S. on business, and a couple of medical reports. It figured. She'd barely been present in Groverton before her untimely death on the platform; and even if she'd lived long enough to make any kind of impression on the town, her existence would most likely have been spent in quiet obscurity, due to the persistently delicate state of her health and the large shadow cast by her powerful husband.

Curt clicked on the first medical document and read it carefully from top to bottom. It was a one-page form, stating a diagnosis of influenza and signed by a doctor whose name he could barely make out, the handwriting was so poor. Nothing unusual about that, he thought, recalling the most recent prescription he'd had filled. He then initiated another search, this time for the names of all the physicians practising in Groverton in 1932. Of the dozen names on the list, none of them came close to matching the scrawled signature on Gertrude's examination record.

Hmm. She'd been quarantined at home, not placed in isolation at the local hospital. That in itself was strange, for Curt had read an archived magazine article that included a photo of the Groverton General Hospital circa 1930, and he had been surprised by how large and well-equipped it was. This little town had apparently boasted one of the finest hospitals in the region, with an entire wing of private and semi-private rooms. So, why wouldn't Hugh have brought his sick wife to where she could receive the best possible care? Why keep her at home?

Struck by a sudden thought, Curt widened his search to include physicians who'd been practising in Groverton earlier but had retired. This time he found a name: Thomas Ostler, retired in 1909.

And Hugh had pulled this doctor out of decades of

retirement to treat Gertrude? It made no sense. Or was there perhaps a Thomas Ostler Jr. or a Thomas Ostler III, MD, who'd been called in from out of town?

Now curious, Curt checked the town's marriage, birth, and death records. He found Ostler and his wife, Margaret, but no sign of any Ostler children. He did, however, come across Ostler's birth and death certificates, the latter dated August 14, 1933. Curt did the math. Thomas Ostler had been 93 years old and twenty-four years out of practice when he'd accepted Gertrude McFadyen as a patient. The thought that this elderly man (who might or might not have had all his wits about him, let alone kept himself professionally current during his retirement) could actually have been entrusted with diagnosing and treating the wife of one of the town's leading citizens was disturbing, to say the least.

Had he had all his wits about him? Could his diagnosis be trusted? More to the point, why on God's green Earth would someone with Hugh McFadyen's clout and resources have turned to him in the first place?

These documents were not going to give Curt the answers he needed. Logging out, he left the room and went downstairs again.

Clara and Ruth were in their usual place, watching for trains. As Curt stepped out onto the platform to join them, he noticed a chill in the air and realized that a third ghost was present.

Gertrude.

Bundled up in a coat that concealed her from neck to ankle and wearing a short-brimmed bucket hat, she was standing with her back to the tracks at the far end of the platform, glaring icily at the double steel doors. On that fateful day in 1933, they would have been flung open to transfer freight to and from the baggage car while passengers were boarding and disembarking. Now, they were shut tight, having become an emergency exit from the exhibit hall of the museum.

Gertrude never spoke. She didn't have to. Everything about her telegraphed rage: the stony set of her features, the rigidity of her posture, the way she kept her arms folded tightly across her chest… and, of course, the drop in temperature of the air around her.

Curt had first seen her—and felt her frosty stare—three years earlier, while exploring the basement of the museum. She'd appeared to be tethered to something on the other side of a locked door with the words "Safe Storage" stencilled onto it. His curiosity instantly aroused, Curt had tried the museum's keys in the lock one at a time until he found one that worked.

Little more than a closet, this room had clearly not been opened in a long while. It contained several cardboard boxes, each marked, "Personal Effects, 1933: Unclaimed". Evidently, some of the items found in the aftermath of the train wreck had not been wanted by the families of the deceased, and someone in authority had decided to put them into safekeeping. Now they were relics, possessing historical significance. They belonged upstairs, on exhibit. And one of them had a mute, unhappy spirit attached to it.

While cataloguing the contents of the cartons, Curt had found the handbag and realized with a start that it looked the same as the one the ghost was clutching. This was clearly a clue to her identity. The historian in him loved a mystery, especially when it involved a ghost. After all, determining who she had been while alive could reveal why she was so angry, and perhaps show him how he could help her to find peace.

He'd immediately begun to delve. Weeks later, after a fruitless search of the Historical Society's archives, he'd finally gone to the public library, where he and Sara eventually succeeded in finding a copy of the incident report filed by the railway company's security department. It included eyewitness statements confirming that Hugh and Gertrude had both been on the platform, and describing Gertrude in detail, right down to the tortoiseshell trim on her brown leather handbag.

That had solved one mystery but presented Curt with another. Both McFadyens (what had been left of them) had been given proper burials in the town's cemetery. So, what was Gertrude doing hanging around the train station? Was there something special about that purse, perhaps, that tethered her to it? Should that be the next direction his inquiry took?

"Hey, handsome! Are you going my way?" Clara's teasing voice broke into his ruminations.

With a final glance at Gertrude, he stepped over to the bench and sat down between Ruth and Clara. "Does she come out here often?" he asked them.

"Only whenever children are inside the station," Ruth replied. *"Being around young ones makes her uncomfortable. She misses her baby, poor thing."*

"There you go again," Clara scolded her, *"spreading gossip."*

"It's not gossip! I know what I saw," Ruth maintained stoutly. *"Just because I've never borne a child of my own, that doesn't mean I can't tell when another woman is expecting one."*

"Wait a minute," Curt said, confused. "When would you have seen Gertrude pregnant?"

"When she arrived here on the train with her husband. Not even the coat she was wearing could hide the curve of her belly. My mother was a midwife and I used to assist her, so I recognized the shape of that curve. I'm telling you, she was at least five or six months gone when he helped her

down onto this platform."

Curt's thoughts were careening around inside his head so hard that for a moment he wasn't sure he could safely stand up. What if Ruth was right, and Gertrude had come to Groverton already with child? Just considering this possibility put a whole different complexion on everything he'd already learned about her.

Maybe it hadn't been influenza that had kept her inside the house for all that time. Maybe it had been what was then called "confinement". If a doctor was in attendance, then a birth—live or still—should have been registered with the town… but if the pregnancy itself was being kept secret, then there might be a reason for that not to happen, and if it were against the mother's wishes…?

That would explain Gertrude's anger, certainly, but not her apparent attachment to the handbag.

Damn! If only he could get her to talk to him!

Three

Tricia Vickery's offices were located at the west end of town. Hearth and Home Realty shared a strip plaza—and an ample parking lot—with a burger joint, a convenience store, a walk-in wellness centre, and an accounting firm. As Selena steered her car into the lot, she noted with some annoyance that a black sedan was angle-parked directly in front of her destination, taking up two slots instead of just one.

If that was how someone parked, she could just imagine how badly they drove. So, not wanting to risk a collision when they backed out to leave, she picked a spot as far from the danger zone as possible and left her own vehicle there.

Shaking her head at the thoughtlessness of some people, Selena walked through the realtor's door and found herself staring at two broad backs clad in identical dark blue. Then one of the men turned to face her, and she saw the PPS patch on the shoulder of his jacket, and Tricia Vickery sitting at the reception desk, dabbing at her eyes with a tissue. That was when things clicked together in Selena's mind. The sedan out front was an unmarked Provincial Police Services car, and

Vickery was evidently receiving some bad news.

"I'm sorry," Selena blurted, taking a step back towards the doorway. "This is obviously the wrong time. I'll come back later."

"No, stay!" Vickery leaped to her feet and thrust a forefinger in Selena's direction. "This is her, Detectives. The client I was telling you about. She was Brenda's last appointment the day she went missing, and she's been insistent about buying that damned house."

"So, you're Selena Watt?" said the first detective, flipping to a clean page in his notebook and preparing to write.

Something had to have happened to Brenda. Her heart slowly spiralling down into her stomach, Selena replied, "Yes. Am I in some kind of trouble?"

"Not yet, ma'am. Would you show me some identification, please?"

Under the polite but official gaze of two pairs of police eyes, she unzipped her purse, fished out her driver's licence, and handed it over to him.

Meanwhile, Vickery had sat back down and was gathering up papers and stuffing them into file folders. "I wish I'd never heard of the McFadyens or their effing house," she muttered darkly between sniffles. "It's been nothing but trouble ever since I added it to my listings."

As the first detective finished with Selena's licence and gave it back to her, his partner said, "Now, how did you know Brenda Ryan?"

Selena's breath turned to dust in her throat. She'd read too many mystery novels not to know what it meant when a police detective used the past tense for a question like that. Brenda wasn't just missing—she was dead. The police were reconstructing her final hours because they suspected foul play. And the last person to see the victim alive had better have an alibi for the time of death or they could become a suspect in a murder investigation.

Choosing her words carefully, Selena replied, "I met her for the first time two days ago, when I walked into this office to inquire about buying a house and found her sitting behind that desk. We spent about an hour in conversation... she took me on a couple of virtual tours of homes on her computer... I picked the one I was most interested in, and we made an appointment for one o'clock the following afternoon, to meet up and go through the place for real. Then I left to shop for something for dinner."

"And that was the last time you had any contact with Ms. Ryan?"

"No. She texted me later that evening. Apparently, there were special permissions she had to get before bringing me into the house, and we agreed to move my tour from one o'clock to three."

"Do you still have that text?" the first detective inquired.

In response, Selena pulled out her phone and let him read the message for himself.

"It's time-stamped 9:45 p.m.," he remarked.

Vickery frowned. "That's nearly an hour after the office closed. I was here alone from nine o'clock until after ten that night."

"So, she could have sent it from anywhere."

Selena's Crime Club reflex kicked in then, and she couldn't help herself. "Or someone else could have sent it using her phone," she piped up.

Both detectives stared at her for a moment. Then one of them said with a triumphant grin, "Selena Watt. Now I recall where I've seen that name before." Turning to his partner, he added, "The Rafferty House case last summer. Staff Sergeant Brassard's going to have a bird when she finds out who's involved in this one."

Both men chuckled gleefully.

Brassard was in Groverton? Fine, then, Selena thought. In for a penny, in for a pound.

"What happened to Brenda?" she asked.

"That's what we're trying to determine, Ms. Watt. Her badly beaten body was found early this morning, on the front porch of a residence at the corner of Beech and Webber. So, I'm afraid your purchase of that property is on hold until the scene has been processed."

With burgeoning excitement, Selena told him, "I think we can help you with that."

"Oh, I doubt it, Ms. Watt," his partner cut in, his expression now severe. "This is a real criminal investigation, and the last thing we need is a bunch of well-meaning amateur sleuths getting in the way. My advice to you is to stay away from the castle and let us do our jobs."

"Then would you please convey a message for me to Staff Sergeant Brassard?" she said sweetly.

"Sure, no problem."

"Tell her I've been inside this house, and have found that it has a great deal in common with Rafferty House. That's why I want it. Tell her I plan to stick around for as long as it takes to purchase it. And here's my phone number," she added, handing him her business card, "in case anyone needs to reach me."

Vickery had been eavesdropping on this exchange. Her mannequin face now wore a deer-in-the-headlights expression. Selena had no idea whether it would last, but the thought of it gave her a certain amount of satisfaction as she made her exit and quick-stepped back to her car.

"Oh. My. God. That's *terrible*!" Sara dropped onto a chair, still clutching the serrated knife she'd been using to slice up tomatoes for their sandwiches. "So, they consider it a suspicious death. What else did they tell you about it?"

"Not much they *could* tell me about an ongoing investigation," Selena replied. "I expect there'll be more information about it in the next edition of the local newspaper. Meanwhile, that poor, lonely house is being processed as a crime scene, which means the police have reason to believe that Brenda was killed somewhere on the premises. It must have happened overnight, after Vickery and I finished our walk-through and locked the place up."

"But you said she'd already been missing for a day before that, so where was she, I wonder?" Sara's blue eyes held a speculative gleam.

Selena smiled inwardly. Larry might not be a fan of crime fiction, but his sister had been devouring murder mysteries since her teens. That shared love had cemented the friendship that had sprung up between the two women the previous summer, while they oversaw Larry's recovery from smoke inhalation. And now a real-life mystery had just fallen into their laps, and Sara was apparently eager to sink her teeth into more than just a BLT.

"I left her at the realtor's office at half past four. She could have gone anywhere after that." Selena eyed the knife, which was now dripping tomato gore onto the tabletop. "Would you like me to help you prepare lunch?" she prompted.

"No, I've got it, thanks." Sara returned to the cutting board at the counter and resumed assembling their sandwiches. "Do you think Brassard will actually contact you?" she called over her shoulder.

"Again, no idea. I hope she will. However, the last time we spoke, she made it clear what would happen if Larry or I ever interfered with another of her investigations. So, how do you feel about bailing us out of jail?" Selena said, only half-joking.

Just then, the tea kettle shrilled, and she got to her feet to silence it.

When both women were seated once more with tea and

sandwiches in front of them, Sara said, "I've been thinking about what we discussed last night. I've never believed in ghosts, but you and Larry sounded so convinced… How certain are you that the castle is…?"

"Sentient," she supplied. "Aware of itself and of what goes on around it. I'm dead certain, Sara. I think this house witnessed Brenda's murder and needs to give a statement to the police. But we're in a chicken and egg situation here, just like on Rafferty Island. The police won't treat the house as a witness if they don't believe it's sentient; and the only way they'll believe it's sentient is if it helps them to solve the case."

"Hmm." Sara took a bite of her sandwich and chewed it thoughtfully. After swallowing it down, together with a sip of apple cinnamon tea, she remarked, "You called Larry a 'house whisperer'."

Selena paused with her cup halfway to her mouth and said, "That was the nickname we gave him after Brassard made him the liaison between her constables and Rafferty House. Apparently, it liked him a whole lot better than it liked them."

"Why? I mean, you know I love my brother, and I get the feeling that you're fond of him too, but why do you suppose the *house* liked him?"

A clever quip jumped to the forefront of Selena's mind. Then she saw the taut expression on Sara's face and decided to give her an honest answer. "Larry was working his way through some pretty raw emotions at the time. I think the house was, too. It probably saw him as a kindred spirit."

Sara let out a sigh. "After Mom and Dad passed, we sort of drifted apart. It's the Holmes way of dealing with great loss, I guess, turning inward, burying ourselves in our work. Once that becomes your normal state of mind, it's hard to change it back to the way it was before. Then he lost Tamara, who was like a daughter to him… When I found out about it, I tried to comfort him, but he pushed me away." She went silent for a couple of heartbeats. Reaching out to take Selena's hand, she added, "I'm glad he met you, and I'm glad he went to Rafferty House. What happened there last August has brought our family closer together than we've been in years. And as far as I'm concerned, it's increased our number by one. I hope you realize that."

Selena replied in a husky voice, "I do, and I'm glad we met too."

Sara gave her hand a squeeze, then shrugged as though to shake off the moment. "Let's finish eating and clean up," she said, leaning forward across the table and wearing a conspiratorial grin. "We've got some investigating to do, and Sergeant Brassard doesn't need to know a thing about it."

Selena's first impression of the Groverton Library as she drove past it to make the turn into the parking lot was how out of place it appeared, as if a slice of the future had been dropped into a part of town still rooted in the past. Four storeys high, clad in yellow brick, and with the afternoon sun reflecting off its many plate glass windows, it towered over the much older structures that surrounded it, like a lighthouse overlooking a sea of red and brown. Clearly, the town planners had been thinking of urban renewal to come when they'd approved its design.

This modern edifice of knowledge was where Sara worked. Today, she had the second shift, from 2:00 p.m. to closing at eight o'clock, so she and Selena travelled there in two cars.

"I can pick the boys up from school and make them dinner if you'd like," Selena offered as they walked together toward the tall double doors of the entrance.

"I appreciate the offer, but it won't be necessary," Sara assured her. "Days when I'm working late, they take the school bus home. If Larry's not there yet, they stay with our neighbour two doors down the street until he arrives. Now that he's switched to the administration track, he keeps regular hours and can spend more quality time with his nephews. Personally, I think it's done all three of them a world of good."

Crossing the terrazzoed foyer, Sara led the way to the main desk, where she logged onto the computer system and proceeded to open a membership account for Selena.

"Okay, here's your library card. Your email is your user name and the card number is your password. Once you're logged on, you can reset your password to be anything you want. And now we can go into the Reference section and begin to dig."

"Aren't you supposed to be on duty now?" Selena asked, confused.

"Yes. And helping a new patron to navigate the library's computerized resources is part of my job. Besides, there's a one-hour overlap between the two shifts, from two to three o'clock. All hands are on deck right now, so no one is going to miss me for at least the next forty minutes, and that gives us plenty of time to get started."

So saying, Sara ushered her into a large room half-filled by rows of double-sided bookshelves. At one end sat a row of a different kind: carrels equipped with computers. Tall dividers on three sides gave each carrel privacy from the others and security from casual or prying eyes. "Sit," she commanded. "Log on, and let's see what the Reference materials and publicly available records have to say about your deceased real estate agent, Brenda...?"

Barbara. Last seen alive on the shoulder of a highway talking to a man in a dark green pickup truck with a painted-over logo on the driver's-side door and mud-obscured licence plates...

Selena's next breath was a sob. She had done this sort of

deep dive before, in a different library, and had come up empty. It had taken her years to accept that she would probably never get closure—that she had to get on with her life. And now this girl's body had been found, perhaps on the very spot where Selena had been standing when the house reached out to her; and it felt as if she was right back at square one, with a pulsing void in her chest and a lump in her throat that refused to be swallowed, being handed her cousin's personal effects at the morgue.

"Hey, the sooner we can help the police get closer to solving this case, the sooner they'll let you back inside the castle to find out what it saw," Sara reminded her, not unkindly. "That's what you want, right?"

Selena nodded numbly. If she couldn't help herself, and she couldn't help the victim, then at least she could try to help the house.

"So tell me, do you know Brenda's last name?"

"It's Ryan," Selena replied thickly. "Brenda Ryan."

The other woman frowned. "Well, it's a fairly common name, and she may not have been from around here, but it gives us a starting point. We'll begin with local birth records. If nothing pops up, we can expand the search, internationally if necessary. She was a real estate agent, so she must have taken courses, joined the Real Estate Board, kept her licence current... no realtor would have hired her otherwise. Don't worry, Selena, we've got access to a wealth of information here and plenty of practice at solving puzzles. We'll prove our value to the police investigation. Then they'll *have* to let us help them."

It was brave talk, Selena thought darkly, but it didn't mean a thing if they couldn't back it up with something the police had overlooked. That was how she and Larry and the Crime Club had won over then-Sergeant Brassard the previous summer—with clues and leads only the house had been able to provide. This time, things were different. The castle had been effectively bound and gagged by a barrier of yellow crime scene tape, and had been put off-limits to anyone who might believe it had something to communicate beyond the physical evidence it contained.

Half an hour and numerous dead ends later, Selena's patience was nearly gone, and Sara had to return to the main desk, leaving her to carry on the search by herself. For several long moments, Selena stared bleakly at the computer screen. Then it occurred to her that they were going about this all wrong. Someone as personable as Brenda had been earlier would not have lived in a social vacuum. She had to have had friends. And they wouldn't live in the Reference section of a library. They would be online.

Mentally crossing her fingers, Selena logged onto her own social media accounts and put up a public post in each one:

Desperately Seeking Brenda! My friend Brenda Ryan, a Groverton real estate agent, has gone missing. Pls DM me if you know anything about her whereabouts since 2 days ago.

There. No more sifting through reams of public data with the feeling of déjà vu weighing down her mind. No more chasing flimsy leads into blind alleys. If anyone out there knew Brenda or had seen her with someone just before she was killed, that information was now going to come looking for Selena instead.

Meanwhile, she was aware of one person who definitely had known the victim. Tricia Vickery had seemed quite upset this morning. Shaken enough to cancel all her showings and appointments for the afternoon? Selena decided to swing by Hearth and Home and find out. And since both Sara and Larry were busy right now and it made no sense to drag Curt along for this, she would just have to do it alone.

*   *   *

"Oh! Ms. Watt. I should have been expecting you, I guess… I was preparing to draw up your offer when the police arrived, and… well, under the circumstances, there didn't seem to be much point… I'm sorry, it's just…"

Vickery remained seated behind the front desk. She'd repaired her makeup, but there was flusterment in her voice.

"Actually, I'm here for a different reason," Selena said, stepping forward to lean over the counter. "I never had a chance to tell you this morning how sorry I am for your loss. Did you know Brenda very well?"

"Not as well as I would have liked, unfortunately. That makes two that I've lost before their time," Vickery added with a sigh.

Selena inhaled sharply. "You've lost *two* agents this way?"

"What? No! Well, maybe, if Rachel had lived a little longer…" Meeting her gaze with pain-filled eyes, Vickery explained, "Rachel was my daughter. She was working towards getting her real estate licence when the cancer was finally diagnosed. By then, there was nothing they could do. At the funeral, Brenda came up and introduced herself to me. She told me that she and Rachel had been classmates in the real estate program and had become good friends, and I told her to let me know when she'd graduated and was ready to start working. She did, and I took her on. That was about a year ago."

"Was she from around here?"

"I don't think so. She didn't talk much about herself or her family, but she once mentioned that the drive to Georgian College used to take her twenty minutes each way."

"Did you tell that to the police?" Selena asked hopefully.

"Of course. I told them everything I knew and gave them everything I had about her: her appointment book, her contact information on file… even my copy of her certificate from the college. I held nothing back," she declared, her jaw at a righteous angle. "As the detective said this morning, sometimes the smallest detail can crack a case wide open."

"And nothing new has occurred to you since then?"

At this, the mannequin brow wrinkled with suspicion. "No. Brenda was a very private person. I only saw her during business hours, and everything we discussed had to do with selling real estate." The note of finality in her response was unmistakable.

Damn! So much for that idea.

Well, it was all up to social media now. Leaving Vickery to her paperwork, Selena walked out the door… and met one of the detectives who'd spoken with her that morning, coming the other way.

"Ms. Watt?" Making no move to go past her, he gave her a mirthless grin. "I'm Detective Izkari. Staff Sergeant Brassard got your message. She wants to see you at the detachment, immediately."

Selena felt a sudden chill. Brassard could have summoned her with a text or a voice call. Instead, she'd sent this burly detective to pick Selena up and bring her in. For questioning, perhaps? This did not bode well.

The Groverton Detachment of Provincial Police Services was housed in a block-shaped building that could not possibly be mistaken for anything but what it was. To Selena, gazing out the rear passenger window of Detective Izkari's unmarked vehicle, it looked disturbingly like a fortress. Or a prison.

Seen from the street, it had a scattering of tall, skinny windows to either side of an area of red brick wall with a door in it that looked as though it was hoping not to be noticed. The wall wore a "patch" similar to the ones on the shoulders of PPS uniforms but many times larger. Not until Izkari made the turn onto a side street and again into the parking lot behind the structure did a set of glass doors appear, raised a couple of concrete steps above the ground and with the same patch image etched into the centre of each one. There were windows on this side of the building as well, just as tall as the others but not as narrow.

"I'm guessing you don't get a lot of walk-in traffic," Selena joked nervously as he ushered her across the threshold and onto an elevator car.

He gave no sign of hearing her. In fact, from the moment she'd gotten into his vehicle, he'd barely acknowledged her presence. Normally, this would annoy her. Today, all she felt was apprehension.

The elevator stopped and the door slid open on the second floor of the building. Guided by his hand on her elbow, Selena stepped out into a carpeted corridor and turned to her right. The room to which she was now shown had an engraved metal plaque on its door, mounted at eye level: *Interviews.*

Uh-huh. Like that was going to fool anyone who'd ever watched *NCIS.*

Izkari swung the door open and stepped back to let her go first. "Make yourself comfortable, Ms. Watt. Staff Sergeant Brassard will join you in just a couple of minutes," he assured her, giving her another of those official, insincere smiles. Then he left, closing the door behind him.

Selena surveyed the room, not sure whether to feel relieved or disappointed that it reminded her of someone's front parlour. There was the requisite two-way mirror, of course, but also a well-upholstered loveseat and two matching armchairs in a conversation grouping, with a low coffee table and a couple of wood-veneered end tables strategically placed among them.

It didn't take a genius to realize where the "interviewee" was supposed to sit. Selena had barely settled herself on the loveseat before the door opened again to admit Staff Sergeant Isabel Brassard, holding a blood red file folder in her left hand.

Tall, sturdy, and stern-faced, the PPS officer had been an imposing sight on the boat dock of Rafferty Island. In this little room, dressed in full uniform, she appeared even more formidable.

"Ms. Watt!" she declared from just inside the doorway, then, speaking with the francophone cadence that Selena remembered so well, added, "Do you know why I called you here?"

Selena mentally crossed her fingers. "Because you got my message and want to discuss the house?" she said, trying to sound more confident than she felt at that moment.

"No." Brassard eased herself onto one of the armchairs, her lips set in a grim smile. "It is because of a discrepancy that we need to clear up. This morning you gave a statement to one of my detectives, in which you claimed to have met the victim, Brenda Ryan, for the first time two days ago, when you happened to walk into the real estate office to inquire about buying a house."

"It wasn't a claim," Selena replied, her dander rising. "It was the truth."

"So, you are confirming that you had no relationship with Ms. Ryan before that moment?"

"None. Our paths had never crossed, and I didn't even know she existed."

"Ah! Then, if you were total strangers to each other, how do you explain this?" Brassard placed a page on the coffee table, turned so that Selena could read it. It was the printout of a screen shot, showing the post she'd put up on social media less than an hour before Izkari had come to fetch her at the realtor's office.

Damn!

"You see my confusion now?" Brassard was saying. "If she was a stranger, she could not possibly be a dear friend you are worried for. These two things contradict each other.

Therefore, one of them must be a lie. Which one is it, Ms. Watt?"

"I did not lie to the detective."

"*B'en*. That is fortunate for you. But now I have to ask: what exactly was the purpose of this post?"

"I—Wait a minute." Selena straightened in her seat, struck by a sudden thought. "You've been monitoring my social media activity?"

"Of course not. We have been searching the internet for anything by or about Ms. Ryan that might tell us how she spent her final hours. Imagine my surprise to discover her name linked with yours in this way. Or perhaps I should not be surprised to find you disregarding my warnings about interfering with our investigation."

"I was only trying to learn something that would convince you to take us seriously."

"Well, you have succeeded, although I imagine it is not what you were hoping for. This is not one of your murder mystery novels, Ms. Watt, with their clever, insightful *amateurs* and bumbling police detectives. My people are professionals who know what they are doing and especially what *not* to do in order to catch criminals.

"There is a reason that we do not shout our questions out to the whole world. We are hunting a killer, and it is very important when hunting not to reveal oneself too early to the prey. It gives them a chance to escape. Or, in a case such as this, to cover up their tracks by harming even more people." With these final words, Brassard's piercing dark eyes focused like targeting lasers on Selena's face.

She swallowed hard. "Oh. I never thought about that."

"I know. It is because you are an *amateur*. I have no desire to charge you—"

"Then don't. But please, hear me out."

"If you are going to tell me the crime scene is cursed, you

can save your breath. The first thing we learned about that house is that half the town believes it is haunted."

"And I know a way to determine or disprove that, if you'll let us."

Pursing her lips, Brassard leaned back in her chair. "Go on," she said with a sigh, and a skeptical tilt to her eyebrow.

"You know what happened at Rafferty House. Your own people experienced it, even if you personally didn't. Even if no mention of it was included in your official reports, even if there's no scientific way to prove that it's true, every human who spent the weekend in that house knows that it was sentient."

"Are you suggesting that this house you are so eager to buy is also sentient?"

"Yes! The one time that I was inside it, it reached out and communicated an emotion to me. And there's a high probability that it also witnessed the crime that you're investigating and can give you a statement about it."

"That can be said about every crime scene, can it not? Our analysts are still gathering and processing evidence from this house. It has already told us a great deal about the death of Brenda Ryan."

"And it can tell you even more if you'll let us back inside. Rafferty House spoke through Larry. I believe the old McFadyen house is trying to speak through me. Please, give us a chance to help."

Brassard paused, her tightly-pressed lips deking from side to side. Finally, she blew out a breath and gave her head a single emphatic shake. "No. Our case must stand up in court. That means the investigation has to be based on rationality. So, we will follow proper procedure and go where the physical evidence takes us, dotting every 'I' and crossing every 'T'."

"But—"

Brassard waved her to silence. "Even if I were to believe

you, Ms. Watt, others won't, and sentient houses do not make credible witnesses. However, once we have taken down the yellow tape, you are free to buy this building and have as many conversations with it as you please."

"I see. And if one of those conversations produces new information relating to the case?"

"As long as there is tangible evidence to back it up, I will expect you to bring it directly to my attention. *Entendu?*"

"Yes. Can you tell me how much longer I will have to wait to go inside the house?"

"There is no hard and fast deadline to an investigation like this. A matter of weeks, perhaps."

Really? Weeks?

Damn!

Four

With questions still whirling around inside his head, Curt was locking up to go home. He hadn't heard from Selena all day, nor was he expecting her call. Sara had phoned him a couple of hours earlier to give him the news that the castle was now a crime scene and there was no telling when anyone would be allowed inside.

A screeching of tires made him turn around in time to see a blue Buick racing toward him across the parking lot. The vehicle halted abruptly in one of the spots near the front door and two women stepped out onto the pavement, one of them in colour, one in greyscale.

"Curt! I was worried I would miss you," Selena declared, hurrying toward him. "I was going to call earlier, but the PPS scooped me up for a chat and then I had to go back and retrieve my car and—Why are you looking at me like that?"

He hadn't realized he was staring. Curt recomposed his features, cleared his throat, and took an educated guess.

"You lost someone, didn't you? Someone you cared deeply about? And you held onto something of theirs to remember them by. Something you're wearing right now that I haven't seen before. Maybe a favourite piece of jewellery…?"

Now it was her turn to stare at him. "My cousin. This was her pendant." She lifted it to show him—a pewter disc engraved with the yin/yang symbol. "I was in such a hurry to talk to you this morning that I left it on the dresser in the motel room and had to go back for it before my meeting with the realtor. But the only way you could know about Barbara—"

"She was about your height but a little thinner, with long hair parted in the middle and tucked behind her ears. They're pierced, and her earrings are shaped like stars, with a pearl in the middle of each one."

Selena's eyes were shining. "She's here, isn't she?" she whispered.

"Yes. I believe she's tethered to that pendant."

His reply opened a floodgate of words. They tumbled out of her in a torrent, her voice rising through a couple of registers as she went on excitedly, "You said that you can communicate with them if they know they're dead. Barbara was raped and murdered and the PPS never did solve her case. If she saw her attacker and can describe him, maybe even identify him—! Do you think you can—?"

He raised both his hands to quell the verbal onrush. "I can try." Taking a step forward, he said conversationally, "Hello, Barbara. My name is Curt Wakefield. I'm the manager of this museum, and a friend of Selena's, and I can see you. Will you see and speak to me?"

Not surprisingly, she appeared at first not to notice him. However, as he stood patiently gazing into her face, their eyes eventually locked and he saw a spark of realization in her expression, followed by something else—fear.

Of course, he belatedly recalled. Ghost time didn't pass the same way as living time did. Emotional wounds remained raw. Pain and memories stayed fresh. A man had raped and murdered Barbara. A man would be the last person she would want paying attention to her.

There was dread on Selena's face as well, as she prompted him, "Will she?"

"No, but I have an idea. Follow me."

Curt led her around the corner of the building, onto the train platform. Ruth waved and Clara grinned at the sight of him.

"Hey, there, handsome! How about introducing us to your friend?" Clara greeted him.

He smiled back at her. What she'd asked for was precisely what he intended to do. As far as he'd been able to determine, these two ghosts had never had a problem getting anyone to talk. Except for Gertrude, of course.

"What do you see there, Selena?" he asked, gesturing toward them.

"That? It's an antique wood and wrought iron bench," she replied with a shrug. "Isn't it? Or is it more?"

"This place is full of ghosts," he told her. "Two of them—two very friendly older women—are sitting on that bench—or rather, on the bench that was in that same spot when the train derailed and took it out in 1933."

"There's a ghost bench?" she said incredulously.

"I told you that some things defy explanation. This is one of them."

He looked at Barbara, who, as he'd hoped, was seeing more than just a piece of furniture in front of them as well and appeared more curious about it than afraid. To Selena he said, "This may sound strange, but humour me. I'd like you to take off the pendant and hang it over the back of the bench so that your cousin can spend some time with Ruth and Clara while you and I chat elsewhere. It'll be safe, I promise. We won't go far."

She stared doubtfully at him.

"I think a comforting female shoulder or two is just what Barbara needs right now," he replied. "And I want to hear about your interview with the police. They can't have been pleased with you if they grabbed you off the street like that."

There was a twin to this bench at the opposite end of the platform, a modern replica with no spirits attached. This was where Curt and Selena sat down and talked, periodically casting glances to their right—Curt to check on the ghosts, Selena (he guessed) to check that the pendant was still there.

"Well, I'm glad Staff Sergeant Brassard decided to let you off with a warning this time," he commented after Selena had brought him up to date.

"It felt more like a threat," she grumped. "And I'm no wiser about the investigation now than I was before she had me hauled in for questioning."

"But you may soon know more about Brenda Ryan, thanks to that message you posted. Once something enters the cloud, it's devilishly hard to pull it back out."

"Not for the police, apparently." She paused, lips pursed. "This is so frustrating, Curt. I feel I should be involved because the house reached out to me for help. I know it did. Or maybe it was something inside the house. Either way, we had a connection before Brenda was killed. Her death had to be traumatic to witness. And now the police won't even let me go inside the building until they've finished gathering their pieces of evidence for forensic analysis."

"So, you've got questions but no way to get answers," he summed up. "Sounds like a dead end to me."

She threw him a jaundiced look. "Really? Is this supposed to make me feel better?"

"No, but sometimes frustration is a choice. It's a poor one when there are more worthwhile and satisfying things on which you could be spending your emotional energy."

"Such as?"

Preparing his response, Curt turned his gaze toward the space where the tracks had once been. It was no wonder Ruth and Clara had loved to while away their afternoons here, train-watching. A series of strong wooden buttresses hugged the wall of the erstwhile station, curving gracefully outward to support the shelf of roof that overhung the platform, and affording anyone waiting to travel a panoramic view of the surrounding countryside. Then he looked up, and for the first time he noticed the resemblance between the roof supports and the ribs of a ship's keel, turned upside-down. Very apt, he thought, for a town that had depended for so long on the steady traffic of large cargo vessels.

He drew a deep breath before replying to her question. "Such as tackling a cold case. We could help each other, actually. I've been working on one for a couple of years and could use a fresh perspective on it. And you know what they say about a change being as good as a rest."

"You're talking about the angry ghost of Gertrude McFadyen?"

"Yes, along with the unsolved murder of your cousin. I've been watching Barbara, and it appears she's connecting with Ruth and Clara. If she can talk to them, then they'll talk to me, and helping you with your cold case will give me a break from mine. Meanwhile, Sara and I can walk you through our McFadyen research to date, and maybe we can even get Larry to join in, since I hear the two of you partnered up really well before. "

Selena heaved a sigh. "It's tempting, but… I don't know for sure whether I'll be able to stick around. Brassard told me it could take several weeks before I'm able to put in my offer on the house, and I still have bills to pay and a business to run back in Standerville. Summertime is the high season, after all."

"I understand. Give it some thought, though. And if you do decide to leave Groverton for a while, it might be a good idea to leave the pendant here as well, so Barbara has someone to talk to who can actually hear her."

"I'll think about it," she said, but he could tell from the set of her features that her mind was already made up.

"That poor girl!" Ruth declared as Curt sat down between her and Clara on the bench.

Selena had collected the pendant and departed, taking Barbara with her, and he was itching to know what the two resident ghosts had found out.

"Did she tell you what had happened to her?" he asked them.

There was a sudden chill in the air. *"Don't make it sound like an accident, Mr. Wakefield,"* Clara warned. Even in black and white, the darkening of her expression was evident, and the fury in her eyes was alarming to behold. *"It was a crime. A man raped and murdered her and got away with it."*

"Only for now," he said emphatically. "Unless he's a ghost himself, we can still bring him to justice. But I need your help to do it. And I ask again, did Barbara tell you anything about the attack?"

"Mainly, she cried," said Ruth, *"but she got enough words out that we could logic our way through it."*

"She wanted to stay here with us," Clara chimed in. *"Will she be back?"*

"I certainly hope so. And then you'll have to get as much information as you can out of her. The police will need every detail she can provide if they're to track down her killer."

"You sound very sure of them, Mr. Wakefield," Ruth observed quietly. *"Will they believe her? Will they even believe that she exists?"*

That gave him pause.

If there was anything Curt hated to see, it was a spirit in torment because of unfinished business on the worldly plane.

He'd helped a number of the museum ghosts to find peace, but this was going to be different, and much more difficult, because it required him to do something he'd assiduously avoided during his entire adult life. He would have to reveal his paranormal ability to the authorities.

Curt swallowed hard. Perhaps this would turn out not to be a bad thing after all, he told himself. Perhaps, after convincing Staff Sergeant Brassard that he was for real and not some deluded crackpot, he could persuade her to resume the investigation into Barbara's murder. Perhaps the detectives would take her statement, and then, by some miracle, take it seriously. Or perhaps they would order him held for psych assessment, or just figuratively pat him on the head and send him away. He was entering uncharted territory. However, as Selena had said at dinner the other night, there was no way to know how events would end up if he didn't at least try.

His parents had always taught him that if something was worth doing, it deserved his best effort. If bringing a rapist-murderer to account wasn't worth doing, Curt decided, he didn't know what was. And so, with renewed determination, he got to his feet, said a good evening to Ruth and Clara, and headed for his car in the parking lot.

Five

The heritage property in which Sara and her two sons lived was a board and batten two-storey structure with gabled upper windows and an ornate front entrance, set in the middle of a tree-shaded block of homes in the heart of a residential area. Painted the Society-mandated shade of grey with white trim, it had originally been built as part of a modest country estate called Greenhaven, with a carriage house and stables contained in a separate building on the grounds. Then the town had sprung up, drawing more and more people to the area; and parcel by parcel, the land surrounding the estate and then the estate itself had been consumed by urban development. The main residence and an oil painting in Sara's living room were all that remained to prove that Greenhaven had ever existed.

Selena had gone directly there from the museum. She'd told herself it was to keep Larry company while he minded his nephews. In fact, with everything that she had roiling around in her mind at that moment, it wasn't company she was after so much as a sounding board.

She parked her car on the street in front of the house, then sat for a while, debating whether to put Barbara's pendant back on. Knowing what she now knew about it—that for the past nine years she'd been dragging her cousin's ghost around with her like a dog on a leash—made the thought of wearing the necklace uncomfortable. But leaving it in the car—or anywhere else, for that matter, including the museum—that didn't feel right either. Finally, she slipped it into her pants pocket.

"Barbara, I'm sorry about this," she muttered as she got out of the vehicle.

Larry opened the door to her knock. "Perfect timing!" he declared. "The kids are working a jigsaw puzzle in the rec room, and I'm just about to shove a frozen pizza into the oven."

"Frozen pizza? I thought food preparation skill was a prerequisite for being a firefighter," she teased him.

"It is," he replied with a grin, "but apparently not for being a babysitter."

"And Uncle Larry is the best babysitter ever!" called a high-pitched voice from the direction of the closed washroom door.

"Attaboy! Butter me up so I'll let you eat this in front of the TV set again, why don't you?" he called back. Still smiling, he murmured to Selena, "I swear, give them an inch..."

"Mom lets us do it too, all the time." Sara's ten-year-old son, Eric, emerged from the washroom, wiping his hands down the sides of his jeans. "Hi, S'lena."

"Hi!"

"Why are you drying your hands on your clothes?" Larry inquired with mock severity.

"Donnie hung the towel up wrong again and it slipped off the rack onto the floor. Now it's only good for the laundry."

"How do you know it was Donnie?" Selena wondered.

"Because it's *always* Donnie," Eric replied with a shrug.

"And of course, there's only one towel in this house," said Larry, deadpan, "so if it's dirty, we're all out of luck. And don't get me started on the toilet paper situation."

Eric rolled his eyes. "I'll get another towel from the linen closet," he said with a sigh.

"Good man! I salute you," Larry called after him in a fair imitation of Robin Williams' voice.

"He looks just like Sara," Selena observed.

"And Donnie is the image of Doug when *he* was seven years old. It was hard on Sara, losing him suddenly like that, when the boys were so young."

Selena and Sara had exchanged stories about their losses over tea one winter afternoon. Now Selena nodded wordlessly, thinking, *Yes, but a burst aneurysm would have been so much easier for me to accept than the way Barbara was taken.*

That day, Sara had also shown her some of Doug's artwork, including one especially cherished piece carved out of driftwood. It depicted two lovers embracing and occupied a place of pride in Sara's bedroom. It made her feel, she'd said, as though Doug was still there. At the time, Selena had admired it for its craftsmanship. Today, acutely aware of the pendant in her pocket, she had to wonder whether there might be more than one ghost currently in this house.

"Anyway," said Larry, his hearty voice rescuing her from the whirlpool of her thoughts, "I've got a couple of pizza monsters to feed, so if you'll join me in the kitchen…"

He stopped and stared into her face for a moment. "I'm sorry," he said. "I didn't mean to get maudlin or anything. Are you okay?"

"Not really. It's been a day and a half, Larry."

"Let me take care of the boys. Then we'll talk," he promised her.

Later, they sat across the kitchen table from each other,

their slices and tea growing cold as she brought him up to date. When she'd finished, he stared at her, slack-jawed for a moment, then blurted, "Holy crap, Selena! Posting to social media about an ongoing police investigation? You're lucky Brassard didn't throw you in jail. Did you think about the kind of responses that post is likely to attract? What if one of them came from the killer?"

Selena's mouth went dry. Brassard had hinted at this same possibility, but not pointedly enough to frighten her. Now, hearing the concern in Larry's voice really pounded the message home. "She told me she would have the post taken down."

Larry shook his head. "I'll bet you anything she doesn't. She'll probably find a way to use it as a tip line, or to bait a trap or something." He paused as though gathering his courage before adding, "I notice you're not wearing the pendant. Where is it now?"

She brought it out of her pocket to show him. "I'm not sure I have the right to wear it anymore," she said brokenly. "In fact, I don't know whether I ever did." As the words left her lips, Selena realized that this was a truth she'd been avoiding for some time.

She fingered the pewter disc for the space of a breath, then laid it with care on the table.

"This was Barbara's favourite piece of jewellery," she explained. "She was wearing it when she was killed. Later, when the police released her personal effects, I was the family member who picked them up and verified that nothing was missing. Handling the pendant was comforting for me then. I could close my eyes and believe that she was somehow still with me, and I wanted to hang onto that feeling... hang onto *her*. So, I removed her necklace from the envelope before passing it along to her parents. It was the only thing of hers that I kept."

"Did they ever question the fact that it was missing?"

"No, but I'm pretty certain they knew I had it. That was nine years ago. It still brings Barbara back to life in my memory whenever I put it on. And today, for the first time, it feels like I stole it from them."

He reached across the table and covered her hand with his own. "Do you remember what you told me at Rafferty House when I was hurting and confided in you?"

Her vision blurring with tears, she drew a shuddering breath. "Not word for word, no."

"You said that life can't be perfect because we're all flawed in some way, and the only way to move forward from a tragedy was by forgiving ourselves and other people for being imperfect human beings. Selena, you're right. I think your aunt and uncle did know where the pendant had gone, and that their silence was as good as a blessing. I think they wanted you to have it, so there's no need for you to feel guilty about wearing it."

"But now that I know it's haunted—"

Larry pulled back his hand, his features contracting into a frown. "Do you? Do you really? Just because Curt said so?"

"He didn't just tell me, he proved it. He saw her ghost shadowing me and he described her, right down to the earrings she was wearing on the day that she died." Selena leaned forward and said in a taut, earnest voice, "Listen, I can't explain all the whys and wherefores of this. I only know what my gut is telling me, and what it's saying is that this man is for real. Like you inside Rafferty House, he wasn't putting on an act. Curt Wakefield is a ghost whisperer."

Larry let out a gusty breath. "Okay, fine. I'll defer to your gut in this matter: he can see and communicate with ghosts. But if you want Barbara's case brought out of cold storage, you'll have to convince Brassard to believe it as well, and good luck with *that*."

*   *   *

Sara arrived home just in time to put the boys to bed. By the time she'd tucked them both in and returned to the kitchen to join the adults for tea and cookies, Selena had come to a decision.

"I'll be going back to Standerville tomorrow."

Sara froze with her cup halfway to her mouth. "I thought you were planning to spend a full week here. And I was really looking forward to helping you with your… research."

Selena cast a helpless glance at Larry. "Don't look at *me*," he warned her, leaning back in his chair. "It's *your* mess. You tell her."

"What mess?" Sara demanded.

Selena filled her in about the online post and Staff Sergeant Brassard's reaction to it.

"Wow," she murmured admiringly. "That was a bold move. And how does your leaving town change anything, exactly?"

"Oh, for the love of—!" Larry exclaimed. "It keeps her out of any further trouble and possibly out of jail while the police conduct their investigation."

"Uh-*huh*." Sara shot him a reproving look. "Her, and by extension, me. This isn't just you trying to protect me, is it, big brother?"

"*Hell*, no! To be honest, ever since the two of you got together I've been wondering whether that's even possible," he assured her.

"Good." Turning her attention back to Selena, she added, "What changed your mind about staying?"

"As long as the castle remains under siege by the police, I can't go ahead with the purchase, which is what I'm supposedly here to conclude. Brassard told me the investigation could take weeks to wrap up. And with what it's costing me for the motel room—"

"It will cost you zero to stay here with me," Sara cut in.

"And you told me earlier that your calendar was clear, correct?"

"Ye-es, but—"

"No buts! There's a lot more to investigate around here than just one possible murder, so we need to put all our heads together, beginning first thing tomorrow," she finished archly.

More than one murder? That sounded awfully familiar. "You've been speaking with Curt, haven't you?" said Selena.

Sara's response was a knowing grin.

Selena did not sleep well that night. Horrific images kept invading her dreams and yanking her awake. The following morning, feeling achy and a little fogged in the brain, Selena slipped the pendant into her pants pocket and packed up her belongings. She checked out of the motel, treated herself to a comfort-food breakfast of pancakes and hot chocolate at a local diner, then drove to the museum.

Evidently, the girl behind the gift shop counter remembered her from two days earlier. She greeted Selena with a cheerful smile. "If you're looking for Mr. Wakefield, I believe he's out on the train platform, contemplating the universe. That's what he calls it, anyway."

Leaning confidentially over the counter, Selena lowered her voice and asked, "And what do *you* call it?"

The girl's smile widened. "When I do it, I'm taking a coffee break."

Uh-huh.

Selena thanked her and went back outside. She found Curt sitting in the middle of the bench where she'd hung the pendant the previous day. Apparently, she was interrupting a lively conversation between him and the ghosts. The moment he saw her, he quit talking and got to his feet, with a resigned expression on his face.

"So, this is what contemplating the universe looks like?" she teased him.

"For me it does." He gave a cordial nod to the space behind her left shoulder. "I gather you're on your way home."

"Actually, I've decided to wait out the week. And I've also decided that you're right about the pendant." Pulling it out and holding it by its chain, she offered it to him. "I think this is what Barbara wants me to do. I had nightmares about watching her get attacked over and over last night." Selena repressed a shudder.

"And you believe she was sending you a message?"

"Honestly, I don't know. What I do know is, she needs help, and I'm not in a position to provide it to her. I'm hoping you are."

He cupped his hand around the pewter disc, and she lowered the chain onto his palm as well.

"Me too. I'll take good care of this," he assured her. "Now, what are your plans for the rest of the day?"

"Other than moving my stuff into Sara's spare bedroom, I don't have any. Why? Do you have something in mind?"

"What you said the other evening, about sensing an emotion from a house that people think is haunted—it got me thinking. Anyway, there's an item I'd like you to have a look at. It's been puzzling me for some time."

"I don't know how much help I can be, but… Sure," she replied with a shrug.

Selena followed him back inside the museum, to the hexagonal display case in the History of Groverton exhibit. The first thing she noticed was a sudden chill in the air. The temperature was especially brisk in the centre of the room.

"Feels like someone's cranked the air conditioning way up in here," she remarked.

"The A/C isn't on," he told her. "That's just Gertrude being her usual angry self. She's tethered to that brown purse, and unless there's some mystical connection between women and their handbags, I'm at a loss to figure out why."

Hugging herself for warmth, Selena moved in for a closer look at the item in question.

"Well, I'm no expert on the subject, but this bag appears nearly new," she commented. "To have survived a train wreck ninety-odd years ago and still be in this good shape, I'm guessing it had to have been really well made, using top-quality materials. This was not an inexpensive purse. You're certain it was Gertrude's?"

"I have it on good authority that she was carrying it when she first arrived in town and also had it on her person when she was killed."

Selena smiled. "Good authority. You're talking about Ruth and Clara?"

"They were retirees who loved to sit on that bench every afternoon, watching trains and people come and go. If they say they saw Gertrude get off a train while holding that purse, I believe them."

"I'm not doubting your sources, Curt. I'm just wondering whether Gertrude came from money. What do you know about her family?"

"Not much. The only thing I found with her unmarried name on it was a public records copy of Hugh and Gertrude's marriage certificate. They were wed in a civil ceremony, conducted in a Chicago courthouse, and her maiden name is given as 'Smith'."

"Really! There was no attention paid to this blessed union in Groverton's local press? No reception? No celebration at all?"

"None. That may be due to something Ruth noticed when Gertrude stepped down onto the platform. She's ready to swear that the brand-new Mrs. McFadyen was about five months pregnant. And before you ask, that's one month less than the duration of Hugh's out of town business trip."

All by themselves, Selena's eyebrows rose precipitously. This changed everything… almost.

Turning to Curt, she asked, "Are you sure it's the purse that she's tethered to and not something inside it?"

"Absolutely. I spilled everything out of the bag and brought one item upstairs at a time to see what she would do. The only thing she followed was the empty purse. And there's one more thing: when a spirit is tethered, it generally means that the item signifies something she deeply regrets," Curt explained, "or that it's part of something of great importance that she left unfinished when she died. If that's the case here, then Gertrude ought to be projecting sadness, not rage."

Selena considered for a moment. "Maybe rage is what she was feeling at the moment she died. Was she still pregnant then?"

Curt glanced to his left and replied, "I'm no expert either, but that ghost does not look like a pregnant woman to me."

"So, what do you suppose happened to the baby?"

He frowned. "If she lost it—or had it taken away from her—that might explain the intensity of her anger… but it still wouldn't answer the question about the handbag."

Selena stared at the item for several seconds. "Would it be all right if I touched it?"

"Certainly, as long as you're careful about it." Curt produced a key and unlocked the glass display case for her, and she reached in and lifted the purse up with both hands.

She could tell from the weight of it that both the leather and the tortoiseshell were natural, not manufactured. A wealthy woman would most likely have owned several handbags like this. She would have had no reason to be as attached as Gertrude was to any one of them in particular. Unless—

All at once, Selena felt a familiar tingling sensation, followed by a powerful wave of emotion. It broke over her, engulfed her, flowed along her skin like liquid fire. For an endless moment she burned. Then a blanket of pure longing seemed to wrap itself around her, and all the heat was gone.

"Selena! Are you all right?" Curt's voice sounded as though it was coming from far away.

She gulped her next breath. "There's a lot of emotion imprinted on this," she told him in a hushed voice, "and it's not just anger. It's—It feels like—Almost like a plea for help. Tell me, did the purse belong to someone else before it came into Gertrude's possession?"

"Of course, it's possible," he replied slowly. "But if that's true, then what you're sensing from the item means there should be a second ghost attached to it, and Gertrude is the only one I'm seeing."

"And you're positive the bag is empty?"

"Yes! Why do you keep asking that?"

"Because if the second emotion is hers as well, then there must be something still inside it that she wants us to find."

He didn't even hesitate. "Open it up and see for yourself. It's survived a train wreck and nearly a century in storage. I doubt that another inspection is going to hurt it now."

Selena set the handbag upright on the nearest flat surface— the top of a waist-high display case. She released the tortoiseshell clasp, widened the opening, then turned the purse upside-down and gave it a good shake.

"Wait! What are you—?" Curt exclaimed.

Selena ignored him. She shook the purse another couple of times, listening carefully... and was rewarded with a rustling sound. She was right. Something *was* concealed inside the handbag, perhaps in a hidden pocket between the lining and the leather.

Sensing Curt's hand reaching for the purse, she spun to put it beyond his grasp.

"Listen!" she commanded him, and shook it once more. "Did you hear that?"

His eyes widened. "Son of a bitch," he whispered.

Using her fingertips, Selena found first the outline of an envelope, then the opening to the secret pocket in which it had been resting for all those years. With reverent care, she extracted a letter, sealed and addressed to "Captain Lewis Granger, 17th Precinct, NYCPD", and placed it beside the purse on top of the display case.

"No stamp, and an incomplete address," Curt commented. "She was planning to deliver this in person, so it must have been important. And it was concealed inside her bag, which probably meant she didn't want her husband to know about it."

"A letter to a police captain," Selena mused. "Whatever is inside that envelope must be the reason Gertrude is angry. Shall we find out what it says?"

Before she could pick it up, Curt brought the flat of his hand down, pinning the item to the glass surface. "Yes, but it's a historical document and it needs to be treated with care and respect," he warned her.

"Meaning what? You open it while I watch?"

"Actually, I have someone else in mind who'll want to be present when it's opened. It's addressed to the police. If this letter bears on a law enforcement matter, the information it contains will need to be forwarded to the proper authorities in New York, in which case it should come from a credible source."

Selena grinned. "Like the PPS? Brassard did tell me she expected me to come to her with any tangible evidence of wrongdoing we discovered."

Smiling back at her, Curt said, "Then that is precisely what we're going to do."

Six

My dear cousin,

It is with the deepest sadness and shame that I bring you this information.

I cannot believe that we were all so thoroughly taken in by the lies of a fortune hunter. It comes as small consolation to know that we were not the only ones he's deceived. Hugh McFadyen has charmed an entire town in Canada, where he is considered to be a public benefactor, all the while plying his selfish influence behind the scenes. I cannot undo the harm he has already done to our family, but it is my hope that with what I am about to tell you, you will be able to cut short his criminal career and prevent him from causing any further heartache.

It was not by coincidence that McFadyen turned up and began insinuating himself into all of our good graces so shortly after Uncle Hermès was killed. I suspect he may even have paid to have Trudy's father taken out of the way. When McFadyen proclaimed his love for her and insisted on "making an honest woman of her" after learning that she was carrying his child, it warmed our hearts and cleared the path to what he was really after, and still is— Trudy's inheritance. Uncle Hermès's will stipulated that it was to remain in trust until her twenty-first birthday. If she died before then, the entire estate was to go to charity. So, all McFadyen had to do in order to get his hands on it was take her back home with him and wait.

Unfortunately, she was already having a difficult pregnancy. Even more unfortunately, he'd made me a part of his cold-hearted plan. No sooner had we arrived in Groverton than his true colors emerged, and before long, Trudy and I were virtual prisoners in his house.

The very next day, she developed a fever, and I begged him to take her to the hospital. He refused, and instead called for a doctor to come and see her at home. After that, her care was given entirely to me, a practical nurse. I was ordered to remain with her at all times.

Even after the fever had broken, her condition did not improve, and I feared for the child in her womb. Again and again, I pleaded with McFadyen to let her have proper medical attention, but he wouldn't hear of it. One day I decided to take matters into my own hands by going to the local police and making them aware of the situation. He caught me before I could get out the front door. When I told him where I was going and why, he manhandled me up the stairs and locked me inside a room.

After that, he moved Trudy and me into a private apartment on the second floor and locked us in at night. I tried climbing out a window to get help for her, but I fell and sprained my ankle, and once again he caught me. The following day, he had metal bars installed over all the apartment's windows. For security, he said.

This nightmare lasted for three months. Meanwhile, Trudy became steadily weaker. She couldn't walk unassisted. She couldn't keep food down. In her eighth month of pregnancy, she had a stillbirth. I couldn't stop the bleeding. I couldn't do anything for my friend and cousin but weep as I watched the life leave her body, one week before her twenty-first birthday.

Hugh McFadyen is a monster. He's disposed of both their bodies on the property and has threatened to put me in the ground if I say anything to anyone about any of this. Now he's forcing me to wear her clothes and answer to her name the odd time he takes me out. I know what he's doing. He's parading me around so that all of Groverton will swear up and down that they saw Gertrude McFadyen, alive and well, weeks after her birthday. Well, there's one thing of hers that he can't make me wear, and that's her wedding rings. He took everything else away from her, so I made sure she got to keep those.

He may not let me talk to anyone in Groverton, but

that doesn't mean I'll stay silent. I am writing this to you in secret so that you can stop him. I feel terrible about the part that I've been forced to play in his charade. He says it will end with "the McFadyens" going to New York City for a holiday, but that once I've helped him to move all the funds from the trust to his own bank accounts, we'll go our separate ways. I don't believe him. He never laid a hand on Trudy but that doesn't mean he didn't kill her. That's why I'm going to give this letter to the first American police officer I meet and hope it reaches you before Hugh McFadyen murders me too.

With love and deep regret,

Lillian

Curt stood beside Staff Sergeant Brassard's chair, reading the letter over her shoulder. As he'd expected, the ghost of its author had accompanied it and now stood in a corner of the room, gazing with taut anticipation at Brassard's face. Lillian's anger was understandable now. She didn't have to drop the temperature in the room—the account in the letter was chilling enough.

Her lips pressed tightly together, Brassard leaned back in her seat. Curt took that as his cue. He bent forward and with latex-gloved hands turned the several sheets of writing paper so that Selena could read them. Then he rounded the corner of the desk and lowered himself onto one of the guest chairs.

For several long moments, not a word was spoken.

Finally, Brassard said, in a voice gruff with emotion, "*Quelle horreur...* and then to be misidentified after the disaster and buried in another woman's grave...! You are certain this letter is authentic?"

"If you're referring to its age, yes, absolutely," Curt replied. "It came out of a hidden pocket in a handbag that's been in the museum's possession for the past ninety years. As for whether Lillian Friendly wrote it herself…" He glanced over to the corner. The ghost was nodding her head. "…that, too, I'm certain of."

"We would never have found the letter without Lillian's help," Selena chimed in, causing his breath to congeal in his throat.

Brassard's eyebrows rose. "Really! I suppose now you are going to tell me that her ghost told you where to look."

"As a matter of fact—"

"Not exactly," Curt interrupted before she could out him completely. "We were examining the purse, thinking it was empty, and Selena heard something from inside the lining."

"So, as well as having empathy with houses, you are able to receive messages from old letters, Ms. Watt?" said Brassard dryly.

Selena's expression became sullen. "I was following a hunch," she replied.

"Ah!"

Curt let out the breath he'd been holding and asked, "What now, Staff Sergeant? We can't leave Lillian's remains in a grave intended for Gertrude."

"You want to get them exhumed and reburied. I understand. After all these years, there could be very little left of Lillian, and almost certainly nothing of Gertrude. If he kept his wife's death a secret, then we must assume she was not embalmed. However," she added thoughtfully, "if she was wearing metal jewellery, it should at least be possible to discover where he buried her. Afterwards…" She eyed him, frowning. "You know that this is normally something the family takes care of, not the police?"

"Yes, and that's where the problem lies. We know almost

nothing about Lillian and Gertrude's family. The address on that envelope is the first clue we've had, and it's the reason we brought it to you. Their cousin was a police captain."

"Ninety years ago," Brassard reminded him sternly. "And New York was a very large city even then. So, unless this Lewis Granger did something that made the newspaper headlines, tracking down his surviving family members is going to be a difficult and time-consuming task—and I wish you luck with it."

"But—"

Her expression now forbidding, she raised a silencing hand. "Listen carefully to me. What Hugh McFadyen did was cruel and despicable, there is no doubt, and his plan to steal his wife's inheritance was definitely illegal. However, the train wreck ended his life before he could carry it out, and everyone who suffered or abetted his domestic abuse is long since deceased, meaning there is no longer a crime to prosecute. As fascinating as the substance of this historical document may be, it is not a police matter, and I am not going to pull my detectives away from their current cases to help you trace a family tree."

"What if we brought you evidence or testimony relating to a more recent PPS cold case?" Selena piped up.

"How recent?"

"Nine years ago, Barbara Cournoyer was raped and strangled to death. Her murder was never solved."

Brassard nodded slowly. "That I would consider. But your evidence would have to be solid."

"It will be," she said grimly.

Curt knew what she was thinking: that her cousin could point them in the direction of her attacker. However, Barbara's trauma was still so fresh that she couldn't even bring herself to put it into words. How she could be expected to help them identify her killer, he had no idea.

Selena, on the other hand, had evidently formulated a plan.

"Like you said earlier," she explained as they drove back to the museum, "she can talk to Ruth and Clara, they can talk to you—"

"And I can talk to Brassard? That's not going to work."

"I was going to say, you can talk to a police sketch artist," she corrected him patiently.

"You're assuming she saw the face of her attacker. We don't know that."

"Not yet. But once we do…"

"We'll still have a problem, you know. Brassard is a 'dyed-in-the-wool skeptic', to use your own words. How can we make her believe in ghosts?"

"She'll believe when one dumps her off her chair and throws a few books at her head," grumped a female voice from the back seat.

"Violence is not the answer, Lillian," he declared over his shoulder. "Not if we want her to help us. Besides, if ghosts could affect material objects, that letter would have been found decades ago."

"Then take it back there and let me show her how quickly I can turn her office into an ice box."

"Nope. Not even as a joke."

"What makes you think I would be joking?"

It had become noticeably cooler inside the car. Meanwhile, Selena had been watching him with widening eyes. "What am I missing?" she demanded.

"Not a thing," he grated. "Not a damn thing."

"The cemetery will require a reason for the exhumation, of course. Absent a formal request from a living relative of the deceased, we need official proof that the wrong person is in the grave before it can be opened."

The president of the Groverton Municipal Cemetery had a

condescending voice that seemed to originate from somewhere up his nose. As they spoke on the phone, Curt's mind flashed the image of a face with beady eyes, pursed lips, and a curly, powdered wig.

He couldn't help himself. "Will a notarized copy of a letter from the grave's current occupant do?"

"From the—! Is this some kind of prank, Mr. Wakefield?"

"No, sir! I'm deathly serious. The letter in question is an authenticated historical document. It describes the death of Gertrude McFadyen in her home nearly a month before the train derailment, as well as the subsequent travel plans of her husband, Hugh, accompanied by Gertrude's cousin, Lillian Friendly. Lillian was misidentified as Gertrude, and her body was therefore mistakenly interred beside Hugh's."

"I see. And would you happen to know the whereabouts of the late Mrs. McFadyen's remains? If the cemetery is going to reopen the grave to remove Ms. Friendly, it would just be more efficient to replace her with the rightful occupant at the same time. This is something we would be happy to arrange for you, for a reasonable fee."

Right. Anything is possible, for a fee…

Curt consciously relaxed his jaw muscles. "We're still in the process of locating them. Meanwhile, what I need from you is an estimate of the cost for all the work: reopening two graves, opening a third one, relocating the remains of both women, and closing everything up again."

"Very well. And who shall we assume will be footing the bill for this?"

Whoever you're willing to give the best deal to, you self-important son of a—! None of us are made of money, you know.

Fortunately, he chose not to say that aloud. Realizing that his jaw was clenched tight again, he opened and reclosed it before replying, "We're also trying to track down surviving family members. For now, however, let's say it will be the Groverton Historical Society."

"Of course. With remains that old, I should have expected it. Give me an hour or so to pull a quote together and get back to you."

Sure, Curt thought darkly. An hour was plenty of time to inflate a list of dollar figures. Everyone imagined an organization like the Historical Society must have deep pockets, when in fact the Society and the museum shared a government grant with more than a hundred and fifty other communities in the province…

The importunate buzzing of the intercom yanked his mind back to the present.

"You've got a visitor," said Amy's voice. "It's Ms. Traynor, the lady from the library. Shall I send her in?"

Curt checked his watch. "No, I'll come out and talk to her, thanks."

The exhibit halls were full of visitors, as it turned out. A tour bus had arrived while he was on the phone—he could see it parked in the lot by the front entrance of the building—and about twenty happily chattering adults were now drifting among the displays, admiring his handiwork. This was good for business, but not so good for having a private conversation with Sara. He would have to take her out onto the train platform.

Curt paused at the front counter and made eye contact with both Amy and Orville. "In about an hour, there should be a phone call from J. D. DeLucci of the Groverton Municipal Cemetery. It's important that I speak with him, so if I'm still outside, don't take a message. Send someone to fetch me."

They nodded their understanding in tandem.

Curt ushered Sara out the door and around the corner, past the bench where Ruth, Barbara and Clara sat engrossed in quiet conversation, and over to its twin at the other end of the platform. Fortunately, the area was sheltered. Rain had been forecast for that afternoon, and grey clouds were already gathering. The air was full of humidity. He could practically smell it, wafting on the breeze.

"Selena has told me what the two of you are up to," Sara said once they were seated. "What can I do to help?"

Her simple question broke Curt's emotional dam. Through sheer force of will, he'd managed to be calm and civil on the telephone, suppressing his growing frustration. Now all that pent-up vexation came gushing out of him in a flash flood of words. "I've been on the phone with a bunch of bureaucratic doorstops for the past two hours, at the Historical Society, and the Health Department, and the Coroner's Office, and the Municipal Cemetery, and the Regional Cemetery Association, trying to get Lillian's body moved out of Gertrude's grave, and it all comes down to two things with those people, neither of which I can provide: money, and a request from the family."

"Even the Coroner's Office?"

"Okay, correction," he snapped, his voice rising. "The Coroner's Office, like the police, flatly refuse to have anything to do with this, since ninety-year-old corpses that are already in the ground do not fall within their purview. However, since Gertrude's body was not embalmed, they did suggest I contact the Health and Environmental Safety Departments." He practically roared these last words.

"Careful of your temper, Mr. Wakefield," said Ruth's voice in his mind. *"You don't want to bust a blood vessel, now."*

The irony of his receiving health advice from a ghost was not lost on Curt. Nonetheless, she made a good point. He paused for several deep, calming breaths before continuing in a lowered voice, "This ought to be a simple matter of putting things right. But everywhere I turn, there are fees to be paid, plus taxes, plus gratuities, and 'may we ask whose name should appear on the invoice?' If I can't track down one of Gertrude's relatives and convince them to cover the expense of giving her a proper burial, then all those fees are probably going to come out of the museum's budget, and I can barely make ends meet as it is. This is infuriating!"

"Mm-*hmm*," she said. "So, if I understand correctly, the first step in solving your problem is to recreate Gertrude's family tree, from the late nineteenth century to the present. That shouldn't be too hard, considering all the genealogical resources that are currently available to us."

"Are you offering to do this research for me?" he ventured.

She gave him a reproachful look. "Weren't you listening before? Of course I am! All I need is a starting point. Selena said there were some names mentioned in that letter you found...?"

Relief was already bringing his blood pressure down, he could feel it. "Come into my office. I'll show it to you."

As she followed him through the exhibit hall and into the tower, he glanced around, searching for Lillian amidst the crowd of tourists. The ghost wasn't there. Unease tiptoed across his shoulders. If she was haunting his office, that could be a good thing or a bad one.

This wasn't Sara's first visit to his sanctum. Immediately making herself comfortable, she pulled up a guest chair and sat down, regarding him expectantly across the desktop, and for the first time all day, he felt he had a reason to smile.

Old documents had to be carefully handled. Curt pulled two pairs of latex gloves out of his upper desk drawer, one for himself and one for Sara. When the necessary protections were in place, the blue file folder came out. Curt set the pages of the letter in front of her, side by side on the desktop.

A moment later, Curt sensed movement behind his left shoulder and turned his head to find a familiar greyscale figure standing in the corner of the room.

Lillian's gaze was riveted on Sara's face as she read. The ghost's expression morphed to mirror the changes that paraded across the living woman's features as she processed each stunning revelation. At last, Sara looked up from the letter and leaned back in her chair, and it felt as though a spell had been broken. It was Curt's imagination, he knew, but the air in his office seemed somehow easier to breathe.

"I'd better write this down," Sara said. "It will be the data for my initial search."

Curt reached into a different desk drawer and handed her what was left of his own lined notebook.

Sara produced a pen from her purse, found a clean page in the notebook, and immediately began jotting. "So, in 1932, we have Gertrude… I don't suppose you happen to know her unmarried name?"

"On the marriage certificate it was Smith, but that could have been an alias," Curt replied. "It felt suspicious to me when I saw it."

"If it was an alias, her father, Hermès, must have used the same one. How else could Gertrude claim her inheritance after he died? And you may find this hard to believe, but there are people on this planet whose actual legal surname is Smith." She flashed him a grin. "To do the math, if Gertrude turned 21 in 1933, then she was born early in 1912, probably in New York City. And logically, anyone who could leave their daughter an inheritance worth killing for in the depths of the Great Depression had to have been a tycoon before it started. Construction… the railway, perhaps… with friends in high places, I'm guessing."

"Or low ones," he muttered dryly, thinking of where McFadyen had probably made his fortune.

She appeared not to have heard him. "Now, there are two cousins with different surnames: Lillian Friendly and Lewis

Granger. Without their years of birth, the whole exercise becomes more difficult. I suppose I can dig into both families to see where the Friendly-Granger-Smith bloodlines crossed…"

Curt threw a glance over his shoulder. Lillian hadn't budged from the corner of his office, only now she was studiously pretending to mind her own business.

Waiting for an invitation, was more like it.

"Sara," he began uncertainly, "what if I were to tell you that we have another source of information, a first-hand one, in this room right now?"

Her eyebrows rose. "Are you talking about a ghost?" she said with hushed excitement.

"Would you believe me if I said yes?"

"I… might be persuaded that such things exist."

"Fair enough. Lillian Friendly wrote that letter in 1933. Her spirit is tethered to it, and we've been… conversing, you might say, from the time it was found."

Sara inhaled sharply. "So you were serious the other night at dinner. You can see and hear ghosts? Can she speak to me? Do we need a seance or something?"

"A seance! Sounds like fun. You can shake the table and practise your ventriloquism and I'll just… cool my heels."

Hearing the sarcasm fairly drip from Lillian's voice made his laughter a little brittle. "Good Lord, no! What I mean is, no trappings are necessary. Just ask her whatever you need to know. She'll hear your question, and I'll repeat her answer word for word."

"How boring. Honestly, some people have no appreciation for theatre."

"You'll know it's her speaking through me because if I make something up or change her meaning, Lillian will be pissed, and she'll turn this room into an ice box. Does that about cover it?" he added, swinging his attention to the ghost in the corner.

She was already pissed. Her arms were crossed over her chest, her chin was elevated, and there was a perceptible drop in the air temperature. Curt held his breath, waiting for her response. It had taken ninety years for her to break her angry silence. If she were to shut down again now…

"I suppose it does," she replied at last.

"Lillian says it does," he told Sara, nearly giddy with relief.

It was short-lived.

"You said you wouldn't change my meaning, Mr. Wakefield," Lillian reminded him sternly.

Sara pulled her cotton jacket closed and hugged her shoulders. Frowning, she said, "I'm getting the sense that Lillian Friendly isn't feeling very friendly. Did you put words in her mouth just now, Curt, to test the system?"

"No. I just omitted a couple that I thought weren't important."

"And they were…?"

"She said, 'I suppose'."

"So she's not really happy with the arrangement but it's all that's available. Those are not unimportant words! I know exactly how you feel, Lillian," Sara declared to the room. "Men can be dense at times, and there's nothing we women can do about it. We'll just have to be patient and work with what we've got."

Curt swallowed a heartfelt sigh. It was going to be a very long day.

Seven

Selena gasped loudly and clapped a hand to her chest, then cried melodramatically at Sara's back, "Oh, no! You didn't actually side with Lillian and gang up on Curt, did you?"

Standing at the kitchen counter, Sara shrugged one shoulder in reply and continued chopping vegetables for dinner. "It was getting pretty cold in the room, and I had to do *something* to calm her down. Besides, I've had my share of being unseen and unheard, not to mention being censored and misrepresented by men, so I could understand her frustration at having to speak through one. Even if it's a man I happen to like."

Selena liked him too, and now that Lillian had finally broken her silence, she couldn't help sympathizing with him. Until everyone's remains were in the right graves, this tethered spirit was apparently going to be a handful to manage.

"I gather you now believe in ghosts," Selena commented.

"Mmm... Let's just say that my mind is a lot more open to the idea now than it was before I met him; and after this morning, it's hard not to believe in Lillian. She's one tough cookie, I have to say, and she's got quite a temper. I can't imagine anyone crossing her and escaping unscathed while she was still alive. If that train hadn't derailed and she'd been able to get her letter into the hands of the New York City police, Hugh McFadyen would have gone to prison and the bodies of Gertrude and her baby would have been found and properly buried ninety years ago."

"Same thing if she'd been able to alert the local authorities," Selena mused. "Then Curt wouldn't be having to fight with them to get the remains exhumed now. Well, at least that murder mystery has been solved."

"Has it?" Sara perched the end of the cutting board on the rim of her largest pot and used the back of her knife to scrape its load of diced raw carrots and squash into the stew she was preparing. "You read that letter she wrote. Did it sound sincere to you?"

Selena considered for a moment. "Sincerely ashamed, you mean? Or sincerely vengeful? People wrote differently back then—"

"Unh-*unh*!" she cut in. "Not that differently. And not that formally. Not in the 1930s. Not when the author is supposedly grieving and desperate. I've read enough old documents to be able to tell a genuinely emotional account from an objective report. Think back now: what did you feel when you handled the purse?"

"Mainly anger, but there was something else, too. It might have been despair."

"The anger sounds like Lillian. The despair was probably Gertrude's, since it was her handbag to begin with. What I keep wondering is how someone as strong-willed as Lillian could have been forced to go along with Hugh's plan, especially once Gertrude was dead. Any leverage he held over her would have been gone at that point. Each time he took her out of the house, she would have had an opportunity to slip a note to someone, asking for help. So, what do you suppose was stopping her?"

Selena's mind recoiled as a terrible possibility occurred to her. "Are you suggesting that she might have been Hugh's partner in crime?"

"Maybe. Or maybe there was another reason for her to cooperate with him. At this point, all I can say is that I think it would be a mistake to take Lillian's letter at face value. I suspect there's a lot more story to uncover. Her memory was spotty when I questioned her this afternoon. So, I'm going to do a deep dive to find out what she *didn't* tell me about her relatives, and figure out why."

Sara dropped several bouillon cubes into a large measuring cup, then filled it with boiling water from the kettle and stirred energetically until the cubes dissolved.

"You believe she lied to you?"

Emptying the measuring cup into the stew pot, Sara replied, grim-faced, "I do. By omission, at the very least. She died in 1933. I don't think she understands how thorough a data search can be in the twenty-first century. But she's about to learn."

Two hours later, Selena and Sara were sitting at the kitchen table, exploring public information web sites on Sara's computer and recording notes on Selena's laptop, while the contents of the stew pot burbled quietly in the background. Then the timer on the stove chimed to announce that dinner was ready to serve, just as Donnie and Eric came thundering through the door of the house.

"Mom! You won't believe what we found at the end of our street!" Donnie hollered from the front hall. "They're making a great big hole in the ground, and the sides of it are all layers of rock, and I saw some dinosaur bones and stuff in there, but

Eric wouldn't let me climb down and dig for them, so when he grabbed me to pull me away, I ducked and fell down."

Sara froze, wide-eyed. "The end of our street?" she repeated in a horrified whisper. "They were supposed to stay in the park across the road."

Then, in case that wasn't bad enough, Eric called to her, "I don't think anything's broken, but we're gonna need some band-aids."

"Oh. My. *God!*" Sara sprang to her feet and rushed out of the kitchen, with Selena right behind her.

The sight that met them in the hall brought both women to a screeching halt: two boys, one looking shamefaced, both in need of a shower. Eric's grass-stained clothing was raining sand onto the floor, and his bare arms and legs sparkled with it. His little brother, meanwhile, was muddy all over. Donnie couldn't have been dirtier if he'd swum in a bog, fully dressed.

"I tried to keep him in the park, Mom," Eric explained, "I really did. But he was off like a shot, and there were these rocks, and a mud puddle—"

"I get the picture," Sara said. "And you don't *think* anything's broken?" Taking her younger son by the hand, she began working the joints in his arm to check for herself.

Sara was a Virgo, Selena recalled. Very detail-oriented.

"Listen, I can drive him to the ER right now, if you're concerned," she offered.

Sara threw her an incredulous look. "Do you really want that mess inside your car? No, I appreciate the thought, but I think Eric's right. And these two need to stand on the porch until I can hose them down."

"Hose them down?" came a hearty voice from the other side of the screen door. "That sounds like a job for the fire department."

Uncle Larry had arrived.

Sara heaved a sigh of relief. "Yes! Please! You know what

to do?”

“I’ve been on the receiving end of enough of these back yard showers to figure it out,” he assured her. “Come on, boys...”

A bar of soap and two sets of clean clothes later, they were all sitting around the dining table, digging into Sara’s delicious beef stew with biscuits.

“Well, I already know what my daredevil nephews did after school today. And what have you two ladies been up to?” Larry asked between mouthfuls.

The ladies exchanged meaningful looks. Then, taking turns, they filled him in. Selena couldn’t help noticing that the deeper they went into their narrative, the more slowly he chewed his food, and the farther back he leaned in his chair.

“So, I left the library early and spent an hour with Curt and Lillian, finding out everything she remembered about the Smiths, Friendlys, and Grangers,” Sara said, wrapping up her account. “And Selena and I were on the computer for a while before dinner just now, trying to verify what she’d told us.”

“Sara doesn’t trust what Lillian put into her letter to the police, either,” Selena added. “She says it sounds insincere.”

“Not so much insincere as rehearsed,” Sara explained. “It’s too detailed, for one thing—answers every question before it can be asked.”

“Maybe that’s because she was afraid she would be dead by the time it was received?” Larry suggested.

“No. It’s too carefully worded. This feels like a narrative she fabricated to put herself in the best possible light while shoving most of the blame onto Hugh McFadyen.”

“That could just be her writing style,” Larry pointed out. “If you could find other things she’s written and make a comparison—”

“We searched the net, big brother,” she cut in. “All the historical document databases that time permitted. There’s nothing from her in any of them. That gave me another reason to look into her family tree, to see whether any of her still-living relatives might have saved a letter or two."

"And...?" he prompted, visibly curious now.

She let out a sigh. "Dead ends. Since Lillian died unmarried and childless, we had to go backwards in order to go forwards along a different branch. We found Upstate New York public school registration forms dated 1910, for two sisters surnamed Friendly. Neither of them was Lillian. However, on the chance that they were her older siblings and she was simply too young to be enrolled, I researched the parents' names provided on the forms."

"And?"

"There's no history for an Alan and Josephine Friendly at all. Or their daughters. It's as though the family didn't exist before 1910. And before you ask, we looked into immigration records, Canadian as well as American, and there's no evidence of a Friendly entering either country at that time."

"So you can't say for certain whether Lillian was even part of this group," Larry said thoughtfully. "That must be frustrating."

"Yes, but it's nothing compared to trying to trace Gertrude's lineage. That branch was surnamed Smith," Sara reminded him, practically snarling the final word.

"Hermès isn't a common given name, though," he pointed out.

"Yes, well... when I looked it up, I discovered that among other things, Hermes was the Greek god of thievery and cunning. I'm beginning to wonder whether Smith and Friendly might both be aliases, and the word 'cousin' might be code for something else."

Meanwhile, Eric and Donnie had been sitting quietly, their eyes wide as saucers, taking in the conversation. Selena smiled inwardly. Fossil-hunting at a construction site might be fun, but this was a real-life mystery, and it was apparently showing them a side of their mother that they'd never seen before. Investigating a murder tended to have that effect.

And people wondered why crime novels were so addictive.

Selena received the text from Tricia Vickery the following morning: *Please stop by the office at your earliest convenience. We need to talk.*

About the castle? Had the police finished processing it already? That didn't seem likely. Then again, Brassard might have purposely exaggerated how long it would take in order to keep the *amateur* at a distance.

Fairly itching with anticipation, Selena gulped down the rest of her breakfast and headed over to Hearth and Home. As she stepped through the door she heard Vickery blurt out, "Oh, thank goodness you're here! I didn't know who else I could talk to about this."

The realtor was sitting behind the reception desk. She'd been crying—her mascara was smudged. Selena glanced around to ensure that they were alone. Then she dragged a chair over, sat down beside Vickery, and gazed into the other woman's anguished face.

"Tell me what's happened," she said softly. "Are you okay?"

"Yes, but I—The police were here earlier, and the questions they were asking me—!"

"What kind of questions?"

"First, they accused me of holding back information about Brenda," Vickery said in a tremulous voice. "They insisted it was impossible for us to have worked together for an entire year without sharing things about ourselves. After I set them straight about that, they—" She caught her breath in a sob. "They wanted to know if I ever caught her doing anything sneaky or unprofessional."

"And did you?"

"No! I told them that we all make mistakes when we're learning the ropes, but that doesn't mean we're criminals."

"How did they take it?" Selena asked, already suspecting what the answer would be.

"Not well. They wanted details. Every little thing she'd done wrong. It was like throwing dirt on her memory, and it made me angry, so I challenged their right to do it. And that was when they said—" Vickery's features crumpled. In a choked voice, she continued: "They said they had reason to believe that she wasn't who I thought she was. That the real Brenda Ryan had died twenty years ago at the age of three. That I should probably have my accounts for the past year audited because it was entirely possible that I was being scammed the whole time by a con artist. That scammers like to target grieving families because the recently bereaved are such easy marks…"

A tear painted a shiny stripe down the realtor's cheek.

Unsure how else to comfort her, Selena reached out, took both of Vickery's hands in her own, and gave them a squeeze. Meanwhile, her thoughts were whirling. There were many different reasons for someone to assume a false identity, most of them benign. However, the police had picked on this one— and warned Brenda's employer about it—so that had to mean they had uncovered something incriminating about the young real estate agent in the course of their investigation.

"I did hold back something from the police," Vickery said with a shuddering sigh. "The reason Brenda didn't talk about herself was that we were always talking about Rachel. Whoever that girl really was, she didn't lie to me about knowing my daughter. They'd spent time together, studied together. They'd been friends and shared secrets. I could tell," Vickery declared in a low voice. "She was mourning her too. Being around each other and sharing memories about Rachel was helping us both to deal with my daughter's death. And now Brenda's gone too, and I don't know who is going to help me deal with losing *her.*"

Selena could think of someone—as long as Brenda's ghost was still around.

"You say you held back some information. Was there something else you held back? Perhaps a gift that Brenda once gave you, or something of hers that you simply couldn't part with?"

Vickery's eyes widened. "I… Yes, actually, now that you mention it. A couple of things."

Excellent!

She patted Vickery on the arm. "I've got an idea. Stay here. I'll be back as soon as I can."

Selena burst through the front entrance of the museum and found Curt deep in conversation with the young woman at the counter of the gift shop. Apparently sensing her approach, he glanced up, then crossed the foyer to meet her, a welcoming expression pinned on his face.

"Do you have any news for me?" she asked, keeping her voice low. "How is Barbara doing? Has she told you anything yet?"

"Nothing yet, sorry. She's gone without therapy for nine years, so this could take a while."

"That's okay. In the meanwhile, I'm here to ask you for a favour."

His eyes narrowed. "Oh?"

"I need you to make a house call, and it needs to be today."

Inhaling audibly, he took her by the elbow and ushered her into the exhibit hall, where a couple of visitors wearing shorts and sandals stood admiring the gallery wall of vintage photographs. She could practically feel the tension flowing through Curt's fingertips as he urged her toward the emergency exit at the far side of the room and stopped her just short of it.

Frowning, he turned to face her and whispered hoarsely, "A house call? I'm not a doctor, Selena, so what the hell does that mean?"

He had evidently not been having a good morning.

"Well, technically it's an office call, not a house call—"

"Stop it!" he hissed over his shoulder. "I am not taking you back there and that's that!"

Startled momentarily speechless by the abruptness of his tone, Selena didn't realize at first that he'd been talking not to her but to Lillian this way. It seemed the ghost took exception to it as well—the air around them was suddenly chilly.

"Listen," Curt continued, addressing Selena this time, "I'm still trying to get the remains of two women exhumed and put into the right graves. You have no idea what a bureaucratic nightmare this is turning out to be. So unless you're here to tell me Sara has identified a family member who can take the matter off my hands—"

"The realtor's office is haunted," she said, raising her voice to cut off his tirade.

It worked. For a long moment, Curt stared at her in mute astonishment.

"At least, I suspect it is," she continued. "I can't see or hear ghosts, but you can. If I'm right, and Brenda's spirit is tethered to something in Hearth and Home, she can answer a lot of questions about her death. And if that helps the police solve their case, Brassard will have to believe that Barbara's ghost can help them find her killer as well. And maybe also that the castle is sentient and has valuable information to give them."

"That's an awful lot of ifs, Selena," Curt pointed out.

"Yes, but they're lining up like dominoes. Once the first one falls, the rest will follow. All I'm asking you to do for now is step inside Tricia Vickery's realty office and look around the place. That's all. Just tell me whether I'm right. If I am, we can decide together what the next step should be." A pause, then, "That house is in pain, Curt. I only want to stop its suffering."

"And help it find peace," he murmured. "All right. DeLucci still hasn't called back with a quotation—I'm not sure I even want to know what the dollar amount will be—so let's meet at the realty office in, say, half an hour?" Turning his head, he added flatly over his shoulder, "No, Lillian. The letter stays here and so do you."

As he walked Selena to the front entrance of the museum, he leaned in and whispered in her ear, "I hope we untether her soon. All she wants to do is refrigerate the living, starting with Brassard."

That was a lot of anger for a ghost to be carrying around. Deep down, Selena couldn't help wondering whether putting Lillian in her own grave would be enough to satisfy it.

Selena and Curt parked their cars side by side in the lot and walked into Hearth and Home together. Vickery appeared much calmer now. She'd fixed her makeup and was able to greet them with a smile as they came through the door.

"Ms. Vickery—" Selena began.

"Please. It's Tricia." The firmness was back in her voice as well.

"This is Curt Wakefield. He's the curator of the museum here in town and he's had a lot of experience with—"

"Research," he said, interrupting her. "As a historian, I handle a lot of old artifacts and investigate their pasts."

"He uncovers the *truth* about their pasts," Selena added, tossing him a significant glance. "The police seem to have decided that Brenda was involved in some sort of criminal activity. You beg to differ. What I'm suggesting is that we test their theory by conducting our own search for the facts, beginning with what is in this office. You told me earlier that you still had something of Brenda's here?"

"Yes. When I hired her last year, she gave me a gift to thank me—a charm for my bracelet." She held out her left wrist to show them a tiny silver house, then rotated her hand rapidly to make all the charms dance. There had to be a dozen of them, all clipped onto an elegantly interwoven chain. "Last week, she gave me another one to mark our first anniversary of working together. This bracelet is precious to me. It was a birthday present from my daughter, before she passed away, and I wear it every day. Do you need to take a closer look at it?"

"That won't be necessary," said Curt, waving away her question as his gaze settled on a corner of the room.

Judging from the expression on his face, he was seeing a ghost, perhaps even two of them. And if they were tethered to that bracelet...!

"Are you sure, Curt?" Selena asked tautly.

"Absolutely," he replied, then turned gentle eyes on the realtor. "What was your daughter's name, Tricia?"

"Rachel."

"I'd love to see a picture of her. Do you have one?"

"Of course. In my private office."

Bemused, Selena followed them into Vickery's sanctum, where a framed photograph hung on the wall, a picture of a beaming young woman wearing a mortarboard on her head and clad in graduation robes. She had long auburn hair, dark eyes, and a proud tilt to her chin. Just like her mother.

"She was beautiful," Curt said.

"That's how she looked before the cancer took hold of her. It's how I prefer to remember her," Vickery responded in the voice of someone holding back tears. "Do you think you can find out the truth about Brenda?"

"I don't know yet," he told her, "but that doesn't mean we won't try. Thank you for sharing this with us, Tricia. We'll let you know if we learn anything."

Selena felt an unusually cool hand on the small of her back. Next thing she knew she was being urged out the door of the office and through the reception area, towards the main entrance of Hearth and Home Realty.

Outside in the parking lot, she whirled on Curt and demanded, "What just happened in there?"

"There's a spirit attached to that bracelet, but it's not Brenda's. It's Rachel's. That was what you wanted me to do, correct? Look around and determine whether there was a ghost on the premises?"

"Well, yes, but… Rachel knew Brenda when they were alive. If you could ask her—"

"How, Selena? The only way I can have a private conversation with Rachel is by separating her grieving mother from that bracelet; and the only way she'll agree to let it out of her possession is if she can be convinced to believe not only in ghosts but also in my ability to communicate with them."

"And if she could be convinced?" Selena persisted.

When he met her gaze, the sadness in his eyes made her heart constrict. "Then my secret would be out, and I'm not ready for the world to know about my special gift. In fact, I doubt whether I'll ever be ready. You're one of only three people whom I've entrusted with the knowledge, and that's where I need it to stop. Do you understand, Selena?"

An icy splash of disappointment erased her earlier sympathy for him. "So that's it, then? You're giving up? On Brenda? On Barbara?"

"I never said that." Improbably, he was smiling. "In the past three years, I've untethered half a dozen spirits without betraying myself. There's always a workaround. We just have to find it."

Eight

C urt had hoped to be feeling better when he returned to the museum than he'd been when he left it an hour earlier, but that wasn't to be the case.

The first thing he heard when he walked through the front door was Amy's chirpy voice, informing him that he'd missed the call he'd been expecting from Mr. DeLucci at the Groverton Municipal Cemetery. Returning it wasn't an option, apparently. Today was Friday, and DeLucci had already departed to spend a long weekend out of town. So, Curt could look forward to another week of playing phone tag with the man... which wasn't necessarily a bad thing, when he thought about it. Perhaps a family member would be identified and persuaded to assume the cost of at least one of the exhumations and reburials by the time they reconnected.

Uh-huh. Dream on.

Letting out a heavy breath, Curt shifted his grip on the bag containing his lunch. It was a salad he'd picked up from the Loblaw store on his way back from Hearth and Home. Spinach, pine nuts, and mandarin orange segments, with a small cup of vinaigrette tucked into one corner of the cellophane-wrapped container. Not his first choice, but it was the most interesting thing they'd had on offer that didn't involve rice and raw fish, and he hadn't relished the thought of hunting for a better selection elsewhere.

Normally, Curt ate in his office in the tower. It was clear as he stepped through the door, however, that today was not going to be a normal day for him. Lillian's letter was kept in his desk drawer, and she had evidently been sulking nearby during his absence. The temperature inside the room had to be nearly zero degrees Celsius.

So, change of plans. Letting Amy know where she could find him if necessary, he headed outside to the train platform to lunch alfresco. As expected, Barbara was sitting between Ruth and Clara on the ghost bench. None of them seemed to take notice of him as he passed. *Good,* he thought. Barbara wasn't flinching or shrinking away from him anymore. It was a small improvement, but he would take it.

Curt lowered himself onto the replica bench and set out the components of his meal atop a serviette: the salad, a plastic-pouched cutlery kit (also plastic), and a small bottle of cranberry cocktail. He'd also grabbed one of the last oatmeal cookies from the batch that Amy had brought in that morning. It would stay in the bag for later. As he was removing the transparent covering from the salad, a shadow fell across his picnic, causing him to look up into the sombre face of Nena Cartier.

Although she wasn't dressed in her Ojibwe garb today, the long grey braid that hung over her shoulder, her dark, deep-set eyes, and the height and prominence of her cheekbones revealed her indigenous ancestry.

"We're not just having problems with a flaky air conditioning system," she said. It wasn't a question. "And I've seen how you are when you talk to yourself. You're not really alone."

A chill pierced his core. "And…?" he prompted warily.

"My late grandfather was a medicine man when he was alive, gifted by the *manitouk* with special knowledge and abilities. Sometimes, when I'm sleeping, he sends me a dream, appearing inside it in the form of an owl when it's meant to tell me something. Last night, he gave me a warning that I believe is intended for you: 'There is an angry spirit inside the museum, and this spirit is going to bring you great trouble.'"

"She's already bringing me great trouble."

"Mr. Wakefield, the trouble is just getting started. There is much worse to come."

Curt heaved a sigh. "And does your grandfather have any suggestions for how it can be avoided?"

"I kept hearing three words: 'Burn the paper.' I don't know what that means, but I'll be sure to share with you whatever wisdom he imparts if I receive any more dreams from him." And with that, she wheeled and strolled away.

Burn the paper? That had to refer to the letter, and burning it was the one thing he didn't dare do. Digitize it, yes. File it, yes. But every fibre of his historian heart rebelled at the idea of destroying an old, original document, especially one that was the only tangible evidence of a past crime. Never mind that it was also the sole justification for ordering the exhumations and re-interments of not one but *two* sets of remains.

Worse trouble to come? Just thinking about what that might mean was enough to pull the taste of bile up the back of his throat.

Curt turned and stared at his lunch for a long moment. Then he put everything back into the bag. Perhaps later, his appetite would return. For now, digesting any sort of food was going to be a challenge.

Lillian was waiting for him near the hexagonal showcase in the exhibits hall, her arms crossed and her lips pressed primly together.

"Well? Was it worth making the trip?"

He glanced around to make sure no one could overhear him, then replied, "I guess. There was a ghost there, but not the one Selena was hoping I would find."

Lillian tilted her head, raising a disapproving eyebrow. *"She's looking for another ghost? Why? Isn't one enough for her? Or is she trading in that weepy girl for a newer model?"*

Biting back an angry retort, Curt informed her tartly, "The 'weepy girl', as you call her, is Selena's cousin, Barbara, who was brutally murdered by someone the police stopped looking for years ago. Now Selena is trying to solve a more recent killing—one that apparently took place somewhere inside Hugh McFadyen's old house, by the way—"

"In the castle?" Lillian cut in, instantly attentive. *"And she's trying to find the ghost of the victim at a real estate office? Not inside the house?"*

"The police have expressly forbidden her to enter the crime scene until they've finished processing it and are ready to wrap up their investigation. Now, if you'll excuse me…?"

With that, Curt headed toward the tower. His office had been turned into a walk-in refrigerator. What better place to store a salad to be eaten later? Then a thought occurred to him that halted him in mid-step and spun him around.

Lillian hadn't budged from her spot, but her lips were now curved in a superior, infuriating smile.

Curt hurried back to the centre of the room and demanded in an urgent whisper, "What do you know about that house that no one else does, Lillian?"

Her grin became positively feline. *"I can't tell you. I'll have to show you."*

His thoughts were racing. "McFadyen was a rum-runner, wasn't he? He had to have a secret place to stash his booze. A room with a hidden entrance, maybe?"

"You'll never find it on your own," she pointed out archly.

Ever since they'd returned from the PPS building, Lillian had been nagging him to take her out again. Now she was baiting him, trying to get him to sneak her into the castle. Whatever trouble she'd already made for him, it would pale by comparison if he were to be arrested for interfering with an ongoing investigation.

Nena's grandfather was right—this woman was trouble, on two planes of existence—but forewarned was forearmed. That letter wouldn't be going anywhere near the castle. Neither would he. However, as he'd told Selena earlier, there was always a workaround. And he had resources to call on.

"Never find it without you?" he mused aloud. "I guess we'll have to see about that."

Curt walked past her and back out the door. Lillian's mention of a "weepy girl" had reminded him that he hadn't checked on Barbara yet today.

"It's a lovely afternoon for train watching," Ruth commented as he rounded the corner and stepped onto the boarding platform.

"Hi, handsome!" Clara carolled, beaming up at him and patting the space beside her in invitation.

"Ladies," he said, giving each of them an acknowledging nod and a smile. "It is a bright and sunny day, isn't it? But I thought I saw Barbara with you earlier. Is she all right?"

"Oh, she'll never be all right, Mr. Wakefield. None of us will, truth be told," Clara replied. *"But she's better than before, now that someone has listened to her."*

"She's deciding whether she's ready for you to listen to her," Ruth said. *"We've assured her that you're good people, and that you'll help her if you can. Now it's up to her."*

"In the meanwhile, have you any idea where she's gone?"

"I imagine she's hiding between the walls," said Clara with a sigh. *"Len came out pushing his luggage trolley and said*

hello to her, and she was off like a shot, poor thing."

"She'll be back when she feels safe again." From the deliberate tone of Ruth's voice and the way she was looking at him, that was his cue to leave.

"I guess I'll see you later, then," he said, and headed back toward the entrance.

To his surprise, a cluster of people had gathered at the museum's front doors. He glanced to his left and saw a tour bus parked on the far side of the lot, and a stream of passengers disembarking to join the seven or eight already waiting to enter the building. Curt pinned an affable expression on his face, then negotiated his way through the rapidly growing crowd and tried the door. It was locked.

What the hell...?

Fortunately, he carried a spare key with him in case of emergencies. He let himself in, murmuring reassurances to the patiently standing visitors as he did so.

"Oh, thank God!" Amy blurted when she saw him come through the door. "It all happened so fast and I didn't know what else to do. The A/C's gone nuts. It's like the Arctic in Exhibit Hall B, and Hall A isn't much better. I turned the thermostat up and switched it to heat, but it's not having any effect. Romy and Nena will be back soon—they've gone home to get their winter jackets."

"Lillian," he muttered darkly. Trouble-on-two-planes hated being denied anything.

"Are you going to request a service call?" Amy asked.

"No," he told her. "I know how to fix it. I just need a couple of minutes." *...and a warm coat,* he added silently, hunching his shoulders as he walked toward the coldest part of the museum.

Exhibit Hall B contained the history of the town, with special emphasis on transportation, agriculture, and the roles played by many of Groverton's citizens in World Wars One and Two. It was filled with old photographs, paintings, scale models, and dioramas, and this sudden cold couldn't be doing any of them any good.

Lillian stood waiting for him in the centre of the hall, wearing a triumphant grin. She'd won and she knew it. The image popped into his mind of a crackling fire with a handwritten letter slowly curling and blackening inside it.

"Okay, fine," he told her, biting off each word. "I'll take you there." His breath hung in the air like mist.

"*When?*" she demanded.

"As soon as I can gain access without getting myself arrested."

She appeared to consider this for a moment. At last, she replied haughtily, *"That would be acceptable."*

"Wonderful. Now will you please put the temperature back the way it was so I can reopen the museum to the public?"

"Since you asked politely, I will."

"Thank you."

"Ohmigod!" said Amy's voice behind him. Curt spun around and saw her staring goggle-eyed at him from the entrance to the exhibit hall. "Were you just—?"

Oh, shit!

"Was I just what?" he asked, playing for time to think.

"Talking to a hacker on your phone. Did someone take remote control of our environmental settings?"

Curt nearly burst out laughing. She thought he was wearing an earpiece. It made so much more sense than pretending that he'd been talking to himself! He couldn't believe he hadn't thought of it before.

He drew himself up. "Yes, Amy," he said with as much dignity as he could muster. "There's nothing wrong with the air conditioning. The temperature is already rising. And in just a few minutes you'll be able to unlock the door and let our visitors come in."

As she raced back to her post behind the gift shop counter, Curt breathed a sigh of relief. That had been a close one.

The Fire Inspector's office was located on the second floor of the main fire hall. Little more than a glass-enclosed cubicle in the administrative wing, it nonetheless had a window, one that afforded an unimpeded view of the ramp to the street from the station's vehicle bay doors. Curt imagined Larry standing at that window, watching as a convoy of trucks departed in response to an alarm, their sirens screaming, and he couldn't help wondering: did Sara's brother miss the adrenalin rush of firefighting? And if he did, would he say so?

Curt was acutely aware of the sacrifices one had to make sometimes for the sake of family. His own mother had drilled that into him from the time he could walk. So, from where he sat right now—on a barely-upholstered guest chair borrowed from someone else's work space—it was safe to guess that the answer Larry gave to both of his questions would probably be no.

Larry rested his leg across the corner of his desk and leaned his butt against the side of it as Curt filled him in about the promise he'd been forced to make to Lillian in order to keep the museum open.

"Uh-*huh*. So, Ms. Friendly is not so friendly after all," he summed up, returning to his seat.

It was the second time he'd heard that play on words in as many days, and it was getting old very fast. Swallowing the irritable comment that had dropped reflexively onto his tongue, he said instead, "She doesn't like hearing the word 'no', that's for sure. But she got me thinking about secret rooms, and that got me thinking about blueprints. I remembered that the castle had been extensively renovated not long ago, which would have entailed filing a set of plans with the town's Permits Office, including an updated set of blueprints."

"I gather you called them?"

"Yes, but I was too late. Apparently, they've switched to summer business hours and had already closed for the weekend. Okay, time to move to Plan B. It makes sense that a secret room installed in 1927 would only appear on the original prints… and who might have kept a copy of those? The Historical Society. So, I went into their archives."

"And?"

"Not much help there," Curt said disgustedly. "The oldest set in their files for that building was drawn up by an architectural firm based in Toronto in 1950. If I could just compare it with the one from twenty-three years earlier—"

"You still might not find the hidden room," Larry pointed out. "Not if McFadyen truly wanted it to be a secret. He could have bribed the construction crew to deviate from the plans that were on file. He certainly had the resources."

"You're right, of course, but that's not my immediate goal. I just want to give Lillian the field trip she wants and get her off my case—"

"And coincidentally determine whether there are any ghosts on the premises?"

Larry's face now wore a knowing grin. Involuntarily, Curt's lips curved as well. "Sure. I can multitask. But I'd prefer to do it without sneaking around behind Brassard's back and potentially ending up in trouble with the PPS."

"You could just wait for the police to finish processing the crime scene, you know. Then you wouldn't need her permission to enter the house."

Curt sighed inwardly. If Larry were actually dealing with Lillian, he wouldn't even be *thinking* about suggesting patience right now.

"Listen, Lillian wants what she wants and she wants it ten minutes ago. And please, don't remind me of all the things I could do with that letter she wrote. The genie is out of the bottle, Larry. Until she's in her own grave, she's capable of wreaking havoc no matter where the letter goes. Lillian has led me to believe that McFadyen had a booze vault inside his house, and she's determined to show it to me as soon as possible. And… she's dropped hints that it's because of something the vault contains that would be of interest to the police."

"I see. Well, you would have to show Brassard something compelling to make her change her mind."

"I know. I was hoping it might be an unexplained difference between two sets of blueprints, but that doesn't look likely."

"I wouldn't give up on that just yet," said Larry, his expression becoming speculative.

"Oh?"

"You may not be able to find the earliest set of blueprints in Groverton, but that doesn't mean there isn't a copy of them somewhere else."

"Somewhere else. Such as…?"

"The first job I ever had was in construction, so I saw a lot of blueprints and overheard a lot of discussions between the foreman and the architect. Those 1950 prints were drawn up by a firm in Toronto, you said. The name and address of the company should appear on them somewhere, and that is where I would begin to search. If they're still in business, they most probably have an archives, including before-and-after files of all the commissions they've completed. Renovators keep before-and-after photographs. Architects—"

"—would keep before and after blueprints, the old and the new," Curt broke in with burgeoning excitement. "And the older ones would also have a name and address on them, and so on. Even if they're digitized, I could keep going backwards to the originals that way. That's brilliant!"

"And you're welcome. Now, I have a report to finish

writing before heading over to Sara's for dinner—I understand you're invited?"

Curt nodded in reply.

"Then you know what she'll do if either one of us is late. Please don't be offended if I tell you to get the hell out of my office and let me work."

Curt rose to his feet, feeling much lighter than when he'd entered, and quietly departed, closing the door behind him.

Nine

Friday night dinner at Sara's place was served at six o'clock sharp, no excuses. Selena had stopped at the supermarket earlier in the day to pick up half a dozen salmon fillets. They were the final ingredient in one of Sara's famous slow-baked, single-pan family meals. This one included small potatoes, baby-cut carrots, onions, and red and green peppers. The boys had ice cream for dessert—rocky road for Eric, French vanilla for Donnie—which they were left to finish at the dining table while the adults moved into the front parlour to have their tea.

Meanwhile, Selena was giving serious consideration to making an excuse and going upstairs to her room.

The conversation over dinner had felt guarded and a little strained, she thought. It might simply have been because the children were present, and not everything was suitable for young ears to hear. However, Curt's reticence was unsettling, and she couldn't help wondering how much of the awkwardness that hung over the table was due to the tension that seemed to linger between them following their discussion in the parking lot of Hearth and Home.

Twice this week, he'd cut her off in mid-sentence when he thought she was about to give away his secret, once in Brassard's office and again that morning at the realtor's. Was she the reason he was regretting having shared it with the group? Worse still, by making him uncomfortable with her presence, was she inadvertently preventing a relationship from developing between him and her best friend Sara?

"Here you go, girl. Enjoy," Sara carolled, drawing her back to the moment.

The fragrance rising from the cup that had materialized in front of Selena was light and citrusy. Earl Grey, hot. This was it—her chance to plead fatigue or indigestion and leave the party.

Then Larry's voice floated back into the dining room. "You know we're going to talk about you whether you're here or not, Selena, so you may as well join us."

"Oh, really?" she called back to him. "You gonna tell stories about me, Mr. Fire Inspector?"

"Only the true ones. Curt needs to know what he's getting himself into." There was an infuriating grin in his voice.

"Maybe this isn't the best—" Curt began.

"It's never the best," Larry cut him off, "but in this case it's *for* the best. If you think Lillian is dogged and difficult, just wait until Selena gets a bee inside her bonnet. Voice of experience."

"Oh, come on—she's not that bad, big brother," said Sara.

"Only because you're worse," he retorted. "Listen, on Rafferty Island, Selena went out in the pitch darkness, using her phone as a flashlight, and climbed down a cliff on the chance that there might be evidence to find."

That did it.

Selena got up, walked her tea into the parlour, and settled onto the loveseat facing his in front of the fireplace. "It was a bluff, not a cliff," she corrected him primly as she deposited her cup on the coffee table between them, "and there were stairs leading to the beach, with railings. You make it sound as if I rappelled down the side of a mountain."

Waving off her objection, Larry continued speaking to Curt, beside him. "The point is, nothing I said or did was going to dissuade her from going out that night. So, if she says to you, 'Let's do such-and-such,' and you're not willing to go along with it, for whatever reason… trust me, she'll do it without you, even if it's risky and might get her into trouble. If it is, you'll be worried and will probably end up following her anyway, just in case the worst happens and she needs help."

"So, you're saying I should go along with whatever she proposes?"

Selena cleared her throat loudly. "I'm sitting right here, guys," she reminded them.

Larry swung his gaze to her face, but he was clearly addressing his words to Curt. "Not necessarily everything, but someone may need to call for backup, so I would keep the cavalry on speed dial if I were you."

He was referring to the police. And now Curt was staring at her as well, and Selena could feel her cheeks heating up. Larry was exaggerating to make a point, of course. She'd never been *that* reckless… had she?

"Thanks. I'll keep your advice in mind," Curt said, before turning his attention to Sara and (mercifully) changing the subject. "Have you had any luck with your research?"

Sara swallowed her mouthful of tea and replied, "It's still baby steps, I'm afraid. There are plenty of Friendlys in the databases, but I still haven't been able to connect any of them to Lillian or her parents. As for the Smiths—hah!"

"Didn't you tell me earlier that Hermès Smith had to be a wealthy and influential man?" said Selena.

"Yes. That was before I failed to find him in the social

register of 1930s New York and realized that I was probably looking on the wrong side of the law. I am becoming more and more convinced that Hermès Smith was an alias, and that Gertrude's inheritance was actually his share of some theft or other. Or maybe it was a fortune amassed over the years through a variety of criminal enterprises. Wherever it came from, I could find no public record of it."

Larry's expression was pensive. "So, if Smith was a crook, what does that tell us about the family relationships Lillian mentions in her letter? She calls Gertrude and the police captain 'cousins'. Do you think that might have been a coded message? Maybe a hidden warning, or a reminder of some private debt owing? Or—hey!—what if she was Granger's informant, and 'cousin' was a verification word they used in communications?"

Selena smiled inwardly. Larry Holmes might not be a fan of crime novels, but he couldn't stay away from a real-life mystery. She'd seen it happen on Rafferty Island, and now it was playing out here. For a while, he would pretend to have no interest in the investigation. Then, at some point, the attraction became irresistible, the sleuth in him took over, and in he would dive, determined to find answers.

"Lillian swore up and down to me that she and Gertrude were first cousins," said Sara. "She was hazy on Lewis Granger, except to say that the relationship was by marriage and they weren't in the same generation, so perhaps he was a second or third cousin…? Quite honestly, I don't know what to think at this point. I'm trying to keep an open mind and look into all possibilities, but it's slow work, and it's not easy."

"Did you check the available immigration records?" Curt asked.

"Yes, and I hit another dead end. No one named Friendly was granted refugee or landed immigrant status to Canada or the United States around the time Lillian said they were.

Either she was misremembering her family history, or there's a secret she'd rather we didn't find out about them."

"You know, people who are choosing a new country will often sever ties with the old one by taking a new name as well, especially if they're escaping from a past they aren't proud of," he remarked, giving each word the weight of careful thought.

Larry levelled narrowing eyes in his direction. "What are you saying?"

"There are different ways to anglicize a foreign-sounding name, so this may be a long shot, but I would suggest you find out how to say 'friendly' in a variety of languages, and then recheck the immigration rolls," Curt said, addressing his reply to Sara. "If you can identify the country Lillian's family came from, that may be where Gertrude's father was born as well."

"It sounds as though you and I should exchange responsibilities," Sara joked. "You can do the family research and let me deal with the bureaucratic doorstops."

"I wish we *could* trade places," he said with a sigh. "I'd do it in a heartbeat. But I have to keep Lillian's letter—and therefore Lillian's ghost—at the museum, and it could be dangerous to have her looking over the shoulder of anyone digging into her past, especially if you're right and there are secrets she doesn't want revealed."

"Family secrets," she mused. "That would explain her giving me incomplete or misleading information. But… dangerous? Really? She's been dead for nearly a hundred years. You've said yourself that ghosts can't affect material objects. That's why it took so long for the letter to be discovered. She couldn't open the handbag where it was hidden."

He blew out a breath. "She's also been nursing a deep-seated grudge for nearly a hundred years, and an angry ghost can do a lot of damage. Trust me. She turned the whole damn museum into a refrigerator earlier today because I refused to take her to the castle. She wasn't even that upset, just determined to bend me to her will. What do you suppose she'll do if she realizes we're about to unearth some heinous crime lurking in her family's past?"

"Whoa!" Selena interrupted him, coming to seated attention. "Back up a bit. That's what your exchange with her this morning was about? Why does Lillian want to go to the castle?"

"I believe it's to show me a secret room that McFadyen had someone put inside it. Like Al Capone's vault. She's being coy, claiming that she can't just tell me where it is or how to locate it. All she would say was that we'd never find it on our own."

"But we're going to look for it anyway, right?" Sara ventured brightly.

The librarian's tea sat in front of her, cooling and forgotten. Meanwhile, she'd slid forward on her seat and was poised for takeoff, her eyes and her voice sparkling with excitement.

Hmm. Perhaps Larry hadn't been exaggerating about his sister's readiness to take risks. At least Selena now knew where Donnie's adventurous nature had come from.

"The police are still processing the building," Curt replied. "However, if I can prove to Staff Sergeant Brassard that there's a discrepancy between the original blueprints and the ones currently on file, she *may* agree to let us inside before the crime scene tape comes down. Then Lillian can have her field trip, and maybe there will actually be something valuable to find there. One can hope."

"To be honest, I'd be happy to settle for simply not being kept in the dark," Selena grumped. "Brassard's like a dragon protecting a hoard of data. On Rafferty Island—"

"That was different, and you know it," Larry pointed out. "By the time the PPS arrived, we'd already begun working the case, so she had no choice but to involve us in the investigation. She's only doing now what she would have preferred to do back then, controlling the flow of information while conducting a by-the-books criminal inquiry."

"And keeping a bunch of nosy amateur sleuths from getting underfoot. I know. She told me," she bristled. "But dammit, Larry, we're members of the Crime Club. Brassard has seen how good we are at solving murders. We're well informed. We understand the rules of evidence and we respect them. And now a civilian like Tricia Vickery is allowed to know that Brenda Ryan was an alias for someone who may have been running a con, but we don't even rate a crumb like the probable cause of death…? That's infuriating!"

The grin that had settled onto his face during her rant was infuriating as well.

"What?" she snapped.

"You don't get it," Larry told her, continuing to smile as he raised his hand palm outwards in a placating gesture. "I think Brassard *does* remember how the Crime Club operates. She's not starving us for information, Selena—she's just providing it through a conduit that puts it at arm's length from her investigation. One that she can moderate."

Comprehension struck Selena like a physical blow, shoving her deeper into the loveseat. "Vickery?" she murmured. "Tricia's the conduit? Do you think she realizes—?"

"I doubt it. But figuring out what happened to Brenda is even more important to her than it is to you, so I would imagine this is part of Brassard's plan for keeping you both out of her hair. And you out of trouble," he added with a chuckle. "That lady cop is nobody's fool."

"How about a recap, then," Sara suggested. "What do we know so far about Brenda?"

Selena began. "Vickery met her for the first time at her daughter Rachel's funeral. Brenda introduced herself as a friend of Rachel's, claimed they'd been classmates in the real estate course, and apparently said all the right things to ingratiate herself with the grieving mother. Then, once Brenda had her licence, Vickery hired her as an agent. That was about a year ago."

"Okay, colour me suspicious," Sara said. "You met with the girl when she was alive, Selena. Did she seem legit to you?"

"More so than Vickery did, to tell you the truth. Brenda had arranged for me to visit the one house I was interested in, but Tricia insisted on showing me others. I got the feeling that she wasn't that anxious to sell me the castle. Later, she remarked that it had been nothing but trouble since she'd added it to her listings."

Sara raised a speculative eyebrow. "Huh! Considering that the realtor makes a commission each time a property is sold, wouldn't you think she would *want* it off her hands? Why her hesitation, I wonder."

"Did she happen to mention how long ago she'd begun listing it?" Curt asked.

Selena thought for a second. "No, but I believe it was before Brenda joined the realty office. I can ask her."

"All right, but you need to understand something about Rachel," he warned. "She's very protective of her mother, and she won't take it well if she feels you're trying to trick or badger Tricia. That's why she pushed us out the door earlier today."

"Excuse me!" Sara blurted. "Are you saying there's a ghost in the realty office?"

"Most likely tethered to the charm bracelet Tricia wears, yes," Curt replied.

"And it actually pushed you out the door?"

"Not literally, but—"

"Wait a second," Selena broke in, frowning. "I did feel something cold against my back, but I thought it was your hand. You're saying it was Rachel's?"

He shook his head. "Again, not literally," he repeated emphatically. "A ghost can't physically touch you, but it can… occupy the same space as part of your body. When it does, that body part feels cold. The angrier the ghost, the colder it will make you feel, and the more rapidly you're going to move away from it."

Sara tilted her head, a wry little smile on her face. "So, instead of pushing you in a particular direction, a ghost will… herd you?" She paused for a beat. "Not sure I like the sound of that."

"Well, like it or not, it works," he declared. "Rachel wanted us to leave Tricia alone and she basically ushered us off the premises." Turning to Selena, he added, "Since we're both sensitive to Rachel's presence, I'm not sure it would be a good idea for either of us to go back there."

"Seriously?" Selena said, raising a skeptical eyebrow. "You're the only one among us who can see and hear her."

"And you're the one with the empathic connection to tethered spirits," he countered. "If I'd let you finger the charms on that bracelet—"

"Two of them were from Brenda," she reminded him sharply. "I might have found out—"

"But Brenda wasn't attached to them, was she? And I couldn't very well ask Rachel about her while her mother was present."

Right. Ghosts aren't the only ones keeping secrets, she thought bitterly.

"Okay, arguing about what didn't happen is getting us nowhere," Larry declared, batting away the air over the coffee table and breaking the growing tension in the room. "Let's focus our attention back on what we know about Brenda."

"Selena?" Sara prompted her. "Did Ms. Vickery tell you

anything else?"

"Yes, but it's not going to carry any weight with Brassard, I'm afraid. Tricia seemed very certain that Brenda and Rachel had known each other before the funeral. She also said that she and Brenda had spent a lot of time talking about Rachel over the past year, and that Brenda appeared to be genuinely missing her and grieving her loss."

"All of which makes me more suspicious, not less," said Sara. "A good con artist always researches the mark. And any skilled actor can counterfeit mourning."

Privately, Selena was beginning to agree. "Also, at one point, Brenda mentioned to Tricia that the commute from her home to Georgian College for the real estate course was twenty minutes long."

"A number! Now, that's something we can work with," Larry said, brightening.

"Not really," she had to tell him. "Tricia has already given that lead to the police. I'm afraid our one remaining chance to uncover something that might impress Brassard and get us inside the castle was those charms on Vickery's bracelet." … *and the ghost attached to them*, she added silently.

"Fine, then!" Sara said briskly. "It's clear what we have to do next. We need to steal that bracelet for an hour or two."

"What?!" Curt yelped. "No! Absolutely not!"

"Unless I've misunderstood the situation, Rachel has information about Brenda that the police are missing, but you have to ask her about it when Tricia's not around. And since Rachel can't leave the bracelet, that means either the bracelet must leave Tricia, or Tricia must leave the bracelet."

"It's more complicated than that. Vickery is also attached to the bracelet. She wears it all the time."

"*All* the time? Even when she's in the shower?" Sara persisted. "What about when she goes to bed at night?"

Curt's expression had morphed into something reminiscent

of a painting by Edvard Munch. "Now you want to break into her house?" he whispered, aghast. "At night? Good grief, Sara, are you trying to land all of us in jail?"

The librarian's spine straightened as though pulled upward by a string. "No, but it's the most reasonable course of action I can think of right now. Unless someone has a better suggestion…?" she said stiffly.

Curt had one. "There may be another way to question Rachel. One that doesn't involve separating Tricia from her jewellery."

"Care to share with the class?" Sara prompted.

"Not yet. I need to be certain it can stand up to scrutiny."

"Scrutiny? Whose scrutiny?" said Selena.

But a tight-lipped shake of his head was the only response he would give them.

Ten

urt had promised Selena that he wouldn't give up on Brenda or Barbara, and he fully intended to keep his word. He hadn't lied to her in Sara's front room that evening. An idea had sprouted in his imagination. But ghosts were involved, the logistics were going to be tricky, and he didn't want to get anyone's hopes up only to dash them if he couldn't deliver.

It was reasonable to assume that Rachel's spirit was tethered to the charm bracelet by some unfinished business it represented. Something to do with her mother's ongoing grief, most likely, since Rachel hadn't reacted to his presence until he'd shifted his interest away from Brenda and onto Tricia's loss.

But what if Rachel's aim wasn't to protect a living person from being tormented by memories? What if the unfinished business was a secret she'd kept from everyone including her mother—a secret that Brenda had confided to her and that Rachel was still determined to protect? It could be the key to solving a murder.

That made it even more important for Curt to find out

what she knew.

There were two ghosts on a bench on the train platform who might be able to get her talking. He could invent a reason for the realtor to come meet him at the museum, and an excuse to keep Tricia inside his office while Clara and Ruth engaged a fellow spirit in conversation. The problem was, the "bench ladies" already had their hands full providing emotional support for Selena's cousin, Barbara Cournoyer.

There was no getting around it—Barbara's unfinished business would have to be resolved first. All of which brought Curt back to the question that had been haunting him lately, more persistently than any ghost he'd ever encountered.

How could he convince Staff Sergeant Brassard that invisible spirits were real—let alone that they made credible eyewitnesses—without inviting a repeat of the debacle that had cost him his contract position with the Royal Ontario Museum three years earlier?

He thought briefly of Nena's grandfather. Did deceased medicine men make house calls? Maybe if he appeared to Brassard in a dream…?

No, he thought with a sigh. Lady Cop was far too much of a realist to put credence in something like that. *Damn!*

Mulling over his frustrating lack of options, Curt placed the contents of his pants pockets on his nightstand and began getting ready for bed.

There was a specific order of operations for this, one his mother had begun teaching him when he was quite young. He'd had to learn many such regimented routines while growing up. Beginning the day. Preparing for travel. Organizing and caring for his belongings. He'd soon discovered that the discipline and predictability of each one calmed his mind, providing a respite from a highly irregular childhood and adolescence. Even in adulthood, he found the old habits comforting in times of stress. Times like this.

And so, he began by laying his pyjamas out on the neatly-made bed, the pant legs hanging down the side of the mattress, straight and smooth.

Next he undressed, putting each item of clothing away as soon as he'd taken it off. Suit jacket and trousers on separate hangers in the closet. One-day shirt arranged tidily over the back of a chair. One-day briefs and socks folded and placed on the seat. Shoes on the floor in front of the chair, left on the left, right on the right, toeing an invisible line.

Putting on his pyjamas was always followed by oral hygiene, a glass of water placed on the nightstand, and lights out. And sleep. It came easily, as long as he didn't skip any pre-bedtime steps.

Not until after his mother's death had it occurred to him that she might have been aware all along of his supernatural gift—in fact, that she could have had it as well, passing it on to him through her genes. If she'd grown up seeing ghosts, her emotional distance and her insistence on discipline could have been the teachings of her own personal experience. He'd often regretted never asking her about this while she was alive. At odd moments, he still sometimes wondered whether she'd tethered herself to something, so that he might have a chance to find and speak with her spirit.

But it never happened. Evidently, she'd felt she had no unfinished business when she departed the mortal plane, because she was gone.

At three in the morning, Curt jackknifed awake, cursing loudly. Driven by an adrenalin surge that shivered and shuddered through every part of him, he threw off his blanket and raced to check the floor of his bedroom closet. It was empty. He'd been dreaming.

Intense relief washed through him then, draining the strength from his legs and depositing him in a gasping heap beside the open closet door.

The Ouija board—or rather, the broken pieces of it—had been left behind in Toronto three years earlier. By now it was probably buried in a landfill somewhere. And yet… in his nightmare, the cursèd thing had followed him north, mended itself in the darkness of his closet, and—propelled by ghostly hands—begun bashing its way through the closed door to get to him.

The varnished, palette-shaped wafer of oak with its Gothic-style inlaid lettering had been an ornament at first. An amusement when entertaining company. Then a friend of a friend dropped by with a tethered ghost in tow, one desperate to make a connection on the mortal plane, and just for that evening the board became a tool. A translation device, as it were.

Curt had done his best after that to downplay what had happened. The Ouija board was meant to be fun, after all, nothing to be taken seriously. But friends had spoken to other friends, and soon, to his chagrin and embarrassment, people were contacting him—sometimes at work—with requests to conduct seances.

Curt had never advertised himself as a medium. He'd never charged a fee or cheated anyone in any way. But none of that mattered to the tabloid journalist thirsty for column space who was looking for "fake psychics" to expose. As far as she was concerned, the use of the Ouija board alone was ample proof of fraud. After speaking to two or three of his "clients"—who had immediately warned Curt of what was coming—the writer finally approached him directly.

They met in the office of Curt's lawyer, where a deal was hammered out. Curt wouldn't sue the pants off the journalist and the tabloid she worked for, and she would look elsewhere for charlatans to skewer in the press. And just for good measure, the agreement was put in writing, signed by both parties, and duly witnessed.

On returning home that afternoon, Curt had taken a literal hammer to the Ouija board and then hurled the pieces with force into his closet, vowing never to touch it again.

That should have been the end of it, but it wasn't. Unfortunately, word of Curt's "dabbling in the supernatural" had already gotten around, tarnishing his professional reputation and ultimately leading to the cancellation of his contract with the Royal Ontario Museum.

Now, he was in Groverton, up to his neck in ghosts and juggling mysteries. And still stressing over what might happen if too many people became aware of his special gift. It was exhausting. His legs felt like rubber. He wasn't sure they could support his weight even if he managed to lift himself off the floor. Maybe he should just stay where he was until morning.

Leaning back against the wall, he swivelled his gaze from left to right around the room. Amidst the dim shadows, the outline of his bed looked very far away. It was just as well he wasn't in it—a line from *Hamlet* had popped into his head: "To sleep, perchance to dream."

He wouldn't have minded dreaming about the Ouija board if the dream had had a purpose beyond simply terrorizing him, like the visit from Nena's grandfather, or even the nightmare Barbara had sent to Selena…

The nightmare that convinced her to leave the pendant with me.

And there it was. Arriving in a flash of insight that instantly cleared the fog in his brain, a plan now lay before him, fully formed. Curt had no idea whether it would work on someone like Brassard. He only knew that he had to give it a shot, and that the hardest part was going to be the several hours' wait until he could begin to implement it, since he was now wide awake.

*   *   *

Step one: get Barbara on board.

As he went through his morning routine—showering, brushing, and gargling—Curt couldn't help wondering: would she be ready for this? Was he? They were about to find out.

The sky was cloudy and grey and threatening rain when he pulled into his parking spot at the museum shortly before eight o'clock. The museum wouldn't open for another two hours. That was plenty of time for his usual Saturday breakfast at Eggsnow—the servers didn't even ask for his order anymore, just brought orange juice, eggs Benedict, and decaf coffee to his table—but today he'd decided to skip it. He was impatient to set things in motion.

As he tore around the corner of the building, he spotted Ruth and Clara sitting on their bench on the platform, conversing with Len who stood leaning on the push bar of his luggage trolley. Barbara was nowhere in sight.

Curt came to a breathless halt in front of them. "Excuse me for interrupting, but this is rather urgent. Do you happen to know where Barbara is right now?"

Three pairs of grey eyes came slowly to rest on his face.

"Well, something seems to have got our Mr. Wakefield into a lather," Clara observed coolly. *"Do you suppose he realizes what he's done?"*

"Or rather, not done?" Ruth chimed in.

Not done? What were they talking about?

Curt's stomach chose that moment to growl. Perhaps skipping breakfast hadn't been such a good idea after all.

"Listen," he said, annoyance making his voice jumpy, "I don't read minds. Why don't you just tell me what's wrong?"

Len was wearing an uncharacteristically smug expression. *"Why don't you go inside and find out?"* he said. Then he raised his chin, tilted his cap forward onto his brow, and pushed his trolley through the metal door, into what had once been the baggage handling area of the station.

Exasperated, Curt turned back to Ruth. "You won't even drop me a hint?"

She seemed to think about it for a couple of seconds before giving her head a single decisive shake. *"Nope. You'll know right away."*

His midsection now churning with more than simple hunger, Curt let himself into the museum and stood in the foyer for a moment, scanning the exhibit halls for something different or out of place. Nothing leaped out at him. Everything appeared to be in perfect order, and the air temperature felt comfortable, so what could possibly—?

All at once, he heard laughter coming from the direction of his office. There were two female voices. And that was when it hit him: before closing up the museum Friday afternoon, he'd locked the letter and the pendant into the same drawer of his desk for safekeeping.

From the sound of it, Lillian and Barbara had become friends overnight.

Damn!

Just imagining the havoc that could be wrought by two angry ghosts working together was enough to send Curt racing towards the tower. With trembling hands he opened his office door, to be met by a sight that momentarily froze him in place on the threshold.

Lillian was sitting in his chair—well, not exactly—she was actually hovering a few centimetres above it, her greyscale body bent at the hips and knees to create the illusion of being seated. Barbara was doing the same thing in the middle of his desktop, only cross-legged. They'd been leaning toward each other, sharing a joke. It had probably been about him, for at his entrance they sprang apart and gave him identical knowing smiles.

Curt debated inwardly about calling them out on it, then

decided it would be a waste of time. The grin on Barbara's face answered the question that had earlier been foremost in his thoughts, and now they all had more important matters to attend to.

"Ladies, if I may have your attention…?" he said, stepping forward and waving them away from the furniture. "I've come up with a plan that will give you both what you want, but it requires your assistance."

Barbara floated backward, then unfolded her legs. A second later she was standing on the far side of his desk, gazing curiously at him. Typically, however, Lillian didn't budge from the chair. Curt swallowed a sigh and remained on his feet, refusing to let a territorial dispute with a ghost derail him from his purpose.

"Our first order of business is to convince Staff Sergeant Brassard to believe in the supernatural," he told them.

"*So nothing's changed,*" Lillian remarked dryly. "*Now will you let me turn her office into an icebox?*"

"No. What I've got in mind will work much better. Barbara, you gave Selena a dream the other night. Was that deliberate or did it just happen?"

She frowned. "*I'm not sure. I was angry because she wouldn't let me stay here with Ruth and Clara, and I sort of… gave her a piece of my mind.*"

Perfect!!

"So, she was preventing you from doing what you wanted and you shared your anger with her in the form of a nightmare," Curt summed up. "Do you think you could do it again, on purpose? And this time slip a message into it?"

"*You want me to give the police officer a nightmare about the day I was—?*" As her features crumpled, Curt felt a pinch of regret at what he was asking her to do. Reliving her death couldn't be easy or pleasant for her, even when the memory was driven by rage.

"Did you see his face?" Curt persisted.

"*Yes!*"

"Then I want you to show her the face of the man who murdered you and tell her—" Curt paused, suddenly uncertain. Tell her what, exactly?

"*Tell her who you are and what he did to you, and warn her that his crime will haunt her dreams for the rest of her life if she doesn't hunt him down and put him away for it,*" Lillian piped up.

"That's a lot to communicate," he said. "And I don't think it's a good idea to threaten a police officer under any circumstances."

"*But it's perfectly all right to scare the bejeezus out of her while she's sleeping? It's a strange world you live in, Mr. Wakefield,*" Lillian commented, shaking her head sadly.

Curt ignored her, addressing himself to Barbara instead. "Tell her you've been waiting for nine years to give her your statement, and that we can help her to close your case."

Lillian perked up immediately. "*We? Does that include me?*" she demanded.

"Eventually, yes," he assured her, "but first things first. I have to find out where Brassard lives. That will determine the tack I take to put the pendant into her hands."

"*Ooh, like breaking into her bedroom and slipping it under her pillow? Sounds like fun!*"

Lillian's entire being was sparkling with anticipation. She was up for a caper. Meanwhile, Curt sincerely hoped it wouldn't come to that. Subterfuge of any kind had never sat well with him, mainly because he was terrible at it, but also because of how dangerous it became when one was dealing with the police. Among the rules his mother had drilled into him when he was growing up, *Never lie to a cop* was still near the top of the list.

That said, Adult Curt had found that in certain cases a

lapse of memory could serve him well—it was also much easier for others to forgive—and so he had spent the long hours before dawn that morning sifting through the known facts in order to assemble a credible story that wouldn't blow apart his own carefully kept secret.

It was Saturday. Brassard might or might not have the weekend off. Curt's first phone call would have to be an inquiry to the PPS station in town, but not until the museum opened. And not until he'd had something to eat.

According to the constable who took his call, Staff Sergeant Brassard was not on duty that weekend, and no, she could not give out the sergeant's personal information. If he cared to leave a message and a number where he could be reached, however, she would gladly pass it along.

This was annoying but not surprising. A previous search had turned up no one surnamed Brassard in the Groverton area phone directory—which made sense considering that the staff sergeant had only recently moved here and was most likely relying on a wireless cell service provider. So, it was on to plan B.

"Please tell her that I have new information regarding one of the cold cases we discussed in her office the other day, and that I'll be at the museum until five o'clock this afternoon."

"Of course, Mr. Wakefield, I'll let her know."

Okay, it was time for step two. As Barbara and Lillian looked on curiously, Curt opened his laptop and booted it up.

"*What are you doing?*" Lillian asked.

"Change of plans. I want to conduct an experiment to find out what, if anything, happens on my screen if a ghost touches it."

"*No!*" Barbara yelped, recoiling as though from a physical blow. "*I already know what will happen. I tried using Selena's computer to send her a message shortly after I—*

anyway, I broke the screen. It cost her a pile of money to get a replacement."

Damn! He would have to come up with a plan C, preferably before Brassard got back to him.

"How could you have managed to break a screen just by touching it?" Curt wondered aloud.

Barbara gave a one-shoulder shrug. *"Selena had left her laptop open on the kitchen table, and I saw an opportunity to contact her. But the alphabetical keys wouldn't work for me. I was getting more and more frustrated, and after a while I just blew up. I gave the screen a shove with the heel of my hand, and that was when it cracked."*

"So you were angry at the time." *...and generating a considerable amount of cold,* he added silently. In fact, that made a lot of sense. Even when a ghost wasn't upset, its touch wasn't warm. Curt recalled the way it had felt when he'd been sitting on the bench with Ruth and Clara, and one of them had patted his hand.

That was when it hit him. His nightmare about the Ouija board had contained a message for him after all, from his subconscious mind. It was plan C, and it was brilliant.

Eleven

So, Sara was combing through data for information about the Friendly and Smith family histories, and Curt was working on a way to question Rachel. That left Selena to follow up on the castle, and on the people who currently owned it.

Shortly before noon, she steered her car into a parking spot by the front door of Hearth and Home Realty, armed with several potentially fruitful questions.

There was a new receptionist at the front desk, an older lady wearing rimless glasses and a white cardigan sweater with a green and burnt orange Fair Isle yoke. She looked up from her computer screen and adjusted her glasses, then said through naturally pursed lips, "Good morning, dear. How can I help you?"

Only momentarily taken aback, Selena cleared her throat and replied, "I'm looking for Tricia. She's preparing an offer for me and I just need a few minutes of her time."

"Oh, she's at an open house today until 1:00 p.m., a lovely property in Bellavon. It's no more than a twenty minute drive from here. You should go have a look at it."

"Thanks, but I've already found the place I want to buy. And… I'm wondering whether *you* might be able to give me the information I need. Are you a real estate agent too?"

"I used to be, before I retired. Now I just hold down the fort from time to time. What's your question?"

"It's actually for the current owner of the house I'm interested in, so I would like to get in touch with them. Are you allowed to give me their address and phone number?"

The woman's eyebrows shot upward, seeming to pull her backward in her chair.

"No, I'm sorry, I can't. However, Tricia can contact them on your behalf and relay your question once she returns from Bellavon. Perhaps if you come back later today…?"

Not good enough.

"Hmm. I was hoping to speak to them directly. Is there some sort of rule against that?" Selena asked.

"No. It's just not something realtors consider to be a good idea. In case one party or the other says something that's taken the wrong way… these business deals, you understand, they can be delicate… people are selling homes they've become emotionally attached to over the years and a single word can…"

…can sink the sale, costing the agent her commission. Yes, Selena understood running a business very well.

The woman shifted uncomfortably in her chair, evidently aware that she had said too much. Well, Prue Davidson might be a professional moniker, but it was also a starting point for an online search.

Selena pinned on a smile and said, "That's okay, then. Please tell Tricia I stopped by and I'll try to come back this afternoon."

"Very well, dear, but I didn't catch your name. Who shall I let her know to expect?"

Selena couldn't resist a good exit line. "I'm the person who's going to buy the castle."

As she walked out the door, she heard a sharp intake of breath behind her.

By 3:00 p.m., Selena was sitting at Sara's kitchen table, sipping green tea and staring thoughtfully at the screen of her laptop computer.

Prue Davidson. Short for Prudence, maybe? An interior designer, based in the Toronto area. As co-owner of the building, she would have been the one to add all the finishing touches to the renovated home at Beech and Webber. She'd probably purchased everything from Groverton's local merchants and artisans, providing Selena with more people to talk to, as well as an excuse for requesting a face-to-face meeting with Davidson herself.

The interior designer's contact information hadn't been hard to obtain. The young man who had picked up the call to her listed business line had cheerfully given out her cell phone number after hearing Selena's story about buying a house out of town and being pointed in Davidson's direction by the real estate agent. (Technically, it wasn't a lie. Tricia had volunteered the information one day after Brenda had taken Selena on that virtual tour, showing her a beautifully decorated home, and the new buyer had naturally taken these together as a recommendation. Who wouldn't have?)

Unfortunately, *reaching* Prue at her cell number was proving to be no easy matter. While the skies over Groverton were threatening rain, the weather in and around the Greater Toronto Area was bright and sunny, making this a perfect weekend to be sussing out "finds" at flea markets and rural antique shops. That was where she was today, and she apparently didn't want to be disturbed. After hearing Davidson's voice mail greeting for the fifth time in two hours, Selena decided she'd had enough. She left a message she hoped would be intriguing, then turned her attention elsewhere.

Hmm… "Friendly." She began punching keys, and in short order was looking at a list on her screen.

In French, it was *aimable*. In German, *freundlich*. In Spanish, *amigable*. In Italian, *amichevole*. In Russian, *druzhelyubno*. In Portuguese, *cordial*. In Romanian, *prietenos*. In Japanese, *furendori*. In Swedish, *vänlig*. In Irish Gaelic… and Chinese… and Hindi…

It appeared Sara was going to have her work cut out for her.

A glance at the clock told Selena she wouldn't be alone in the house much longer. Sara's shift at the library had just ended, and the neighbour down the street who minded Eric and Donnie when Larry wasn't available was probably getting them ready to return home at that very moment. Was it too soon to check in with Curt about his plan to speak with Rachel? Did it make any sense for Selena to return to the realty office, knowing that her questions were now moot?

Just then her phone rang, the sudden noise breaking into her thoughts with nerve-jarring force.

She snatched up the device and managed an almost-calm, "Hello?"

"Hello. This is Prue Davidson. Am I speaking with Ms. Selena Watt?"

Finally! Selena sagged backwards in her chair with relief. "Yes! Thank you for calling back."

"Not a problem. You said in your message that you're in the process of buying a home in Groverton?"

"Yes. Tricia Vickery is my realtor and she mentioned that you were also a client of hers, so I was wondering whether you could answer a couple of questions for me."

"About decorating your new property?"

Selena hesitated for a couple of heartbeats. Deception did not come naturally to her. She was a terrible liar and knew it.

However, her years spent dealing with people at Watt's Greatest Travel and Leisure (and its various events) had taught her a thing or two about carefully choosing her words. And so, she mentally crossed her fingers and replied, "Not yet. I'm actually more interested in knowing about *you*." (Which was, of course, the absolute truth.)

"Ah! Yes. To make sure we'd be a good fit before you engage my services. I quite understand. How would you like to do this?"

It was working. Fighting to keep her excitement under control and her voice conversational, Selena heard herself say, "Well, since I'm up here and you're down there, I thought we might video chat, either this evening or some time tomorrow."

"I have a social engagement tonight, but tomorrow afternoon would work. Shall we say two o'clock? I can set it up and send a link to your phone. At the number you're using now?"

"That would be fine."

"Wonderful! See you then," Davidson concluded, and ended the call.

Seconds later, Selena's heart was on its way to the pit of her stomach. A virtual meeting? What had she been thinking? A video call could be ended with the click of a button, and that was probably what the other woman would do as soon as she realized what Selena's true purpose had been in contacting her.

"I'm back," Sara called from the front hall, a moment before Selena heard the door close. "And I'm not cooking. I spent most of my shift repairing books, and I think sniffing all that glue has addled my brain."

"Yay! Pizza!" came a chorus of young voices.

Apparently, Eric and Donnie had slipped inside behind her. Selena watched as Donnie followed his mother into the kitchen. "Uncle Larry likes pizza. Can we invite him here for dinner?" he asked.

Sara sank with a weary groan onto the chair across from Selena's.

"I suppose," she replied. "But he may be a little late. He's on fire pit patrol."

That sounded interesting, and a little dangerous. Selena stared a question at her.

"It's not really a patrol, it's just what he calls it," Sara explained. "This is the time of year when people remember they'll need a permit if they want to build a bonfire on the beach or burn yard waste on their property, or whatever. So, there's a sudden spate of permit applications, and each one requires a personal visit from the fire inspector before it can be approved. Larry likes to get them all out of the way at once, so he dedicates a weekend to them, during daylight hours. And since the sun won't set until about nine o'clock tonight..." She let out a gusty breath before continuing, "... he'll probably only join us for dessert."

"I don't suppose you were able to find a moment to work on our family history project...?" Selena ventured.

Sara yawned and shook her head. "Saturdays are always busy at the library. But I'm off for the next three days, so I should be able to make some progress then. What about you? Any news?"

Selena filled her in on the day's developments.

"An online chat? Really?" Sara remarked.

"I know. But I couldn't imagine making her drive all the way up here—it's two hours on the highway, for heaven's sake—just so I could ask her a single question. It didn't seem right."

"It didn't—? Do you know what your problem is? You're too considerate, even for a Canadian. If Davidson thinks she can win you as a client, she'll happily travel to wherever you happen to be *and* treat you to lunch, and—trust me—she'll consider the time and money well spent."

"Mom! Donnie hit his head and he's bleeding!" came Eric's voice from the rec room. "And he's talking to his imaginary friend again!"

Wearing a martyred expression, Sara filled and emptied her lungs. "If you'll excuse me, I have a crisis to attend to." Then she got to her feet and left the kitchen.

A moment later, Selena had arrived at a decision. Coming to stand at the top of the stairs, she called down to the basement, "I'm going out. Do you need anything?"

"Yes!" Sara shouted back. "Band-Aids and antibiotic ointment. And if you could toss me down a clean towel, please...? Evel Knievel has been at it again."

The welcoming smile on Tricia Vickery's face morphed into an expression of wary hopefulness as she watched Selena walk through the door of Hearth and Home Realty.

"Is there any news about Brenda?" she asked.

"Not yet, I'm afraid. I'm here with a question about my offer on the castle."

At this, the realtor's demeanour shifted, becoming business-formal. "I'm sorry, Ms. Watt, but the police have put a halt on that until they've finished their work at the crime scene."

"I'm not surprised. But I was just wondering—have you let the current owners know that I'm interested in buying the property?"

Vickery frowned. "No, that's not how it's done. We wait for everything to be in writing in case the buyer has a change of heart before the offer can be presented. Have you? Had a change of heart, I mean."

"No, not at all. I was just curious about the procedure. So, they have no idea who I am or that I have my eye on their castle?"

Tricia came to seated attention and declared, "If they're

aware of that, they got it from someone other than me."

"Is there any chance *Brenda* might have…?"

"Absolutely not!" she cut in, her voice a horrified whisper. Then she added in more normal tones, "But even if she did let something slip to them, surely there's no way that could have led to her death… could it?"

"It's highly unlikely that it did," Selena assured her. "But in the interests of being thorough, we have to consider every possibility, even the most remote ones. By the way, you told us earlier that you wear your bracelet all the time. Did you really mean *all* the time? Like, in the shower? Or to bed at night?"

Tricia giggled and relaxed back in her chair. "Don't be silly. Nobody does that."

"Well, thank you for your time. We'll let you know if we find out anything new about Brenda's case."

Selena smiled to herself as she headed toward the door. Larry had been right the other night. She'd learned quite a bit from Vickery just now… and she would learn even more from Prue Davidson tomorrow afternoon.

Next stop, the pharmacy. Sara's boys went through a lot of first aid supplies.

Twelve

W hen Staff Sergeant Brassard finally returned Curt's phone call, he'd resigned himself to letting her in on his secret and knew exactly what to say to her.

"Mr. Wakefield, you say you have uncovered new evidence in one of the cold cases. Can you be more specific?"

"Yes, but I'm afraid it will have to be just between you and me for now. An eyewitness has surfaced, someone who needs to remain anonymous but who is anxious to give you her statement."

"And which cold case is this regarding, if I may ask?"

"The murder of Barbara Cournoyer, nine years ago."

A pause, then, "I see. Well, we follow up on anonymous tips all the time, so I have no problem with this. I assume you are going to suggest we meet privately somewhere?"

"In my office at the museum, after 5:00 p.m. She'll be here when you arrive, so please come alone. Oh, and one more thing: could you bring with you whatever you need to create a computer-assisted sketch of the murderer's face?"

He heard the sound of an expelled breath at the other end

of the line. "And if I need to bring a technician with me who is familiar with the software?"

"Make sure it's a woman. This witness has been traumatized enough."

"You should know that since it was last mentioned to me, I have reviewed the file of this case. The crime scene was processed quite thoroughly during the investigation, and no sign was ever found of a third person being present. How certain are you that your alleged witness is telling the truth?"

"Staff Sergeant, I am dead certain, and you will be also by the time she's finished speaking."

Another weighty pause followed. At last, she said, "The museum closes at five o'clock, is that correct?"

"It is."

"*B'en alors,* we will be there. And Mr. Wakefield, I would like to remind you that there are legal consequences for making false statements and wasting police time and resources. So, if this is some kind of game you are playing..."

"Trust me, Sergeant Brassard, it's the furthest thing from it."

"In that case, I will see you in about one hour."

At ten minutes past five, Curt unlocked the museum's entrance to admit two uniformed officers, one carrying a leather briefcase. In contrast to Brassard's imposing presence, the woman introduced as Constable Rutledge, the police artist, wasn't a threatening figure at all. Quite the opposite, in fact. Short and slender, she appeared to be not a day over twenty years old. That was good, as long as she could keep a secret. And wouldn't bolt out the door the moment she realized who and what the "witness" actually was.

With fingers firmly crossed, Curt led them through the foyer and the darkened exhibit hall, into his office in the tower.

"You said the witness would be here," Brassard reminded him, scowling.

"She is, but before Constable Rutledge sets up her gear on the desk, I need you to indulge me for a bit while I show you something. I promise you, it bears directly on why you're here this evening."

Curt reached into his desk drawer and pulled out the pendant, holding it up by its chain.

"This was Barbara's. She was wearing it when she died. Selena has had possession of it for the past nine years." So saying, he lowered it onto the desktop, face up. "She recently told me that being around this necklace made her feel as though Barbara was still with her. Well, it makes me feel the same way. Would you agree that fighting to stay alive can unleash powerful emotions?"

"*B'en sûr.* But I do not see how—"

"I have considerable experience in this area. It's *documented* experience, by the way—I can even give you references. When emotions are very strong, they can imprint themselves on objects or places. Some people are sensitive enough to pick up on those emotions and experience them through one or more of their five senses. For Selena, it's the tactile sense. With me, it's visual."

Brassard uttered a rude syllable. "You are saying that you see ghosts?"

"Yes. In fact," he added, gazing over her shoulder, "I'm looking at Barbara's ghost right now. A spirit can be tethered to something associated with unfinished business on the mortal plane, and hers is attached to this pendant. I can prove it if you'll let me."

Brassard and Rutledge exchanged *Why not humour him?* looks.

"Go ahead, then," the sergeant said.

Curt dipped into his drawer again, this time for a felt-tipped marker. "I got the idea for this from a Ouija board," he explained as he printed a large 'Y' on the back of his left hand and an 'N' on the back of his right one. "Ghosts can't interact with physical matter, so pushing a pointer around on a board isn't possible for them. However, their touch feels cold to human skin. That's how she's going to communicate with us, by tapping 'Y' for yes and 'N' for no."

Rutledge drew back when he reached for her hand. "Oh, don't worry, it's not permanent ink," he assured her. "And you're going to need this for when she's picking out eyebrows and noses and such on the screen."

"The witness..." she said faintly, "is a ghost?"

"The witness is the murder victim, and her attacker's face is burned into her memory," he replied, adding a flourish to the 'N' on Rutledge's right hand. "And when she's done, you'll have a detailed, accurate image of him for your investigation."

"On the basis of an anonymous tip," Brassard said pointedly, then turned and addressed her next words to Curt: "And assuming, of course, that this isn't simply an elaborate hoax."

"It's not." He printed letters on her hands as well, then recapped the marker and said, "And to prove it, I invite you to take the pendant and go anywhere you like, inside or outside of the museum, and ask questions that can be answered yes or no. You can ask about things that only the police and the murder victim would know, for example, and see what she says. I'll keep my distance the whole time, and once you're satisfied that she exists and is really the person I say she is, we can get on with creating the artist's sketch of her killer."

"Inside the car?" Rutledge suggested quietly. "It's the one place we know will be clean."

Brassard responded with a nod.

Curt handed her the pendant and accompanied them to the parking lot door. The threatened rain appeared not to have materialized, he noted. The pavement was dry and the cloud cover had broken up, revealing patches of sunlit blue sky.

As he watched the two women climb into the front seat of a silver-grey Rav 4, he heard Lillian's voice inside his head: *"You're taking a big chance. What if the questions bring back memories Barbara can't handle and she freezes up and doesn't answer them?"*

"Then her fear and anger will drop the air temperature in the cab of that vehicle until Brassard can see her own breath, thus proving that Barbara's ghost is real. The questions aren't the point of this exercise, Lillian. Convincing the police to take a murder victim's statement—that's what we're trying to do here."

"You really think that will free her from her pendant?"

"It's hard to say. However, helping to bring her killer to justice has got to make her feel better—as you of all people should understand."

"Well, I hope you're right, Mr. Wakefield, but I'm not holding my breath."

Since ghosts had no breath to hold, she was absolutely correct.

He didn't have long to wait for the results of Barbara's "private interview" with the police. Scant minutes later, Brassard and Rutledge tumbled out of their car and came racing back inside with Barbara close on their heels. Brassard's expression was stern. Rutledge looked… well, she looked as though she'd just seen a ghost. Which, of course, she had, sort of.

"I have decided to follow up on this anonymous tip of yours," the sergeant announced to the room. (And to any ghosts that it might contain? Inside Curt's mind, Lillian's voice was chuckling.)

Brassard took off the pendant and placed it with visible relief on Curt's outstretched palm. Meanwhile, the police artist set about booting up her laptop, and Curt watched Barbara manoeuvre herself into a spot from which she could both see the screen and reach the constable's hands.

He hated to admit it, but Lillian had apparently been a good influence on her. Anger was a great motivator, and everything about Barbara's demeanour reflected the focus and determination of a huntress tracking prey. Curt was aching with curiosity but didn't dare speak to her. There would be time later to ask her how things had gone inside the officers' vehicle.

As the facial sketching program opened on the screen, Rutledge asked, "How am I supposed to do this?"

"Well, how does it usually work?" Curt responded, more for Barbara's benefit than for his own.

"There's a numbered menu of shapes for each feature. The witness picks out the one they remember. Then I click and drag it to the composite drawing on the left."

"Maybe you can ask her about each shape in turn, and she'll tap either yes or no on your hand."

Barbara glanced up, frowning. *"That doesn't sound very efficient. It would be a lot simpler if I described him to you and you did the picking out for me,"* she said.

Curt swallowed a sigh. Actually, it wouldn't. Brassard was willing to believe in the direct contact of a spirit's icy touch. Inserting himself as a middle-man in the process was what had gotten him in trouble back in Toronto those three years earlier. It was how charlatans operated, and the last thing he wanted to do right now was undermine the credibility of Barbara's testimony.

"Okay," said Rutledge with a helpless shrug. "Let's give this a try." She brought up a screen that showed a featureless oval on the left side and a column of possible jawlines on the right. "I'm going to pause the cursor on each one of these in turn. Tell me yes or no for each one."

"This is ridiculous," Lillian grumped. *"Do you* want *to be here all night? Which one comes closest, Babs?"*

"Number three. The square-ish chin with the cleft," Barbara replied.

"All right, then. Watch and learn."

Before Curt's disbelieving eyes, Lillian reached out and tapped the 'Y' on Rutledge's hand three times, rapidly.

"Yes-yes-yes?" said the artist. "Are you telling me you want number three?"

"I knew she was smart enough to figure it out," Lillian crowed, then tapped the 'Y' once more. *"And you're welcome, Mr. Wakefield—you didn't have to give away a thing."*

Fifteen minutes later, a human face was coming together on the left side of the screen. The ghosts were engaged in lively discussion about the various menu options, and the selection process was expedited by Lillian's gleeful poking at Rutledge's hands. And she was right—neither Brassard nor Rutledge had reason to suspect that he was more than he'd told them he was.

Then they hit a snag.

"Ears?" Rutledge said. She clicked on an icon at the bottom of the screen, and the right side refreshed itself to show a numbered menu of ear shapes.

"It's not here," Barbara fretted. *"He had strange ears. The tops were tight to his head but the bottoms stuck out. It was like he'd originally had jug handles but the surgery to correct them hadn't been completely successful."*

"You saw that face and still got into his truck?" Lillian reproved her.

"He wasn't the pickup driver. The driver was a good Samaritan, taking me to a service station that had a tow truck. That man," Barbara said, pointing a shaking finger at the image on the screen, *"tricked my driver into stopping for him, then shot the driver, threw us both into the trunk of*

another car, and—!" The rest of it came out as a sob.

Hearing that, Curt had to struggle to remain calm. It was no wonder the police hadn't been able to solve the case. They'd been chasing someone whose body had probably been mouldering in its own shallow grave for the past nine years. It was now more important than ever that Brassard receive this information… but how? Clearly, a series of yes or no questions was no longer the answer.

Curt cleared his throat and asked the artist, "What if a feature is a combination of two of the options presented?"

"You mean, if his left and right ears are different, say?"

"Or if the tops are one shape and the bottoms are another. What do you do then?"

"The program lets me specify left and right, top and bottom. And if a shape isn't in the menu, I can draw it manually. Why? Is there a problem with this guy's ears?"

"Well, she seems to be hesitating, so I'm guessing there is. Maybe you should get a little more detailed with your questions…?"

Barbara gave him a grateful smile. Brassard was smiling too, he noted, but she had a calculating gleam in her eyes. Putting two and two together and getting twenty-two, no doubt. He wasn't sure how he felt about that, only knew that the prospect of waiting to see what she would do next was planting butterflies in his belly.

"Bravo, Mr. Wakefield!" Lillian said dryly.

It took a little longer, but eventually the killer's ears were the right size and shape. After that, his aquiline nose was a snap. Four taps. Hair? Blond and straight—five taps—medium length—four taps—and parted on the left—two taps. No beard or moustache, just thin, tweezed-looking eyebrows—one tap—above deep-set blue eyes. Three taps.

"Scars?" said Rutledge.

Once again, Barbara paused. *"None that I could see, but he had plenty of tattoos, on his neck and both arms."*

Lillian poked the 'N' on the artist's hand, then turned to Curt and said, *"Your turn again."*

"Does your program include tattoos?" he asked. "Because it occurs to me that body art could improve the chances of identifying this guy."

"No, I'm sorry," Rutledge replied. "I usually draw them myself, from the witness's description."

"Which she can provide in her written statement," Brassard cut in.

The artist looked bewildered. "How is a ghost supposed to—?"

"I believe Mr. Wakefield is resourceful enough to come up with a way. And when he brings the document to my office Monday morning, he will need to bring the pendant as well, so that Ms. Cournoyer can swear to the truthfulness of her account." Turning to Curt, she added, *"D'accord?"*

Darting glances at the stern expression on Lillian's face and the look of utter relief on Barbara's, he responded, *"D'accord,* Staff Sergeant."

Thirteen

"**A**ha! Found it!"

Sara's whoop of triumph carried all over the house. Not only did it bring Selena racing downstairs from the guest bedroom, but it also pulled Eric and Donnie away from their video games in the basement. This in itself was no mean accomplishment. Sara and Selena both did double-takes when the thunder below their feet was followed by two boys piling through the kitchen door in search of something other than food.

"What did you find, Mom?" Eric demanded. "Is it a clue?"

Clearly enjoying the presence of an audience, Sara leaned back in her chair, beaming with pride. "It's the trunk of the Friendly family tree. Curt was right. Their surname *was* a translation, from Italian. There's a record of an Alfonso D'Amico, his wife, Giuseppina, and their three daughters travelling from Florence to Manhattan Island in 1908. The youngest child was a one-year-old named Liliana."

"…who would have been twenty-five in 1932. Good work!" said Selena.

"Oh, it gets better," Sara assured her, grinning. "They

arrived on the same ocean liner as a single male relative of Giuseppina's. His name was Hermès Ferrari, and *ferrari* is Italian for 'iron worker'."

Selena's eyes widened as she realized: "In other words, a blacksmith. A Smith. Wow. I would have kept the name Ferrari, to be honest. Smith is so… ordinary."

"Very true. And that makes it difficult to trace, making the family itself hard to track down. Remember what I said earlier about Gertrude's inheritance probably being Hermès's share of a heist or something? I suspect they came to America to disappear, most likely so they wouldn't have to face the consequences of something that happened in Europe. Something that made them rich."

Selena frowned. "Why would you assume that?"

"Because unlike the other emigrants on that ship, the D'Amicos were able to pay for first-class passage for themselves and Hermès. That means they lived and ate well during the crossing. And if the information on the liner's official records is correct, they were also not detained on Ellis Island along with their fellow passengers, for Customs and Immigration inspection. So, no medical exams and no background checks."

"But how——?"

"Bribery. It's a documented fact that for a couple of dollars under the table, some of the Immigration officers were willing to 'streamline the process' and send newcomers directly to Manhattan Harbour. Of course, a couple of dollars back then was like a couple of hundred now."

"So, they were able to bypass Immigration and avoid any inconvenient questions about how much wealth they were bringing into the country," Selena said, following the reasoning. "And once they'd left the ship, they could simply melt into the population, change their names, and make the D'Amico family disappear. How much of this did Lillian remember?"

Sara uttered a syllable of laughter. "She was only a year old when they made the Atlantic crossing. She has no memory of being anyone but Lillian Friendly. All she could tell me about her family history consisted of bits of information that got dropped when the adults were talking—in English, always—and forgot that she was in earshot. She said that for the most part, no one spoke much about coming from an 'old country', or things that happened before she was born... which further supports my theory that they'd come to America to put a criminal past behind them."

"Are you going to share with her what you've found?"

"To what end, Selena? She's dead. What can she possibly do with it? No, I'm just going to continue keeping my promise to Curt. I'm going to follow the various branches of the two family trees and find a living relative who's willing to help us put Lillian and Gertrude in the right graves."

"What's a family tree, Mom?" Donnie piped up. "Is it like the one in our back yard?"

Smiling, Sara explained, "It's a diagram, Sweetie, like a drawing that shows who all the members of a family are and what their relationships are to one another. For example," she added, turning to a blank page in her notebook and picking up a pencil, "Daddy and me and you and your brother would look like this."

She printed their names and drew the lines joining them, then inserted their birth years and, for Doug, the year he'd died. She paused, her jaw wobbling as she stared at the second number beneath his name. Then she drew a deep breath and shrugged off the moment.

"But I have a brother too, so Uncle Larry goes here, and then there are Gramma and Grampa Holmes..."

"And Nanna and Poppa Traynor?" said Eric.

"Yes, and lots of other family members too. Aunts and

uncles and cousins. It's a pretty big tree, because each time someone in our tree gets married, another whole family tree gets connected to it."

"Can we build a family tree?"

"You know what? I think that would be a great summer project for this year," Sara declared. "I'll pick up the supplies and we can get started the day after school lets out."

That settled, the boys drifted away to resume playing their game.

"Where do you plan to begin?" Selena asked her. "Finding Lillian's relatives, I mean."

"The two older sisters—Eleanora and Carlotta D'Amico. Lillian remembers them as Nora and Carol Friendly. They're my best bet, since Gertrude was apparently an only child."

"Mmm... I wouldn't rush to rule out other siblings. Just because Hermès left everything to Gertrude, that doesn't mean he had no other children."

"You're thinking illegitimate offspring?"

"Illegitimate, estranged... disowned, maybe? This family tree has been growing for more than a century in the western hemisphere alone, and we still don't know how the Grangers fit onto it. And who knows how many other families may be connected to it?"

Sara gave her a strange look. "Like the McFadyens? He *was* legally married to Gertrude at the time of her death, after all."

"Oh, shit..." Selena muttered. She hadn't thought about that.

At five minutes before two o'clock that afternoon, with her list of carefully worded questions written out and close at hand, Selena sat down in front of her laptop and opened her email. As expected, there was the text message she'd earlier forwarded from her phone, containing the link to a video conference with Prue Davidson. She clicked on it.

Moments later, Selena was looking at the face of a woman who appeared to be only a few years older than herself, but a whole lot better at applying makeup. Her dark brown hair was styled into a fashionable updo. Her smile was practised and deep, deep red. And her bright blue eyes held something Selena couldn't define. She only knew in her soul what it was not, and that was happiness.

Either the decorating business or Davidson's personal life had to be in trouble. Choosing not to speculate, Selena refocused her thoughts on the actual purpose for this meeting.

"Hello!" she said, mirroring the decorator's welcoming expression as best she could. "It's good to put a face to the name."

"It is. I'm glad you decided to contact me. I… spent some time in Groverton last year, so I'm familiar with the area. What kind of house are you preparing to purchase there?"

"Well, it's old, but it's been well-maintained."

"Is it on a residential street in town, or is it on the outskirts?"

"It's in town." Mentally crossing her fingers, she added, "On a corner lot."

Davidson's smile broadened. "So. Many small rooms, one large veranda. I'm picturing it in my mind as we speak."

"I know you've worked on at least one home like that in the past. The realtor showed me some photos, and I was very impressed."

A shade seemed to come down over the light in the other woman's eyes. Pressing her scarlet lips together, she nodded tersely in acknowledgement of the compliment.

To keep her from shutting down, Selena took a step backward. "Do you source everything locally?" she asked, then held her breath as Davidson's expression visibly relaxed.

"In a town like Groverton, that's well supplied with shops

and talented artisans, yes. As much as possible, I try to support the local economy while creating a beautiful yet practical space that will reflect each client's personality, interests, and lifestyle."

It sounded as though she was quoting from a brochure. Well, Selena had a script as well. She glanced at—and instantly revised—the next question on her list. "And how do you determine all that?"

"First, I have to decide whether I can help them. I do that by chatting with them, and by taking a peek at their online presence. If I think we would be a good fit temperamentally, I'll ask to have a look at the room or rooms in question. Most of the people who request my services are already living in the spaces they want decorated, and I can learn a great deal about them from what they've done to their current surroundings."

"I see. Have you ever changed your mind about a client? Or walked away from a commission before it was completed?"

"Ah. I understand your concern. I've heard those stories, about small-town contractors who disappear for weeks on end halfway through a renovation. Be assured, Ms. Watt, that interior design is more than just a job for me—it's a calling. Should we enter into a client-decorator relationship, your personal satisfaction will be my primary goal. I can put you in touch with any number of my former clients who'll attest to it."

"That's good to know."

"If you're thinking of upgrading or making other changes to your new home, I can also recommend a couple of contractors in your area who are dependable and do quality work. We've used them ourselves."

It was the opening Selena had been waiting for.

"Yes, Tricia told me about your extensive renovation of the property you and your husband purchased," she said.

Davidson's face fell. "She discussed that with you?"

"She also told me that right after you'd finished decorating it, you abandoned it. Since I'm the one planning to buy it from you, I would very much like to know why."

"You're—?" she squeaked.

For several moments after that, Davidson appeared at a loss for words. Her lips were moving, but no sound came out.

Selena decided to help her. "Was it something you heard that frightened you?" she prompted. "Or something you saw? Or was it just a strange feeling that crept under your skin whenever you were alone in a room?"

The decorator's eyes went saucer-wide. "Wh—What? How could you—?"

Selena leaned closer to the screen. "I had a feeling like that, as soon as I stepped onto the veranda. It was as if the house was alive and trying to communicate an emotion to me—a terrible sadness."

Davidson clasped her hands together as though in prayer. "Oh, my God!" she whispered harshly. "Ben told me I had to be imagining it, that the house couldn't possibly be haunted, but—You're saying you felt it. Did you hear it too?"

"I was only inside for a short while. What exactly did you hear?"

Her eyes welled up with tears. "A woman sobbing. It kept me awake at night. I searched the whole house but couldn't find where it was coming from. It broke my heart to hear her."

"And Ben—your husband?—he couldn't hear her at all?"

"No. In fact, he kept suggesting I see a psychiatrist. Finally, I couldn't stand it anymore. I told him he could live in his castle if he wanted to, but he would have to do it alone. Then I packed a bag and went back to Toronto. Do you know what's going on? Is the house haunted?"

"We're not sure yet, but we're getting close to the truth. And I have a friend who can explain to you why hearing voices doesn't necessarily mean you're losing your mind. He's the curator of our local museum. Shall I give him your phone number?"

"Yes, please!"

"One final question: if not for the woman crying, would you and your husband be happily living together in that house right now?"

Frowning, Davidson pursed and unpursed her lips. "Happily?" she said at last. "I don't know. Ben was furious at me for forcing him to give up our dream home, especially after he'd liquidated so many of his investments to pay for the renovations."

"He had his own investments?"

"Ben's a lawyer. We have a prenup. I suppose I should be grateful for that. It means I retain half-ownership and will get something when the house is sold."

That probably explained why the asking price was so low, Selena realized. He couldn't whip the house out from under her, but he could minimize the amount she received from the sale.

"We've been separated for a couple of months now, barely on speaking terms," Davidson continued sadly. "A solid marriage should have been able to weather something like that, wouldn't you think?"

Selena had no answer for her. However, the thought did cross her mind that Ben Davidson was probably another person who would benefit from a heart-to-heart with Curt Wakefield.

After a day spent staring at a computer screen, Sara had settled on comfort food for dinner: her own version of mac and cheese, ladled into bowls from a large pot on the stove top. The cheese sauce was made from scratch, and she'd added plenty of finely chopped vegetables to give it a bit of crunch (and some extra vitamins).

Once the boys had eaten, it was reading time. Donnie and Eric went upstairs with a couple of books each, leaving Sara and Selena to enjoy leisurely cups of rooibos tea and catch each other up on the day's revelations.

"Any luck with the two older sisters?" Selena asked.

"Some." She got up and fetched a large spiral-bound notebook from beside her computer, then sat down again. Finding a page filled with handwriting, Sara read aloud from it. "Nora Friendly was the oldest, born in 1901, according to the school registration form. Carol was two years younger. They both graduated from high school and studied nursing. Nora never married or had children. She completed her studies, enlisted in the military, and made a career for herself as an army nurse, attaining the rank of Lieutenant Colonel shortly before her death in 1950. According to the available records, she'd been posted to a base in Seoul and was on an inspection tour of MASH units in Korea when the Jeep she was driving was hit by friendly fire and exploded, killing her instantly."

Selena nearly choked on her mouthful of tea. "You're kidding! Friendly fire?" she managed between coughs. "The thing that took her out literally had her name on it? That's so—"

"Ironic. And frustrating, because it's another dead end—pun intended."

"That just leaves Carol. Please, tell me she had children."

"I can't. I had to stop researching and make dinner."

"Will you know something tomorrow, then? Before I head back to Standerville?"

Sara gazed at her for a moment over the rim of her mug. "It depends on how early in the day you plan to leave, but I'll try. Now it's your turn. How did your meeting with the interior decorator go this afternoon?"

"Better than I expected, actually. I found out why she abandoned the house only weeks after moving into it. Turns out the place is haunted after all, by a weeping female ghost. It can't be Brenda—she was too recently killed—so my money is on Gertrude."

"Wait a minute! Davidson can see ghosts too? Now I'm *really* feeling left out!"

"She didn't say anything about seeing the ghost, only that the constant sound of a woman's sobbing was making it impossible for her to sleep at night and driving her to distraction during the day. And her husband couldn't hear a thing, and was convinced his wife was losing her mind. She wants me to put her in touch with Curt so he can reassure her that she's perfectly sane."

Sara's jaw dropped. "You told her about him? Selena, Curt has made it very clear—"

"Relax. I did not betray his secret. All I said was that he could explain things to her. Then she can explain them to her husband, and maybe they'll get back together again."

"The haunted castle broke up their marriage? That's sad. But you're not thinking of—? I mean, you still intend to put in your offer on the place, don't you?"

"Of course." *If not on this property, then I'm sure Tricia can find me another...*

"Mom!" came a wail from upstairs. "Donnie's doing it again!"

"The imaginary friend?" Selena ventured.

"Unfortunately, yes," Sara replied with a groan. "Our pediatrician says not to worry, that he'll outgrow the need for one eventually. I just hope it happens before Eric decides he wants one too."

Fourteen

It was a good thing Curt had eaten a late lunch today. The museum closed at 4:00 p.m. on Sundays. As soon as all the other living beings had departed, he locked himself inside the building. Then he sat down at his desk with a pad of lined, legal-sized paper in front of him and a couple of pens at hand, ready to take Barbara's statement for the police. He'd anticipated that this would be a rather long and stressful exercise, but he was shocked by just how arduous it turned out to be, for both of them.

By the time the final 'T' was crossed and the final 'I' was dotted, the sun was riding low in the sky; and Curt was disgusted with himself for having forced a young girl to relive the most traumatizing experience of her too-short life. That neither one of them had a choice, that every harrowing detail was important to the investigation and needed to be recorded, that he wasn't doing anything more to her than the PPS detectives assigned to her case would have done had she survived the brutal attack—none of that mattered to him at the moment.

Dinner? It was the last thing on his mind. Barbara's ordeal

nine years earlier had become his own, tying his stomach in knots and robbing him of any desire to eat. He was going to have nightmares about her death, he was certain.

For both their sakes, he decided not to read Barbara's statement back to her. Conjuring the face of her murderer on Rutledge's screen had been distressing enough for her. Dredging up the memories of everything she had endured at his hands—that had been much, much worse. The pain Curt had seen on her face, the hoarseness of her voice as she struggled to get each word out, had clouded his vision with tears more than once.

Lillian had remained at her side meanwhile, providing emotional support, but not even she had been able to distance herself from the horrors Barbara had suffered. At the end, Curt felt as though he'd just run a marathon, and the other two looked as though they might dissipate into mist at any moment.

"It's getting late," he said. "Tomorrow morning, we're going to deliver this to Staff Sergeant Brassard so she can resume investigating Barbara's case. Until then, I'm locking it inside my desk drawer so that there can be no suspicion of tampering."

"Oh? Is there a reason we should suspect you of tampering, Mr. Wakefield?" Lillian asked with renewed interest.

"No. But Brassard is going to ask her whether it's a truthful and complete recitation of the facts, and I want the answer to be a prompt and unequivocal 'yes'. Make sense?"

Lillian paused. When she replied, there was a pout in her voice. *"I suppose."*

Curt didn't want to imagine what sort of trouble he had just headed off.

As instructed, Curt arrived in Brassard's office the following morning, carrying both the statement and the pendant.

Barbara appeared much more self-composed today, so, over Lillian's objections, he had left the letter in his desk drawer. With luck, this would be a simple in-and-out visit.

He should have known he didn't have that kind of luck.

As Curt watched, tautly perched on the edge of the guest chair, Brassard perused Barbara's account. Then, frowning, she plucked a highlighter pen from her desk drawer and painted a couple of broad pink lines across the middle of the first page.

"What are you doing?" he demanded. "Isn't a victim's statement supposed to be an official document?"

She glanced up, still frowning, and replied, "Not unless it is signed and witnessed and added to the case file. And for reasons that I should not have to explain to you, Mr. Wakefield, that is simply not possible in this instance. What you have brought me is called 'a report by an anonymous source', and I am highlighting the parts of it that I find questionable."

"Questionable!" Before he knew it, Curt was on his feet, heat rising in his cheeks as he leaned across the desktop. "Have you any idea how painful it was for her to talk about what happened to her that day, and how difficult it was for me to hear and record it? And now you're suggesting that I made things up?" His voice rose precipitously on the final three words.

The staff sergeant's frown hardened into a scowl. "Sit down," she commanded him sharply, and, suddenly aware of Barbara staring wide-eyed at him, he complied.

"I was not questioning your honesty, Mr. Wakefield," Brassard continued sternly. "However, now that you have brought up the subject, I must ask: did you omit or embellish anything that you say Ms. Cournoyer told you?"

"No!" The word fairly exploded from his lips. "And I'm certain that she didn't omit or embellish anything either."

"*B'en*. Nonetheless, I must consider this document to be unverified, and there are places where I need to ask follow-up questions. For example, the driver of the pickup truck, the man she refers to as 'Nando' and claims to have seen murdered by her attacker—"

"It's not a claim, it's a fact!" he cut in firmly.

"Did Ms. Cournoyer see or hear anything that might suggest this Nando and her killer knew each other? Is it possible that one of them was an accomplice and they had a falling out?" she persisted, clearly running out of patience.

She wasn't the only one. As Barbara's complexion darkened, the air temperature around Brassard's desk plummeted. Curt pulled his jacket more tightly around him and crossed his arms over his chest, for warmth. With evident reluctance, the staff sergeant did the same.

"I believe you can take that as a no, to both questions," Curt replied. "As I wrote in her dictated statement, Nando was a good Samaritan, driving her to his place of employment where there was a tow truck, and the killer flagged him down, posing as another motorist in trouble."

"And this does not strike you as a strange coincidence?" said Brassard.

Curt paused. In retrospect, the timing did seem a little contrived... Then Barbara's angry voice sliced into his thoughts.

"Nando was not an accomplice! As soon as he saw the gun, he fought to defend me!"

...or perhaps he realized that his own life was now in peril and he was fighting to save himself...?

"No matter. You should know that we have matched the composite image of Ms. Cournoyer's attacker to the face of a man who is also wanted for questioning in two other sexual assaults. Thankfully, both the victims survived, and we are hoping that once he is in custody, we will be able to build a case that will stand up in court based on *their* statements and identifications. Unless something comes to light that I can use to procure his confession for the double murder, it is the best that I can promise. This is not a perfect conclusion for Ms. Cournoyer, I realize—"

"But you've got a name, right? There's a manhunt underway?"

Letting out a sigh, Brassard pulled a red file folder from one of her desk drawers.

"A name alone does not mean much," she replied. "Criminals use aliases all the time. They can also change their appearance. The match I mentioned just now was close, but not one hundred percent. And that is why..."

The sergeant opened the folder on the desktop in front of her. "To justify my connecting Ms. Cournoyer's nine-year-old murder to the more recent investigations, I need her to confirm that this is, indeed, the man who attacked her. Shall we say one poke for 'yes, it's him', and two for 'no, it's not'?"

Brassard flipped to a page in the file folder, then leaned back in her chair and placed her right hand flat on the desktop.

The full-face photograph she had uncovered was a portrait of evil, a "Mr. Hyde" version of the "Dr. Jekyll" image they'd created on Rutledge's computer two days earlier. This man took pleasure from causing others pain. His thin lips stretched in a reptilian smirk, and his eyes held the promise of a slow, cruel death.

Curt had seen eyes like those before, on the faces of some of the ghosts in the concentration camps in Europe. He'd had nightmares about those eyes, those faces, for years after that trip abroad. Encountering their predatory gaze again, in the here and now, triggered a surge of adrenalin that he could practically feel pushing him into overdrive.

Then he thought to check on Barbara. She was backing

away, hugging her shoulders, as an expression of abject terror emerged on her face like a mask rising from water. In that instant, Curt's mind filled with a single thought: *Enough!*

In one smooth motion, he rose from his seat and slapped the file folder shut.

Then, still leaning toward Brassard over the desk, he told her in a voice that slammed the door on any objection she might make, "She's shown me it's him. You have your confirmation, Staff Sergeant. Now you need to find this man and see that he gets what he deserves, and Barbara Cournoyer's spirit needs to begin healing."

With that, he snatched up the pendant, slipped it into his jacket pocket, and stalked out of the office.

Barbara was silent all the way back to the museum. Meanwhile, Curt's thoughts had begun wandering into dangerous territory. By the time he'd parked his car in the lot, they sat squarely in the darkest part of his mind.

What had he just done?

Striding past the gift shop counter, he made for the tower with Barbara close behind him. Lillian joined the parade when they were halfway there. She said not a word but held her head at a haughty angle. As he opened the door to his office, Curt felt as if his own head was about to explode.

He dropped the pendant back into its desk drawer and himself onto his chair with a despairing groan.

"Lillian, you should have seen him," he heard Barbara say wonderingly. *"He totally took over and told that horrible woman where to get off."*

"Sure he did. He's a regular Sir Galahad," came the other ghost's sour reply.

I don't need this right now, he decided. Curt got to his feet and walked away angry for the second time that morning.

His steps led him onto the boarding platform at the side of

the building, where two familiar greyscale figures sat on a bench, watching for imaginary trains.

"Hey, handsome! You don't look very happy. What's wrong now?" said Clara.

"He doesn't eat enough," Ruth declared, adding, *"Are you sleeping well, at least, Mr. Wakefield?"*

"Not if he's sleeping alone, he's not," her friend sniffed.

"Clara!"

"Don't you 'Clara' me! I know what he needs, and so does he—confidence. That young lady he's sweet on is only going to wait so long for him to work up his nerve. If he doesn't snap her up soon, someone else will. Then he'll really be miserable."

In other words, timing was important. Well, he'd certainly learned a lesson about times and places today, hadn't he?

"I made a right royal mess of things this morning," he moaned, easing himself onto the bench beside them.

"Oh?" said Clara. *"Do tell."*

"I was in such a hurry to keep my promise to Lillian that I rushed Barbara as well. I took her to the police station to verify her statement. But she needed more time to recover from the trauma of reliving the event, and when Staff Sergeant Brassard began asking further questions about it… I'm sure it triggered a flashback. I could see it on her face."

"Did she know she would be going to the police station?" Ruth asked. *"Did you tell her why, so it wouldn't be a surprise?"*

"I did," he replied, frowning thoughtfully, "and she seemed okay with it before we left here this morning." …*'seemed' being the operative word…* "Still, I should have given her more time. I could have, you know. Brassard's not my boss. When she told me to bring the statement in on Monday morning, I could have stood up to her. I could have told her she would just have to wait until Barbara was able to handle it, but I didn't. Instead, *I* waited while Brassard pushed Barbara to her breaking point."

"And what did you do then?" said Ruth.

"I cut the meeting short, in the rudest, most aggressive way possible, and got Barbara the hell out of there."

"So you did come through for her, even if it was a bit late in the game," Ruth observed. *"And how does she seem to you now?"*

"She's back to not talking to me, but I heard her say something to Lillian about how I defended her from 'that horrible woman'."

"So, your mistake has set things back between you a little, but she appreciates that you rescued her, and in the end, no real harm has been done. If you were to ask, my advice to you would be this: you can go ahead and feel depressed about your behaviour this morning if you wish, but at some point you have to emerge from your 'slough of despond' and move forward; and, trust me, the longer you wallow in it, the more difficult getting out of it is going to be."

"Perhaps he deserves *to wallow for a while,"* Clara remarked, biting off each word.

Ruth gave her a look. *"Your advice would be different?"*

"I think it depends on who he's actually feeling sorry for. Is it because of the effect his decisions have had on poor Barbara? Or is he rueing the fact that he blew up in Brassard's office and is now on the outs with someone he was counting on to grant him a favour?"

As usual, she had cut straight to the heart of the matter, regardless of how much it might bleed.

"Why couldn't it be both?" he protested. "There's nothing wrong with that, is there?"

Once again, he decided he didn't need this. Curt sprang to his feet and headed back inside the building, thinking dark thoughts. Ruth and Clara could dry Barbara's tears. They'd all three had high expectations of him, and he had clearly fallen short. Meanwhile, cynical, self-serving Lillian was much better suited to help him carry out the next step in his plan to breach the walls of the castle.

She was waiting for him in his office, lounging on his chair this time but still wearing a sardonic expression on her face. He didn't even attempt to get her to move.

"Where's Barbara?" he asked.

Lillian waved a negligent hand. *"Around here somewhere. She won't go far. None of us can, as you well know."* Slowly pulling herself to seated attention, she gestured rather imperiously to him to take a guest chair. *"I gather your visit to the police station was less successful than you'd hoped it would be."*

Now he was being called on the carpet by a ghost. Nena's grandfather had been right about her—Lillian Friendly was trouble. Curt felt a return of the heat to his cheeks. The urge to burn her letter and be rid of her was becoming irresistible. However, he needed her help with Rachel, and so he paused to damp down his rising anger before speaking again.

"If you're about to say 'I told you so', don't bother," he snapped. "Brassard ambushed Barbara with a photograph of the man who'd attacked her. He may as well have been in the room in person with her. She panicked when she saw him."

"Of course she did!" Lillian thrust an accusing forefinger at him, shaking it for emphasis. *"She wasn't ready for that and you knew it, and you took her there anyway. But you did finally stand up for her—which counts for something, I guess—so I'll let you off the hook this time."*

"Gee, thanks," he growled.

"So. What's the next step in your plan, Mr. Wakefield? I'm assuming there is one. A plan, I mean, not a step."

Ignoring the disdain evident in her tone, he told her, "Actually, there is, and it requires your assistance if I'm to pull it off."

"*Oh?*"

"I've met another ghost, named Rachel. She was a close friend of Brenda Ryan, the real estate agent whose body was recently found at the castle."

"*The one whose death is the reason the place is crawling with cops, and until they leave you can't take me back there? That Brenda Ryan?*" she sniffed.

"Right. Rachel knows more about Brenda than anyone else does. The problem is, Rachel's ghost is tethered to a bracelet that she gave her mother, and Mom never takes it off."

"*Let me guess: Mom has no inkling the bracelet is haunted, and if you're to keep your secret safe, then that's the way she has to stay.*"

"Correct. I can't talk to Rachel directly, but you can. If I bring her mother here for a meeting, will you walk Rachel out of the office and have a chat with her?"

"*To find out what, Mr. Wakefield?*"

"Whatever information you can glean about Brenda Ryan. At the very least, it could help us dig up a fresh piece of evidence to present to Brassard. That would convince her to let us enter the castle and look for Brenda's spirit. If she was killed in or around the house, it's where her ghost is most likely to be."

"*You sound quite certain of that. Have you checked to make sure it's not tethered to her body?*" When he didn't respond right away, she demanded, "*Do you even know where her body is?*"

Reluctantly, he replied, "It will be in the morgue, being autopsied and then waiting to be claimed by a relative, along with about a dozen other bodies." *...and a dozen other angry, fearful ghosts,* he added silently.

Curt had learned at a young age to avoid places where murdered bodies lay together. Even now, just thinking about the "educational" trip his mother had taken him on to visit Auschwitz and Bergen-Belsen was enough to send a violent shudder through his entire body.

Lillian inhaled sharply. *"You're afraid to go there, aren't you?"* she said wonderingly. *"A ghost whisperer who's afraid to be around the dead. How strange! And interesting."*

He batted away her remark. "It's complicated. Listen, I'll visit the morgue later. For now, let's just stick to the plan. I'll phone Tricia and tell her I'm tired of renting and want to buy a house in town. Then I'll set up a meeting with her, here in my office. When she arrives, you sidetrack Rachel for some ghost-to-ghost conversation. And please, be discreet with your questions. If she realizes you're pumping her for information, she'll get angry. And then the temperature will drop and it'll be game over."

"Fine, then. You're the boss," she declared. *"I'll handle her with kid gloves."*

He was the boss? Right. Curt didn't believe that for one second.

Fifteen

Selena came downstairs for a late Monday morning breakfast and found the dining room table fully occupied by sheets of Bristol board, pads of sticky notes, rulers, pencils, and felt-tipped markers. Sara sat at the kitchen table meanwhile, still wearing her robe and slippers. A half-eaten bowl of cereal had been shoved aside to make room for her laptop in front of her. Hunched over her keyboard and surrounded by a sprawling mess of notebooks and sheets of marked-up paper, this was not the neat-and-tidy Sara everyone knew. This Sara was engrossed to the point of obsession.

"Please, tell me you didn't pull an all-nighter just to have something to tell me before I left," Selena begged her.

Glancing up, Sara threw her a bright smile. "Don't worry. I got my beauty rest. I also had a hunch, and I got up early to follow it… all the way to Lewis Granger."

Stunned, Selena dropped onto the chair adjacent to hers. "You're talking about *Captain* Lewis Granger of the Seventeenth Precinct, New York City Police Department?"

"Yep, the very one. It turns out he's been the key to this puzzle all along. Selena, the Smith-Friendly extended family tree is enormous. There are cousins by marriage sprinkled all through it, some of them several times removed, and at least a dozen surnames that I've found so far. And the moment it truly began to spread was when Lillian's sister, Carol Friendly, married Kevin Gallagher in 1923."

"Gallagher. Not Granger?"

Sara let out a syllable of laughter. "That would have been too simple. No. Kevin's aunt, Lucy Gallagher, was the one who married into the Granger family, in 1887. Lewis was her oldest son. I figured a police captain had to be in his late thirties or early forties, at least, and worked my way backward from there. That's how I found the connection."

"So, if Kevin was Lucy's nephew and Lewis was her son, that made Lewis and Kevin first cousins, and Carol a cousin by marriage, along with her two sisters. And her offspring. She did have offspring, right?"

Sara nodded, her gaze once more riveted to her screen. "Four kids altogether. I'm running them down now. This has really mushroomed, Selena, literally overnight. It's been a ton of work digging it up, but the good news is, our chances of locating a living relative of Lillian Friendly just increased exponentially."

"Why?"

Sara paused with her fingers hovering over the keyboard and shot Selena a look. "Why have they increased?"

"No. Why has it been so much work? Lillian had to have known about the connection between the Friendlys and the Gallaghers. She knew how important it was for us to locate a living family member. And Carol was her *sister*, for heaven's sake! You don't just forget the name of your brother-in-law, not even if you're dead. There's something very fishy about this."

"I totally agree. As I've been saying right from the start, Lillian is not a reliable source of information. That's why I've gone to such pains to verify from public records and databases everything that she told me in Curt's office the other day. Listen, I don't mind any of this. I went into it with my eyes open, and I enjoy a deep dive, so you shouldn't feel the need to be angry on my account." A pause, then, "Have you changed your mind about returning to Standerville? I'm only asking out of curiosity—you know you're welcome to stay here for as long as you like."

"Thanks, I appreciate it, but I really have to get back there. It's been six business days. There may not be a lot of walk-in traffic in a town that size, but there's still some, and there are in-person meetings I've got lined up. I'll stay in touch and drive into Groverton when necessary—it's not that far to go."

Sara turned and stared wistfully at the supplies on the dining table. "So, I'm working on this project on my own, then?"

"Not necessarily. Why don't you invite Curt to help out? Dealing with bureaucrats can't be *that* time-consuming. And it's no secret how you feel about each other. Of course," she added with a grin, "it'll probably drive Larry around the bend seeing the two of you together so much."

Sara's cheeks dimpled. "I guess we'll find out."

Selena's low estimate of her travel agency prospects in Standerville had been spot on. Curating her email and voice mail inboxes during the past week had taken no more than five minutes each day. And once she'd returned home and disposed of all the junk in her snail-mail post office box, she was left with a couple of bills and a postcard from a local couple she'd sent to Scotland for their honeymoon. Thank goodness for the event planning side of her business! Corporate retreats, AGMs, and the Crime Club convention were all that had kept her afloat over the past few years.

She spent the rest of Monday drawing up her to-do list.

The bulk of the planning for the Crime Club Report and Investigation had happened over the winter, but there were still some last-minute details to be ironed out. As well, it was time to touch base with the several companies that regularly hired her to organize their team-building and creative brainstorming weekends. She also needed to cold-call additional potential clients, in case the worst happened and she was stuck in Standerville for another year.

Tuesday, she was on the phone and in virtual meetings all day, too busy (she thought) to worry about what was going on in Groverton… except when someone in a call used a phrase or a vocal inflection that triggered a swell of anticipation in her chest—and for just a moment she was back in Sara's kitchen, feeling the warmth of Larry's sympathetic gaze across the square wooden table.

That evening, there was a text from Sara on her phone: *Get back here. U r not going to believe what I've found.*

Selena replied: *Wed night earliest. C u then.*

No sooner had she pressed *Send* than the phone buzzed, signalling an incoming voice call.

"Hello, Ms. Watt? This is Prue Davidson."

Selena's brain stumbled. She'd forgotten about Prue, about mentioning her to Curt. And about the pendant, and Tricia's bracelet, and probably a few other things as well. Now everything was coming together at once, colliding inside her head, and she was momentarily at a loss for words.

Eventually, she managed to respond, "Hello! It's… so good to hear from you."

"Listen, I've been thinking over what you said the other day, about your friend, the museum curator. I realize he must be busy, since I haven't heard from him yet, but I had a strange dream last night and I really need to talk to him about it. How soon can you set up an appointment for me?"

"How about the day after tomorrow? Afternoon, maybe?"

After I've had a chance to warm him up to the idea…?

"Perfect! Where shall we meet, then? At the museum?"

"Actually, we should have lunch together first," Selena said on impulse, startled at first to hear the words come out of her mouth but then realizing what a brilliant move this was, on several levels. Ben was a lawyer, but also a stakeholder, which meant he would be working for himself.

"Good idea. If you're still considering having me decorate the house it will give us a chance to get to know each other."

Well, there was that, of course, but… "There will be three of us at the table. My friend Sara is a librarian, and she's made a project out of researching the history of the house. I promise you, I still intend to make Ben an offer on it, and you will be meeting the curator of the museum to discuss the experience you had while living inside it, and you will feel much better about it afterward."

A pause, then, "All right. Name the restaurant."

"The kitchen table."

"I'm not familiar with that one. Is it new?"

"Not really. I've eaten there many times and can personally vouch for the food. Here's the address for your GPS…"

Wednesday was a relative blur of activity. In-person meetings that couldn't be moved online or postponed for a week had to be hastily prepared for and taken that very day. Granted, there weren't that many of them—nailing down floral and catering arrangements for an on-again-off-again end-of-June wedding and securing a day's worth of local entertainment for Standerville's Canada Day celebration were the most urgent items on her to-do list. However, clearing the decks to accommodate a trip that had been planned for weeks was quite a different proposition from doing it with only a few hours' notice. Meetings and auditions became rushed and chaotic, causing stress levels to rise and achievement levels to drop.

This was no way to run a business.

By the time Selena had finished packing for the return to Groverton, she was exhausted and having serious second thoughts about getting behind the wheel of her car. Then, as though reading her mind, Sara sent her another text: *Found a living relative. It will blow ur mind!*

That did it. A two-hour drive, most of it in daylight? *No problemo, señora!*

Selena pulled into Sara's driveway at 9:45 p.m., hauled her weary self out of her vehicle, and was immediately swarmed by three very excited people.

"Thank goodness you're here!" Sara exclaimed. "I was afraid you would beg off coming until tomorrow morning and I'd have to wait to show you—"

"How about we get her inside first?" Larry cut in. "You go ahead. I'll grab the luggage."

"And I'll put on the kettle for tea," Sara added, making a beeline for the front door.

That left Selena and Curt standing on the walkway, trading looks. His was amused. Hers was quizzical.

"I gather there's been a breakthrough?" she said.

"A big one," he replied, offering her his arm. "Totally unexpected."

"Wow. If that's what happens when I'm not around, I should leave town more often."

He laughed.

"Baggage coming through!" Larry announced.

They stood aside to let him pass, then followed him into the house. Curt ushered her to a seat at the kitchen table, where clean cups and saucers sat waiting. Apparently, this was also where dinner had been served earlier, since what Selena could see of the dining room through the adjoining door was entirely taken up by Sara's project. Two large sheets of Bristol board lay flat on the dining table, their surfaces covered by a mosaic of various-coloured sticky notes.

"You texted me about locating a living relative of Lillian's," Selena said, returning her attention to the other three people in the kitchen.

"Yes, and I'll show you on the chart, after you've had your tea and heard what Curt has been up to," Sara told her, raising her voice above the whistling of the kettle.

"He's been busy," Larry confirmed.

"Just doing my part in the investigation, is all." He cleared his throat before continuing, "She's probably going to deny it, but I think Staff Sergeant Brassard may now believe in ghosts. I had to convince her that they're real so she would accept Barbara's statement and her description of her murderer, and act on them."

"And did she accept them? And act on them?" Selena asked, leaning forward from the edge of her seat.

"She did. And she says she will. But if she names the victim's ghost as her source, no one in the PPS will take the sketch or the statement—or Brassard herself, for that matter—seriously. So, as far as the police are aware, she is following up on an anonymous tip related to a cold case. She's identified your cousin's assailant and put out an all-points bulletin on him. And once he's in custody, she'll do her best to get a confession out of him. Under the circumstances, that's the only way the murder case will stand up in court."

Sara brought the teapot to the table and set about filling everyone's cup. "And how is Barbara?" she asked between pours. "Just knowing that things are finally moving forward must be a huge weight off her mind."

"Actually, she's not doing so well," Curt replied. "To produce the statement she had to relive the event, and it traumatized her all over again. Now she's hiding from me. Lillian knows where she is. She's been trying to comfort her, but it's going to take longer than a couple of days—"

"Wait a second—Barbara and *Lillian* are friends now?" Selena blurted. "I thought Ruth and Clara were supposed to be supporting her."

"And they were, for a while. Then, I guess she discovered she had more in common with Lillian."

"Really! Like what?" Selena demanded, her cheeks growing hot while her tea sat forgotten. "We already know Lillian isn't someone to be trusted, that she'll do anything to get her way, so what could she and Barbara possibly have in common?"

"They're both dead, for one thing," Larry said flatly, expressing a truth so blunt and obvious that it instantly knocked the wind out of her sails. As she stared wordlessly into his face, he continued in the same hard voice, "They're both tethered to material objects on the mortal plane, and they're both relying on us to complete their unfinished business so they can be released to rest in peace."

Flushing with shame now for forgetting that, she said, "I'm sorry. It's been a long and busy day, and I'm tired. And frustrated. Lillian has been trapped among the living for more than ninety years. I can't help wondering at what point Barbara will be able to find peace. Will it be when her murderer is arrested? When he's convicted? When he *dies?* Will it even be within my lifetime?"

"Hey!" Larry brought his hand down over hers and gave it a comforting squeeze. "It will be whenever she feels she has received justice. It's not our call to make, Selena. It's hers."

Curt replaced his cup in its saucer and chimed in, "Listen, when I first came to this museum, there was a woman's ring on display. It had been found by a diver exploring one of the shipwrecks in the bay, and the ghost of a young man was tethered to it. This ring was nothing special—in fact, it was cheap costume jewellery—but it was the best he could afford.

He told me he'd bought it to put on his girlfriend's finger when he proposed to her, and the biggest regret of his life was that he hadn't been able to do that.

"He gave me her name, and I did some research. She was a local girl. I found her grave in the old cemetery, and I knew what I had to do. Using my own money, I had a replica made of the ring. I switched it with the one in the museum. Then I took the original to the graveyard. He came with it, of course. He watched as I dug a little hole near the base of her tombstone, placed the ring inside it, and covered it up. I heard him say, 'I love you, Elaine'. And next thing I knew, he was gone. She had received the ring, and he could finally be at peace."

"And is the ring still in her grave?" Sara asked.

"The replica is. I switched them again once he was free. The point is, he knew they were both dead, that he would never actually get to put the ring on her finger. It was enough for him that she and the ring were finally in the same place. Barbara knows that she's dead, and that we're striving to get justice for her. She will decide what is enough for her to be at peace. When that happens, assuming you leave the pendant with me, I will know, and I will give it back to you so that you can wear it and be at peace too."

Her vision clouding with tears, Selena whispered, "Thank you."

"Now tell her the rest, about the blueprints," Larry prompted him.

"Why? It was a dead end," Curt protested.

"Because a negative answer is still an answer. Tell her!"

"Fine. I was able to locate the blueprints used for the construction of the original castle in 1927, and there's no sign of any secret room anywhere in them. That means either Lillian has been stringing me along so that I'll take her out for a field trip, or…"

"Or McFadyen had an extra dividing wall put in after the building was completed, creating a hidden space," Larry supplied.

"Either way, we'll have to wait for the yellow tape to come down before we can go in there looking for ghosts, or booze vaults, or anything else. End of report," Curt said with finality.

"Now it's my turn," said Sara, her eyes sparkling with excitement. "Finish your tea, everyone, because we're moving to the dining room table for show and tell."

This was what Selena had been waiting for. With burgeoning anticipation, she downed the last of her beverage and followed the others out of the kitchen.

When they were all gathered around the brightly coloured paper mosaic lying on the table, Sara went on, "It took me a while to find the Smiths and the Friendlys, and another while to realize just how extensive their complete family tree was going to be, and how much of my time would be chewed up if I tried to explore all of it. So, since our goal was to locate a living relative of Lillian Friendly as expeditiously as possible, I finally decided to limit my search to the descendants by blood of Carol and Kevin Gallagher, from 1926, when Bridget was born, to the present. As you can see, there were a lot of them. These people loved kids. With only a couple of exceptions, the ones who had families of their own had large ones. I've colour-coded the chart using sticky notes so that we can see at a glance who's deceased and who is still living."

"It's getting late, Sara. Can we cut to the chase here?" Larry asked. "How many living relatives does Lillian have?"

"If we eliminate the deceased and the minors, there are nineteen, ranging in age from elderly to millennial."

Selena was still waiting for her mind to be blown, as Sara had promised in her text. Impatiently, she prompted, "You told me you'd found something unbelievable...?"

"Have a look at these two," she replied, pointing to a couple of orange sticky notes near the centre of the board.

Selena leaned closer. Neatly printed on the notes were the names of two sisters, evidently twins since they were both born in 1983: Phoebe Anne and Prudence Leigh Brickman.

Prudence?

She lifted her gaze to meet Sara's. "No way! This has to be a coincidence."

Growing an impish grin, Sara replied, "I don't think so. Look at who she married."

Selena glanced at the board once more and had to remind herself to close her mouth.

The name linked to Prudence's was Corben Davidson Jr. It struck with almost physical force, knocking Selena a step away from the table.

"She called him Ben," Selena murmured incredulously. "Damn! She's been under our noses the whole time."

"Would someone please fill me in?" Curt asked. "I feel as if I need a program."

"I second that motion," Larry said. "Who is Corben Davidson?"

"Prue and Corben Davidson are the current owners of the castle," Selena replied.

Male jaws dropped in unison.

"And Prue is a descendant by blood of Carol Friendly," Sara added. "That makes her Lillian's great-great-grandniece… I think." She stared for a moment at the chart on the table, then nodded her head. "That's right. From Margaret to Emily to Elspeth to Prudence."

"We need to reach out to this lady," said Curt, "and the sooner the better."

"Actually, she reached out to *me*," Selena informed him. "She phoned me yesterday to ask if I could arrange a meeting for her with my friend, the museum curator, about a dream she'd had, and I suggested that she might want to join Sara and me for lunch as well. She's driving up here tomorrow."

"She is?" Sara said, frowning. "Lucky for you that I'm working the second shift, then."

Meanwhile, his expression darkening, Curt lowered his face. *Like a bull about to charge,* she couldn't help thinking as the ground seemed to shift beneath her feet, fracturing the foundations of her already-crumbling composure.

In a quiet, restrained voice he asked, "And why, if I may ask, does she think *I'm* the one who can help her with a dream?"

At this, a flare of anger found its way to Selena's mouth. "I know what you're thinking, and you're wrong—again!" she snapped. "When she told me earlier that the reason she'd abandoned the house was that she kept hearing the disembodied voice of a sobbing woman, all I told her was that I had a friend who could explain to her why that didn't necessarily mean she was losing her mind. Whatever this dream of hers was about, she didn't share it with me. She just asked for a meeting with you to discuss it, and I told her I would set it up for tomorrow afternoon. So, when the time comes, you can present yourself to her however you want—as a psychologist, or an expert in the field of supernatural phenomena, or whatever else you please. Just know that whether you choose to believe it or not, I *can. Keep. A secret!* Now," she added, with effort modulating her tone if not her mood, "it's late, and I'm tired, so if you'll excuse me, I'm going to bed."

With that, she wheeled and headed upstairs.

Several minutes later, there was a timid knock on her bedroom door. "Selena?" said Sara's voice from the hall. "I'm alone. May I come in?"

Only if it's to deliver an apology, was her first thought. Then she reconsidered.

"Sure. I'm decent."

"Thank you for not slamming the door and waking the boys up, by the way," Sara said as she let herself into the room.

Selena shrugged a shoulder in response. In truth, she hadn't been thinking of that. She'd just been weary to the point of tears and unable to muster the energy required for a physical show of anger. But if Sara wanted to believe Selena was being thoughtful, so be it.

Remaining tentatively just inside the door, Sara said, "I want to apologize for earlier. It was my decision to hold off on the general sharing of information until you arrived to hear it, and when you finally got here… It must have felt like an ambush. I should have realized you'd be tired after a long day and postponed everything until tomorrow. I'm so sorry about that."

What was done was done. Selena's eyes were welling up. Not trusting her voice, she gave Sara a brief smile and a nod.

"I just have one question," Sara continued. "Why did you invite Prue Davidson to join us for lunch? She's welcome here, of course, that goes without saying, but—did you already know who she was?"

Sinking down onto the edge of the bed, Selena drew a deep breath and raised a hand palm outwards to pause the conversation while she recomposed herself.

"No, I didn't," she finally replied. "I thought that if we told her about the work we'd been doing, she might agree to contact her husband for us. Corben Davidson isn't only half-owner of the house—he's also a lawyer, and it made sense to me that when we were ready to approach the living descendants of those families, he should be the one to do it. As a lawyer, I mean, so they wouldn't suspect we were trying to scam them and call the police on us. After all, if some stranger called you out of the blue to tell you that you're related to a woman who died in 1933 and got buried in the wrong grave, and could you please pony up a few hundred dollars so she can be moved to the right one, what would probably be going through your mind?"

"You're right. It will have to be someone official, and considering how much trouble Curt is having with the bureaucratic doorstops in town, as he calls them…"

In spite of herself, Selena had to laugh. "That's what he calls them?"

"It is, and speaking as someone who's been forced to jump through more than a few of their hoops to get things done around here, I can't say I disagree with him." Sara stepped forward and settled down onto the bed beside her. "Listen, I think we all need to cut Curt some slack, Selena. He hides it well, but he's been under enormous stress the past couple of weeks. Dealing with Lillian especially has not been easy for him. And what he had to do for Barbara took a lot of courage on his part. He's not just being paranoid, you know—he's had some bad experiences in the past when people found out about his gift. It literally cost him his job at the ROM."

After the story he'd just told them about the ring, Selena thought she could understand why.

"So, we'll be three for lunch then," Sara said briskly. "What time can we expect Ms. Davidson to arrive tomorrow?"

"Between 11:30 and noon."

"Good, because I still have to report for work at two o'clock."

Struck by a sudden thought, Selena said, "About that meeting I promised her with Curt…"

On her way to the door, Sara turned and replied, "He's already agreed to it, and I know he won't let you down. He knows how important it is that we get Prue Davidson onside. Now, go to sleep. We've all got a big day ahead of us. Except for Larry," she added, frowning. "I'll have to do something about that."

Sixteen

Curt did not sleep well that night. Lillian kept popping up in his dreams, nagging him to do things that were blatantly against the law and shrilling at him, *"You know you want to do this!"*

The sad thing was, she was right. If not for his terror of being arrested for trespassing, he would have stolen past the yellow tape and broken into the castle much earlier—with or without Sara and the others. The sobbing woman Selena had mentioned had to be Gertrude's ghost, longing to be set free, but he was also itching to find McFadyen's hidden vault and uncover whatever terrible secret lay within it, and his curiosity had only grown stronger with each passing day.

Lillian knew the truth about him: he was a coward. And now she was haunting his sleep, giving him nightmares. Clearly, Curt wouldn't be free until *she* was, making it more important than ever that she be untethered from that damn letter and sent away to wherever spirits were supposed to go when they left their mortal shells.

The following day dawned bright and sunny—quite the opposite of the way he felt as he walked through the front entrance of the museum at 9:30 a.m. Amy's first comment after "Good morning" was delivered with a sympathetic smile. "You don't look very well, Mr. Wakefield. Are you sure you're not coming down with something?"

"I'll live," he grumped back at her. "What's on the schedule for today?"

She consulted her computer. "A couple more school groups, one at ten and one at one o'clock. Nena's got both of those. Romy can handle any tour buses that stop by. And a realtor phoned just now and left her number. She said she would appreciate it if you could get back to her sometime before noon."

"I'll certainly try," he said, taking the slip of paper from Amy's outstretched hand. "If anyone needs me, I'll be in my office, chasing down bureaucrats. If Ms. Vickery calls again, put her through. Oh, and I'm supposed to have a meeting this afternoon with someone named Prue Davidson, but I'm not sure when she'll be arriving."

Amy's fingers flew over her keyboard. "Not to worry," she assured him. "I'll let you know the moment she gets here." Behind her, Orville made the OK sign with his thumb and forefinger.

Curt met his gaze and nodded acknowledgement, then paused to watch Amy at her job. He recalled what the outgoing curator/manager had told him about her three years earlier.

She'd been helping out at the museum since her junior year of high school, managing the gift shop so that the regular staffer could switch to providing day care for her grandchildren in July and August while their parents worked. The month of June had been added when Amy began her university studies, so that she wouldn't be tempted to look for full summer employment elsewhere. This next academic year would be her last in the undergraduate program, meaning that this summer was most probably her last at the museum.

Orville Mead wasn't the only one who would miss her when she left in September. Amy was the best-organized person Curt knew, almost as obsessed with details as he was. She was also a quick study and a compulsive learner. By now, she could probably pass a museum management exam and take over running this place.

"There!" she declared, and flashed him a grin. "We're all set for the day."

Of course, they were. Curt headed toward the tower to make his first phone call.

"Mr. DeLucci is currently walking the grounds," said the pleasant-voiced woman who answered the phone at the Municipal Cemetery.

"Really! Does he do that very often?" Curt asked. *...or only when my number comes up on call display?*

"He goes out periodically to check on the condition of the older established FRPs."

"FRPs?"

"It's an acronym he coined. It stands for Final Resting Places. He's quite proud of it—even had it put on the licence plate of his car."

Somehow, Curt wasn't surprised.

"Well, when he's finished inspecting gravesites, would you please tell him I have some important news, and ask him to contact me as soon as possible?"

"Of course, Mr. Wakefield."

As he ended the call, he noticed a familiar greyscale figure standing in a corner of his office, and for just a moment he couldn't be certain whether he was truly awake or still asleep and dreaming.

"You look like hell, Mr. Wakefield."

"Lillian," he said through clenched teeth, "I'm in no mood for this right now."

"Fair enough," she conceded, approaching his desk and

appearing to sit down on a guest chair directly facing his. *"But I gather something has changed, and I'm curious to know what the important news is… and you're going to tell me. Aren't you?"*

Already knowing what the alternative was, he decided it was best to figuratively throw in the towel right away. "We've located a living relative of yours, someone who can make a formal request for the exhumation of your remains and their relocation to an accurately marked grave. More to the point, it's someone who might actually have an interest in doing it. I'll know more after we've spoken this afternoon."

"A relative?" Her eyes widened, with anticipation, he presumed, until he heard the tremor of fear in her voice. *"So quickly? I wasn't able to give you much information. Are you sure you have the right person?"*

"Yes, we are. Information technology has come a long way since the 1930s, Lillian. She's your great-great-grandniece, and you're going to meet her this afternoon."

"A niece? Descended from Nora?"

"From Carol, related by blood, through four generations."

"Oh." She sounded disappointed.

Curt's interest was piqued. "Is there a problem?" he inquired.

"It's just that Nora and I had a special connection. It went beyond blood. She… understood me when no one else in the family did. Carol disapproved of my lifestyle. So did Pop. Mom didn't mind it, and as long as she and Nora were around, the others kept it to themselves. But once Mom passed away and Nora was posted to Panama, all that dislike of me came spilling out."

"I don't understand. According to the records Sara found, Nora reported for duty in Panama in 1925. You were—what? Eighteen? So, what could you possibly have done while still in your teens that would turn your family against you?"

"My father and Uncle Hermès had very strict rules about how young women should behave. Trudy was better at pretending to follow them than I was. And, as you said, it was the 1920s. Things were different back then."

He nearly laughed. The "terrible thing" wasn't so abhorrent after all.

"Lillian!" he chided her gently. "Are you telling me that you and your cousin were rebels? That beneath that long woollen coat beats the heart of a flapper?"

"Among other things, yes. We smoked, we drank bootleg liquor, and we liked to sneak out wearing fancy clothes and have some fun. Carol said I was a bad influence and cut me off, and when Pop died, shortly after her wedding, I learned that he'd left everything to her and her future children, and not a cent to me. I had to go to her, begging for enough money to put me through a practical nursing program so that I could at least have a means to support myself. She made me a deal: she would pay my rent and my tuition, on the condition that I disappear from her life right after graduation and never trouble her or her husband's family again."

"Ooh! That was harsh."

She shrugged. *"That was Carol, the family prig. And I had no choice but to agree to her terms. Four generations later, there's no reason for anyone in her bloodline to know that I even existed. So don't be surprised if your 'sure thing' isn't as certain as you think it is."*

"I'll bear that in mind. But what about Gertrude? You still had a relationship with her, right? Even if her father didn't approve?"

"Uncle Hermès took pity on me when he saw I was trying to change my life, so he let Trudy and me stay close friends, even if I was no longer considered family. That was how I found out she was pregnant. When she told me—" She caught herself up, then continued, *"I realized immediately just*

how bad it was and insisted on accompanying her to Groverton. You know the rest, from the letter."

But Curt's attention had been snagged by that unfinished thought. "When she told you what, Lillian?"

Silence. She pressed her lips together, as though to prevent the words in her mouth from escaping.

"Come on. It happened ninety years ago, and everyone who was involved is dead," he pointed out. "Is there really a reason to keep it a secret anymore?"

The ghost appeared to draw a shuddering breath. *"I guess not,"* she replied in a small voice. *"When I stopped partying, Trudy sometimes went out alone. That was how she met Hugh McFadyen. One day I caught her sneaking a drink that I didn't recognize. I asked her what it was, and she broke down in tears. She told me that Hugh McFadyen had drugged her and had his way with her in one of the back rooms at a party. Now she was carrying his child, but she wouldn't be pregnant for much longer. She said she had been dosing herself with a concoction purchased from some back-alley chemist who'd guaranteed her it would bring on a miscarriage."*

Comprehension dawned. "That was why she was having a difficult pregnancy. She was poisoning the fetus."

"And herself at the same time. I made her stop. Assured her that things could be worse—after all, it wasn't as if she had to marry the guy." A pause, a sad shake of her head, then, *"What we didn't realize was that getting Trudy pregnant was just the first step in Hugh's plan. He waited until she started showing, then convinced Uncle Hermès to let him 'make an honest woman of her' before any more damage was done to her reputation. Hermès agreed, of course. By then Trudy had become too ill to fight them off or run away, and before either of us fully knew what was happening, she was Mrs. Hugh McFadyen."*

"And then Hermès was killed. I gather you suspected foul play."

"It was hard not to. He was run over by a car while crossing the street. I saw the look on Hugh's face when the will was being read. He was not happy about having to wait several months to steal Trudy's inheritance, especially considering how sick she was. She was dying, Mr. Wakefield, and he knew it."

All at once, Curt understood with painful clarity where McFadyen's "bagfuls of American money" had very likely come from. Being crushed by a derailing train seemed too easy a death for such a heartless predator.

"So, he switched to plan B—remove her to Groverton, keep her sequestered from the locals, and then, if necessary, find a way to convince everyone that she'd survived past her twenty-first birthday. And force you somehow to go along with it."

"He told me that if I tried to report him to the Canadian authorities, he would have me arrested and charged for the deaths of his wife and his unborn child. He said that it would be his word against mine, and with his reputation as a pillar of the community, he was the one who would be believed, and I would be presumed guilty."

"And that's why you wrote the letter to an American police captain. Lewis Granger might not know you well enough to trust you, but he was certain to be acquainted with Trudy's story and would perhaps care enough to look into McFadyen's American past. I must say, that makes a lot of sense."

She relaxed visibly in her chair. *"Thank you. And Mr. Wakefield? Thank you for listening to me."*

He nodded thoughtfully in response. Listening hadn't been difficult—she told a gripping story. Could he believe it? Not entirely, he suspected. It had answered some of his questions, but others still remained, such as how she had known to address her letter to someone two marriages away from her on the family tree, yet had struggled in vain to recall the name of Carol's husband when briefing Sara earlier.

There were many more pieces to this puzzle. Curt was certain they would all fall into place eventually. He just had to be patient and keep himself in the loop… while simultaneously playing phone tag with a real estate agent and a clutch of regional bureaucrats.

As if on cue, his land line buzzed. Raising a hand to signal a pause in his conversation with Lillian, he picked up the receiver and found Tricia Vickery on the other end of the call.

"Hello, Mr. Wakefield," she said brightly. "I know our appointment isn't until this afternoon, but it happens that I'm practically around the corner from you, with the next hour free, so I'm just wondering if you can possibly make some time for me this morning instead. Have you had a chance to check out the houses I emailed you about earlier this week?"

Casting a sidelong glance in Lillian's direction, he consulted his watch. It was half past ten o'clock. On the plus side, getting this meeting out of the way before lunch would clear his schedule for the one with Ms. Davidson, whenever she happened to arrive. On the minus side, there weren't many places in the museum for two ghosts to have a private conversation when the exhibit halls were full of schoolchildren and one of the spirits was averse to being around them.

Curt mentally flipped a coin and made up his mind. "I'm afraid I've only had time for a cursory look at the listings, but I would still like to meet with you this morning to discuss them and perhaps narrow down my options. How does eleven o'clock sound to you?"

Vickery replied firmly, "Sounds perfect. I'll see you then."

As he recradled the receiver, he noticed Lillian staring at him, her eyebrows arched inquiringly.

"That was the real estate agent I told you about, the one with the haunted bracelet," he told her.

"And just like that, you've shifted to sleuthing into Brenda's untimely death. It must be exhausting for you, Mr. Wakefield, having to juggle all these investigations," she observed, without a trace of sympathy in her voice or on her face.

Exhausting? That was putting it mildly. What sane person would be trying to solve three mysteries at once?

Tricia Vickery was nothing if not punctual. She walked through the museum's front entrance at precisely eleven o'clock with her skinny leather briefcase tucked beneath one arm and a professional smile on her face... and the greyscale figure of a young woman following a short distance behind her. Curt recognized her from the photograph in Tricia's office.

The school group had departed, leaving the exhibit halls empty for now, and Rachel appeared eager to explore. Her wide-eyed gaze leaped in fascination, from the books and pamphlets on the carousel inside the gift shop, to the tall hexagonal display case in Exhibit Hall B, to the birch bark canoe slung from the ceiling in the indigenous part of Exhibit Hall A. Then it settled on Curt's face and she recognized him as well.

Instantly, her jaw set and her eyes narrowed. *"This had fucking well better be about buying a house,"* she warned him.

Feeling the chill in the air but purposely not responding to her, he mentally crossed his fingers and ushered her mother toward the tower, where Lillian awaited.

Since Curt wasn't actually planning to move from the place he was renting, all he wanted was to engage in a pleasant half-hour conversation with Tricia about real estate while Lillian teased information out of Rachel. That was the plan. It was also the best case scenario, the one that depended on everything else coming together as expected. By now, however, Curt knew how unpredictable ghosts could be, so he'd already run a number of other possible situations through his mind.

By the time he opened the door to his office, he was sure he'd prepared for every eventuality and could not be surprised. Then he saw Barbara standing mournfully in the middle of the room and Lillian nowhere in sight, and for several heartbeats he was dumbfounded.

"Is there a problem?" Tricia's voice snapped him back to the moment.

"Oh! No, no," he assured her, forcing his lips to curve in a smile. "Please, have a seat."

The realtor dropped onto one of his guest chairs, reached into her briefcase for her laptop, and busied herself setting it up on his desk. Meanwhile, Curt settled down in his usual place, keeping both ghosts in view.

Rachel had noticed Barbara as well, and had come to stand beside her. However, Barbara remained staring straight ahead, giving no sign of awareness that the other spirit was there. Rachel frowned and looked her up and down, then passed her hand in front of Barbara's face.

No reaction. The frown deepened, along with Curt's anxiety.

Where the hell was Lillian? He knew she and Barbara could see each other. How was Rachel any different?

"So! You said you've looked at the listings but haven't taken any virtual tours, is that correct?" Tricia asked briskly.

"Uh, yes."

Reluctantly, he dragged his gaze away from the scene being played out behind the realtor and paid attention to the woman sitting across from him instead. She'd pulled up one of the listings onto her screen and turned it to face him.

"This one recently came onto the market. It falls at the high end of your price range but has had some lovely upgrades and is in absolutely pristine condition. Take a look inside," she urged him, initiating the tour with her forefinger.

"Barbara! There you are!"

Startled, he glanced up in time to see Lillian come charging through the wall of his office, the portrait of exasperated relief.

"I've been looking all over—! Oh, hello," she said, pretending to suddenly notice the third ghost in the room. *"I'm Lillian. And you've just arrived, I gather. Well, whoever you are, welcome to the museum. Do you know which exhibit your item is going to be part of?"*

"Thank you, but... My name is Rachel. Rachel Vickery. And I'm just visiting here."

"Oh! In that case, let me give you a quick tour. And I'm sorry if Barbara bothered you. I've been taking care of her, but she gets away from me sometimes."

As Lillian shepherded the other two out of the office, Curt heard Rachel's voice asking, *"Is she going to be all right?"* and Lillian replying, *"Eventually. Some passings are more traumatic than others. I died instantly in a train derailment ninety-some-odd years ago. What was your death like?"*

This girl was good. A little *too* good, in fact. She had the skills of a con artist. They cast doubt on the reliability of anything she had previously told him. And he really wished she hadn't used Barbara as a prop just now. Nonetheless, he decided, if she was able to dislodge information about Brenda's past from an otherwise uncooperative ghost... and if it secured them access to the castle before the police tape came down... and if there really was a secret space to be found there... then Lillian's walk on the shady side would have been worth it.

Seventeen

Sara had the spinach salad prepared and the bruschetta ready to pop under the broiler by 11:30 sharp on Thursday morning. Ten minutes later, Selena heard the crunching of tires on gravel outside—the Historical Society was dead set against paving a century-old driveway—and went out to greet Prue Davidson.

The decorator was casually dressed today, in khaki slacks, a black and white striped short-sleeved blouse, and strappy, flat-heeled, brown leather sandals. As she emerged from her car, she glanced around in confusion. Then she saw Selena standing on the veranda and strode around the rear of the car to the walkway.

"I thought we were meeting at a restaurant...?" said Prue.

"Well, we have things to show you, and Sara's work shift starts at two. It's simpler to lunch here. I didn't lie to you, though. We'll be sitting at her kitchen table, and she's a great cook."

"But I'm empty-handed. If I'd known, I would have brought a hostess gift."

"Trust me, Ms. Davidson, your presence by itself is a

hostess gift. You have no idea how much work Sara has put into finding you."

"I don't understand. And call me Prue. Please."

"You will. Come inside, Prue. Lunch is ready."

Introductions were made and smiles were exchanged. As the three women sat enjoying their meal, the discussion turned mainly on Sara's home: on its heritage features, on the decor she had chosen for its interior, and on the places where she'd found the treasures with which to create her personal living space. It would have been easy to segue from there to the decorating decisions Prue had made for the castle. Selena formulated a question for the purpose, but something at the back of her mind kept saying, *Not now. Wait.* And so, she sat and spectated, marvelling at how well the other two were getting along, and how smoothly the conversation flowed between them. It was as though they'd known each other all their lives. This boded well, she thought.

After Sara had brought out a plate of store-bought biscotti for dessert and poured out three cups of sweet green tea, Prue asked, her brows drawing together, "Selena said earlier that you had been looking for me…?"

Sara swallowed her mouthful of tea and replied, "Well, not for you specifically, but—" A pause, then a decision. "Leave everything here. Come into the dining room and we'll show you."

Prue's eyes goggled when she saw the chart Sara had created. "Oh, my! That *was* a lot of work!" They widened even more when she spied the three sticky notes side by side near the centre of the diagram. "That's me!" she said wonderingly, thrusting an index finger at the one in the middle.

"Yes, and here is where I started the search," Sara told her. She found and indicated the note bearing Carol's name, then drew a line with her finger on the chart as she continued,

"Carol Gallagher was your great-great-grandmother. She had an older sister, Nora Friendly, and a younger sister, named Lillian Friendly, and they had a first cousin, named Gertrude Smith McFadyen."

"Hugh McFadyen was the first owner of the home that you and your husband purchased last year," Selena added. "He had it built in 1927, and Gertrude was his wife."

"And you're saying that I'm related to her," said Prue, shaking her head.

"We're not just saying it," Sara declared. "It's a verifiable fact, and I've printed out the documents to support it. You're related by blood to Carol Gallagher, and that means you're also related to Gertrude and Lillian. Both of those relationships are very important right now."

"And why is that?"

"Because a train derailment at the Groverton Station in 1933 caused the deaths of a number of people, including Hugh McFadyen and Lillian Friendly, who was with him at the time. However, there was no DNA testing back then, and because Lillian was wearing her cousin's clothing and carrying her purse, she was misidentified as Gertrude. Her remains are buried next to Hugh's in our local cemetery, with a grave marker that has Gertrude's name on it."

Prue's eyes narrowed suspiciously. "You expect me to believe that Gertrude would have allowed such a thing to happen?"

"Yes, because there's much more to this," Selena cut in. "According to a letter Lillian wrote before she was killed by the train, Gertrude died giving birth to a stillborn infant in the castle, and her husband chose to keep those deaths a secret. I believe that the sobbing woman you heard was her ghost, trapped inside that house. When you speak with our friend Curt at the museum this afternoon, ask him to show you the letter. It will explain a great deal."

"Ever since that letter came to light," said Sara, picking up the story again, "we've been trying to correct the earlier mistake, but none of the cemetery officials are willing to exhume a body—or what's left of it—without authorization from a living relative of the deceased. You're the first one we've approached, because of your interest in the house."

"And because it's not just Lillian's remains that are in the wrong place," Selena chimed in. "We have reason to believe that Hugh disposed of Gertrude and the baby somewhere on the grounds or perhaps even inside the building, but in order to search for them…"

"You need permission from the owners of the property," Prue supplied. "Now I understand. But what would you do if I said no?"

"To the exhumation? You're our first choice but you're not the only one," Sara said with a shrug. "There are eighteen other living relatives on the chart. I would begin cold-calling, beginning with the oldest and working my way down."

It made sense to do it that way. The oldest were more likely to have heard family tales about earlier generations. But Selena was pretty sure none of them had had to lie awake listening to Gertrude mourning her dead baby.

"And I assume that there would be an expense involved…?" Prue's eyebrows were rising. She still wasn't convinced that this was for real. Mentally, Selena crossed her fingers.

"Of course," Sara replied. "There always is with things like this. Curt can tell you more, since he's the one who's been dealing with the Historical Society, the municipal cemetery, and all the other bureaucratic doorstops. And if you ladies will excuse me, I have to report for work in less than twenty minutes."

A smile was playing at the corners of Prue's mouth. When Sara had left the room, she turned to Selena and asked in a low, amused voice, "Bureaucratic doorstops?"

"That's what Curt calls them. Small town officialdom can be very stubborn when it comes to following the rules," she replied. "You heard over lunch about Sara's adventures with the Historical Society. Well, Curt has been juggling a bunch of similar organizations, and he's been ready to tear his hair out at times. I suspect that if you offered to take on even one of them for him, he would feel indebted to you for life." *...or if Ben would agree to do it... Come on, Prue, connect the dots...*

As though capable of overhearing her thoughts, the other woman drew and expelled a reflective breath. Finally, she said, "I want to meet this friend of yours. Is it too early to go to the museum?"

Selena gave her a smile. "No, but Sara would probably appreciate it if we cleared the table and finished loading the dishwasher first."

At about 3:00 p.m., Selena pulled into the museum's parking lot and found a tour bus straddling all three handicapped spaces and blocking access to the slot beside them near the main entrance where she usually parked her car. The museum was busy today, she noted. Only a few empty spots remained, scattered at the far end of the lot. That probably explained why the bus was where it was, but it didn't make the situation any less annoying. Letting out a sigh, she drove on, selected the widest spot available, and backed into it.

"I thought you said people followed the rules in a small town," Prue remarked as they began the short trek to the front door.

"What I said was that town officials could be stiff-necked about enforcing them. I never once mentioned people. Or tourists. And these ones," she said, lowering and sharpening her voice in imitation of a bureaucratic doorstop and aiming a weaponized index finger at the offending bus, "had better all be senior citizens with mobility issues, including the driver."

Prue laughed.

Joking or not, Selena had been half right. The museum was apparently a stop on a seniors' tour, for the areas visible from the foyer contained large numbers of grey- and white-haired visitors, some using canes.

"Welcome back, Ms. Watt," said the girl behind the gift shop counter. "Are you looking for Mr. Wakefield?"

"Yes. This is Ms. Davidson. He's expecting us."

"Last time I checked, he was outside on the boarding platform. And here he comes now," she added, shifting her gaze to look behind them.

Selena turned in time to see Curt walk through the door.

"Ms. Watt," he greeted her. "And this would be Ms. Davidson?"

His welcoming smile had a forced quality to it, she noticed. Today had apparently not been going well for him. Or perhaps it had been, until now. Selena felt a pinch of guilt. She'd been presumptuous on Tuesday, promising Prue a meeting with him on such short notice. However, since they were already here…

"Prue, this is Curtis Wakefield, the gentleman we were telling you about."

"It's good to meet you," she said. "Is there somewhere private where the three of us can talk? Away from all these people?"

"Private," he muttered to himself. "Right."

Wrong. Selena could imagine what was going through his mind. For someone like Curt, who could perceive beyond the mortal plane, the world was a much more crowded place than anyone else could envision. She held her breath, waiting for the rest of his response.

"We could go back outside to the platform, I guess," he

finally said.

"And I understand that my great-great-grandaunt left a letter behind. I'm told I need to read it."

He let out a sigh of resignation. Selena watched it deflate him a little.

"In that case, we'll need to use my office. Follow me, please," he instructed them.

Selena noticed the chill in the air the moment he opened the door, but said nothing. There had evidently been an angry ghost in here not long ago. Or perhaps it hadn't left. That might explain why Curt had been outside when they arrived.

Gesturing them towards the two guest chairs in front of his desk, Curt unlocked one of the drawers and pulled out a blue, letter-sized file folder. Then he produced and put on a pair of latex gloves. "This letter is nearly a hundred years old," he explained as he carefully removed the pages from the folder and arranged them one by one on the desktop in front of Prue. "It was recently found inside a hidden pocket of a handbag that was salvaged back in 1933 from the wreckage of a train derailment and placed in storage along with other unclaimed personal effects. The only reason the paper isn't too brittle to handle right now is that the museum's storage vault was originally an environmentally controlled space. When the station was restored to its pre-disaster condition, the vault was as well."

"So this is authentic?" said Prue.

"Yes, as best I can determine."

"And that's why you've lowered the temperature in your office? To reproduce the environment inside the vault?"

He shot a warning look into the air between and behind them before replying. "No. We seem to be having a slight problem with our air conditioning system. But it will be fixed soon," he told her, crisply enunciating each syllable.

Selena felt a shiver that owed nothing to the briskness of

the air around her. Lillian was present, she was certain, and the ghost was not happy.

Prue leaned forward and proceeded to read the letter in its entirety. When done, she sagged backward in her chair with a stricken expression on her face.

"Oh, my… those poor women," she said faintly, then fell silent.

Curt set about replacing the pages inside the folder and the folder inside the drawer. "J. D. DeLucci, the president of the municipal cemetery, is willing to accept this letter as proof that the exhumation is justified, but Gertrude's body was almost certainly not embalmed, and Lillian's has been in the ground for more than ninety years. As a result, switching the remains is not going to be a simple matter.

"I won't lie to you, Ms. Davidson. DeLucci is standing on a stack of rules and procedures that we have to follow, and securing authorization from a living relative is only the first step. By the time this is done, not only the cemetery and its employees but also the Health Department and possibly the police will have become involved. As well, there could very likely be scientific lab work required. And at each additional stage of the process, costs will be incurred. This is not going to be an inexpensive exercise, so you may want to seek legal counsel before making any decision in the matter."

There was dawning respect in Prue's eyes as her gaze met Curt's, and Selena realized with a thrill of relief that the other woman must finally be convinced of their honesty.

"Thank you, Mr. Wakefield. That's good advice."

"You're welcome. Now, I understand you wanted to discuss something in particular with me?" said Curt.

"Selena says you're some kind of expert, and… I need to know that what I think happened to me inside that house months ago actually happened. Because I had a disturbing dream earlier this week about being back there. The rooms were strangely furnished, the woman's voice I'd heard before was moaning in pain, and I was searching desperately for a piece of jewellery that I was certain would make her stop."

"Do you remember what the piece was?"

"Yes, and that's what I found so unsettling. I already owned it. When I woke up, I checked to make sure it was still in my jewellery box, and it was. I've brought it with me." Prue reached into her purse and pulled out a small, tissue-wrapped bundle. "This is a family heirloom, passed down through five generations," she explained as she opened the wrapping, exposing a beautiful cameo brooch.

It was clearly very old. Delicate gold threads wove an intricate pattern around a polished obsidian oval with an ivory inset in the shape of a woman's profile. Holding it carefully in the palm of her outstretched hand, Prue told them, "Because of its age, I've always been afraid to wear it, and—Ow!"

Her hand jerked suddenly as though stung or struck. Frozen in place, Selena watched as the brooch dropped onto the desktop. In that same moment, Curt shouted, "No!" and leaped to his feet, glaring into the centre of the room. Then he scooped up the brooch, rewrapped it, and returned it to its owner.

"Grab your purses. We have to go outside," he said urgently. "Now!"

The air temperature was already plummeting. Wordlessly, the two women made for the door, with Curt right behind them.

He chivvied them through the exhibit hall, out the main entrance of the museum, and across the parking lot, all the way to Selena's car.

"What happened in there?" Prue demanded, flexing the fingers of her wounded hand while still clutching the brooch in her good one. Her voice teetered on the edge of hysteria.

Curt uttered a heavy sigh. "I lied to you earlier. The problem isn't with the air conditioning. There's a ghost in the museum. When she's angry, it gets cold. And even though she can't affect material objects, I believe she tried to snatch the brooch from you just now."

"It's Lillian, isn't it?" said Selena.

He nodded. "We're safe out here. She can't travel far from the letter."

"Wait a minute," Prue said. "Are you saying that my great-great-grandaunt is haunting that letter you showed me?"

"I prefer the phrase 'tethered to'," he replied, "but yes, that is exactly what I'm saying. I believe that ghosts tend to be attached to things and places that were emotionally significant to them in life, or that represent some business that they deeply regret leaving unfinished when they died. Lillian's letter was never delivered to the police, but bringing it to the PPS did not release her. So we're assuming, from the contents of the letter, that the misidentification and wrongful burial are what needs to be corrected. That's why it's so important that we locate Gertrude's remains, and that both cousins be laid to rest, each in her own, correctly-marked grave."

Prue was working hard to wrap her brain around all this. Her features contracted into an expression that reminded Selena of a child concentrating on a difficult math problem. "And you think Gertrude's ghost is haunting the house for the same reason? Because she needs to be found and properly buried?"

"That's our working theory, yes," he replied.

"But it still doesn't explain why I could hear her voice and my husband couldn't," she pointed out.

Curt cleared his throat, buying himself a moment to think, most likely. "I'm not sure that what you heard was actually her voice," he said. "Don't get me wrong—I'm not saying you imagined it. In fact, I'm sure you didn't. You know that our five senses don't reside in our physical organs, right? That it's the brain that processes sensory stimuli and translates them into images and sounds and so on?"

"Of course."

"Well, what I suspect is that the house is filled with Gertrude's intense sadness, and that the only way your brain could handle it was by translating the pure emotion into a sensory stimulus and processing it as a woman's voice. Selena experienced the same thing, but as a tactile sensation. As for why it happened to you and Selena but not your husband, I do not know. Some things simply defy explanation. However, the history of the castle is documented, and all the evidence that I've read clearly indicates that over the past ninety years, people must have been hearing or seeing or feeling some profoundly disturbing things inside that building. So, I can tell you with confidence that you are not losing your mind, and anyone who thinks that you are is welcome to come and experience Lillian at first hand."

Now Prue was frowning. "Why do you suppose she tried to steal the brooch?"

"I don't know that either. But I assure you, I will do my best to get you an explanation. When are you planning to head back down to the city?"

"Sometime after rush hour. I won't be spending the night here."

"You're welcome to join us for dinner, Curt," Selena chimed in.

"All right," he replied after a pause. "The museum closes at five today. Text me the where and when and I'll meet you there."

And, shifting his features to a stern expression, he wheeled and strode across the parking lot to the front door of the building.

Eighteen

Curt sucked in a steadying lungful of air, drew himself up to his full height, and opened the door to his office. It was bloody cold in there—he could see his breath. No matter. Dragging Barbara into her con this morning had been bad enough, but Lillian had gone too far this time, and he was a furnace on legs, ready to chew iron and spit out nails.

"Show yourself, Lillian!" he roared into the room.

A moment later she emerged from the far wall and came to stand in front of his desk with her arms crossed tightly over her chest and defiance written all over her face.

"What the hell was *that* all about?" he demanded.

"*That thieving bitch stole my brooch,*" she declared, elevating her chin even more.

"Are you talking about Prue Davidson? Because she wasn't even alive when you were killed."

She let out an exasperated syllable. "*Not her, you —! I'm talking about Carol, my erstwhile backstabbing sister! She knew how much I loved Mama's cameo brooch. I played dress-up with it when I was a child. Mama promised it would be mine when she passed away, and yet, after she was gone, it mysteriously disappeared from her jewellery case. I knew deep down that Carol had taken it—it was already a family heirloom by then and wouldn't simply have been misplaced—but she denied it and Pop supported her, so there was nothing I could do. Not until the piece turned back up. And now it has. And it's mine, dammit!"* she shrilled.

On the face of it, she made a good case. After all, artwork stolen by the Nazis before the Second World War was still being recovered and returned to the descendants of its rightful owners, more than eighty years later. However, if she was correct, this brooch hadn't been stolen by strangers. It had never even left the family. And there was also, of course, the pesky fact that Lillian had died before she could produce any heirs, meaning that one of Carol's children would have ended up with it anyway... which raised an interesting question at the back of Curt's mind: did Carol already know that? Was that why the brooch had been kept out of Lillian's hands?

"All right, let's say I agree with you. The heirloom is rightfully yours. To do what with, Lillian? Think about this for a minute. Even if Prue is willing to surrender it to you, it's not as if you can wear it, or bestow it on anyone, or even touch it. Not anymore. You're a ghost."

A spark leaped to life behind her eyes. *"Yes, and I can haunt it, Mr. Wakefield,"* she informed him with a triumphant toss of her head.

As visions of paper being devoured by flames danced inside his mind, he wondered: was that even possible? According to Nena, a powerful enough spirit could move at will between the planes of existence. Once Lillian had been freed from the letter, could she simply reattach herself to the brooch and begin meddling in Prue Davidson's life the way she'd done to his?

Just thinking about that was enough to drain all the

strength out of his legs, dropping him onto the chair behind his desk.

"Where is Barbara?" he asked wearily.

"I left her with the two old gals on the bench."

"Well, then, since we're alone here, do you mind answering a question that's been rattling around in my head?"

"If I can," she replied guardedly.

"When I suggested you might be a flapper earlier, you said, 'among other things'. Since then, it's occurred to me… Your lifestyle that your family disapproved of so harshly… did it involve lesbianism?"

Everything about her stiffened. He braced himself for another cold snap, but it never came. Instead, she said softly, *"Would it matter to you if it did?"*

He relaxed again and replied honestly, "No, not a bit. But it would explain a great deal. Especially if Gertrude tended that way as well."

"She hadn't decided yet. She was still experimenting. Until her father boxed her up and shipped her north with her rapist, Hugh McFadyen," she concluded bitterly.

"And what about Nora? You said she understood you in a way that went beyond being an older sister."

"Nora liked men just fine, but she wanted a military career. Marriage and children would have ended that for her." A pause. Then, in a much smaller voice, she asked, *"What are you going to tell people about me?"*

That she even cared what others might think of her caught him by surprise. Nonetheless, he managed to school his features and keep his voice even. "What would you *like* me to tell them, Lillian?"

"The truth. That I never intentionally hurt anyone. That I would have given my life for Trudy's if I could. That if I had survived the train wreck, I would have done the right thing."

"And if it turns out that there's a way for you to be

attached to the brooch…?"

"Then I'll finally be back in the family, even if only as an observer."

Curt met up with Prue and Selena at Mom's Kozy Kitchen, a moderately-priced family restaurant on one of the larger side streets at the west end of town. The women had arrived before him and taken a booth for four against the far wall. They glanced up and smiled as he approached, and Selena scooted over to make room for him to sit down.

"We haven't ordered yet," she said, passing him a menu, "but just so you know, we've already told the server it will be separate checks."

"Did you find out why Lillian was so angry, and why she tried to take the brooch, Mr. Wakefield?" Prue asked.

Fortunately, their server—Danny, according to his name badge—chose that moment to materialize at Curt's elbow, thus saving him from having to reply immediately. He was going to be winging it either way, since the drive from the museum to the restaurant hadn't given him much time to figure out the best response to that question.

"A Greek salad and a glass of water," he said when the turn came around to him.

After Danny had collected their menus and spun away, Curt felt the weight of two inquiring stares, one from beside him and the other from across the table.

He paused to choose his words. "Apparently, the brooch had been promised to Lillian by her mother—Ms. Davidson's three-times-great grandmother—but it was not among her effects after she passed away. I'm told there were accusations of theft… and a rift between the sisters that was never mended while Lillian was alive."

"That's terrible!" Prue exclaimed. "So, when she saw the brooch in my hand, she tried to claim it." She inhaled sharply and leaned across the table towards him. "Would she know that I'm Carol's descendant?" she whispered anxiously. "Would she hate me for that?"

"You did call it a family heirloom, so I'd guess the answer to your first question is yes. As for the second one, I suspect that's up to you."

"Are you referring to my decision regarding the graves? Because I've already texted my husband about the two of us coming up here for a few days next week to look into that situation."

"Corben Davidson is a lawyer," Selena informed him. "We're probably going to need one before this matter is settled, and who better to represent the interests of the woman who died in that house than its current co-owner?"

Curt's world took a sudden leftward tilt. Hire a lawyer? The museum's budget had no money for something like that, even if the Historical Society were willing to approve it. Clearly, things were getting out of hand.

Feeling both bone weary and outnumbered, he decided there was no percentage in arguing. Not yet. Maybe this Davidson fellow would take the case pro bono, if it meant getting Gertrude out of his house and his wife back into it. One could hope.

Eventually their food arrived, interrupting a discussion between the two women about interior decorating that Curt had been listening to with half an ear. Pasta for Selena, stir-fry on rice for Prue. Not exactly gourmet fare, it was nonetheless attractively presented and quite tasty. The three of them ate in silence for a while. Then Prue put her fork down and said, "Tell Lillian that she's right. The brooch belongs to her, and the next time we're in the same room, I intend to hand it over to her, to dispose of as she sees fit."

Curt nearly choked on his mouthful of salad. When he could once more trust his voice, he asked her, "Are you sure about this? It's a family heirloom, most likely valuable. What if she decides it should go to the next person to step through the museum's front door?"

Prue cocked her head curiously. "You honestly believe she would be that spiteful? Considering how much it obviously means to her?"

"I was thinking more about how much it must mean to *you.*"

A knowing smile crept across her face, thoroughly confusing him. "Mr. Wakefield, as soon as I inherited the brooch, I had it appraised. It's a piece of costume jewellery, worth maybe fifty of today's dollars. Whatever value it seems to have had for the women in my family was sentimental. So, if Lillian wants it badly enough to claim it from beyond the grave, who am I to keep it from her?"

When the meal was over, Prue got up from the table, said her goodbyes, and departed for home, leaving Curt and Selena sitting across from each other in the booth.

Danny came over to offer them coffee or tea.

"Green tea for me, please," Selena replied.

Sure, why not? "Make that two," Curt told him.

"A fake? Well, *that* was unexpected," she remarked after the server had pivoted away again. "Sara and I were certain the D'Amicos were wealthy when they arrived in North America."

Curt shrugged. "We don't know anything for sure about them, Selena, or about the brooch. The original may have had a lot of monetary value a century ago, but it could have been sold and replaced by paste at any point since then."

"You're right," she said with a sigh. "Since I've become drawn into Gertrude and Lillian's story, everything about it feels so immediate! I have to keep reminding myself how much time has actually passed. It must be even worse for you, having to deal with Lillian every day. For her, the train wreck is practically a current event." She paused for a couple of beats, then added, "Speaking of current events, have you learned anything new about Brenda's case?"

"Not a thing," he said disgustedly. "I invited Tricia Vickery to my office for a meeting, specifically so that Lillian could take Rachel aside and trick some information out of her about Brenda, but Lillian dragged Barbara into it, turning the whole thing into a therapy session for your cousin. I'm not saying that's a bad thing, not for Barbara, at least. But now I think I may actually be buying a house."

Selena's cheeks dimpled. Involuntarily, he returned her smile.

"Well," he continued as the server placed two mugs, two teabags, and two pots of hot water on the table between them, "I've been renting for the past three years, thinking that Groverton would be just a temporary pause in my career—a stepping stone, if you will, on my way back to a major urban museum somewhere. Now I'm thinking differently."

"Because of Sara? I know you two like each other."

Feeling a sudden heat in his cheeks, he turned his full attention to unwrapping his tea bag and dropping it into one of the pots. "For a number of reasons," he told her stiffly. "Anyway, a couple of the homes Tricia showed me on her computer looked promising. I'm going to view them tomorrow."

And he was going to do something else as well. It was his last resort, the only trick left in his bag, and it scared the dickens out of him. Just thinking about it gave him a chill. But dealing with Lillian if he couldn't tell her he'd at least *tried* to find Brenda's ghost at the morgue—that was going to be much, much worse.

Nineteen

The hour and a half spent waiting for Sara to return home from the library that evening was, by far, the most difficult part of Selena's Thursday. She had such important news to impart! Fortunately, Larry was there, minding the boys. His ear was available to be bent, once Eric and Donnie were fed and cleaned up and ready to be tucked in by their mother as soon as she arrived.

Of necessity, Sara ran a tight ship. So, it was a good thing Larry was a firefighter, accustomed to a strict routine interrupted by periods of pure adrenalin rush. As Selena walked through the front door at half past six, she noticed with some admiration that the children were out of sight and the kitchen was spotless.

"Where are the kids?" she asked, settling onto one of the wooden chairs.

"Upstairs, poring through the old comic books I brought over as a distraction. I knew those superheroes would come in handy someday."

She gasped and reared back dramatically, feigning shock. "Comic books? Considering what we've been doing lately, shouldn't Eric, at least, be into murder mysteries by now?"

Larry sat down facing her across the table and replied earnestly, "Listen, I know you're joking, but you have to realize that I'm in this for the long haul. It's important that Sara's boys be exposed to as broad a variety of people and experiences as possible. That's why I signed them up for four weeks of day camp this summer, and I've been taking them to places like hockey games, and theme parks, and art galleries. It's what Doug would be doing if he were still here."

He gave her a look that plainly advised her it was time to change the subject.

So, "Tell me about your day," she prompted him.

Larry grimaced. "Trust me, it was nothing you want to hear about. I spent my whole shift catching up on paperwork. Then I picked up Eric and Donnie from Mrs. Grayson's. She looked a little frazzled, but I didn't think anything of it until I got the boys home and they started bouncing off the walls. Summer vacation begins on Monday. Apparently, there's going to be an all-day party at school tomorrow and they're warming up for a monumental sugar high."

"Hence the comic books?"

"Hey, whatever will tame the savage beast. And now it's your turn," he informed her. "How did it go with Prue Davidson this morning?"

She told him about both their meetings, finishing up with, "Curt's looking at houses tomorrow. After three years, he's finally decided to make Groverton his home."

As Larry leaned back thoughtfully in his chair, Selena held her breath. She was expecting some disparaging remark about Curt just wanting to be around Sara; it came as a surprise, therefore, to hear Larry say, "So, you believe this ghost thing is for real, then."

"And you don't. You are a very strange man, Larry Holmes," she declared. "You're willing to accept that a house can have and communicate feelings, but resist the idea that a human consciousness can exist outside of a physical body."

"In the absence of first-hand experience, yes, I'm a skeptic. But Curt's explanation about the brain translating a residual emotion inside a building into something that can be processed...? After the weekend we spent at Rafferty House and everything that I've heard about the McFadyen place, it's not so far-fetched anymore. And now, if you'll excuse me, I have a couple of boys to hose down and put into their jammies."

As Larry got to his feet, Selena bit back her next comment. Curt had tailored his logic in order to turn doubters into believers without giving away the fact that he could see and hear disembodied spirits. That was why it sounded so reasonable to people like Prue Davidson and Larry Holmes. The problem was, it could not explain those ghosts who were self-aware and possessed agency, like Lillian Friendly.

Once again, the thought occurred to her: what if correcting the misidentification and laying Gertrude's remains to rest turned out not to be enough to send Lillian away? What if she'd already decided to stick around the museum? Or around Curt? Or—now that she'd seen the brooch and knew that Prue was Carol's descendant—what if Lillian were planning to attach herself to one of *them*?

These dark ruminations were cut short by Larry dropping with a groan back onto his chair, followed a moment later by the sound of the front door firmly closing and Sara's singsong, "I'm ho-ome!"

"Are you spending the night here?" he asked Selena.

"Planning to, yes."

"Good. Then *you* can put the kettle on and bring out the mugs and stuff. I'm tired."

"So, let me get this straight," Sara said between sips of her lemon tea once the boys had been put to bed. "The 'family heirloom' that caused a permanent rift between Lillian and her sister may have been a trinket purchased at the dime store, but Lillian's ghost is still determined to claim it? And do what? Wear it? She does realize that's impossible, right?"

"I don't think she cares about that," Selena opined. "I think for her it's a matter of principle. The original brooch was supposed to be her inheritance. Her mother wanted her to have it. Lillian's lifestyle and what the rest of the family thought of it was a separate issue entirely and shouldn't have had any bearing on the situation."

"There must be a lot more to the story than what we've learned so far," Larry mused aloud. "Or maybe Curt is holding out on us. We know he's been keeping his own secrets. Why not Lillian's as well?"

"Only until now," Sara cut in deliberately, aiming dagger looks at her brother across the table. "He's been keeping secrets because until now he hasn't felt safe enough to reveal any of them. Prue Davidson may suspect, but we three are the only ones who know for certain what he can do. We should feel honoured that he believed he could entrust us with what is probably the biggest secret of his life. Instead, you resent him for not sharing more? How could you, Larry?"

He let out a weary breath. "Well, *that* didn't come out the way I intended. Just for the record, I don't resent Curt. Okay? In fact, I can't help feeling sorry for the guy. He's a bundle of nerves, and every time I see him, I wonder if this is going to be the day that he finally breaks down. Look, all I meant to say before was that he's known Lillian long enough that maybe *she* now feels comfortable confiding secrets to *him*. And if so, that he's being a good friend and keeping them."

. . and assuming that everything she told him was the truth, of course, which was by no means a safe bet. Fortunately, Selena chose not to express that thought aloud.

"And with that, ladies, I'm going to take my leave," said Larry. He stifled a yawn and rose from his chair. "Evel Knievel and his brother have totally worn me out."

"Thank you for looking after them," Sara told him. "And for cleaning them up. I can only imagine the mess they must have carried home with them."

He smiled. "With those two, I figure it comes with the territory. But you're welcome. See you tomorrow."

As he let himself out the door, Sara put the kettle back on to freshen their tea.

"He's only trying to protect you, you know," Selena told her.

"I know," she said with a sigh. "He feels he needs to make up for the time we lost after Mom and Dad passed. And then Doug died… and Tamara. I think that was when Larry finally understood how much we both needed to lean on each other. I just wish he'd cut Curt a little more slack, though. It's hard enough being stressed out by things no one else can see, much worse when talking to someone about it gets you branded as delusional."

The whistling of the kettle drew her back to the stove.

"But enough about that," she continued over her shoulder as she topped up the teapot. "Tell me your honest impressions of Prue Davidson."

Selena waited to reply until Sara was back in her chair and the pot was on the table. "She seems genuine to me. She believed in Lillian right away, which came as no surprise. And I think she's miserable being separated and wants to save her marriage. But I'm curious now. Did you get a different vibe from her than I did at lunch today?"

"No, I liked her. I was just wondering…" She paused, visibly choosing her words. "How badly do you want to buy that property? Because assuming we're able to 'exorcise the castle', as it were, and also assuming that it's enough to mend

Prue's marriage, what do you think the chances are that the house will stay on the market?"

"It's hard to say. Both assumptions would have to be true, but in any case, I expect her husband will be the one making that decision."

"Her husband, the lawyer?" Pursing her lips, Sara poured more tea into their mugs. "Well, if you had your heart set on owning that place, I think you'd better brace yourself for some major disappointment. If the Davidsons get back together, it's a safe bet that he's not going to simply walk away from his investment. Either they'll move into the house as he'd originally planned, or he'll recoup what he sank into it by setting a more realistic asking price, putting it beyond your means. Either way it won't be yours. If I were you, I'd be preparing a plan B."

"So, you're saying that the only way to ensure that I can afford to buy the castle—"

"—is if it remains haunted, and/or the Davidsons remain separated."

On her way upstairs to bed, Selena replayed the situation in her mind. It wasn't just the desolate spirit in the house that affected the marital status of Prue and her husband. What about the matter of the exhumations and reinterments that they would be coming to Groverton—together—to look into in a few days? What if settling this problem brought them back together? Or—worse—what if hearing how much it was going to cost ignited an argument that deepened the chasm between them and created one between the Davidsons and Groverton? What if they decided that Lillian's problem wasn't theirs to solve, resetting everything back to square one?

All this what-iffing was giving her a headache. However, Sara's remark about plan B had also sparked an idea. Tomorrow was Friday. Hearth and Home Realty ought to be open. Tricia Vickery had told her before all this madness began that there were other homes to be seen.

It only made sense to give them a look.

Selena had called right after breakfast to make an appointment. At 9:30 sharp, she walked through the realtor's doorway and found Tricia—perfectly made up and put together, as usual—conferring with the Fair Isle-sweatered lady behind the reception desk.

They looked up and welcomed her with identical practised smiles.

"Good morning, Ms. Watt," said Vickery. "If you're here about the castle—"

"I'm having second thoughts about that."

She nodded sadly. "To be honest, with everything that has been happening lately, I'm not surprised. Is it still your intention to move your business to Groverton?"

"Yes. You mentioned earlier that there were other properties available...?"

"Of course. Why don't we continue this in my office?"

Glancing meaningfully at the receptionist, Tricia led the way into her sanctum. She pulled a guest chair over for Selena, then took the one behind the desk, where her laptop sat open and waiting. "There were four that I wanted to show you last time," she said, her fingers busy on the keyboard. "Let's see what their status is. Your requirements haven't changed, I trust?"

"Not since I discussed them with Brenda, no. I need a duplex with living quarters on the second floor and room for offices and storage space on the first. An older building is acceptable, as long as it doesn't need extensive repair or renovations, and the total amount payable has to be within my price range. Oh, and I want it to be no more than two blocks away from a main street."

"Well, that last condition just knocked two of them out of the running. The other two are still available, and both are currently vacant. When would you like to view them?"

"Anytime today would be fine."

"Excellent!" She pulled the top page off a memo pad, scribbled something onto the square of paper, then held it out to Selena. "How about this morning? I have a couple of things to do in preparation, but we can meet at this address at 10:30. Does that work for you?"

"It does," she replied, slipping the page into a front pocket of her denim pants. "By the way, you said something earlier that I've been puzzling over."

"Oh?"

"You said that the castle had been nothing but trouble ever since you added it to your listings. May I ask why?"

Tricia leaned back in her chair. "It's not the property that's the problem. It's the Historical Society. The building is a year or two away from the hundredth anniversary of its construction. That's when it's officially designated as a heritage home, and the rules for preserving its appearance kick in. For about a decade before that, the Society monitors. During that time, they issue warnings and reminders to the owners, and anytime the property goes on the market, prospective buyers are required to be made aware that certain restrictions will apply as of such-and-such a date."

"I know. Brenda mentioned it while giving me the virtual tour of the house."

"Good. And before I presented his offer to purchase, two years ago, I made sure the current owner was informed of the rules as well. A few weeks after taking possession, he applied for permits to renovate the interior of the building. When the Society saw his plans and drawings and realized how extensive the changes would be... well, they were incensed. And I have to say, in all the years that I've been involved in real estate in this town, I had never before seen them move this fast.

"First, they found a magistrate who would issue an injunction, blocking the permits from being approved. Then they filed a lawsuit against the owner personally. I guess they figured that if they could tie him and the project up in enough legal red tape, it would take him until the castle's hundredth anniversary to unravel it—at which point it would become a heritage home, the rules would automatically apply, and the problem would no longer exist."

"I gather they figured wrong. Didn't they realize the owner was a lawyer?"

"I'm sure they did. They just underestimated what *kind* of lawyer he was, and how bulldog-determined he was to renovate his property.

"After a couple of months, he counter-sued them. Whatever he'd spent the interim doing, I would rather not know. All I *do* know is that it worked. It took more than half a year for the proceedings to begin, and less than a day for the Society to capitulate. They withdrew their lawsuit and had the injunction lifted. The homeowner was finally able to go ahead with his remodelling plans."

Something told Selena that wasn't the end of it. She waited patiently for Tricia to speak again.

The realtor heaved a heartfelt sigh. "When they realized they couldn't touch Mr. Davidson without getting stung, the Society found another target for its wrath. They haven't explicitly forbidden me to handle the properties on their monitoring list—it would be an overreach if they did—but they've made it clear that they're keeping an eye on me and, by extension, on the people I sell those homes to. They won't hesitate to drag me into court if there's even a *rumour* of a repetition of what happened with the castle."

"That's why you were hesitant about showing me the

property, isn't it? Once bitten, twice shy." After a pause, she added, "Of course, you could always hire Mr. Davidson to represent you."

Tricia's peal of laughter held a bitter note. "That would show them, wouldn't it? And then I would be done here. I would have to pack up and start my business over in a different place. Some things about small towns never change, Ms. Watt, regardless of how physically large they may grow."

Twenty

A phone inquiry to the Public Affairs Office of Provincial Police Services the following morning led Curt to the basement of Groverton General Hospital. According to the clerk who'd taken his call, this was where a dead body found in the local area would have been brought to be autopsied and then stored pending final disposition.

The first thing Curt noticed as he stepped out of the elevator was a chill in the air. A certain degree of coolness was to be expected in a basement, but this was something more. He wasn't imagining it. The young woman in baby blue scrubs who emerged from the door in front of him was rubbing her hands together to warm them up.

"Can I help you?" she asked with a polite smile.

"I'm here to view a corpse. Brenda Ryan."

"Are you a relative?"

He hesitated. This woman might not be a cop, but she was in a sort of uniform. And she had to know that Brenda's death was being investigated by the PPS. If he said yes, they would surely be notified of his presence. If he said no, he might be denied access and politely escorted back to the main floor.

So, he obfuscated. "We're still trying to find one," he said.

Her eyes widened. "Oh, right! I got a call from upstairs last week about a police consultant who might need a look at her. That's you?"

"Guilty as charged," he returned, forcing his lips to curve in a smile as his thoughts careered around inside his head. Last week? Had Brassard engaged someone else to assist with the investigation? If so, what would happen when *that* person showed up at the morgue?

"It's outside of viewing hours, but you're with the police, so I guess it will be okay. Follow me, please."

With each step, Curt's anxiety deepened. Not only was he an imposter, potentially setting himself up to be charged with interference in an ongoing criminal case, but as he had feared—there were ghosts down here. He couldn't see them yet. He didn't have to. Their sonorous moans and whispers already filled his mind.

He hoped these spirits would be like most of the ones at the museum, barely seen shades imprisoned in the moment of their death and unaware of the living. Except for Brenda's, of course. She had to be somewhere on this level—it took a very angry ghost to refrigerate such a large area. With luck, she would still be rational enough after witnessing her own autopsy to give him the information he needed.

The basement hallway was all business, no visitors—a stark white tunnel punctuated by plain slab doors bearing doctors' names and/or room numbers engraved on raised plaques. The message they sent was clear: Hospital Staff Only. And in case that wasn't enough to deter curious members of the public, the air around the elevator fairly reeked of antiseptic cleanser. It made him wish he were wearing a mask.

"In here," said the attendant, holding open one of the

numbered doors and gesturing to him to enter. "Normally I would stay with you while another AP prepared the deceased for viewing, but there's only me right now, so if you don't mind being alone…?"

Actually, he didn't mind a bit. If Brenda's ghost was able to join him in here, it would be preferable if their conversation remained private.

The viewing room, it turned out, was an observation booth separated from the autopsy room proper by a wide glass panel that began at waist height and stretched to the ceiling. An opaque white curtain hung on the other side of the window. After a couple of minutes, the curtain parted to reveal a sheet-covered figure lying on a metal table and the morgue attendant standing on the other side of it.

Curt scanned the rest of the autopsy room, as much of it as he could see past the curtain, and spotted something else as well: a greyscale figure making itself as small as possible beside a desk against the far wall. It was a young girl, no more than twelve years old. His heart writhed as he realized that one of the moaning voices inside his head had to be hers.

"Are you ready, Mr. Wakefield?" the attendant called through the glass.

Curt nearly fell over. She knew his name! But how? Then he spied the telephone on the desk. Of course. She would have called someone for verification before actually showing him the body. Soon Brassard would know that he was here. There was no time to waste.

"I'm ready," he called back.

She lifted and folded over one end of the sheet, revealing the head and shoulders of a petite blonde-haired woman who might have been peacefully sleeping on that table if not for the unmistakable marks of a savage beating on her face. Morgue assistants could wash away the blood, but bruises and gouges were impossible to hide. Likewise a ghost, if it were tethered to such a corpse. The emotions associated with a prolonged, violent death tended to create stronger connections. Brenda's spirit should have been hovering nearby. However, Curt saw no sign of it anywhere in the autopsy room.

"Oh, Brenda, where are you?" he murmured to himself.

"Not very pretty, *hein*?" Brassard's voice behind him was not unexpected, but it startled him nonetheless.

He spun to face her. "Are you here to arrest me?"

"No. Why? Do you wish to be arrested?"

Her lips twitched in the briefest of smiles, and all at once he understood.

"You're the one who told them to expect me," he said.

"I knew you would eventually come here, unable to resist your investigative impulses, and I did not want any additional paperwork. It was selfish of me, I know, but I have been learning about your history with my predecessor, and so, in the interests of simplicity, I have made you a consultant on this case. Now I need you to behave like one and share with me what you have learned about it."

"It's not much," he confessed. "I thought Brenda's ghost might be attached to her corpse, but I was wrong."

"Ah! And what made you so certain that there was anything more of her than her corpse to be found?"

Mentally crossing his fingers, Curt replied, "Because it's been my experience that the spirits of murder victims don't simply dissipate into the air like smoke. They hang around, tethered to something that was present when they died. Something that held deep emotional significance for them in life, like Barbara Cournoyer's pendant. So now I'm wondering whether your Forensics team could have scooped that something up in the course of processing the house. I don't suppose you'd be willing to authorize me to visit your evidence storage…?"

"No. That would be a step too far. However, if I were to sign out an evidence box and have it brought to my office while you were there, would that be satisfactory?"

"Absolutely. And thank you."

She nodded acknowledgement, then added, "By the way, you may tell Ms. Watt that we are making progress in her cousin's murder. Based on the information given in her statement, we were able to locate the remains of a body, which we have positively identified as Fernando Galliardo, the driver of the pickup truck. Our forensic analysis is still ongoing, but it appears promising."

"And what about the killer? Have you had any luck in locating him?"

"He was apprehended while attempting to escape into the United States. That is all I can reveal to either of you for now, since we do not make public every detail of an active investigation, but I will try to keep you apprised of further developments. And I presume that you will in turn inform me of any new discoveries you make relating to the Brenda Ryan case," she added, handing him her business card. "Use the number on the back."

"Of course."

With his thoughts and his stomach somersaulting in tandem, it was all Curt could do just to walk a straight line to his car in the hospital's parking lot. He'd held something back from Brassard just now: the disturbing possibility that Brenda's killer might have unknowingly taken her ghost with him after leaving her body on the castle's front veranda. That she might have kept fighting him, even after death. A ghost's touch was chilling. Barbara had broken the screen of Selena's computer by giving it an angry shove with the heel of her hand. What would have happened if Brenda's spirit had punched its fist into her murderer's head, or his chest?

What if he were lying on a slab in some other pathologist's

morgue right now, confusing the hell out of everyone by having apparently died of a frozen brain?

No. There were limits to what even a believer ought to be thinking about.

As Curt stepped through the door of the museum, Amy beckoned him over to her counter. "The real estate agent called. She's set up those evening showings you asked for," she said, and handed him a sheet of paper with times and addresses written on it.

Three houses. The first appointment was for 6:30 p.m. As he recalled, these walk-throughs didn't take long. He could have a decent meal after locking up the museum and still make it to Sara's place for tea and dessert. Best of all, though, Tricia would be wearing her charm bracelet, which meant Rachel would be present, and if he could get her to talk to him about Brenda…

…the news he would be able to report would blow them all away.

"Okay, then," he said, nodding as usual to Orville before heading to his office.

What the hell…?

The knob on his door was so cold that there was a layer of frost on it, making him afraid to touch the metal with his bare hand in case his skin stuck to it. So, he improvised a glove using the hem of his shirt before attempting to enter the room. As he expected, it was like stepping into a walk-in freezer.

A haunted freezer. Barbara's ghost was whipping furiously back and forth in front of his desk, making a strange growling noise. When she saw him, she pulled up and declared, *"You have to get it back! We have to help her!"*

"Help who?"

"Lillian, of course! She's been kidnapped!"

"She's been—? How is that even possible?" he demanded.

"A man came in here earlier. He searched your desk, found the blue file folder, and walked away with it. When he brought it back, Lillian wasn't with it. We have to find her, Mr. Wakefield! And you have to rescue her!"

"All right, we will!" he exclaimed, then added in a calmer voice, "But I need you to simmer down, Barbara, and think. You say he 'found' the file folder, but I keep that drawer locked. Are you telling me you watched him break into it?"

As he spoke, Curt went to examine the keyhole on the drawer in question. It was still dangerously cold to the touch, but showed no outward sign of having been forced or jimmied. Then he saw the sticky note clinging to the corner of his computer screen:

PER HIST SOC PROTOCOLS ORIGINAL DOCUMENT IS UPSTAIRS

"He had a key. He brought it with him."

Of course he did. As comprehension dawned, Curt wanted to kick himself. The "kidnapper" had been a member of the Historical Society, with lawful access to every part of the museum (including the manager's desk drawer, it seemed) using the Society's keys. This was not a break-in, nor a theft. It was, simply put, the result of his own thoughtlessness.

The company that had installed the museum's security net was contracted to perform regularly scheduled diagnostics. After each check-up, an e-notification was sent out, the system was returned to its default settings, and Curt had to disable the monitoring camera in the manager's office so that he would have privacy somewhere in the building besides the washroom. The last time there had been a diagnostic sweep, with all that had been going on in his life, he'd apparently forgotten to do it.

So, if his concealment of a fragile old document in the middle drawer of his desk had become a matter of Historical

Society record, why bother sneaking around? Why not just confront him about it?

Nena. The answer came to him as though delivered in her own voice. Curt had always had the feeling that she knew more than she let on, including the fact that there were things he couldn't talk about. Couldn't explain to anyone, not even the highest-ranking members of the Society. If they demanded answers, he would have to resist, and probably resign. For reasons she'd kept to herself, Nena had already used her influence with the Society twice to save his job. Perhaps that was what she was trying to do now, by ensuring that the protocol regarding the preservation of historical documents was followed before Curt's integrity could come into question… "trying" being the operative word.

By sheer willpower keeping his hands steady, Curt used his own key to unlock the drawer. He brought out the blue folder and opened it in the middle of his desktop. Then he exhaled heavily—his breath hanging like a stray cloud in the air—and stood staring in displeasure at several pages of computer printout.

Lillian's original letter had been scanned, filed, and replaced with a certified copy. And now there was an angry ghost tethered upstairs in the archives room and no doubt refrigerating the premises.

That couldn't be good for all the old paper in those bankers' boxes.

"I know where she is, Barbara. Don't worry, I'll get her back."

Gripped by urgency, Curt scooped up the blue folder and raced up the stairs of the tower. He'd been right: the chill of Lillian's rage could be felt on the second-floor landing. He paused to check whether the Society's office was occupied (it wasn't), then turned his attention to the archives across the way.

There were cameras trained on the entrances of these two rooms, and at least one to monitor activity inside the archives. They were visual only, but that was enough to be damning. Curt hesitated for the space of two breaths before deciding, *Fuck it!*

"Lillian, it's me," he called through the door. He fitted his key into the lock and let himself in.

She was perched on the hard wooden chair with her arms crossed over her chest and a martyred expression on her face. *"Well, it's about time!"* she scolded. *"Who was that dreadful man, and why weren't you there to stop him?"*

Curt glanced around. Locating the camera tucked into a corner of the room, he moved to stand with his back to it and replied, "I'll tell you later. Now, would you dial it down, please, and show me where he put your letter? Barbara's been climbing the walls, worrying about you."

As though by the flip of a switch, Lillian's demeanour changed. Now grinning happily, she said, *"She has?"*

Such an abrupt turnaround was disconcerting, to say the least. Considering what he knew about her, however, it could mean only one thing: these two ghosts had become more than just friends.

Shaking off the image that had arisen in his mind's eye, he repeated tautly, "Your letter?"

She pointed to one of the bankers' boxes. Carefully keeping his body between the camera and what his hands were doing, he wrangled the box onto a lower shelf to be searched. In short order, he'd switched the contents of the folders, replaced the box on the shelf, and was on his way back downstairs with his fingers mentally crossed and Lillian close behind him.

Noticing Amy on determined approach, Curt hurried to meet her before she reached the door of his office. Meanwhile, Lillian rushed past him and through the wall to where Barbara was presumably waiting.

"I didn't want to go to lunch without giving you your messages," Amy told him. "You've missed a couple of phone calls. Mr. DeLucci would like an update on the cemetery matter you've been handling. And Tricia Vickery needs you to phone her back as soon as possible about changing the time of your viewing appointment this evening. And finally, you asked me to remind you that it's the last Friday of the month."

Payroll. Of course. The museum's budget was one more thing for him to stress about today. "Thank you. I'll cut the cheques first thing this afternoon."

She flashed him a grin and disappeared back into the exhibit hall area.

His office was empty of ghosts, thank goodness. Once the file folder was safely locked back inside his desk drawer and his privacy was restored, Curt glanced at his watch. It was nearly noon. DeLucci and Vickery would both be going to lunch soon, and he was in no mood to play phone tag with them. Eating was out of the question for him right now—as the tightening knot in his midsection was telling him in no uncertain terms. So, he headed outside to the boarding platform, to decompress.

"Hello, handsome!" Clara called, waving to him to join her and Ruth on their bench. *"Why so glum?"*

Taking the offered seat, he replied wearily, "I think I may be in over my head. I've taken on too much." *...and I may not be working here much longer...*

"Nonsense!" said Ruth. *"You're doing a fine job managing the station."*

But Clara had been watching him closely. *"I don't think he's talking about his work, Ruth. Is everything all right between you and your special young lady, Mr. Wakefield?"*

"Not everything is about romance, you know. He's got

important responsibilities," the other woman pointed out.

"Mm-hmm. And none of that matters if there's no love in his life. Love doesn't just make the world go 'round, Ruth, it also makes it shine with promise."

"I'll have to remember that for the next time I'm cross-stitching a cushion cover."

Feeling a chill in the air, Curt decided to put an end to their argument. Truth be told, neither his work nor his love life was something he felt like discussing right now, but if those were his only choices...

"Clara's right," he said with a sigh. "For one thing, I can't even say whether she *is* my special young lady. It seems to change from one day to the next. When we're working together to do research or solve a problem, we're in sync, and the conversation flows, and I know she enjoys my company as much as I do hers. But there are times that aren't that comfortable for me—like when her children are around, or when she and her friends are talking about memories they share. That's when I wonder whether I'm fooling myself by thinking there will ever really be a place for me in her life."

Ruth nodded sagely. *"You are in love, my friend. I remember those days. When you're young, love is like a roller coaster ride at the amusement park. It's thrilling and suspenseful and terrifying, all at once. Half the time your heart is in your throat. The other half it's in the pit of your stomach, because you know how little it would take to send everything off its rails.*

"And then you get older, and you want something more. You want a love that will last, that will stand the test of time. Someone you can laugh with and cry with, and who will stay with you no matter what. That was my Henry. Steady and dependable, Henry was. Definitely not a roller coaster ride. More like a horse on the merry-go-round."

Clara let out a snort of laughter. *"He was as romantic as*

taxes."

"*Maybe so, but that didn't matter,*" Ruth returned mildly. "*All I cared about was that he was a kind and gentle man who loved me and let me know it, in many different ways. Sometimes the littlest things are the most important. Others tried to discourage the match—didn't think it would last— but for fifty years, we shared a life, and it was a good one. We looked after each other. Henry took the train to work every morning, and I met him here every afternoon when it brought him home again.*"

"Forgive me if this question is inappropriate, but it sounds like you were devoted to each other," Curt remarked. "And yet here you are, attached to a bench. Shouldn't you be with Henry?"

She gave him an indulgent smile. "*My dear man, what makes you think I'm not?*"

Curt returned to his office with his thoughts spinning even harder than before. He'd been dealing with ghosts all his life, and yet there was still so much he didn't know about them!

He announced himself before opening the door, in case Barbara and Lillian were inside, doing whatever ghosts in love did. Relieved to find the room empty, and with nothing better to do until it was time to return those two phone calls, he pulled his laptop and the museum's cheque book out of their respective desk drawers and took care of the payroll.

Writing Nena's cheque reminded him of the warning she had relayed to him from her grandfather: that an angry ghost in the museum was going to create trouble for him. Unfortunately, predictions like this were always much easier to understand in hindsight.

Curt had assumed that the ghost in question was Lillian— a rebel while living, a pain in the proverbial butt after death— but the medicine man's warning had arrived before Barbara entered the picture. Now the two spirits were a couple. Did that mean Curt had inadvertently headed off a disaster by letting them become emotionally attached to each other? Or had their mutual love been the very thing that ensured the prediction would come true?

What if something were to happen that separated them permanently? Would the one left behind fly into a rage and freeze the museum solid? Or—worse—figure out how to kill the living and lash out at whoever she felt was responsible? Was that what the warning had been about?

Curt heaved a sigh of resignation. He could waste the rest of the day second-guessing himself, but what was done was done. Let Lillian ride Ruth's roller coaster—after all, she was the one who was in love, not Curt Wakefield... right?

Ignoring the insistent grumbling from his stomach, he firmly refocused his attention on the task at hand, signing the paycheques and putting them into envelopes, then placing the envelopes in the Out basket on the corner of his desk.

Next, the phone messages. He consulted the slips of paper Amy had given him earlier.

J. D. DeLucci could wait for his update until there was actually something new to report. Curt dropped that one into the circular file. Tricia Vickery, on the other hand...

He picked up the handset and punched in the realtor's number. She answered on the second ring.

"Oh, Mr. Wakefield!" she exclaimed on hearing his voice. "I'm so glad you called back. Something unexpected has come up, and I'm afraid I won't be able to show you those three homes this evening. However, I am free this afternoon. So, I can either reschedule the viewings for another day, or, if you can possibly get away for an hour or so between now and 5:00 p.m. to visit the properties...?"

Perfect. He was still owed his lunch break, and it would be best if he were unavailable when DeLucci called again.

"This afternoon will be fine," he told her. "How about two o'clock?"

"Wonderful! I'll set it up and text you the address of the first showing."

After recradling the handset, he found a notebook in his desk and set about preparing it for his next meeting with Rachel's ghost. This time she would *have* to talk to him.

Curt arrived at the house on Elm Street with his notebook in hand and his hopes high. As expected, a greyscale figure was standing on the front lawn, a couple of metres away from Vickery. Wearing a jaundiced expression, Rachel's ghost surveyed him narrowly as he approached.

"I thought we should begin with your first choice, so you can see how the others compare to it," Tricia said, reaching into her briefcase for an information sheet and handing it to him.

Curt scanned the page to refresh his memory. "The price has dropped," he commented.

"That typically happens when a property has been overvalued, leading to lack of interest. This one has been on the market for a couple of months. The asking is still higher than what I would advise as an opening offer, but now the difference can be negotiated."

On his way to the front door, Curt looked directly at Rachel and nodded in greeting. Then he purposely turned away, giving his full attention to the house.

It was a boxy, raised, stone-and-siding bungalow with a full, unfinished basement. No garage, but a carport large enough for one vehicle. Two bedrooms (one decorated for a small child), one bath. A smallish kitchen with well-used appliances and a pass-through to a decent-sized dining area. A living room with enough space to accommodate a couple of bookcases, a media centre, and seating for four.

"Why are they selling this place?" he asked Tricia.

"It was their 'starter home'. Now their family is expanding and there's nowhere to put another bedroom, except in the basement," she replied. "They're expecting in the fall, which gives you some leverage in the negotiations, if you decide this is what you want."

Curt opened his notebook. "I'd like to check out the basement."

"Of course. This way."

Manoeuvring himself to stand between Tricia and her daughter at the top of the stairs, he turned to the first page he'd prepared and held it out for Rachel to read: I'M WORKING WITH THE POLICE TO SOLVE BRENDA'S MURDER. PLEASE TALK TO ME.

Silence. No problem—there were still two houses to view, and more messages for her to see.

The basement was clean and dry, with a cement floor and concrete block walls. Nothing seemed out of place or overly complicated, and nothing was missing as far as he could tell. He found the circuit panel and opened it up. Circuit breakers, not fuses, all clearly labelled. This was a promising sign.

Rachel stood at the corner of his vision, watching him as he conducted his inspection and made his notes. Still not convinced that he was a serious buyer, apparently.

When he reached the washer and dryer, Tricia told him, "These are only a couple of years old, but the sellers are leaving them behind, along with all the other major appliances."

That was good. With luck, they were all in solid working order. He doubted whether he could afford to replace any of them.

A few minutes later, he'd seen enough. Tricia gave him the address of the second house, and they headed outside to their respective cars.

This property was located in an older part of town, a single-storey brick house with a gravel driveway and no garage, on a smaller and less tidy lot than the first home she'd shown him. It had also been occupied by a family with children at some point, judging from the wooden swing that hung from a branch of the mature maple tree in the back yard. As he followed Tricia into the house, Curt opened his notebook to a different page and made sure Rachel could see it.

YOUR MOTHER CAN'T SEE/HEAR YOU AND I WON'T GIVE YOU AWAY. PLEASE!

Silence. Next page.

I NEED TO KNOW WHAT BRENDA TOLD YOU ABOUT HER PAST.

More silence… and they were inside the house. Curt swallowed a sigh. He was running out of time. And nearly out of prepared pages.

"They've done some recent upgrading," Tricia said, holding out the second information sheet for him to peruse. "Mainly the roof and the windows, though. The current owners live out of town. This place has been rented out for the past four years, which is no doubt why they had a full inspection done before putting the property back on the market. Nobody likes surprises."

"It's furnished," he said, eyeing the shabby brown recliner in a corner of the living room. "Are there renters living here now?"

"No. It's been vacant for a few weeks. You'll notice that the appliances are all about twelve years old, and the neighbourhood has been retrofitted with sewers and town water."

"But not the house?"

She shrugged. "There's a fee for getting hooked up. Owners' choice. Or buyer's choice. The well and the septic system have both passed their inspections. But if you chose this place and wanted it to be switched over to the town services, you could either deduct the fees from your offer or make it conditional on the seller paying them in advance of the possession date."

"*Or you could get the hell out of my house and leave me alone! I've had it up to here with you people!*"

A sudden chill in the air raised gooseflesh on Curt's arms, and a second greyscale figure materialized, sitting on the recliner—a cranky old man to match the voice inside Curt's head. This ghost sprang into the air and rushed toward the intruders. At the same time, Rachel moved to stand in front of her mother, who was shivering and gazing around in consternation.

Curt took a step forward as well. Purposely making eye contact with the old man and pointing to the chair that he was most likely tethered to, Curt declared loudly, "That recliner is a piece of garbage. I think it should be taken to the dump."

That pulled the spirit up short. "*You can see me?*" he demanded.

Curt nodded, then stared a stern message at him. The old man got it. As he fled through a wall, the room temperature rose back to normal, and Curt glanced at Rachel, hoping he wasn't imagining the gratitude he saw in her eyes.

"You're right, it shouldn't be here," said Tricia, oblivious to the ghostly byplay. "When the renters moved their own belongings out, the current owners brought all of the previous occupant's stuff out of storage. That item should have gone straight to landfill. The old man was lying on it when he died."

And now Curt could understand why Rachel had remained on the mortal plane. In a town like Groverton, containing so many old homes, there had to be a fair number of resident spirits like this one.

"Okay, then," Tricia said briskly. "Would you like to walk through the house now?"

"No. It's a non-starter and I have to get back to work, so let's move on to the third property," he decided.

This one was located on the outskirts of town. About ten metres square, it was clad in weather-treated wooden siding and had a separate but matching single-car garage. As he scanned the information sheet, Curt realized what it was: a winterized cottage, on town water but not connected to the sewer system, sitting in the embrace of a veritable forest of birch, ash, maple and poplar.

"This one is my favourite," came an unfamiliar female voice inside his head.

Curt repressed a smile. "This isn't one of the ones I picked out, is it?"

"No," the realtor replied. "I just had a hunch that you might find it interesting. As you can see from the sheet, it was built recently and has all the amenities of a year-round home. Shall we go inside?"

Curt opened his notebook and took out his pen. "Let's."

Sensing Rachel's presence behind his right shoulder, he flipped to the next page he'd prepared: WHAT DO YOU KNOW ABOUT BRENDA THAT THE POLICE WOULDN'T?

After a moment's hesitation, she replied, *"I know that Brenda Ryan wasn't her birth name. It was Janet Cookson. She had to change it when she escaped from her boyfriend, Tommy Stankov. He treated her like dirt, smacked her around, kept telling her how lucky she was to have him because nobody else would have put up with her stupidity. At the same time he warned her that if she ever left him he would track her down and make her pay."*

"This is such a lovely kitchen," Tricia enthused. "I thought about buying this property myself the first time it came on the market, for Rachel and me to live in. Then she got her cancer diagnosis and the seller changed their mind…"

"One day Tommy got drunk and beat her so badly that she was more afraid of staying than she was of leaving. She waited for him to fall asleep, then grabbed her coat and her purse and ran to a women's shelter. The workers there protected her. They got her medical attention, helped her to change her identity, and gave her what she needed to make a fresh start in another city."

He printed rapidly at the bottom of the page: POLICE?

"She wouldn't let anyone call them. Refused to press charges, insisted that everything be done in secret so Tommy couldn't find out where she was and come after her. She swore me to secrecy too."

"These bedrooms are larger than any of the ones I've shown you so far. And what do you think of the view from the living room window, Mr. Wakefield? …Mr. Wakefield?"

Scribbling furiously in his notebook, Curt paused and glanced up. "It's beautiful," he said automatically, then walked into the washroom. Rachel came through the wall and joined him there.

FAMILY?

"None that she told me about, although she did say that I was the closest thing she would ever have to a sister. I guess that was why she confided in me."

WHEN ESCAPED?

"It happened years before we became friends. Five or six, at least. By the time we met, she'd lived as Brenda in several different places, working low-paying jobs and saving up for the real estate course. She was excited about being accepted into the program. I got the impression that she was just beginning to enjoy her life."

"Mr. Wakefield, are you all right?" came Tricia's anxious voice through the door. "You've been in there for a while. Is there a problem?"

"Not at all," he called back. "Everything's perfect."

SEEN HER GHOST?

"No, and that worries me. Like you, I was sure the charms on Mom's bracelet would keep part of her close to us. They represent such important moments of her life."

That was all he needed to hear.

THANK YOU!

She gave him a smile and a nod in response, then drifted through the tiled washroom wall, presumably back to her mother's side.

Curt closed the notebook and walked back out and down the short hallway to the open concept living/dining/kitchen area. He swept his gaze around the room, took in the view of the back yard, then revisited the two bedrooms, actually seeing everything this time. The house had a spacious yet cozy feel to it. An out-in-the-country vibe, just ten minutes from the centre of town. Best of all, he wouldn't have to do a thing to it, other than move in.

So, the answer he'd tossed off earlier had been right after all—assuming he could afford it, this place *was* perfect for him.

Twenty-One

S elena wasn't the only one bursting with news to share that evening. Everyone came together for dinner at Sara's place, making it a veritable hive of activity. It was Italian night at Casa Traynor, and she'd prepared a pasta feast: fettuccine Alfredo, tortellini in a savoury marinara sauce, Caesar salad on the side, and lemon gelato for dessert.

"Don't ask how much of this is made from scratch," she warned her guests. "I have a reputation to maintain."

"Where's the pizza, Mom?" Donnie demanded. "I know pizza is Italian, 'cause Eric said so. We should have that too."

Sara pressed her lips together, lowered her head, and inhaled deeply through her nose. Evidently, this was a signal that Mommy was losing her patience. Both boys went still and silent.

"Hey, you've had pizza three times this week," Larry reminded them. "Tonight we're having something different. Something special."

Eric shrugged in acceptance, but Donnie wasn't won over yet. "I don't like that white sauce. It looks icky."

"Then it's a good thing I made the red sauce," Sara told him firmly as she ladled some plump tortellini from the serving bowl onto his dish.

His seven-year-old features twisted into an expression of defiance. "I hate the red sauce," he muttered.

"Oh. Well then, I guess you won't be eating any more pizza," his mother commented. She remained on her feet, serving pasta onto plates and passing them to the other diners.

Donnie gazed at her in shock. "But I *love* pizza!" he protested.

"Even though it's covered in the dreaded red sauce?" said Larry.

"That's a different red sauce," Donnie insisted. "It's pizza sauce."

"That's funny. They both taste the same to me. You know, there's an easy way to settle this," Larry told him.

Warily, the youngster asked, "How?"

They'd evidently done this dance before. Sara produced a teaspoon and handed it across the table to her son. "Put a little of it in your mouth. If you still don't like it, I'll microwave some tortellini for you to eat without any sauce. Deal?"

Everyone watched in amusement as Donnie studied the pool of tomato sauce on his plate. He appeared to be sizing it up, as though determining the best direction from which to sneak up on it. Slowly and with great care, he touched the narrow end of the spoon to the surface of the sauce and then to the tip of his tongue.

"Well?" Larry asked. "What's the verdict?"

"It's okay."

"Are you going to finish what's on your plate, then?" said Sara.

He shrugged one shoulder. "I guess."

As the adults resumed eating their dinner, Selena heard Eric say softly to his brother, "Way to be the centre of attention, kid. You know you like that sauce."

The answering grin on Donnie's face was easily worth a thousand words.

One hour later, the boys had finished off their gelato and gone downstairs to play a video game. Four mugs and a steaming teapot appeared on the dining room table, and the information sharing began in earnest.

Sara had gone back over the Friendly-Gallagher family tree to identify other living relatives who might take an interest in resolving the problem of Lillian and Gertrude's final resting places. "Our first choice is still the Davidsons, of course," she said. "But there are a couple of cousins we could contact who are old enough to have heard family stories and are both Canadian residents. They could be our plan B. If we're lucky, they may even have the wherewithal to cover the necessary cemetery fees."

Selena nodded her agreement. It was always good to have a plan B.

"Regardless," she chimed in, "I think we ought to ask Ben Davidson to represent us in case we need to keep the Historical Society at bay. After all, there's reason to believe that Gertrude's remains are on his property, and he's locked horns with the Society before, over a similar issue."

As the other three listened raptly, Selena recounted what Tricia had revealed to her earlier that day, finishing with, "I doubt whether he would charge us—not his full rate, anyway. He might even relish the thought of a rematch."

"Well, he's clearly got something that gives him leverage over the Society or its members," Larry mused, "but I'm not sure it would be a good idea for us to take advantage of it. Davidson doesn't have to live and work here. We do… and small town officials have been known to carry grudges. I'm not saying it's true of Groverton, only that it's a bet I would advise against making." With that, he subsided, frowning, into silence.

All eyes now turned toward Curt.

He told them about his visit to the morgue that morning, and about his conversation there with Staff Sergeant Brassard.

"So, you're a police consultant now. Going to review some evidence from the crime scene. Well done!" Larry said with a smile.

Meanwhile, Selena was gripped by urgency and fairly vibrating in place. "Never mind that!" she blurted. "Barbara's killer is in custody. This is huge! Does she know yet?"

Curt hesitated. "I—No, she doesn't. I've put off telling her because I'm not sure what will happen when I do."

"Wait just a minute," said Larry, leaning forward and speaking in a voice tinged with suspicion. "Aren't you the ghost whisperer? The guy who specializes in this sort of thing? You've supposedly been liberating tethered spirits for years. How can you not know what will happen?"

"Of *course* I know what will happen to Barbara," Curt protested, rearing defensively away from him. "That's not the problem. It's just—"

"Unless you've been lying to us. Have you?" Larry challenged, making the other man shrink even farther back in his chair.

"Hey!" Sara bounded onto her feet, glaring reproachfully at her brother. "Let the man talk." In a much softer voice, she continued, "You were saying, Curt?"

He moved forward again and pushed his glasses firmly up the bridge of his nose. "I was saying that although I know what will happen to Barbara, I'm not sure what the effect will be on Lillian. You already know that they became friends."

"Yes," Selena replied "You told us earlier."

"Well," he said, looking as though he wished he were somewhere else, "there's something I didn't tell you earlier because I wasn't certain of it until yesterday. Don't ask me how it works, because there's still a lot that I don't know about ghosts interacting with other ghosts, but—how well did you know your cousin, Selena? Did she date?"

"Was she gay, you mean? I believe she was. Not that it was anyone else's business, of course." Selena inhaled sharply. "Are you suggesting that she and Lillian—"

"There's no suggesting about it," he told her. "Those two are in a relationship. Lillian is volatile, and there's no way of knowing how much damage she might do if Barbara were suddenly to disappear."

Larry's eyes narrowed. "Damage," he echoed. "To the museum?"

"To anywhere and anyone in her vicinity. She's talking about attaching herself to Prue Davidson's brooch."

"Oh. My. God." Sara sank back onto her chair, a stunned expression on her face. "Can she do that?"

Curt gusted out a breath. "Two days ago, I would have said it's impossible. Now I'm not so sure."

"So, whatever else happens, we need to keep them together," said Selena. "Otherwise, all hell could break loose?"

"Yep. The medicine man was right," he muttered.

"Come again?" said Larry.

Curt batted the question away. "Never mind, it's not important. To continue with my report—"

"There's more? You've been a busy boy."

Curt shot him a look. "While Tricia Vickery was showing me houses this afternoon, I finally got Rachel to talk to me about Brenda."

By the time he finished telling them what he'd learned, jaws had dropped all around the table. For several long moments, everyone was speechless.

Then Larry broke the silence. "So, you believe Brenda's ghost will be found attached to something in the PPS evidence vault?"

"I believe that it's possible," Curt replied. He gave them all a lopsided smile and a helpless shrug. "Listen, I may be completely wrong about this. As I keep learning over and over, there's a lot that I do not know about ghosts. But if Brenda is inside that vault and I can get her to talk to me, we'll finally find out the truth about her death. Then Staff Sergeant Brassard will be able to move forward with her case, the yellow tape will come down, and I'll be able to get inside the castle and determine whether Lillian's story is true. Selena will finally be able to proceed with her purchase of the property."

Selena cleared her throat. "Maybe not that last one."

Under the curious stares of two pairs of male eyes and Sara's knowing gaze, she went on to describe her dilemma regarding the Davidsons' marriage and the house at the corner of Beech and Webber.

"I don't believe this," Larry exclaimed, throwing his hands up in the air. "This entire exercise began with you being intent on buying that place, despite Sara's warning about it. And now that we're up to our necks in solving two murders that probably happened inside it, you're telling us you've changed your mind?"

Sara's expression darkened. "She's allowed to change her mind, big brother. And to be honest, I'm just as glad she's doing it. Having to deal with the Historical Society is an aggravation I wouldn't wish on anyone. When that house turns a century old, trust me—"

"I haven't changed my mind about wanting it," Selena cut in, raising her voice to be heard above the din of their clashing opinions. When she had everyone's full attention once more, she continued, "It's a beautiful home and it's perfect for me and my business, but I have to be practical. The sobbing woman was what drove the Davidsons to separate, which directly caused the husband to put the castle on the market. If that ghost turns out to be Gertrude and we're able to give her peace—which is something we all want to do, right? Find her remains and put them in a proper grave?—then the reason for the separation will be gone, along with any motivation for the Davidsons to sell their property. Besides, Tricia showed me a couple of places this morning. They're both about fifty years old, and one of them had interesting possibilities."

Sara tossed her brother a triumphant smile and nod. It was such a Donnie-like gesture that Selena had to grin.

"Well, there is a silver lining here," Curt remarked thoughtfully. "If the Davidsons are going to live in the castle after all, then they'll have to do something about Gertrude's remains, if only to silence the sobbing woman. And if Corben Davidson could bring the Historical Society to its knees in a matter of just a couple of months, just imagine how quickly he'll be able to bring the board of the Groverton Municipal Cemetery to heel."

Canada Day was on a Tuesday this year, and Standerville's annual picnic, concert, and fireworks display was mostly arranged. Selena went over everything in her head and figured she could spend another day in Groverton before she would have to head home to supervise the final details.

She had understated her interest in the second property Tricia Vickery had shown her. Now she wanted to go through it again, this time as a serious prospective buyer with pen and paper in hand for notemaking. And with Curt at her side. If there were any ghosts in this house, she wanted to be sure they were friendly.

And with Larry, on the pretext of a fire inspection. Selena had a pretty strong hunch as to why he'd been in such a prickly mood at dinner the previous evening. Despite his protestations, Larry Holmes was a sleuth at heart. Listening to the other three at table deliver their progress reports on not one but three investigations, all going on around him but not involving him, had to have been frustrating.

Larry loved his sister and adored his nephews. He didn't begrudge a moment of the time he spent with them, Selena was certain. However, he had never struck her as the sort of man who could be content pushing papers around on a desk. The transition from firefighting to office duty was probably still ongoing, and might never be a comfortable fit.

Selena came downstairs for breakfast on Saturday morning and found Eric and Donnie at the dining room table, already fed and working on their family tree, and Sara sitting in the kitchen with a pot of tea at her elbow. "It's apricot spice," she said. "Shall I pour you a mugful?"

"That sounds delightful," Selena replied, taking a seat as well. She gestured toward the other room. "I know you intended that project to keep them busy for most of the summer. Do you still think it will?"

"Actually, I'm sure of it," Sara said, setting the steaming beverage in front of her. "They're a committee of two, and you know what *that* means. Right now they're arguing over which colour of sticky note to use for what."

Arguing was the right word. Donnie's voice in particular was becoming shrill. Meanwhile, Sara sipped her tea, seemingly unconcerned.

"Are you going to step in?" Selena asked.

"Only if they come to blows. It's unlikely to happen, though, since the alternative activity for the morning is yard work, which isn't much fun when Uncle Larry isn't around to help."

"Oh? Where is he?"

She shrugged one shoulder. "Apparently, it's his turn to make a community outreach presentation on fire safety in the home. He'll be here after lunch."

"I need to borrow him for about an hour. It's to inspect the two homes I'm viewing and help me decide which one to submit an offer on."

"Uh-*huh*," Sara said archly. "Well, you can talk to him about that when he gets here. Until then, it's the cook's day off, so you're on your own for breakfast."

Not a problem. Selena threw together a bowl of cold cereal with slices of banana and some dried cranberries added, then poured herself another mug of tea. After that, she phoned Curt at the museum to find out when he would be available, and Hearth and Home to make mid-afternoon appointments for the two walk-throughs. Finally, she got in her car and went grocery shopping. Sara had more than earned a day off from meal preparation, but that didn't mean the rest of them had to settle for frozen pizza for dinner.

Three hours later, Larry walked through Sara's front door, holding a suspiciously familiar box in his hands. "Hey, everyone! Guess what the host community ordered in for lunch!"

At half-past two o'clock, Selena, Larry, and Curt met Tricia at the first address. Larry was carrying a clipboard with an official-looking printed form on it. Selena and Curt had both brought pens and spiral-bound notebooks with them.

Selena stood on the sidewalk for a moment, surveying the front of the two-storey brick building. Then she jotted her first observation:

SEPARATE OUTER ENTRANCE TO UPSTAIRS APARTMENT. UP 15 WOODEN STEPS, RAILINGED, WEATHERED. INSIDE ACCESS AS WELL?

While waiting for Tricia to unlock the door, she paused on the concrete-slab front porch, closed her eyes, and reached out with her senses.

Nothing. This place was not only vacant, it was apparently dead.

Feeling vaguely disappointed, Selena followed the realtor inside the house, ahead of Larry and Curt.

"This was built as a duplex, back in the 1970s," Tricia explained as she handed out information sheets to all three of them. "The owners lived down here and rented out the upstairs. Since then, the property has changed hands several times. It's currently part of an estate, and the executors have indicated their willingness to be flexible regarding the asking price if it will lead to a firm offer."

"How long has it been vacant?" Larry asked.

"It came on the market looking like this nearly six weeks ago," came the reply. "But it had been unoccupied for about a month before that, while the owner was in hospital with a terminal illness. Her family saw to it that all her possessions were removed and that the place was cleaned top to bottom before it was listed."

Selena stared inquiringly at Curt. He smiled at her and shook his head.

So, no ghosts on the premises. That was reassuring.

While Larry set out on his fire inspection, Selena and Curt wandered around, making notes.

LARGE DOWNSTAIRS LIVING ROOM—GOOD FOR RECEPTION AREA

DECOR A LITTLE DATED BUT PRESENTABLE

1 DOWNSTAIRS BEDROOM—COULD BE PRIVATE OFFICE

KITCHEN, BATHROOM—CLEAN, SERVICEABLE

The exterior staircase to the second floor led to a small, balcony-style landing, where a locking door led into a two-bedroom apartment with a smaller kitchen and living room than in the one below. It wasn't an ideal proportioning of space, and nothing about it screamed *modern*, but this place was move-in clean, and she could visualize her furniture inside it. Selena completed her notes, then headed back down and inside to join the others.

They were in the basement, the door to which had evidently been left ajar so that she could follow them.

Tricia hadn't been kidding when she'd said "top to bottom". Selena had never seen a basement this empty. The floor and walls looked as if they had been vacuumed and damp-mopped. In the uneven light of several cheap overhead fixtures, Larry had found the electrical panel and was checking out the wiring attached to it. Curt was in the laundry room, scribbling into his notebook. Tricia stood like a ringmaster in the centre of the main room, ready to answer questions.

Eventually, Larry closed the panel and recorded something on his clipboard. As he turned away from the wall, he did a double take and pointed at something with his index finger.

Selena sent her gaze in that direction and spied a door she hadn't noticed before.

"What's on the other side of that?" she asked the realtor.

"Oh, that?" Tricia replied. "That's the cold cellar. It's mentioned on your info sheet." She walked over and opened the door, giving them a view inside what appeared to be a fair-sized pantry equipped with bins and shelving. "Back when this area was still mainly rural, people would dig out an underground root cellar for storing food that needed to last them the winter," she explained. "Now it's a common feature in just about every home in the town."

Struck by a sudden thought, Selena asked Larry, "Does Sara have one?"

"Of course," he said. "It's under the front porch, closed off from the heated part of the basement." His eyes widened briefly as the same possibility apparently occurred to him. "She puts all her home-canned stuff down there because the air is cool and dry year-round, so it's as good as keeping it inside a fridge."

"So, even century-old buildings would have them," she mused.

Curt and Larry exchanged meaningful glances.

"Would this sort of thing appear on a blueprint, do you think?" Curt asked him.

Larry paused for a moment. "If it were located under a raised front porch, and assuming that the porch was both a concrete slab *and* part of the builder's original plan, then I would say yes. The foundation would have to be extended outward and bricks laid on top of it to support the weight of the slab, and all of that would show up in the drawings."

"Oh." Curt's shoulders sagged.

But Larry wasn't finished. "On the other hand, three fellow firefighters and I added a wooden deck to the back of my house a few summers ago, and as far as I know, it didn't change the blueprints on file with the town offices one iota."

Selena could sense their rising excitement. She wanted to share it. However, there was still one property to be vetted, and Tricia was wearing the mannequin smile that signalled she was becoming impatient to move on.

So, after clearing her throat, Selena said loudly, "Gentlemen, are we done here?"

And with that, they were off to the remaining address on the list.

Twenty-Two

Curt hadn't missed the change in Tricia's expression, nor the way she'd begun tapping the corner of her business card on the banister of the basement stairs. Out on the street, he joined the caravan of vehicles headed to the second address, and five minutes after that, he stepped out of his car feeling even more impatient than the realtor had evidently been. The sooner he could confirm whether this property was haunted and be on his way, the happier he would be.

There was a reason for this. Not only had the discovery of the cold cellar suggested a possible location for Gertrude's remains inside the castle, but his discussion with Rachel's ghost in the laundry room had provided information relevant to the Brenda Ryan case.

Curt now had a couple of solid arguments to present to Staff Sergeant Brassard for letting him and his fellow investigators into her crime scene. First, however, he had a house to get off his plate: a weathered-looking, two-storey, brick and siding structure on a corner lot, two blocks away from a major intersection. Seen from outside, the first floor of the building had clearly been converted for business use. The large "CLOSED" sign hanging in what ought to have been the living room window was hard to miss.

Built in the 1970s, this house had the same kind of square, cement-slab porch as the first place they'd viewed.

"This was a gift shop until a couple of months ago," Tricia told them over her shoulder as she led them up a pair of poured-concrete steps to the front door. "The owners lived upstairs. There's a back entrance providing separate, locking access to both the shop and the apartment. The advantage here is that the stairs to the second floor are indoors, making them much safer to climb in the winter."

Being a ghost, Rachel hadn't had to wait for her mother to turn a key in the lock to gain entry to the building. She'd hurried through the wall and now returned with an impish grin on her face.

"The pastor has no pants on," she carolled gleefully.

What the hell...?

Once inside the shop, Curt understood. A tall, portly, greyscale figure stood glowering at them from behind one of the empty glass display cases. This spirit appeared to be a well-groomed, middle-aged man wearing a bowler hat, a white shirt beneath a dark suit jacket, and a tidy moustache... and he had the promise of fire and brimstone written all over his face.

"Get out!" he shouted at them, making extravagant gestures with both arms. *"This den of iniquity is no place for God-fearing folk!"*

His warning would have carried a lot more weight if he hadn't been naked from his waist down to the garters anchoring his socks.

Caught off-guard, Curt blurted out, "It's a gift shop, for heaven's sake!"

"Is that what lustful young sinners are calling it now?" the

ghost thundered at him. *"They'll burn in hell, all of them!"*

"Yes, a gift shop," Tricia repeated sharply. "That's what I said."

Meanwhile, Rachel was laughing too hard to speak.

Curt wanted to laugh too, but didn't dare. With effort, he recomposed himself and remarked, "I get the feeling that this is one of those properties with a colourful history."

"Well, there is a story—not about this building but rather one that sat here much earlier," Tricia said.

"Let me guess. It was a brothel?"

"It's the gateway to damnation!" the ghost fulminated. He was now pacing back and forth, his shirttails flapping.

"A whorehouse," Tricia confirmed. "And by all accounts, quite a successful one. The madam running it apparently had a lot of business savvy. By the year 1920 or so, it had become well known in the area. At around the same time, an evangelical preacher who called himself 'the Reverend Upworthy' undertook a tour of the province. His stated purpose was to find and curse all the 'palaces of perdition' that were leading young people astray. Apparently, there was a test that he performed to make sure he wouldn't be raining down fire from heaven on a legitimate enterprise."

"Uh-*huh*. Did this test involve taking off his trousers, by any chance?"

He'd caught Selena's attention with that question. She shot him an inquiring look. He responded with a single nod, causing her eyes to widen and her mouth to form an O of comprehension.

"I would not know about the details of that," the realtor replied primly (despite the fact that she'd clearly done some research on the subject). "All I do know is that he died in Groverton and was buried in our churchyard, where he rests to this day."

He was resting? Curt begged to differ.

"It's a good thing my mother can't see this," Rachel commented, prompting him to check on Upworthy.

The angry ghost was now stalking back and forth along the top of the long glass case, huffing and puffing. His arms swung fervently with each step. His genitals were flapping in time as well. It took every gram of Curt's self-control not to react with hilarity.

"And what happened to that earlier building?" Larry interjected.

"It was struck by lightning during a storm and burned to the ground," Tricia told him. "Not at all surprising, since it was one of the last all-wooden structures left in Groverton. It was quickly replaced with something much less flammable. Eventually, a developer purchased the lot, knocked down what was on it, and put up the house that we're standing in right now. Please, feel free to wander… make your notes… I'll be right here if you have any questions."

Curt scribbled on the next blank page of his notebook: DON'T LEAVE MOM ALONE WITH HIM

"Believe me, I wasn't planning to," came Rachel's answer over his shoulder.

Curt made short work of his "inspection"—the blustering clergyman was the only resident ghost he could find—and took his leave, promising to meet up with Larry and Selena at Sara's house later to compare notes. Then he headed back to the museum to confirm a suspicion.

Ruth and Clara were in their usual place, sitting on the bench on the train platform.

"Hey, handsome!" Clara called out when she saw Curt approach. *"How's every little thing?"*

Smiling, he took the seat Ruth had made for him between them and replied, "Doing fine, thanks. I heard about your brothel burning down. My condolences."

"Oh, it wasn't mine when that happened. I'd already sold

the place and changed professions. It turned out matchmaking better suited my temperament."

Ruth made a rude noise with her lips.

Uh-huh. "And was that before or after the visit from Reverend Upworthy?"

"That horny old man," she said, letting out a syllable of wicked laughter. *"He claimed he was going to save our souls. When we saw how well-endowed he was, every girl in the house wanted to try him on. And they did, one by one. Ilse was the last one. Very strong. Incredible stamina and flexibility. She'd been a circus acrobat before coming to me."*

"And she killed him with sex?"

"Not deliberately. I prefer to think of it as 'she gave him everything he'd asked for'. That final climax must have been more than his poor heart could take. Stopped it cold. Out of respect for his social status, not to mention his clergyhood, we washed and dressed him before sending for the doctor. And every one of us attended his funeral," she concluded in a sing-song voice, her chin raised in righteous triumph.

"What if I told you that his ghost is tethered to the place where the bordello once stood?"

Her eyes widened. *"Really! Doing what?"*

"He's half-naked and threatening eternal damnation. Still believes he's in a whorehouse. Which is a little sad when you think about it, since the current building houses a gift shop."

"Sounds like he's the one who's been damned," Ruth sniffed.

Her comment made a disturbing amount of sense.

Selena had prepared dinner that evening: sweet and sour chicken over rice, with coleslaw and steamed mixed vegetables on the side. She'd also picked up an apple pie, which was now cooling on the kitchen counter and would be their dessert.

Having opted for the *à la mode* minus the pastry, Eric and

Donnie finished their meal early and left the table. Donnie went upstairs to his room to read. Eric cast a resentful glance at his brother's back before choosing the unfinished jigsaw puzzle in the rec room.

Watching the byplay, Curt couldn't help wondering whether the boys had had a falling out. Then Sara brought four cups and a large pot of jasmine tea to the table, distracting his attention with thoughts of dessert.

"So," she said to the group as she poured their beverages, "what were your impressions of those two houses?"

Selena had fetched the still-warm pie from the kitchen and was busily serving it onto small plates. "The second one has a much better layout," she replied without missing a beat. "The first floor is already a commercial space, complete with fixtures, and the apartment upstairs has been modernized. The decor may not be to my taste, but a fresh coat of paint will take care of that. Plus, I prefer having the stairs to the second floor indoors."

Sara reopened the ice cream container, stuck the business end of the scoop into it, and slid it down the table on a trivet, over to where her brother was sitting. This was evidently Larry's cue. He stood up and put a chunk of French vanilla on each of the four pie wedges, then handed them out.

"Of course, there is the matter of the ghost," Curt remarked, hovering his fork over his dessert.

Sara nearly choked on her first mouthful of pie. "The building is haunted?" she got out between coughs.

"It is. If you're interested, I did some research on it before coming here," he told her.

"On the building? Or on the ghost?" Larry asked.

"On both." As the others continued to eat, Curt proceeded to share Clara's account of the death of Reverend Upworthy. By the time he'd finished, three plates were empty and there was laughter all around the table.

"He sounds like a comical character to have around," Selena said. "And the previous owners clearly had no problem with him… It could be interesting, having a haunted house."

"Really?" Larry challenged her, scowling. "Think again, Selena. Ghost or not, a horny old man with his package unwrapped is roaming the building. You may not be able to see or hear him, but he can see you… getting undressed for bed… taking a shower… and you're comfortable with that?"

Her face fell. "Well, when you put it that way, it is kind of creepy."

"Kind of?" he echoed incredulously.

"Damn!" she muttered. "I really *like* that property, too."

"What if we could get rid of him?" Sara suggested. "Is there any way to exorcise him?"

"He's a ghost, not a demon," Curt reminded her, "but I can look into it. Maybe he's tethered to something besides the location of his death. And maybe what Larry and I learned today can crack a murder case or two," he added, with a hand gesture passing the mic to the fire inspector.

Sara shivered—Curt hoped it was with excitement—and said, "Do tell!"

Now it was Larry's turn to spin them a story, about cold cellars and how they were built, and blueprints and what they did or didn't show.

"So, you figure that's the 'secret room' Lillian has been hinting at? A cold cellar that was added after the plans for the house were already approved by the town?" Selena said.

"It makes sense," Curt replied. "McFadyen could have bribed the builder to deviate from the blueprints on file during the original construction, or he could have brought someone else in afterwards to break through a section of the foundation and excavate the room while the veranda was being added on. Gertrude died in the middle of winter, when the ground would have been frozen. Where better than a cool, dry place to store a body while waiting for the spring thaw?"

"Now we just have to convince the owners to authorize a search of their basement… and persuade Brassard to conduct it," Larry pointed out. "And since Curt is the PPS consultant in our midst, that job would naturally fall to him."

"Wrong. I'm only consulting on the Brenda Ryan case," Curt countered, feeling a knot tighten inside his chest. "Brassard has made it quite clear to me that she wants nothing to do with Gertrude and Lillian's problems. However, I've gotten her to agree to help me locate Brenda's ghost. If it's not tethered to any of the evidence in PPS storage, my next request will be to enter the castle, since that is where she died."

"So, in order to learn whether Gertrude's remains are inside that building, we need to hope that Brenda's ghost is there as well?" said Sara.

"I know, it's complicated, but Curt's got a handle on this, and I'm sure he'll keep us posted," Selena told her.

Keep them posted? The knot turned to ice and fell to the pit of his stomach.

Brassard had bestowed on him the title and status of 'consultant', and had warned him to behave like one. That meant there were rules to follow. Okay, what were they?

She had instructed him that anything he learned about the case was to be shared with her personally. He also recalled her saying that the police routinely withheld certain details from the public. Without knowing what constituted privileged information regarding the death currently under investigation, his safest course of action was to keep secret everything he found out. But he'd just reported his conversation with Rachel to the other three at Sara's dinner table.

Had he compromised the Brenda Ryan investigation? Should he come clean and tell Brassard he'd done it? And why, oh *why*, hadn't he realized this earlier, before he'd opened his big mouth and spilled the beans about the victim's abusive ex-boyfriend, Tommy Stankov?

"Curt? Are you all right?" Sara's anxious voice penetrated the wall his thoughts were building and yanked him back to the moment.

"Huh?" Shaking his head to clear it, he muttered in reply, "Yeah. I'm fine."

"You went pale all of a sudden. I was afraid you might faint."

He gave her a feeble smile and pointed to his uneaten piece of pie. "Low blood sugar, I guess. I think I may need some more ice cream."

"Now you're reminding me of Donnie," she teased as she placed another scoop of French vanilla on his plate.

Curt woke up Sunday morning feeling mentally and physically exhausted. He'd spent the night running away from Staff Sergeant Brassard in a string of unpleasant dreams. A couple of them had included Tricia Vickery as well, and he could swear he'd spotted both Reverend Upworthy and Nena's grandfather lurking in the background of at least one more.

Foggy-brained and operating on automatic pilot, Curt completed his morning routine and drove to the museum, arriving two hours before it opened to the public.

Lillian stood shaking her head at him as he walked through the door of his office.

"*You really are in a bad way today, Mr. Wakefield,*" she said. "*More than usual, anyway. What have you been doing out there?*"

He sank onto his chair with a groan.

"Sleeping," he grumped. "Dreaming. Keeping secrets. Blabbing secrets."

She tilted her head and elevated her eyebrows. "*Blabbing none of mine, I hope.*"

"I'm not sure. There are so fucking many of them, it's hard to keep track."

His voice felt thick and gravelly in his throat. For a moment he debated whether to bother clearing it.

Meanwhile, Lillian had gasped melodramatically and clutched a hand to her chest. *"Such rude language, sir!"* she scolded him with mock severity. Then she laughed.

She wouldn't think it was so funny if *she'd* been the one having nightmares, he thought—and that raised an interesting question in his mind.

"Do ghosts sleep?" he asked her. "Do you ever dream?"

He'd evidently caught her off-guard. She opened her mouth as if to reply, then wordlessly closed it again, frowning in bewilderment.

"You don't know, do you?" he said. "Are you aware of the passage of time? You spent ninety years inside that storage vault. Did it feel that long to you?"

"No," she told him after a pause. *"But I wasn't in there the whole time. I watched them at first, after the train derailed. The workers. There were a lot of them. They crawled all over the wreckage, removing chunks of concrete, winching the twisted metal cars out of the way... Then they started bringing out the bodies. It was hard to believe these had once been living human beings. They were mangled, crushed—one was missing pieces. It was sickening.*

"Still, I believed I had survived until I saw the purse I was carrying pulled out of the rubble, along with what was left of the woman who'd been clutching it. In that moment of recognition, I felt a terror such as I had never experienced before. I shut my eyes tightly, wishing myself somewhere else—somewhen else—and when I opened them again, I was inside a little room, staring at a cardboard box marked 'Personal Effects, 1933: Unclaimed'. For me, it had been a blink, nothing more, and yet time had obviously passed. Is

that what you would call sleep, Mr. Wakefield?"

"In a way, I would. You were apparently able to 'shut yourself off'. For how long, would you say? About ninety years?"

"No, unfortunately. I became aware each time a living person came down those stairs—which seemed to happen frequently—but none of them could see or hear me. And each time I tried to go back up with them, something blocked me. It was frustrating, to say the least."

In fact, it was her tether, attaching her to the letter, but she couldn't have known it at the time.

"Is that what you were doing when I first saw you? You rushed toward me with an angry expression on your face. I thought you were attacking me until I saw the way you stopped. It looked as if you'd bounced off an invisible barrier."

"I didn't realize you could see me. I'm sorry if I frightened you, but I was just trying to escape. I thought that if I passed you while you were still approaching... Never mind. You found the purse and brought it upstairs, freeing me from my prison, if not from my chains."

She concluded her speech by striking another dramatic pose, and involuntarily, Curt smiled.

"Once you knew that I was different, why did you wait so long to identify yourself?" he asked her.

She appeared to sit down on one of his guest chairs. Frowning, she replied, *"I wanted to. I tried to. But something stopped me. It felt like a hand around my throat, blocking the words from getting out. The harder I tried to say them, the tighter its grip became, and the angrier it made me. Then you found the letter, and the hand just... disappeared. I can't explain it."*

Ruth probably could, though, and as the other ghost's earlier question bobbed to the surface of his mind, Curt realized that he could as well: *"My dear man, what makes you think I'm not?"*

Hugh McFadyen had had unfinished business to tend to when he was killed. In Curt's experience, that meant his spirit should have lingered on the mortal plane, tethered to something related to that matter. Odds were, it had been on his person at the time of his death and had either been destroyed in the disaster or claimed by someone and taken away in the days or weeks following it. The item was not in the museum—that much was certain. However, if Ruth's spirit could be in more than one place at a time, why couldn't McFadyen's?

He'd had secrets when he died—had threatened Lillian with death if she ever revealed them. What if that was part of his unfinished business? What if his ghost had somehow attached itself to Lillian's to ensure that she couldn't betray him, and the "business" was concluded once the letter—and the secrets—came to light?

One ghost tethered to another? Undetectable even by someone like himself? Just thinking about that made him break out in gooseflesh. On the other hand...

"You believe me, don't you, Mr. Wakefield?" Lillian's voice and facial expression were both strained. *"I know it sounds far-fetched, but it's the truth."*

"I do believe you, Lillian," he assured her, rising from his chair. "If you'll excuse me, I have to verify something."

Curt went outside to the boarding platform, where Ruth and Clara sat on their bench, chatting with Barbara.

"Look who's come to join the party!" Clara announced with a grin.

"Good morning, ladies," he greeted them. "I just have a couple of questions for Ruth, if you don't mind."

She leaned forward attentively.

"I've been thinking about something you said earlier," he told her, "and it's got me wondering. Where was Henry that terrible day?"

Her cheeks dimpled. *"He was in the first passenger car on the train, as usual."*

"So you're saying he died in the derailment?"

She nodded in affirmation.

"And where is his spirit now?" Curt inquired.

"By my side, of course, where he's been ever since."

"Then why can't I see him the way I see you?"

"Don't fret, Mr. Wakefield," Clara chimed in. *"I can't see him either, and Ruth and I have known each other for years."*

Ruth's features contracted in thought. *"Perhaps…"* she began, *"Perhaps it's because you never loved him the way he and I loved each other."*

And once again she had given him a great deal to think about.

The rest of the day plodded along quietly. The museum opened to the public at precisely eleven o'clock in the morning and would close again at four in the afternoon. Meanwhile, there were emailed requests for Curt to reply to, end-of-month reports to prepare for the Historical Society, and periodic circuits to be made of the exhibit halls. And research, of course. Research was a constant in his line of work.

This time of year seemed to follow a regular pattern: once school had let out for the summer, the museum fell into the doldrums until the week after Canada Day. Between now and then, visitors would be few and invariably adult. The previous end of June, a local author had whipped up some unaccustomed excitement around the former train station by making the boarding platform the venue for her book launch, but that had been an anomaly. Curt couldn't count on anything similar happening again.

Nena was away, spending time with her grandchildren. Romy was keeping herself busy by cleaning and tidying the various exhibits. Amy stood at her post, probably surfing the web on the gift shop computer. And Lillian and Barbara were off somewhere together, doing something Curt chose not to speculate about.

Despite the emails, the inspection patrols, and the paperwork, he still had plenty of time to think, and his mind kept circling back to the last house Tricia had shown him. It hadn't been his original intention to buy a home, but the more he thought about that property, the righter it felt for him to live in it, and the more disappointed he knew he would be if somebody else got to it first.

Eventually, fuelled by burgeoning certainty, he picked up the phone and punched in Tricia Vickery's office number. The voice at the other end of the line informed him apologetically that Tricia was out doing back-to-back open houses. Would he care to leave a message? Already deflating, he gave the receptionist his number, asked that Ms. Vickery call him back at her earliest convenience, and terminated the connection.

Then he gave himself a hard mental shake. What was he thinking, sitting around waiting for things to occur when there was so much that needed doing?

Curt found the card Staff Sergeant Brassard had given him earlier and called the phone number hand-printed on the back of it. Expecting a recorded greeting, he was startled to hear her answer, "Hello?"

"Hello! This is Curt Wakefield. I... have some further information to report regarding the Brenda Ryan case, and I was wondering when we could meet."

"I see. Is there some reason that you cannot give me this information over the telephone?"

She sounded the way a ghostly touch felt, but he wasn't about to back away now. Swallowing hard, Curt continued, speaking rapidly in a voice half a register higher than usual,

"Well, you said that I could look at the evidence the Forensics team had removed from the McFadyen house, and I thought… you know, two birds with one stone…?"

Silence. Curt held his breath, the knot from the previous evening returning to his midsection as he waited for her reaction to the temerity of this suggestion.

After what seemed an eternity, she asked, "And would you be bringing anyone else with you to this meeting? In spirit, perhaps?"

"N—No," he replied. "It would just be me." …and with luck, Brenda's ghost, willing to confirm what Rachel had told him, he added privately.

Another pause. Then, "*B'en alors.* Come to my office tomorrow morning at ten o'clock."

Twenty-Three

Selena drove back to Standerville early Sunday morning and found herself caught up in a whirlwind of final preparations for the July 1st celebration. The next two days were a blur of organized chaos, punctuated by moments of panic. In the end, though, everything managed to fall into place. The bandstand was built in time for the concert. The food order was delivered in time for the picnic. The swag was created in time to be handed out (even if Selena did have to drive to the next town to pick it up herself). And the fireworks display went off without a hitch, finishing up shortly after 11:00 p.m.

In other words, it was a typical town-wide Canada Day.

Except for the part where she'd felt like a fraud, handing out buttons and cards as if to solicit more local business when she knew she wasn't going to *be* local for much longer.

First thing Wednesday morning, she threw her packed overnight case into the back of her car and headed west, for Groverton. Breakfast could wait. According to Sara's text message, the Davidsons had arrived in town the previous evening, and Selena was anxious to find out what she had missed over the past three days.

As she carried her things up the walkway to the heritage home's front door, Sara emerged onto the veranda to greet her, holding a forefinger to her lips to signal for quiet. "The boys are still asleep," she said in a hushed voice. "Larry let them help with the fireworks yesterday. They were so hyper afterward that I couldn't get them to bed until nearly one o'clock. Good thing day camp hasn't started yet. Put your stuff in the parlour, then join me in the kitchen. We'll have some tea while I bring you up to speed."

Moments later, Selena was sitting at the square wooden table, watching Sara rifle through her collection of herbal teas as the kettle burbled merrily on the stovetop.

"It turns out you were right about getting a high-powered city lawyer involved," Sara told her. Then, brandishing a couple of dark purple packets, she announced, "Ah! Here it is. I *knew* I still had some Blueberry Sparkle left. Have you eaten? I could whip you up something."

"Just the tea will be fine, thanks. And I gather Ben Davidson has agreed to take the case?"

"Even before leaving Toronto, apparently." She brought the brown earthenware teapot down from the cupboard, along with a couple of mugs. "He's got meetings already lined up for today, with the Historical Society, the Regional Cemetery Association, the Public Health Department, and the PPS. And somewhere in there he wants to see you and Curt as well, at the museum."

"About the ghost in the castle?"

Sara looked up from warming the pot, one eyebrow elevated. "About Lillian's claim to the brooch."

"He's not planning to start a fight over it, is he?" Selena moaned. She was having visions of the tabloids jumping on this story. They would have a field day with it. "I mean, she's dead, and the dead can't inherit... or accept material gifts from the living. Legally, it's cut and dried."

"Perhaps not. To hear Curt describe her, Lillian behaves a lot like a living person. So does Barbara. And who knows how many others? Maybe Davidson wants to break ground on a whole new branch of jurisprudence—the legal rights of human ghosts."

Sara set the filled teapot on a trivet in the middle of the table and brought the mugs over from the counter. "We could be on the cusp of history being made here," she said, her cheeks dimpling.

But the mention of Barbara had dredged a feeling back up—the sickness that had settled at the back of Selena's throat at learning that she'd been dragging her traumatized cousin's spirit around with her for the past nine years.

"Speaking of Curt, how is he doing?" she asked, if only to change the subject. "Has he made any further progress?"

"Actually, he has, and so have I," came the response. "Two days ago, he met with Brassard and was able to confirm two things. First, that Brenda's ghost was not tethered to any of the evidence the police removed from the castle while processing the scene—"

"The evidence she decided it was safe to show him, you mean," Selena cut in.

Sara frowned at her for a moment. "Are you sure you don't want me to make you some toast or something?"

"Nothing, thanks. I'm good."

"You're hungry, and it's making you testy."

She batted Sara's comment away. "What's the second thing Curt found out?"

"Fine. Brassard assured him that after their earlier discussions she had ordered the Forensics people to check the building's interior from top to bottom, and there was nothing in their reports to indicate the presence of a 'secret room'."

Selena scowled. "That doesn't mean there wasn't one there,

only that they didn't find it."

"True. But what it does signify is that, deep down, Brassard is taking us seriously. Otherwise, she would never have given that order."

"Okay, then," Selena mused aloud, depositing her mug back on the table. "Let's consider this logically. If Brenda isn't with her body in the morgue and she's not attached to anything that was carried away from the castle, then there are only two places where she might be: she's either haunting the house or haunting her killer. And since that person has yet to be identified, let alone located, that leaves us with just one way to go—Curt needs to check out the inside of the castle.

"Assuming that Lillian's 'secret room' is a cold cellar that's been sealed off or covered up by a previous owner… Davidson can give us permission to damage the property and find it, but he's bound to demand some proof beforehand that there's actually something to find. And *that's* assuming that either the yellow tape is gone or we have police permission to go in there while it's still off-limits to civilians. Talk about a Catch-22…!"

"Well, rather than spending our time going in circles while we wait to learn the outcome of Davidson's meetings, let me tell you about the interesting wrinkle in the Brenda Ryan case that *I* found out." Sara's face was now wearing a decidedly feline smile. "While you three were viewing properties with Tricia Vickery on Saturday, Curt had a second conversation with her daughter Rachel's ghost. Rachel remembered that Brenda was extremely interested in genealogy, and that she'd been researching the Cookson family."

That snagged Selena's attention.

"Brenda's birth name was Janet Cookson," she said.

Sara's smile widened. "Indeed. So, when Curt had his meeting with Brassard on Monday morning, he mentioned this to her. She had Brenda's phone and laptop brought up from evidence storage and found Brenda's research file, which she was kind enough to let him copy. He then gave the copy to me."

"And...?"

"Do you remember how we talked earlier about the possibility that there might be other heirs to Hermès's fortune besides Gertrude?"

"Yes. Wild oats sown after his arrival in America."

"He was single, so I've no doubt that he sowed an entire field of them," Sara said, "but that's not what Brenda found. If the records are correct, Gertrude had an older brother. He was born just three months after Hermès married his mother. It's no mystery what probably happened there. One year later, in 1912, Gertrude came along, and three months after that, the Smiths separated. Mrs. Smith took little Enzo with her, and Hermès ended up with baby Gertrude."

As far as Selena was concerned, there was no mystery there, either. Forced into a loveless marriage with a man who apparently wanted to keep her pregnant and in the kitchen, Mama had opted for freedom. From what they already knew about that family, it was a safe bet the separation had been anything but amicable. But there was still one question...

"I can understand splitting up the children if both parents are judged to be fit, but why would a mother not take the younger child, especially since Gertrude was an infant?"

Sara shrugged. "Who knows? Maybe the daughter was a child of rape and she didn't want to raise a constant reminder of that experience. Or maybe this was his way of punishing her for leaving him, by making the loss of her baby a condition of his agreeing to the separation. In any case, there had to be a lot of animosity between those two for him to disown his son like that."

"Unless Enzo wasn't his...?" Selena suggested.

"Huh! That's an interesting thought. And it might explain

why Lillian forgot to mention her other cousin when I interviewed her for this project." She shook her head sadly. "Lord, what a family!"

"So, are you saying that Brenda was able to trace her lineage back to Enzo Smith?"

"According to the file on her laptop, yes," Sara said. "And if he was, in fact, Hermès's biological son, and all the information she managed to unearth connected up accurately, then Gertrude was her great-great-grandaunt. And Lillian was—and is—her cousin."

"Carrying this train of thought to its logical conclusion, then, it would appear that before she was killed, Brenda was Gertrude's living relative, making her an heir to the castle." Selena paused to roll that around in her mind for a moment.

Meanwhile, Sara had gasped, inhaling her mouthful of tea. When her coughing subsided and she could speak again, she blurted, "The Davidsons are going to have a bird when they find this out."

"What do you mean?"

"The Cooksons are part of the Smith family tree, which means they're also part of the Friendly family tree. Prue is related to all three of the bodies that will have to be moved and buried—Lillian, Gertrude, and Brenda."

"You're afraid the police won't be able to track down Brenda's family so they can claim the body and make the funeral arrangements?"

"I'm saying we'd better keep our fingers crossed that they do step forward and claim the body. Otherwise, this entire project—and the Davidsons' marriage—could very easily fall apart."

On a hunch, Selena turned down Sara's repeated offer of toast and headed directly to the museum after finishing her tea. Davidson had made specific appointments to meet with the local representatives of the three organizations, but not for getting together with her and Curt. Apparently, they were going to be squeezed into whatever time slot happened to open up over the course of the day. If so, it would probably smooth the process if they were both on site when the Davidsons arrived. This was already a trickier situation than anyone had anticipated, and Selena saw no point in testing the patience of the man who could resolve it.

That Davidson had made one of his appointments with the Public Health Department was a promising sign. It meant he was at least willing to look into the possibility of removing Gertrude's remains from his property. As to the rest of it…? That was anyone's guess.

Summoning all the confidence she could muster on an empty stomach, Selena stepped through the entrance of the museum. The girl at the cash register—Amy?—took one look at her, pulled a box of cookies out from behind the counter, and beckoned to her to help herself.

"If you're looking for Mr. Wakefield, then you'd better take two, Ms. Watt. For the energy," she advised quietly, handing Selena a paper serviette. "He's not alone in his office. Ms. Davidson is back, and this time she's brought her lawyer. They barged through here about ten minutes ago, and neither one of them looked happy."

Amy didn't look happy either. She pointed surreptitiously to a large, stern-faced man who was closely inspecting each of the exhibits in turn, then sweeping the air around them with some sort of handheld device.

"He came in with them," she said. "When I asked him what he was doing, he flashed an ID card in my face and told me to mind my own business."

"What did it say on the card?"

"Security something or other. He put it away before I could read the rest of it. I warned him that the museum *is* my business, and that the artifacts on display are valuable, and if he damaged any of them he would be answering to the Historical Society."

Selena gave her an admiring nod. "You stood up to him. Good for you! And how did he react?"

"He wasn't intimidated, if that's what you mean. I'm about a centimetre away from calling the police. First our air conditioning gets hacked by ransomers, and now this," she fumed. "It's infuriating!"

"You're right, it is. But I think I know why these visitors are being so unpleasant, and I've got a feeling the PPS is already on their way here. I'm going to go join the meeting. You just sit tight and give that guy a dirty look from time to time. Okay? Let him know you're watching him like a hawk."

Amy narrowed her eyes and nodded grimly in response.

Selena squared her shoulders, dropped the serviette into the waste bin, and directed her steps to the tower. She paused in front of Curt's office door to arrange her features into an impassive expression. If her suspicion was correct, she would be walking into a fraught situation. Diplomacy would be needed, and diplomacy required calm.

When she could feel herself practically radiating zen, Selena turned the door handle and stepped inside, drawing the immediate attention of three pairs of eyes and freezing their owners into an eloquent tableau.

Curt sat behind his desk, his spine rigid and pressed against the backrest of his chair. Prue and Ben Davidson occupied two of the three guest chairs that had been set up facing his. Ben leaned forward, his face lowered, his limbs bunched. He looked like a predator about to pounce. Prue's body language, meanwhile, said she wanted nothing to do with him. She was tilted away from her husband, staring at him in shocked disapproval. Her lips were pressed tightly together. She looked on the verge of tears.

Selena made an educated guess as to what had just transpired. Then, firmly quashing her rising anger, she pasted a friendly smile on her face and said, "Sorry if I'm late. I got here as soon as I could."

The contempt in Ben Davidson's eyes as he watched her take the third guest chair seemed to chill the air. Or perhaps the drop in temperature meant Lillian was in the room, becoming annoyed with his attitude. Selena hoped it was the latter. It was always good to have a secret weapon in one's arsenal when dealing with a hostile opponent.

"Ah. The other one," Davidson said. He squeezed out each word as if it were juice from an orange.

Taking hold of her temper with both hands, Selena replied, "Excuse me? The other what?"

"The other one who has been putting nonsense into my wife's head. Or are there more accomplices waiting in the wings in case the two of you can't convince her that ghosts exist? Just how extensive *is* this con, anyway?"

At this, Curt got to his feet and leaned on his knuckles on the desktop, his complexion darkening.

"You think we're running a con?" he said hoarsely. "How *dare* you make an accusation like that!"

Selena glanced at Prue, who was now shrinking away from both men and looking as if she wished she could disappear altogether. *Hmm.* Perhaps it would be a mistake to try to mend the Davidsons' marriage. Perhaps these two were better off living separate lives.

And perhaps Selena would be buying the castle after all. Now, *there* was a thought...

"Did you really believe I wouldn't do my due diligence before coming up here, Wakefield?" Ben's strident voice yanked her back to the moment. "I know about the magazine article debunking fraudulent psychics, and I know how you forced the publisher to take you out of it."

"No, you don't," Curt informed him, putting an icy edge on each syllable. "You only know *that* I did. You don't know *how* I did."

"You threatened to drag both the journalist and the magazine into court and ruin both of them if that article so much as mentioned your name," Davidson declared.

"It's true that I threatened to bring a libel suit. But that's not what made them back down."

"Oh, yeah? Then what was it?"

"Proof that what the article said about me was a wishful fabrication," Curt countered loudly. "And if you'd kept digging past your own cognitive bias, you would have discovered that."

"Oh, please! If you're about to tell me that you turned them all into believers, don't bother. Any rational person knows that ghosts aren't real."

Prue closed her eyes as though surrendering to a physical blow. Seeing the tear that slid silently down her cheek, Selena couldn't be still any longer. "So, rather than admit to the possibility of something you can't explain, you're willing to let your wife live in fear that she's losing her mind?" she bristled.

"You keep out of this!" he snapped. "And why is it suddenly so cold in here?"

"Maybe you've pissed off a ghost, Mr. Davidson," she retorted, throwing each word like a dagger. "Lillian, is that you?" she added on impulse, and felt a momentary confirmation on the back of her hand.

Meanwhile, he had clenched his jaw so hard that she could see his facial muscles bulging. Through gritted teeth he told her, "There are... no... *ghosts!*"

"Actually, this building contains a number of them," said Nena pleasantly from the doorway.

No one had seen her arrive. Curt dropped back wearily onto his seat as she stepped into the room.

"And who the hell are *you* now?" Davidson snarled at her.

She didn't even blink. In a measured, dignified voice she replied, "I am Nenokaasi Cartier, the most senior member of the Historical Society available to meet with you today. And in response to your earlier statement, I would like to remind you that this museum was previously the Groverton Railway Station, the scene of a terrible accident that ended the lives of two dozen people in a most abrupt way. It would be unusual if none of their spirits remained on the premises."

"Really?" he said mockingly. "If you think I'm going to put even a gram of credence into that, you must take me for a fool."

Improbably, she beamed at him. "Oh, I know you're not a fool, Mr. Davidson, or you would not have been able to renovate your home. You see, you're not the only person present who has done their due diligence. Now, you and I have a meeting scheduled to begin in twenty minutes. The Society's office is upstairs and to the right. I'll be waiting for you there." She paused while turning to leave and added, still smiling indulgently, "By the way, the last time I checked, believing in ghosts was not a crime."

And with that, she was gone.

The expression on Ben Davidson's face as the door closed behind her was priceless. Lillian was probably laughing herself silly behind his back. Selena stole a look at Prue and was glad to see her sitting upright in her chair again, dabbing at her eyes with a tissue.

Curt cleared his throat. "You heard the lady. The clock is ticking. So, let's discuss the more mundane reason for your visit, shall we?"

Davidson started and looked around him as though suddenly wakened from a dream. He took a moment, apparently to gather his thoughts, then replied, "You're referring to the gravesites, I presume. The exhumations and reinterments… and the costs associated therewith."

"Yes. Since you're the owner of the property on which we expect to find Gertrude's remains, we felt it would expedite matters if the two of you were involved. As a living relative of both Gertrude McFadyen and Lillian Friendly, Ms. Davidson can provide the authorization required for the cemetery to move forward, and—"

"—and as her wealthy husband I can absorb all the expenses?" he supplied, sneering.

Curt drew himself up and continued firmly, "I was about to say that as the registered homeowner, you can give legal permission for the search for remains to proceed, both on the grounds and inside the house."

That took the wind out of his sails. "Oh. Of course."

"As for the various fees that will be charged, given that the Historical Society operates on a very tight budget—"

Eyes narrowed, Davidson cut in again. "Uh-*huh*! Here it comes…"

"—we were hoping that you could help us convince the participating organizations to reduce or waive them." Curt paused, his expression an outward reflection of what had to be a vigorous internal debate. Selena held her breath, waiting for the other shoe to drop.

Finally, he continued, "And because we sincerely believe that a successful search and reinterment will result in you and your wife being able to move back into the castle, as it's called hereabouts, thus providing you with a large, non-monetary benefit, we are respectfully requesting that you take our case pro bono as well."

Davidson had clearly not been expecting this. He leaned back thoughtfully in his chair.

"That's all you want from me? That I not invoice you for my time?" he asked.

Curt pulled the blue file folder out of its drawer. "We've

already done an enormous amount of research and legwork," he said, pulling on a pair of latex gloves before spreading the pages of Lillian's letter across his desktop. "This was the discovery that got everything started. It's the original. And in case you're wondering, it's been authenticated by an expert who works at the Royal Ontario Museum. He owns a cottage not far from here, and he owed me a favour."

The room went still as Davidson moved forward, read the letter, and returned to his seat.

"We estimate that Gertrude died in early February," Curt said, carefully placing the pages inside the file folder and the file folder back in the drawer. "The ground would have been frozen, and her husband wouldn't have wanted a mouldering corpse lying around, so we believe that he must have concealed it somewhere that had already been excavated, perhaps in a cold cellar under the veranda."

"Not necessarily," said Davidson. "All it says in that letter is that McFadyen disposed of her body. He might have thrown it into the furnace with some coal and burned it, leaving nothing for anyone to find."

Curt had been staring at something behind them. It was Lillian, most likely. He gave his head a sudden shake—as though to clear it, but Selena knew better—then said, "Perhaps, but isn't that a conclusion that should be reached after eliminating other possibilities? We believe our theory has merit, Mr. Davidson. All we're asking is that you permit us to test it."

"How? By tearing up my finished basement? By digging up my lawn? Dismantling my porch? Who's going to absorb the cost of repairing my home when you're done prospecting for bones, Wakefield?"

And just like that, the belligerent lawyer was back. It took all of Selena's self-control to quash her indignation and leave his questions unanswered…

...because they wouldn't be prospecting, would they? Lillian knew where Gertrude was and could lead them right to her. Unfortunately, the very mention of a ghost would not be a good idea right now.

"I understand your concern, but there are ways to minimize the damage," the curator replied mildly. "Ways that the police may have access to. I understand you have an appointment with Staff Sergeant Brassard later today. I'd like to sit in, if you don't mind, and perhaps we can come to some sort of arrangement with them...?"

Davidson's lips quirked in a calculating grin. "Persuade them to loan us their technology and expertise, you mean, without levying a fee?"

Curt smiled back at him. "Think you can accomplish that?"

"I don't know. But I'm certainly up for the challenge."

"Pro bono?" he ventured.

"We'll see. It depends on the outcome of my meeting upstairs."

He'd said "my", not "our". Prue had caught that as well, Selena noted. Ms. Davidson remained firmly settled on her chair when her husband stood up to leave. She responded to his inquiring stare with an elevated chin and a toss of her head.

"Had enough of him, have you?" Selena murmured as they watched him shrug and stride out the door.

Prue's shoulders sagged. "He told me we were coming up here to challenge Lillian's claim. Talked about her as if he believed me when I told him she was real. And the whole time he thought—" She paused to wipe away the tears that welled once more in her eyes. "I'm so sorry, Mr. Wakefield. I had no idea he would be so... so..."

"Suspicious? Badgering?" Selena offered.

"Stubbornly skeptical," Curt concluded, locking his desk drawer and pocketing the key. "Don't worry. Nena's got him now. And Brassard is on our side. He'll come around. In the meanwhile, if you ladies will excuse me, I have a security specialist to deal with. Apparently, Amy told Nena that our environmental controls had been hacked, and Nena reported it to the Chair of the Historical Society, who then alerted the security company, who sent us an expert this morning to scour the museum for unwanted technology. He'd better be finished and waiting to give me his report, because it's time to open our doors to the public."

As he ushered them out of his office, Selena turned to Prue and said, "I skipped breakfast this morning and am wishing I hadn't. What say we find a little restaurant and get something to eat?"

"That sounds good to me. And we can leave a trail of breadcrumbs for Ben to follow... to a different place," she added darkly. "I think I would lose my appetite if he joined us for a meal right now."

So. It seemed there was some Friendly in this woman after all, Selena mused.

Twenty-Four

"The museum is clean, sir. Your computerized systems show no unauthorized access, and security around the exhibits is tight as a drum."

"Good."

Curt took the offered stylus and signed the form on the iPad the inspector held out to him. The Society had opted for the premium package, meaning that extra sweeps of the entire building could be requested as needed at no additional charge. So, the annoyance and intrusiveness of the past couple of hours had been for nothing, in both senses of the word.

As Security Plus marched out the front door, Ben Davidson emerged from the tower. He halted in the space between the two exhibit halls and turned his head this way and that, shooting displeased looks into them by turns.

Curt was suddenly aware of a throbbing sensation at his temples.

Terrific.

He took a moment and several deep, calming breaths before approaching the lawyer.

"Looking for someone?" he asked.

"What have you done with my wife, Wakefield?" Davidson huffed.

Purposely keeping his own voice light and chatty, Curt replied, "Not a thing. She's gone out with Selena. They're having coffee somewhere. Or maybe it's brunch. Then I believe they're planning to spend some time shopping. They said they would text you when they were ready to meet up again. So, it appears you're on your own for a while."

Davidson fixed an icy grey stare on his face. "This was *your* doing, wasn't it?"

Widening his own eyes, Curt protested, "Mr. Davidson, your wife is an adult. If she wants to go have a cup of coffee while you're busy in a meeting—"

"You're right. It was *her* doing," he muttered angrily.

The throbbing at Curt's temples was morphing into an ache. Nearing the end of his patience, he blurted, "Does any of that really matter? You came here to do something. What was it?"

The lawyer drew himself up and informed him in menacing tones, "It was to have you arrested for fraud."

Inside Curt's brain, something snapped. Through a scarlet fog, he heard himself say, "Okay, then! Let's do it! What time do you want me to meet you in the parking lot of the PPS detachment?"

"My appointment is at one o'clock, but—"

In for a penny...

"Good! I'll see you there." With that, Curt marched past him, on his way to the tower. He was itching to know what had transpired during the lawyer's meeting with Nena. And then he had an important phone call to make.

Curt pulled into the PPS parking lot right behind Davidson's car. Driving into a spot in the visitors' area, he turned off the ignition and said to the two greyscale figures in the back seat,

"Remember what I told you, now. Brassard is the only one besides me who knows you'll be present, so you'd better behave yourselves in there."

"*Sir, yes, sir!*" Barbara and Lillian replied in unison.

He groaned under his breath. One of these ghosts had been a bad influence on the other. He just wasn't sure which one was which.

Curt checked to make sure both the letter and the pendant were securely concealed in his inner jacket pocket. Folding the pages and putting them back into their envelope had been a calculated risk considering their age, but he'd felt that carrying the blue file folder—or anything like it—into this meeting would pose a much greater one.

As he left his vehicle and fell into step beside Davidson, Curt's pulse was racing. Today was a first for him—a gamble that could have serious consequences for someone besides himself.

In the past, every lie he'd told, every misconstruction or wrong assumption he'd fostered had been for the sole purpose of protecting the secret of his paranormal gift. There had always been some stress associated with these deceptions, but years of success had dulled its sharp edges. By now, the tightening at his temples and across his shoulders was a familiar sensation, one he could anticipate feeling whenever ordinary folk came nosing too close to the truth. Until now, Curt had lived his life, comfortable in the knowledge that the odds were with him, and that even if he lost his bet, the only person harmed would be himself.

This time was different.

This time, he was banking not on his own memory but on the word of a ghost, whose recollection of events might or might not be reliable. Not to mention that while still alive, Lillian had shown herself capable of doctoring the facts to suit her own purposes.

What made it even worse, though, was that this time he wasn't taking the chance alone. Others were counting on him to win. Having Brassard in his corner was a plus, to be sure, but Davidson had the instincts of a predator, and Curt had never preyed on anyone in his life. The outcome of this match was uncertain. Just thinking about all the ways it could go wrong was pulling sweat from his palms. He wiped them surreptitiously on the sides of his trousers.

The two men entered the building, identified themselves to the constable at the front desk, and got into the elevator car together. From the corner of his eye, Curt caught glimpses of Lillian leaning casually against the stainless steel handrail, her head tilted appraisingly. Barbara was probably standing behind him. With effort, he resisted the urge to turn around and look.

Davidson pushed the button for the second floor, then stood, ramrod-stiff, glaring straight ahead. "I don't know what you're up to, Wakefield, but it's not going to work," he growled.

Not trusting his voice, Curt responded with silence.

"Don't you worry, Mr. Wakefield, we've got your back," Barbara's voice assured him.

And Lillian chimed in, *"We won't let him lay a glove on you."*

He swallowed hard. Imagining how they might defend him wasn't exactly helping his nerves.

When the elevator doors slid open, he let Davidson precede him into the corridor and then into Brassard's office. The staff sergeant had evidently been warned of their arrival. She stood behind her desk, nodding a greeting to each of them as they entered the room, then gesturing an invitation to them to take the two guest chairs already drawn up across from her own.

"Your timing is excellent, gentlemen," she told them as she sat down facing them. "I have just received word from

Forensics that their work at the crime scene is completed. This means you can proceed with your search of the premises."

Davidson reared back in surprise.

"That is why you requested this meeting, is it not? Why you have come up here from the city? To authorize the search of your home in a matter unrelated to the suspicious death that recently occurred there?"

His cheeks flushing pink, he corrected her sharply, "No, I asked to meet with you to discuss the possible arrest of this charlatan."

Brassard's expression hardened. "You wish me to take Mr. Wakefield into custody?" She pulled a letter-sized notepad from beneath her desk and picked up a pen, preparing to write. "*B'en alors.* Bearing in mind, of course, that the filing of false charges is a punishable offence under Canadian law, would you please tell me what crime you believe he has committed?"

"He has fraudulently misrepresented himself as a medium, on more than one occasion."

"I see. May I assume, then, that you are acting on behalf of multiple complainants in this matter?"

She gazed at him expectantly.

"Just one," he admitted. "My wife."

"Liar!" Barbara and Lillian exclaimed together.

"She would never—! She was horrified by his accusations!" Barbara declared, and Lillian commanded him, *"Tell them, Mr. Wakefield!"*

Throwing his shoulders back, Curt silently shook his head. Brassard was handling this, and she knew what she was doing.

"As you must be well aware, Mr. Davidson, there are steps that need to be followed before a formal charge can be laid," she was saying. "Were you an eyewitness to this alleged fraud?"

"No. My wife told me about it, though, in detail."

"Ah. In that case, since you are here without her, she must have given you a signed affidavit. May I see it, please?"

Davidson opened his mouth as though to speak, then closed it again.

Watching the conversation unfold, Curt felt a surge of admiration. He'd heard about the intelligence and efficiency of this PPS officer from Sara's brother, and now he was seeing it for himself. Brassard hadn't wasted a minute. With a single question, she had just pulled the rug out from under a big city lawyer who was used to getting his way.

Davidson stiffened in his chair, clearly realizing that he was about to land on his ass. "I don't have it in writing," he replied tersely.

Behind Brassard, two ghosts high-fived each other. Curt saw that and had to cough to disguise the beginning of a chuckle.

"Well, then." Brassard set her pen down on the desktop and leaned forward on her elbows. "If you did not consider your wife's complaint grievous enough to warrant either taking a written statement from her or bringing her here to give one to me, then there is nothing to be done at this time."

"I *did* plan to bring her here, dammit, but—" Shooting a dagger look at Curt, he grated, "We got separated."

"She's out with a friend, doing some shopping," Curt supplied pleasantly.

"Oh? It seems to me that you and your wife are not on the same page, Mr. Davidson. Perhaps you should discuss this matter further with her before proceeding with any legal action," said Brassard, sharpening her tone to add, "And in the meantime, I can give you some information that your 'due diligence' would not have uncovered… but mine did."

The lawyer's already-flushed face grew even redder.

"Damn! This girl is good!" Lillian remarked.

Brassard reached under her desk again and came up with a thickly-papered file folder. "I can't make you a copy of this, but I can let you see it," she said, opening the folder and sliding it towards him. "These are all crimes that Mr. Wakefield helped my predecessor in this office to solve, by pointing him in the direction of evidence that he had not previously considered. He has broken six cases since three years ago, and I am about to close two more thanks to the verifiable information Mr. Wakefield has provided me of late.

"Where this investigative gift of his comes from, I cannot say for sure. Perhaps he possesses a remarkable combination of observation and deduction, like Sherlock Holmes, or some form of ESP, or—who knows? Its source is not important. All that matters to me is that its reliability has so far been perfect."

"So, you're telling me he's the proverbial gift horse and I shouldn't be looking into his mouth?" Davidson's expression reminded Curt of someone who had just bitten into a lemon.

"I am not telling you to do or not do anything, sir. I am only saying that I have seen enough evidence to be convinced that I can trust his crime-solving instincts. You are, of course, free to examine the evidence available to you and come to your own conclusions."

"You're referring to the human remains that he claims are concealed somewhere on my property, I take it."

"If the results of that search would help you make your choice, then yes," she replied evenly. "But since you own the home and our forensic interest in it has reached an end, your consent is required in order for that search to take place. With an indemnity provision, *b'en sûr*. The house is insured, I presume?"

"It is," he said grimly. "All right, then, you have my con-sent, but only on the condition that there be witnesses present from every entity or organization involved in the process. I want as many eyes as possible on the person or persons who instigated it, so that when the search comes up empty, people will know who to blame for wasting their time." Turning to Curt, he added, "And then I'll have evidence that you're a fraud, and I will take you and your accomplices to court."

"*What a horrible man!*" Barbara exclaimed.

"*There won't be any blame, Mr. Wakefield,*" Lillian assured him. "*I know exactly where to look.*"

Nena had apparently been busy during Curt's absence. When he returned to the museum, he found her sitting behind his desk, speaking on the land line phone.

"He just walked in, J. D.," she said, glancing up and waving to acknowledge his arrival. "Hold on for a second and I'll ask him." Addressing Curt, she added, "Has Mr. Davidson given his consent for the search to proceed?"

"Yes. He did it in front of an unimpeachable witness. Now we have to assemble a live audience for it. Including you, J. D.," he added, raising his voice to be heard at the other end of the call.

She put the phone on speaker for DeLucci's response.

"Well, if I must," came the pinched tenor voice of the president of the cemetery. "Do you know when this event will be taking place?"

"It depends. When can the third grave be ready?" Curt asked.

He heard a loud and disdainful-sounding sniff. "Tomorrow afternoon, at the earliest. I was just telling Ms. Cartier that we have two funerals scheduled for today."

"*Right,*" Lillian remarked sardonically. "*People in Groverton are dropping like flies.*"

"That's enough," Curt warned her.

"Indeed it is," DeLucci responded. "May I assume that

there will be no question as to the identity of the deceased this time?"

"None," he replied, mentally crossing his fingers. "But just in case someone feels the need for a DNA test, we should probably plan for a Friday reinterment at the earliest. Davidson is anticipating property damage and wants to have an insurance adjuster on the premises, someone he's bringing up from the city. And it wouldn't surprise me if he pulled strings and dragged a CBC news crew out to cover the event as well."

DeLucci made the snorting sound that was his version of laughter. "You know what they say, Wakefield—any publicity is good publicity. I'll get Andrew and Farhan working on that third grave first thing tomorrow morning. Goodbye for now. And thank you for the update, Ms. Cartier. Much appreciated."

Nena terminated the connection but made no move to vacate Curt's chair.

"I gather your meeting with the police went as well as could be expected?" she ventured.

"For the first act of what could turn into either a tragedy or a comedy, yes," he said, sinking with a sigh onto one of the guest seats. "What were you and DeLucci discussing when I walked in?"

She gave him a triumphant smile. "We were arriving at a compromise solution to one of our problems. You're going to love it."

"Oh?"

"Rather than digging Lillian up and moving her to the third grave, I've suggested simply giving her a different tombstone, one with accurate information on it. The third grave marker will have to be made regardless, and a third burial site excavated. However, it occurred to me that Gertrude probably wouldn't have *wanted* to be buried next to her abusive husband, so it would make more sense to put her into the third grave, wherever in the cemetery that happens to be, with the existing stone relocated to mark it."

Lillian perched herself on the corner of the desk and crossed her legs, frowning as she considered Nena's proposal. After a moment, she said, *"I could live with that."*

The irony of her statement drew a hoot of laughter from Barbara, who had been standing in the middle of the room. *"Not if you were living, you couldn't,"* she pointed out.

"Then I guess it's a good thing I'm dead, isn't it?" Lillian returned with a knowing grin and a lilt in her voice.

Pushing the distraction of their banter aside, Curt said to Nena, "And you're certain DeLucci is in agreement with this?"

"Yes. J. D. isn't hard to get along with if you know how to approach him. I reminded him how messy and time-consuming a job it would be, moving those two sets of remains around, and how happy it would make his nephew Andrew—and by extension Andrew's mom—if a way could be found to simplify the task. Anyway, my solution cuts the bill from the cemetery by more than fifty percent."

Curt did the mental math. "That would drop the cost enough that Davidson just might agree to cover it."

"Or split it with the Society. That would probably be an easier sell," she told him.

"You're right. I love it," he declared. "Now let's see what kind of magic we can work on the Department of Public Health."

Twenty-Five

Dinner at Sara's place Wednesday evening consisted of Chinese takeout—and a grilled cheese sandwich with microwaved fries for Donnie, who kept insisting that the honey garlic spare ribs were sticky, the beef with mushrooms was slimy, the fried rice was dirty, and the chicken chow mein was full of worms.

"They're not worms, sweetheart," his mother assured him. "They're vegetables."

To seven-year-old ears this probably sounded worse. Selena had a hard time keeping a straight face as she listened to their conversation. Larry didn't bother even trying to suppress his smile.

Donnie leaned toward Sara and stage-whispered, "That's what they want their enemies to think."

"But they're crunchy," she pointed out reasonably. "Worms aren't crunchy."

He leaned back in his chair and crossed his arms stubbornly over his chest. "They are when they're wearing armour."

In the face of this childish logic, Sara could only throw up her hands in defeat. "Okay, fine! I'll stick our dinner in the oven to keep it warm while I make you a sandwich."

Meanwhile, Larry was laughing uproariously. "Hey, Sis," he managed between guffaws, "do you remember Mom telling you that she hoped you would one day have a child just like you? I think she got her wish."

Eric waited until the plate of crispy fries was placed in front of his brother. Then he leaned over and said quietly, "You know what those are, right? They're dead worms in coffins."

"*Mo-om!!*"

Wearing a martyred expression, Sara turned to Larry and declared, "I think she sent me one like you as well."

When at last the boys had finished eating and excused themselves from the table, the grown-up conversation could begin. Larry paused between mouthfuls of jasmine tea to ask Selena, "Now that you've met Ben Davidson, what do you think of him?"

"Quite honestly, not much," she replied. "For one thing, I'm having second thoughts about the future of that marriage. After he accused both Curt and me of running a con on his wife, and then insinuated that our only purpose in helping her was to scam him out of a bunch of money, Prue didn't even want to be in the same room with him. If Nena hadn't come along when she did, he and Curt might have come to blows."

"Nena," Sara repeated. "You're talking about Nena Cartier, Vice-Chair of the Historical Society?"

"She's the vice-chair? She didn't identify herself that way."

"She wouldn't. It's not her style. But she's the real power behind that throne. It was her vote that got me permission to renovate this place."

Selena smiled. "Davidson had a scheduled meeting with her this morning. He didn't recognize her when she came into Curt's office, but she clearly knew all about him."

"Yep. Nena does her homework. If she's in our corner, that big-city lawyer had better have his A game ready," said Sara.

"Speaking of Curt, I received a text message from him just before leaving the office this afternoon," Larry told them. "If you check your inboxes, I'm pretty sure you'll find a similar one. It's an invitation to witness the discovery of the secret room in the castle on Friday afternoon."

Both their smiles wilted, and Selena had to close her mouth in order to speak.

"Curt... is inviting us to our own search?"

"Don't shoot the messenger," Larry said. "I texted him back and found out that this is Davidson's doing. Apparently, our permission to search the property for Gertrude's remains has a string attached. He knows the Historical Society will be recording the whole thing, and he wants a copy of the video, and the right to do whatever he chooses with it, including upload it to the web."

"Great. He'll turn it into a reality show." Sara shuddered visibly with disgust.

"Trust me, Curt is no happier about it than we are," said her brother. "It's pretty obvious to me why Davidson is doing this. We haven't done anything he can sue us for, so he's hoping we'll come up empty and he can publicly embarrass us instead. It'll be Al Capone's vault all over again."

"Curt will be destroyed if that happens," Selena murmured sadly.

Two pairs of eyes stared questions at her.

She told them about the lawyer's "due diligence" and the damning magazine article he'd figuratively thrown in Curt's face earlier that day.

Sara's expression darkened. "That man is despicable," she fumed. "He doesn't deserve Prue *or* that house. You should submit your offer to buy it, Selena. Do it before he has a chance to take it off the market. And make it conditional on the property being returned to the way it was before Brenda died there."

"He won't go for it," she replied. "He won't want to be a penny out of pocket on any of our accounts."

"Isn't that what home insurance is for?" Sara said. "He does have insurance, right?"

Selena shook her head. "Insurance is for damage that happens without your permission, like a roof coming apart in a severe windstorm. Unfortunately, Davidson has given his full consent for whatever we have to do to the castle, so it's a safe bet that the repair jobs and clean-up following the search won't be covered by any homeowner's policy. Even if it were, there would be a deductible to pay, which in this case is likely to be a hefty amount."

Improbably, Larry was grinning like a Cheshire cat.

Sara stared at him with narrowed eyes. "What do you know, big brother?" she demanded. "Spill!"

"Curt didn't give me the details," he replied, leaning forward confidentially, "just told me that Nena had hammered out a deal with Davidson during their meeting, and that it was a compromise—not an ideal solution, but something both sides could live with. Apparently, one of the points they discussed was whose insurance company would be called in to assess the damage afterwards."

Sara inhaled sharply. "I'll bet the Society is designating the castle as a heritage property!"

Of course, Selena thought. Curt had probably set that process in motion when he'd tracked down the original blueprints and added them to the archives. And it made sense for the Society to fund the search for the cold cellar if it was part of an official restoration project. Once Gertrude was found and her sobbing spirit finally at peace, there would remain only one question: assuming it remained on the market and Davidson could be persuaded to sell it to her at a price she could afford, did Selena really want to live all alone in the castle?

She would have to reconsider that.

Curt wasn't the only person who had texted Selena while her phone was off. Sitting cross-legged on the bed in Sara's guest room that evening, she checked her inbox and found messages left by Tricia Vickery, Staff Sergeant Brassard, and Prue Davidson.

Tricia had found three more properties that she could view. Morning or afternoon worked just fine.

Brassard wanted to meet with her one morning soon regarding the progress being made in her cousin's murder case. Barbara was welcome to sit in.

Prue just needed to get away from Ben for a while and was wondering whether they could spend some time together.

Selena hadn't planned on remaining in Groverton on Thursday, but she made a couple of snap decisions and sent her replies.

To Tricia: *I'm interested. Please set up for tomorrow afternoon and text me the first address.*

To Brassard: *Is tomorrow at 10 a.m. okay? I suspect we'll both be busy Friday.*

To Prue: *Care to lunch and then go house hunting with me tomorrow?*

To Curt: *Need to pick up Barbara's pendant for a meeting with Brassard. Is 9:30 tomorrow morning convenient for you?*

Minutes later, her inbox was filling again.

From Tricia: *Will do. Thanks!*

From Prue: *Delighted! When and where shall we meet?*

From Curt: *No problem. We'll be expecting you.*

Brassard's text was an auto-response promising that she would be in her office at nine o'clock sharp the following morning. That worked.

Selena texted Prue back: *Let's meet 11:30 a.m. at same*

place we brunched before. I have a 10 a.m. meeting at PPS and don't expect to be late but will keep you posted.

Perfect! was the immediate reply.

And with that, Selena's whole next day was filled.

At exactly 9:25 Thursday morning, Selena parked her car in a spot near the entrance of the museum and approached the double front doors. Amy waved at her through the glass and hurried to let her in.

"Welcome back, Ms. Watt," she said, smiling. "He's waiting for you in his office."

"Alone this time, I hope?"

"Yes! And looking happier than I've seen him in weeks."

This boded well, Selena thought.

She knocked on his door, heard a cheerful "Come in!" and stepped through the doorway.

Curt glanced up, appearing as relaxed as though he'd just downed three glasses of retsina. He closed the magazine he'd been reading and set it aside. "So, you have an appointment with Staff Sergeant Brassard this morning?"

"She's going to update me on Barbara's case and suggested I bring her along."

"Then it's probably good news. She knows what ghosts can do when they're upset. You'll be attending the event tomorrow afternoon, I trust?"

"Wouldn't miss it for the world. Is there anything you need me to help with?"

"Nope. Nena's taken charge. She assures me that everything is well in hand. However, there is one favour you can do me, if it's not too much trouble." He gestured her toward the guest chairs in front of his desk.

"Name it," she said, settling onto one of them.

"Remember those two properties we viewed with your realtor last week?" She nodded. "I need to have a word with the ghost in the second one—Reverend Upworthy."

"It shouldn't be a problem, since I'll be seeing Tricia this afternoon, to visit three more places. I can ask her to give us another look at that one while we're at it. And now you've made me curious."

He shrugged dismissively. "It's just an idea I've had. I don't want to jinx it by talking about it before I've spoken with him. Text me the time when you want me to meet you there, and… trust me when I tell you that if this works out, it's going to make a lot of people very happy."

Curt reached into his desk drawer and brought out the pendant. Selena hesitated briefly. Plagued by a feeling of guilt, she hadn't worn the necklace in weeks, hadn't even wanted to carry it on her person. Today, however, that feeling was gone. For this meeting, regarding this matter, it seemed appropriate to let the pendant be seen, and so she took it from him and put the chain around her neck.

As she left the building and walked toward her car, she couldn't help wondering how many of those people Curt had mentioned were living, and how many were not. And whether Barbara would be one of them.

"Ms. Watt," Brassard acknowledged, waving Selena toward one of the chairs on the other side of her desk. "You are right on time. Thank you for coming. I trust your cousin is here as well? Excellent," she added, glancing down at the hand that Barbara had evidently touched to signal her presence.

"You indicated that there had been some progress made in her murder case."

"Yes. Fernando Galliardo's remains turned out to be a trove of evidence. Not only is the man charged with the unlawful deaths of both Ms. Cournoyer and Mr. Galliardo currently awaiting trial in Toronto, but we have been able to connect him to two additional sexual assaults in Ontario, and he may also be involved in the disappearances of a half-dozen young women in Manitoba and Saskatchewan. We are continuing to work in coordination with the police authorities in those provinces.

"Since the shared investigation is ongoing, I cannot give you any more detail than that. However, I want your cousin to know that her testimony, while unofficial, was the critical element leading to the apprehension of a dangerous criminal, and we are grateful for her assistance."

"And if she were able, I'm certain she would be thanking you for saying that," Selena told her. "Obviously, she won't be able to testify in court. Nonetheless, I think she should have the option of attending the trial, whenever and wherever it takes place. Do you have that information yet?"

"Not at the moment, I am afraid. The best I can promise is that I will notify you as soon as a court date has been added to the calendar."

"Then I guess we'll just have to wait to hear from you. Was there anything else?"

Brassard flashed her a pro forma smile. "Perhaps later, Ms. Watt. That is all for now."

The brunch place Selena and Prue had selected was a fair-sized family restaurant located at the traffic-lighted intersection of two secondary streets near the middle of town. Since the driving time from one end of Groverton to the other was never more than about fifteen minutes and their lunch date didn't begin for another hour, Selena had plenty of time to arrange the extra house-showing with Tricia Vickery and return Barbara's pendant to Curt at the museum.

She found him sitting on a bench on the boarding platform, his gaze captured by something on the far side of the railway track. Another ghost, maybe?

"So?" he said as she lowered the pendant by its chain onto

his outstretched palm.

"The case against Barbara's killer is solid, but it could be a while before a trial date is set."

"That's a shame," he said. Meanwhile, the grin on his face belied every word.

Selena understood. The longer it took for her attacker to be put away, the longer Barbara could remain on the mortal plane with Lillian.

"And Tricia wants to show us the former brothel at one o'clock," she continued. "Does that time work for you?"

"I guess," he replied. "My business there shouldn't take long."

"Prue will be joining us, by the way. I'm meeting her for lunch in a few minutes. Okay, I've given you my news. Now, what have you got for me?"

"Not much. Nena and Davidson have taken over my office, as well as the burden of arranging for tomorrow's festivities. They're expecting quite a turnout. They've been talking to the Coroner's office, Public Health, lining up muscle from the trades to handle any demolition that needs doing, renting equipment... even alerting the paramedics and the fire department to be ready, just in case they're needed. It's the whole kit and caboodle, as Lillian would say."

"So you get to be a bystander, like the rest of us."

"Not quite. I get to bring Lillian, who's going to be pointing us in the right direction... I hope. *And* Barbara," he added after a pause. The rise in his voice and the exasperation on his face were clear indications that he was responding to a ghost determined not to be left out of things.

"And...?" Selena prodded him.

"And what?"

"You're going to make me ask you?" she said impatiently. "Okay, then. Has the castle been designated as a heritage property? Yes or no, Curt."

When he replied, she heard a note of resignation in his voice. "It hasn't yet, but before anyone sets foot inside it tomorrow, it will be. Nena's called a meeting of the Historical Society this afternoon to rubber stamp her deal with Davidson, and that's part of it."

Huh. As she headed back toward her car, Selena added this complicating factor to the decision she would have to make. Home maintenance could be expensive. Did she want to live all alone in a building that was not only large enough to house a family of four but was also subject to the Society's laundry list of rules?

"Thank you for letting me tag along with you today," Prue said as she scooted over to the middle of the padded bench in their booth at the restaurant. "If I had to spend another minute listening to him go on about—well, you already know how he feels." She turned over one of the menus their server had left on the table and perused the lunch selections. "He's obsessed with that house," she muttered.

"And how about you?" Selena asked, genuinely curious. "Once the excitement is past and the dust has settled, are you going to want to move back into it?"

Prue lifted her gaze from the menu and replied earnestly, "To be honest, I'm not sure. I *could* move up here. I like what I've seen of Groverton, and I've got a wonderful staff who can take over running my Toronto branch while I expand the decorating business northward. That was the original plan, anyway. Ben was going to do much the same thing—sell his share of the practice to his partner and open a law office in Central Ontario. Like there isn't a spot in the province that can't use another civil litigator," she concluded darkly.

Civil? That wasn't the word that came to mind when Selena recalled their last encounter. Prue huffed out a breath. Evidently, she remembered it the same way.

Selena returned her attention to the menu, a moment before their server—Pam, according to the badge on her vest—came to take their orders. They chose identical lunches: chicken Caesar wraps and water to drink.

Birds of a feather.

As Pam spun away with the menus in hand, Prue sighed and leaned back in her seat. "You were asking about the house." She bit her lower lip, then continued, "I really like the house. I do. I absolutely loved furnishing and decorating it, and I would jump at the chance to do it all over again. Moving in, though...? The answer to that depends on whether I would have to share it with Ben."

Selena stared a question at her.

As though reading her thoughts, Prue said, "I've decided to contact a divorce lawyer. Ben doesn't know yet. And even if he did, he's too distracted by other matters right now to care. However, since you asked me first about the house, I have a similar question for you. Once the castle is no longer haunted, will you still be interested in buying it?"

"I'm not sure I'll be able to afford it. By this time tomorrow, it will be a heritage property, and the asking price will probably be closer to its actual market value. That's why I'm looking at homes today—I'm exploring alternatives. Like you, I'm very attracted to Groverton and ready to relocate my business here."

That caught her attention. "Really! What sort of business is it?"

For the next half hour, they ate their wraps and compared notes. By the time they were ready to leave the restaurant, they'd given each other crash courses on event planning and interior design, and Selena was impressed by how similar she and Prue were in taste and temperament. It was almost as if they were fated to be friends.

Prue had taken a taxi to this meeting, so Selena would be

driving both of them around. As they walked toward her car in the parking lot, a cool breeze tumbled Selena's hair, prompting her to gaze skyward. Thick, grey-bottomed clouds were gathering overhead. Had showers been forecast for this afternoon? She couldn't remember. With luck, the rain would hold off until after they'd viewed all four properties. She was wearing sandals today and didn't want to be wandering around someone else's basement in her bare feet.

Tricia and Curt had already arrived by the time Selena pulled up at the curb in front of the first place on the list. Tricia turned around to face them as they approached. Meanwhile, Curt remained scowling at the front door of the former gift shop as though daring it to make a wrong move. Or maybe he was just listening intently to something Rachel's ghost was telling him.

Selena stepped up to stand beside him. "How much time do you need?" she murmured.

"Fifteen or twenty minutes ought to do it," he replied quietly, shifting his letter-sized, spiral-bound notebook from his right hand to his left.

Prue had stopped to talk with the realtor. Whatever she'd said was clearly something Tricia wanted to hear, because both women were smiling as they led the way inside the building.

"Did you have any lingering questions about this property, Mr. Wakefield?" the realtor asked.

"Not really. I'm here to answer any that Ms. Watt may have about its history," he replied pleasantly.

Her smile evaporated. "You're monitoring the visit for the Society?"

"Monitoring?" he repeated, and shook his head. "No, I'm just a friend of Selena's, offering support. And until she needs some, I think I'll stay right here while the three of you do whatever you need to in the rest of the building."

"Thank you. We will," she said firmly, adding for Prue and Selena's benefit, "beginning with the apartment upstairs. Shall we?" With that, she swept out of the room, clearly expecting the other two to follow her.

As she climbed after Prue and Tricia to the second floor, Selena looked down at Curt, visible through the door to the storefront. He had opened his notebook to a page with words on it, hand-printed in large block letters, and was turning it to show to the ghost behind the glass-topped counter. Selena was able to read the message as well:

I CAN SEE YOU.

LET'S TALK.

From the apartment, the realtor led the two women down to the basement. Warned in advance to play for time, Selena had drawn up a series of questions to ask whenever Tricia sounded as though she was about to return them to the main floor. But the other woman had been ready with quick answers, and Selena was running out of things to say that might prolong the showing. All she could do was hope that the conversation in the gift shop had proceeded with equal efficiency.

Then Curt came clattering down the stairs. "I'm sorry to leave so suddenly, but I have to get back to the museum," he announced excitedly. "When you've finished looking at houses, stop by—both of you. We need to talk."

Prue and Selena exchanged curious looks.

Meanwhile, Tricia Vickery heaved a sigh, most likely of relief.

"What did you say to her earlier?" Selena asked Prue when they were once more in the car, on their way to the next address.

"Pretty much what I told you over lunch—that I was considering opening a branch of my business in Groverton and might therefore need her services. What were you and Mr. Wakefield whispering about before we went inside?"

Mentally crossing her fingers, she replied, "I was asking him how much time he could spare me. Apparently, it was only a few minutes."

"Has he gone out looking at houses with you before?"

"Yes. I value his opinions. He... notices things that I wouldn't."

"Well, I'm sure we'll find out what tore him away from you when we see him at the museum later. In the meantime, I'll gladly be your second pair of eyes."

Selena cast her a sideways glance. "And my second pair of ears?"

"I beg your pardon?"

"Did you hear anything unusual while we were in that building?"

Prue thought for a moment, frowning. "Not really, no. A house that old won't still be settling. But if I detect the sound of small scurrying feet overhead or between the walls, I'll be sure to let you know."

The remaining three properties were pretty similar to one another—Selena's list of requirements had narrowed the field of search considerably—but the next-to-last building came closest to touching the bar set by the castle. It had recently been built and was on a residential street, two blocks from a main intersection, and the first floor had a large front room that could easily be converted into a business space. Tricia promised to look into the zoning regulations but didn't feel that getting a variance would be a problem. Now, if only Selena could be sure the place wasn't haunted!

Perhaps she could convince Curt to view it with her on the weekend...?

No, she decided, considering what would be happening the

next day it was probably wiser not to raise the subject with him until the dust had settled from "Operation Hidden Vault", however long that took.

After cards and promises of future meetings had been exchanged with the realtor, Selena and Prue headed to the museum, per Curt's request.

Amy smiled at them as they entered. "He's expecting you," she said, and sent them straight along to his office.

"You've learned something interesting," said Selena as they sat down facing him across his desk. It wasn't a guess. His face was wearing an expression that trod the line between satisfied and smug.

"I've been looking into our friend, the Reverend Upworthy," he replied. "Apparently, he began his ecclesiastical career under a different name. He was Joshua O'Donnell, a deacon of the Anglican Church in Ontario. For reasons unknown to him at the time, the synod kept moving him from parish to parish, then offered him a missionary posting in Nigeria."

"It sounds like their way of sweeping him under the rug," Prue remarked.

"My guess is they felt he needed to shape up. While he was there, someone took him aside and read him the list of rules he had to follow. That was when he figured out that he had no real future in the Anglican Church. He would never be more than a deacon, and he would most likely never have his own parish. He left Africa before his mission trip was up. Came back to Canada, changed his name and his approach to religion, and took his show on the road. And with every performance, every come-to-Jesus rally, he was symbolically giving the finger to the governing body of the Church. Or so he thought. At the end, he had a lot of deep regrets."

"How did you find all this out?" Prue asked. "Did he write his autobiography or something?"

Selena knew the answer but said nothing. This decision wasn't hers to make.

"I… got the information from Upworthy's ghost, while you two were keeping Tricia busy in other parts of the house."

Prue's eyes went saucer-wide. "There's a ghost in the house? And you spoke to him?" she whispered excitedly.

Curt looked pleased by her reaction. "Not out loud. That would have drawn attention. I showed him some printed questions and he answered them."

"But how did you get him to open up about his feelings?"

"When a ghost is angry, the temperature drops. The first thing I noticed about Upworthy was that he was making all kinds of angry noises, but there was no chill in the air. That told me he was putting on an act. Whatever he was feeling, it wasn't anger. And it wasn't sadness, or Selena would have picked up on it. The more I learned about him, the more I realized that the emotion had to be shame, and my interview of him this afternoon confirmed it. All that fire and brimstone bluster he dished out while still living was just Josh O'Donnell compensating for his failure to measure up to his calling. And what keeps him tethered to the mortal plane is the knowledge of his final, worst possible failure—the man of God, dying in the midst of committing a deadly sin.

"As soon as I knew how I could help him, I made him a promise. Do you still have the heirloom brooch with you?"

"Of course. It's in my purse."

"Would you mind leaving it with me over the weekend? I'm working on a way to transfer Lillian's spirit from the letter to something else that matters to her, and you told me earlier that she could have the brooch if she wanted it. So I was thinking—"

"Take it," Prue interrupted him, fishing in her handbag for the tissue-wrapped bundle. "And keep it. I meant what I said. It belongs to her."

"Is this going to create a problem between me and your husband?" he asked warily.

"No. He'll probably be glad I got rid of it."

"I'm referring to the ghost part of it. He's already convinced that I'm a fraud. If he decides I must have scammed you out of a piece of your jewellery—"

She drew herself up, a determined expression on her face. "Trust me, Mr. Wakefield, after tomorrow he's going to have much bigger things to worry about than the fate of a fifty-dollar pin."

Twenty-Six

Friday dawned surly, and its disposition didn't improve as the morning progressed.

The same could be said about Curt's mood.

His sleep had been shredded by nightmares, more than one of them about himself dying and becoming a ghost, tethered for eternity to the museum.

Knowing where these dreams had come from hadn't helped. The last time he'd felt this anxious had been on the eve of his and his mother's tour of the death camps of World War II when Curt had been nine years old. Even at that young age, he'd understood how severely and inevitably he was about to be tested. It hadn't mattered how neatly he'd laid out his clothing the night before, or how cleanly he separated the food on his breakfast plate. Following the rules hadn't been enough to protect him then, and it wouldn't save him this afternoon either. Not with all those uncomprehending eyes watching him succeed or fail.

The only bright spot on his horizon was the cameo brooch sitting on the desktop in front of him, but even that was a test. As he stared glumly at it, something his mother had once told him surfaced in his memory: *"Everyone you encounter in this life is going to have expectations of you, Curtis, and you must do your best to meet them. That is how we get along with others."*

Had she realized that "everyone" included people who had died decades or even centuries earlier? He would probably never know the answer to that.

Heaving a heartfelt sigh, he placed the brooch carefully in the drawer that already contained Barbara's pendant and Lillian's letter. Then he headed out to the boarding platform.

"That is a marching-to-the-gallows face if ever I've seen one," Clara declared as he rounded the corner of the building.

"Whatever is the matter, Mr. Wakefield?" said Ruth.

The two ghosts slid apart on their bench to give him room to sit between them.

"Something tells me I'm not going to be here much longer," he said.

"Well, why on earth not? You're a wonderful curator." Ruth gasped and put a hand to her mouth. *"You're not dying, are you? At your young age?"*

"No," he assured her, "but I'm about to do something that could get me fired, and I don't see any way around it."

"What can we do to help?" said Clara. *"Name it and we'll do it."*

It was sweet of them to offer, but the only thing these ladies were capable of was listening. So, he talked. He told them everything that was scheduled to happen that afternoon, and described all the planning that had gone into it. He enumerated the conflicting expectations of the people (both living and deceased) who would be present to witness it—who was counting on him to succeed, and who was hoping he would fail. And he confessed to not knowing which of these he was hoping for himself.

"In some ways, it's simpler if we *don't* find Gertrude's

mortal remains," he said. "As long as there's a cold cellar under that veranda. That's the thing I was most definite about, and it's the one part of the search that isn't backed up by a single piece of evidence on the mortal plane. The Historical Society pays my salary, so there's more riding on the outcome of this exercise than just a couple of tarnished reputations and some wounded feelings. In fact, I'm surprised Nena didn't simply fire me and take over when the kerfuffle first began."

"Is that what you would have done in her place?" Ruth inquired.

He had to consider for a moment. "Well, no, but that's because—"

"Because you're special?" Clara supplied. *"Don't be modest, Mr. Wakefield. It's true. I've been saying so right from the start, and I'll bet she recognizes it too."*

"I was about to tell you that it's because I have friends that I care about on both planes."

"Yes," said Ruth. *"And that's because you've had one foot on our plane and one on the mortal plane, which means you've been living a half-life in each place... which, if you think about it, isn't really living at all, is it?"*

"It was never my choice," he pointed out hotly.

"Perhaps not," she allowed. *"But it seems to me that you've got one to make now. You said that both people and ghosts have expectations of you. If you focus on satisfying the living, you risk failing the dead, and vice versa. But what do you think will happen if you try to please everyone?"*

The answer was obvious. "Then I may end up disappointing everyone," he admitted miserably.

"Or you might satisfy everyone," Clara cut in. *"For heaven's sake, Ruth, the man is teetering on the verge of the Slough of Despond. The last thing he needs is a shove from behind."*

The other ghost shot her a wounded look. *"I was merely showing him that there is a third alternative,"* she sniffed.

Sure she was, Curt thought wryly. Clara was rolling her eyes, but Ruth was right about one thing: Curt couldn't go into the afternoon's endeavour without a plan, and that meant making decisions. The assault on the castle was scheduled for two o'clock sharp. The involved parties were already assembling at the corner of Beech and Webber. If Barbara and Lillian were going to participate in this event, they needed to be briefed on their roles before it began.

"Thank you, ladies, you've been most helpful," he said, getting to his feet.

Overhead, the looming cloud cover was breaking up, dropping shafts of sunlight down onto the ground. He took that as a sign.

Two hours later, the sky was clear and sunny, the air temperature was about to reach a mid-afternoon high, and Curt was running fifteen minutes late. Turning onto Webber Street, he cruised past an entire convoy of vehicles that occupied the curb around the castle. Among them were a PPS van, an SUV with a Fire Department badge painted on the driver's side door, a flatbed truck with a small backhoe on it, and two pickups marked respectively with the logos of the cemetery and a construction company. Meanwhile, the coroner's wagon and an ambulance sat on the gravel path beside the building.

Davidson had said he wanted a lot of eyes on this event. Apparently, he'd gotten his wish. Other than a vacant stretch of curb beside a fire hydrant and the entrances to several driveways, there was no street parking available around the house at Beech and Webber for more than a block in any direction.

Curt swore under his breath. Well, he'd bent or broken so

many rules already. What was one more?

Driving around the block again, he yanked his steering wheel clockwise at the foot of the castle's driveway, then kept going right, coming to an abrupt halt in the middle of the front lawn. Curt looked in the rear-view mirror and saw two greyscale women in the back seat, both staring at him in disbelief.

"Desperate times, ladies," he told them over his shoulder.

Then his common sense kicked in. This situation was more frustrating than desperate, but what was done was done. The car was well and truly parked. What was the worst that could happen? A ticket under his windshield wiper? A tow to an impound lot? A lawsuit filed by Ben Davidson for… what? Trespassing? He'd already consented to a wholesale invasion of his property, for heaven's sake!

"Welcome to the party, Mr. Wakefield."

Brassard's voice jolted Curt back to the present. He glanced up and saw her standing, arms crossed, beside his left front fender. Her expression was stern, but her lips were twitching.

Oka-ay… He wasn't sure about this, but he liked it. Curt checked his pockets to make sure both the letter and the pendant were securely in place. Then he stepped out onto the grass.

"Is it all right if I leave my car here for a while, Staff Sergeant?"

"That is for the homeowner to decide," she replied. "For me, it's not a problem. Shall we go inside? The others have been waiting to begin."

"The room is in the basement," Lillian reminded him. He heard anxiety in her voice and fortified himself against it. They had a plan. It was going to work.

As they approached the entrance to the castle, Curt paused to take in the front of the building and give Barbara a chance to deke inside and look around. The steps up to the veranda were wooden, he noted. They didn't lead directly to the front doorway but were offset from it by about a metre. The veranda was a good two metres deep and made of wood as well. It was painted off-white, and the space beneath it was completely enclosed by stout-looking vertical planks.

"The veranda was not shown on the original blueprint," he commented to Brassard. "That means there could have been other modifications as well, such as a cold cellar under the front porch, entered via the basement. If so, and if your team couldn't find any sign of it earlier because it had been covered up by renovations or by McFadyen himself, then that's probably the 'secret room' we should be looking for."

Brassard hesitated for a couple of beats, then nodded once, decisively. "*B'en.* That will be our starting point." Unclipping a handset from her belt, she said into it, "Detective Izkari, would you please lead everyone into the basement? We will begin the search down there."

At that moment, Barbara emerged from the wall beside the front door, her expression triumphant. "*You were right! She's here! On the gallery overlooking the foyer. She cried when I told her about you, and that you want to help her, and her voice was kind of blubbery, so I didn't catch all of it, but I'm pretty sure she said she has something important to show you,*" she finished breathlessly.

Curt allowed himself a smile. Something important? That could only be evidence that the police had overlooked. So far, things were proceeding according to plan. It was still too soon to uncross his fingers, though. A couple of wild cards were in the mix, and one of them would welcome the chance to derail this entire rescue operation.

As Curt and Brassard stepped into the now-vacated foyer, he gazed upward and saw a greyscale version of the corpse he'd viewed in the morgue. Fully dressed this time, Brenda Ryan stood at the top of the stairs, staring wistfully down at him and wringing her hands. As their eyes locked, hers widened, and she began beckoning excitedly to him.

"What are you looking at, Mr. Wakefield?" Brassard asked.

Looking *at*. Not looking *for*.

In for a penny, in for a pound.

He drew a steadying breath and replied, "Brenda Ryan's ghost. I believe she may have hidden something on the second floor, something relevant to her death. She wants us to join her up there so she can show us where it is."

"This is all very well, but I am afraid we do not have time for a detour right now. There are people waiting for you to show them where to look in the basement, and you have already tried their patience once this afternoon," Brassard reminded him.

"That's my cue, isn't it?" Barbara piped up. *"If you'll just help me up the stairs...?"*

"I only need ten seconds, Staff Sergeant. Please."

"*B'en alors*. Be quick about it," she replied, frowning.

Curt raced up to the second floor landing and hung the pendant by its chain from the knob at the head of the banister. Then he hurried back down and kept going. There was no need to look over his shoulder. He could hear the voices of the two young women inside his head, already engaged in animated conversation.

Brassard hadn't overstated the impatience of the group milling around in Davidson's windowless, wood-panelled basement. The only friendly faces Curt saw as he walked into the middle of the room belonged to Selena and Larry, and even they weren't smiling at him.

"Ready when you are, C.B.," said Lillian. There was a ragged edge to her voice, as though she could sense that his plan was about to stall.

Maybe it was. Gertrude was one of the wild cards, and she was nowhere in sight. However, he could hear her moans.

They seemed to be coming from every direction at once. Prue Davidson could hear them as well. She had apparently backed herself into a corner, putting as much distance as possible between her and her husband. Now she was standing, stiff as a broomstick, with her hands over her ears and her features compressed in anguish. Selena was suffering also. She was sitting with her back to one of the walls, shuddering and hugging her shoulders as Larry stood helplessly nearby.

She shouldn't be here, Curt thought. *None of them should. We were so eager to solve this mystery that we've turned Gertrude's suffering into a public event. And now...*

"Are we going ahead with this or not?" Lillian demanded. *"Let's get it over with."*

"Where's Gertrude?" Curt muttered angrily.

"You need her to show you the door? Leave that to me," Lillian said, and drifted through a section of wall.

"What's the matter, Wakefield?" Davidson jeered. "Is your crystal ball on the fritz?"

Thankfully, no one laughed.

A moment later, Lillian poked her head back into the room.

"Here," she said, grim-faced. *"They're both in the cold cellar with me."*

Curt estimated the distance from her head to the end of the wall and announced, in a voice that he hoped would discourage anyone from questioning him, "Measure three metres from that corner and you should find the concealed entrance to a space under the veranda. Plus or minus a couple of feet."

"Okay! Masks and goggles, guys!" one of the construction workers—evidently the foreman—commanded the other two. "Everyone else, please go upstairs and wait for my all clear. Once we set to work, this will be an active demolition site, and we will not be able to guarantee the health or safety of any casual onlookers."

"Casual onlookers?" Davidson braced his legs and crossed his arms over his chest. "Let's get something straight, pal. My interest is hardly casual. The only reason I agreed to even allow you and your crew onto the property was that I was promised a video recording of this wild goose chase from start to finish."

"And you'll get it," Nena put in, smoothly inserting herself between the two men, then turning to face Davidson down. "The Historical Society makes and maintains a complete digital history of every property we protect, including, as of yesterday afternoon, this one that we're in right now. We also make copies of the edited footage freely available to anyone with an interest in the history of a particular building. We have an agreement, Mr. Davidson, and it will be honoured... by both sides."

"Oh, yeah? If you video stuff like this," he challenged her, "then why don't I see any cameras?"

"Perhaps because you're looking in the wrong places." She pointed upward, at the pot lights in the ceiling. Three of the bulbs were sharing space with small devices showing glowing green dots.

His jaw dropped. "Oh."

"Don't feel bad, Mr. Davidson. Many people fall into the trap of equating a small town with technological backwardness," she consoled him. "Our archivist has set up a live viewing station in one of the rooms on the main floor, where the air will be much safer to breathe while the work is going on. You can monitor its progress up there."

Defeated by reason, the lawyer could make no further objection. Davidson let himself be shepherded along with the other spectators toward the staircase.

Meanwhile, Curt was faced with a dilemma. As long as Lillian was in the cold cellar with her cousin, the letter to which she was tethered could not leave the basement. He didn't dare entrust it to one of the workers, and anyone else he might have handed it off to was a "casual onlooker", banned from the demolition site. If the basement were furnished, he could tuck it under a seat cushion temporarily. Unfortunately, that wasn't an option. Curt swore under his breath. Surely there was somewhere down here that could serve as a hiding place!

Casting increasingly frustrated glances around the room, he noticed something for the first time—a sliding pocket door. A hasty exploration revealed a modern two-piece washroom, with a medicine cabinet above the basin. Perfect!

Brassard was waiting for him when he reemerged. She held out a mask for him to put on. "Now would be an excellent time to pursue that other matter, would it not?"

He had to agree.

Oblivious to Gertrude's inconsolable moaning and Lillian's efforts to comfort her on the other side of the basement wall, the three workers had already begun ripping their way through a metre-and-a-half-wide swath of it, stripping away the layers one by one. They told a story of successive renovations and redecorations, these overlying layers—the laminated wood panelling atop the several-times-papered wooden board, and beneath it all an apple green painted surface, no doubt covering an abundance of modern blown insulation. As Curt and Brassard crossed the site, the air was already filling with dust and pollutants. What it would be like when the crew began hammering at the original concrete foundation, he didn't want to find out.

The viewing screen had been set up in the downstairs kitchen. On his way to the second floor, Curt heard two sets of voices, one from above and one from behind.

"They have to help someone else first, a woman who's been trapped in the basement for a very long time, but they'll be here soon, I promise!"

"…a shame… that's really nice panelling…"

"I tried so hard to reach her, but I couldn't get past the top of the stairs."

"Well, they're making short work of it, that's for sure."

"…because you're tethered to whatever you were thinking about when you died. With me, it's a pendant…"

"You'd better hope your insurance covers all of this, Ms. Cartier."

"It was supposed to be my insurance policy. I let him know I had it, and that he was safe as long as he kept the hell away from me. But then he came after me and… I was hoping he wouldn't find it, and terrified that no one else would…"

"Oh, wait! I hear someone coming. Let me check…"

"Wait—are those bricks? Son of a bitch! There really is a door under there…"

"Language, Andrew!"

"Sorry, Uncle Jeff…"

Barbara stepped through one of the upstairs doors and beckoned to him. *"We're in here, Mr. Wakefield."*

Curt retrieved the pendant and slipped it into his pocket. Then he turned to Brassard, who had come to a halt beside him. "They're in the middle room," he said, pointing. "Was that the crime scene?"

"No. The fatal beating took place in the bedroom at the end of the hall. But the blood evidence suggests that she did not die there."

Okay, that was enough talking. Barbara had crossed her arms and stood staring at him, her lips pressed tightly together. Any second now, the temperature around her would plummet.

"Shall we?" Curt said. He turned the knob and swung the door wide open… and walked into a roomful of cold air that pulled an involuntary shiver from him.

Strange. The greyscale figure in the corner of the room was

surveying him warily, he thought. Then he realized that it wasn't himself she was gazing at that way, but rather Brassard.

Barbara had noticed this as well. *"It's all right, Brenda,"* she said. *"Staff Sergeant Brassard can't see or hear us, but unlike the other cops, she knows we're real and—what's most important—she'll believe you."* Turning to Curt, she added, *"She's still getting used to being a ghost. And being alone and ignored up here for the past couple of weeks with Gertrude wailing non-stop in the basement… Well, you can imagine."*

Yes, he could, and normally he would sit and listen to her tell her story in full, but today there was no time for that.

"Ladies, I apologize for making you wait, and I'm truly sorry to have to rush you now, but we have to get back to the group before we're missed," he said, in as placating a voice as he could manage. "Brenda, please, tell us what you're tethered to and show us where it is so we can get you out of here and you can help Staff Sergeant Brassard solve your case."

"You promise? You promise you'll get him and make him pay for what he's done? For all the lives he's ruined?" Brenda's voice sounded on the verge of tears.

"Absolutely," he assured her, although that last bit had raised a red flag in his mind.

She stepped forward and pointed to the cold air return near the bottom of the wall. *"It's in there,"* she said, *"taped to the back of the cover."*

The moment Curt repeated this information to Brassard, she got on the radio and summoned a Forensics tech to the second floor. When he arrived with his kit, she told him, "Acting on an anonymous tip, I checked the rooms on this floor, and I think I saw a shadow inside that return cover. Would you process it, please?"

He gave her an odd look, then hunkered down with screwdriver in hand. "We seem to be getting a lot of anonymous tips lately," he remarked.

"*Ouais*," she replied tartly, "that tends to happen when there has been a major crime in a small town. This tip was in connection with the Brenda Ryan case."

Curt held his breath as the tech set the pair of screws from the return carefully to one side, then flipped the cover over for what was apparently supposed to be a cursory look at its backside. He saw the small brown envelope at the same time as the tech did.

"Huh! Good catch, Ma'am. And there's a number printed on it." The tech used his phone to snap a picture of the envelope before detaching it from its hiding place and spilling its contents into the palm of his latex-gloved hand. "This is a safe deposit box key. Did the anonymous source happen to mention which bank keeps the other one?"

Curt nodded encouragement at Brenda.

"*It's the Dominion Bank of Canada at Main and Elizabeth Streets,*" she replied. "*I used my mother's maiden name to open the account. She doesn't know about it.*"

Meanwhile, Brassard was replying to the tech, "No, but that is why we have detectives assigned to the case. Finding out such things is their job. And since you will be needed in the basement shortly to process another scene, you can seal the key and its envelope into an evidence bag for now and sign it over to me."

"Not a problem, Ma'am." A moment later, Brassard was tucking the bag into her inside jacket pocket and the tech was packing up his kit. "Is it just me," he remarked, "or is this room awfully chilly for a day in July?"

Curt and Brassard exchanged looks.

"It is a little cool," he said, "but… did you skip lunch? Low blood sugar can give you chills sometimes."

"Never mind," said the tech. He stood up and dusted off his trousers.

They all headed down the stairs together, three living people and two ghosts. Brenda hesitated briefly on the landing, but Barbara urged her forward, and she reached the foyer with a whoop of glee and a huge smile on her face.

"*I'm free!*" she exclaimed.

Well, not quite, he corrected her privately. The key had been liberated, and Brenda would be joined at the hip to whoever carried it around. For the time being, that was Brassard. And once it had been forensically processed…? Curt was willing to bet it would end up in his desk drawer, along with the pendant, the letter, and the brooch. He was amassing quite a collection of ghosts lately. Fortunately, they didn't take up much room.

The main floor kitchen was emptying out just as Curt, Brassard, and the tech arrived there. Clearly, they'd spent more time upstairs than they thought. The workers had broken through the bricked-up doorway and the dust had had a chance to settle. The foreman had pronounced the site safe for "casual onlookers". Now everyone was headed back to the basement to witness the discovery of Gertrude's remains.

Curt knew that they were there to be found. Hers and the baby's, according to Lillian. For him, the only suspense hinged on two questions: first, what condition might they be in after more than ninety years had passed; and second, what exactly was Gertrude tethered to?

Behind him, he could hear Barbara filling Brenda in on the reason for this gathering of living beings, and the path that had led them here.

"*Wait—Rachel's a ghost too? That is so cool! I mean, not that she's dead—that was a tragedy—but that we can still be friends, even though we're both—well, you know.*"

He swallowed a sigh. Barbara was right. This young woman had a lot to learn about being a ghost.

Meanwhile, the basement was much chillier than it had

been earlier, he noticed.

"As soon as we broke through, there was this sudden blast of icy air," one of the workers was saying as Curt walked by, on his way to fetch the letter from its hiding place. "No idea what it was or where it was coming from, I swear. I thought we were going to be flash-frozen and found years later, like woolly mammoths inside a glacier."

Curt could have told them what it was. It was the pent-up anger of a ghost that had been tethered to something in this cold, dark room for nearly a century. Best not to say it out loud, though. Brassard understood, and Nena, and Larry, Selena, and Sara. They would have to do for now.

Lillian had brought Gertrude out into the light, then had taken her to the end of both their tethers. Curt followed the sound of whimpering and spied them crouching together in a far corner, near a door but unable to go through it. The sight of them gave his heart a twist.

Gertrude was a sad little mouse of a ghost, a portrait of suffering. Barely out of her teens when she'd passed, she had the same hollow expression in her eyes as the spirits Curt had encountered at Auschwitz. In her letter to Granger, Lillian had apparently downplayed the level of abuse her cousin had endured under McFadyen's roof.

Once the foreman had declared the cold room safe to enter, Brassard sent her Forensics team in to look around. For a while, Curt heard nothing but the subdued murmur of Lillian's voice as she reassured Gertrude that her ordeal was finally over and she was safe. Nobody living spoke a syllable. Even Barbara and Brenda stood silently by, gazing with stunned sympathy at the other two ghosts.

Then, the female tech stuck her head back through the jagged opening in the wall, her eyes searching the room for Brassard, and finding her. "There are two bodies in here, Staff Sergeant," she reported. "An adult female and an infant—and they're mummified, which is not surprising because it's really cold and dry in this room. There are also some rags with what could be blood on them. We'll know more once we get everything back to the lab."

On impulse, Curt asked, "Is the woman wearing wedding rings?"

"She is, as a matter of fact." The tech tilted her head inquiringly.

"That matches one of the details in the letter," said Brassard, replying to her unspoken question. "It will help us to identify her. Continue with your processing, Sergeant. As soon as you are done with the mummified remains, there is an ambulance outside that can transport them to the hospital morgue for further examination. After that, it will be up to the nearest living relative to determine how they will be respectfully disposed of."

DeLucci chose that moment to clear his throat loudly. In a voice even more starched than his shirt collar, he pointed out, "The grave is already dug, and a tombstone has been ordered by the Historical Society."

"And an urn can be buried just as easily as a coffin, Mr. DeLucci," Nena Cartier said mildly. Meanwhile, her facial expression was telling him, *Don't worry, J. D., you'll get your money.*

"Trudy mustn't be taken to the morgue by herself, Mr. Wakefield," Lillian reminded him. *"She's been going mad trapped down here with no one to talk to. I promised her when we were living that I wouldn't abandon her. I can't leave her alone now. Please!"*

Curt's heart began death-spiralling into his stomach.

Lillian's request made perfect sense and was the decent thing to do. No argument there. And for a change, only two obstacles had to be overcome in order to make it happen. But they were doozies.

First, Lillian could only go where her letter did. That meant someone would have to ride in the ambulance with her and Gertrude. Someone who could be trusted with her letter and who understood why their own presence in the ambulance was necessary.

Second, this person had to have either an officially acceptable reason for accompanying mummified human remains to the morgue or the ability to bully or bullshit their way aboard the vehicle carrying them.

Try though he might, Curt could not think of anyone present who fulfilled both requirements.

Then there was a gentle tap on his arm. "Mr. Wakefield?"

He spun and found himself face to face with Prue Davidson.

"I... couldn't help overhearing. You need someone to help Lillian. Please, let me carry the letter."

His jaw dropped. "You heard what she said?"

She shrugged one shoulder. "Not so much in words, but I caught the gist of it. Lillian is my great-aunt. Gertrude is my cousin. I can do this for them." She held out her hand. "Please," she said simply.

And without another word, he placed the letter on her upturned palm.

Twenty-Seven

With no digging to do, DeLucci and his staff took the backhoe back to the cemetery.

The coroner's assistant supervised the transfer of the remains to the ambulance, then returned to the office to write up his report.

The Forensics team scoured the cold cellar for possible evidence, bagged it all up, and transported it to the police lab for analysis. Brassard and Izkari followed them in a separate vehicle.

Prue Davidson talked her way into the ambulance and rode it to the hospital morgue.

The Public Health officer decided that ninety-year-old mummified remains did not pose an immediate threat to the community. She drove away right after the ambulance did.

The construction crew did a stellar job of tidying up after themselves, then left Ben Davidson to decide how to deal with the gaping hole in his basement wall.

Nena Cartier and the archivist wrapped up their video, loaded the cameras and recording gear into the trunk of Nena's car, and went to the museum to begin editing the footage.

Larry still had a work day to finish, so he said a quick goodbye and departed for the firehouse.

Curt and Selena stood together on the veranda, watching the street and the driveway empty of vehicles until only one was left, sitting like an ornament in the middle of the castle's front lawn.

"Do you need a lift somewhere?" Curt asked her, followed immediately by, "Barbara, that's enough."

Selena could just imagine what the ghost had said to him. She had bitten back a couple of choice quips herself when she'd realized whose car she was staring at.

"No, thanks, I'm good," she replied, glad that a smile wasn't out of place in this situation. "I parked in the supermarket lot around the corner." After a pause, she added, "I overheard Nena telling you not to worry about locking up the museum, and I can't see anyone wanting to hang with Ben Davidson in his current foul mood, so—where are you going, and would you care for some company?"

"Actually, I was thinking of taking Barbara to visit her friend in the hospital. Lillian won't leave Gertrude without a fight, and it's not fair to expect Prue to stay at the morgue by herself the whole time."

"Good idea. We can take turns spelling her off until the bodies are released for 'respectful disposal'."

He gazed at her, frowning. "Are you sure this is how you want to spend part of your weekend, Selena? Alone in the morgue for maybe hours on end, safeguarding a letter?"

"Helping a friend," she corrected him. "Lillian has already told us the cause of death. The autopsies won't take long. And who says I'll be alone?"

"Ah! I'm guessing you plan to invite Larry to keep you company?"

Involuntarily, her smile broadened. "Larry... Sara... maybe

even Tricia Vickery. We'll see."

Prue's cheeks dimpled when she saw them walk through the door of the viewing room together.

"The reinforcements are here," Selena announced cheerfully. "What have we missed?"

"Well, I haven't heard any moaning or sobbing from the other side of that glass since we got here. I'm hoping that's a good sign," she told them. "Meanwhile, Staff Sergeant Brassard stopped by to update the pathologist, and that I did overhear. Apparently, due to the age of the remains, the Coroner has declined to be involved in the case, and the PPS have washed their hands of it as well. So, all that's left to be done is determine the two causes of death and the age of the baby. I offered to provide a DNA sample to prove that I'm related to the deceased, but the pathologist said it wasn't necessary since the fellow running the cemetery had already accepted my authorization for the disinterments." She grinned. "You did say he was a stickler, Mr. Wakefield. It seems you're not the only one who knows that."

"Small towns," he replied, returning her smile.

Selena peered through the glass and saw an autopsy in progress. "Is Barbara in there?"

"Yes," came Curt's reply over her shoulder. "The three of them are together now."

She inhaled sharply. "They're not watching—?"

"No. They're in a group hug in the corner," he told her.

That was interesting. "Ghosts can hug one another?"

"Apparently," he said with a shrug.

Just then, another medical worker wearing blue scrubs and a surgical cap entered the autopsy room.

"That'll be the pediatric pathologist," said Prue. "They sent for her earlier. She has to be present when the baby is cut open. Let's change the subject now. I'm learning more than I ever wanted to know about what happens after death, and quite frankly, it's depressing. I just wish I could do more for them."

"You're already doing it," Curt told her. "What are your plans for next week?"

She gave him a look. "Does this have anything to do with the cameo brooch?"

"Indirectly. Can you make yourself available on, say, Monday afternoon?"

"It depends." Turning to Selena, she said, "Do you still want me to help you decorate your home in Groverton, whichever one you buy?"

Almost before Prue had finished speaking, Selena heard herself reply, "Yes, of course!"

"Assuming the price is something you can afford, and in light of what we just witnessed in that basement, is the castle still a 'maybe'? Or have you moved it to the 'definitely not' column?"

"I haven't decided yet. Now that I know about Barbara, it isn't just myself I have to think about anymore. But we talked about this yesterday at lunch. Why are you asking me so soon after—?" Struck by a sudden thought, Selena gasped her next breath. "You have plans for that place, don't you?"

Prue's expression became impish. "Let's just say that a host of decorating possibilities opened up for me when I saw what lay beneath Ben's precious wood panelling, and I'm pretty sure the Historical Society would approve of my proposed changes. That's assuming, of course, that Ben doesn't find a purchaser for the property within a reasonable length of time. In that case, I have the option of buying him out and taking full ownership—which I have the resources to do as long as he doesn't hike the price on me."

"Would he really be that spiteful?" Selena wondered.

"It's hard to say. In court, he's had to be adversarial—

abrasive, overbearing, and at times downright belligerent. When we were first married, that was just a persona. The side of himself that he showed me and our family and friends was charming, considerate, and even-tempered. Then something happened, I have no idea what, but in the last few years, he's changed. Some couples try to save their marriage by having a baby. Ben bought me a castle. It might have worked, too, except for Gertrude. If she were alive, I've no doubt he would be suing her for alienation of affection. But she's not, and he can't, and that was evidently the final straw. We're done. When I return to the city I'll be making it official.

"And in answer to your question, Mr. Wakefield, I plan to spend some time up here consulting with my new client, Ms. Watt, which means I can be available to you on Monday for as long as you need me."

One hour later Selena was standing at the viewing window, alone. Curt and Prue had gone out to get a bite to eat and presumably discuss whatever he was setting up for Monday afternoon, leaving her with custody of Lillian's letter, and Barbara's pendant around her neck, and some weighty questions roiling around in her mind.

Apparently, Prue was planning to restore at least part of the castle to its period decor. And then what? Sell it? That made sense—it was a lot of house for a woman living on her own. It also held too many ugly memories for either Lillian or Gertrude to want to stay there, and since Lillian and Barbara were now a couple (according to Curt), that meant Barbara was bound to reject it as well.

…which led to the next conundrum: what was going to happen to these ghosts once the current excitement had settled down? Assuming Curt's efforts to move Lillian's tether from the letter to the brooch were successful, someone would have to take—and maintain—ownership of both pieces of jewellery. Would have to remember that wherever one piece went, the other would have to go as well, in order to keep the lovers together.

It couldn't be Prue, not if she moved back into the castle—nor Selena, if she bought the place—nor an unbeliever, who might split the pieces up at the first opportunity, just to prove a point. And continuing to store the brooch and pendant in Curt's desk drawer wasn't a practical long-term solution either. After all, how much time could anyone be expected to spend inside a museum without becoming bored—and in Lillian's case, mischievous? Or around a particular house or apartment? Sara worked in a library, but ghosts couldn't manipulate material objects like books, so even that environment would eventually become tiresome for them.

It was even worse if Lillian had to remain tethered to the letter, which was a piece of local history, destined for the Society's archives room in the tower. Selena didn't want to think about the possible consequences of that.

"It is disturbing, I know."

Selena gasped and spun around. Staff Sergeant Brassard was standing just inside the entrance to the viewing room.

"I am sorry if I startled you," she said. "Autopsies are never pleasant to watch, especially when the subject is a child."

"You're probably wondering why I'm here and Ms. Davidson is not, since she's the one who's related to the deceased," Selena began, sifting her brain for a plausible reason.

Brassard raised her hand in a dismissive gesture. "I used to wonder about such things, Ms. Watt. Lately, however, I have learned that it is best sometimes to simply accept what is, without demanding an explanation. I am here because I just spoke with the forensic pathologist and thought you might appreciate a preview of the report they will be filing."

Pulling a small, spiral-bound notebook from her pocket, she flipped to a page and continued, reading from her notes, "They have determined that the infant mummy was not carried to full term, and that it was most likely a spontaneous abortion due to deformities that made it nonviable. As well, their examination of the adult mummy found nothing to suggest that she had been the victim of foul play. This corroborates the information provided in the letter that Mr. Wakefield showed me earlier." So saying, she snapped her notebook shut and put it away.

"Thank you, Staff Sergeant. Do you know when the bodies will be released?"

"Not exactly. However, since the autopsies were expedited and there will be no police investigation, it is reasonable to believe that this will happen soon. The hospital has Ms. Davidson's contact information. They will let her know. Have a good evening, Ms. Watt."

And with that, the officer left, dropping another question in her wake for Selena to mull over: it was highly unlikely that anyone would be permitted to camp out in the viewing room overnight, let alone for an entire weekend. How would Lillian react to being separated from her cousin for that long?

"Lillian? Barbara? Is one of you in here with me?" she asked hopefully, extending her hand to be ghost-tapped.

Nothing.

Oh, dear…

Selena had been staring into the darkened autopsy room for some period of time, questioning her recent choices, when she heard a door open somewhere down the hall and the sound of something being dragged along the floor.

Good grief, what now?

Then the entrance to the viewing room swung open and Larry stood there, wearing jeans and a T-shirt with the Fire

Department logo over the left breast, and giving her the same heart-melting, lopsided smile she'd seen on his face the first time they'd met. He was brandishing a paper bag in one hand and pulling a chair behind him. Her knight in shining armour had come to her rescue once more.

"You missed dinner at Sara's." He offered her the bag while simultaneously lifting and swinging the chair through the doorway. "She was worried when your phone went directly to voicemail and called Curt to see whether he knew where you were, and he texted me. I figured you must be starving by now, so I picked up something for you on my way here. Why didn't you get in touch with me earlier?" he chided her. "You know I would have come to keep you company."

"I tried to, but my battery died." Selena blew out a frustrated breath. "So much has been going on lately. I must have forgotten to charge it."

"Uh-huh. Well, tuck into your sub, lady. A lot more has happened in the last couple of hours, and your vigil will soon be over. Apparently, Prue and Curt analyzed her 'respectful disposal' options over high tea and she decided on a quiet, semi-private graveside service—just you, me, Curt, Sara, the Davidsons, and the ghosts. To avoid the media circus that was bound to happen once word of the discovery got out, they alerted Ben, who hopped on the phone and did what he does best.

"I'm not sure I want to know how he managed it. Suffice it to say, though, the undertakers are on their way here as we speak, to collect the mummies and box them up. Most of the paperwork is already done and the cemetery is on standby, so in a few short hours, there will be nothing left for anyone to gawk at or photograph but a freshly-covered grave and a transplanted tombstone."

And, with luck, that's all it will take for Gertrude's ghost to finally be free.

*   *   *

"Do you want a dirge during the procession?" asked the fresh-faced young man at the funeral parlour. Behind him, two men in shirt sleeves were occupied with moving the body bag containing Gertrude and her baby into a plain wooden box on a rolling cart, and then, presumably, into the hearse.

"A dirge?" Prue echoed doubtfully.

It was warm inside this room, much too warm to be wearing a dark blue suit and tie. Selena watched the young man run a finger around the inside of his shirt collar and guessed that he usually spent his time elsewhere in the building—in the chapel or the casket showroom, perhaps, where the comfort of the living was a practical consideration. Those spaces would be air-conditioned at this time of year.

"Sure," he replied. "One family requested it, and now we've got a playlist. There's 'My Way', sung by Frank Sinatra, 'Take Me Home, Country Roads' by John Denver—"

"We don't need music," Ben told him flatly. "Or a procession. If I'm footing the bill, this coffin is going into the ground with all due haste and a minimum of ceremony."

Prue's spine went rigid.

"Take it easy," Curt murmured. He patted his trouser pocket, where the letter once more resided.

Selena knew who he must be talking to, and it wasn't the Davidsons. Lillian was probably itching to give Ben frostbite right now. Prue's decision to divorce her husband was the best one she could have made. If only Gertrude had been given that option!

Selena felt Larry's hand on her elbow. "Come on," he said quietly, "we're meeting up at the cemetery."

The sun was still shining when the hearse finally arrived on the scene, but daylight was waning. There was no time to lose.

A tall man with a shovel stood beside a pile of dirt, five or six metres away from the road. This was where the grave had been prepared. There were six handles on the coffin. The hearse driver gripped one of them and the living witnesses to the burial each took one of the remaining five, and together they carried Gertrude and her baby to their final destination.

As the box was slowly lowered into the ground, Curt delivered a brief eulogy: "This funeral should have taken place in 1933, right after Gertrude Smith McFadyen died giving birth to a stillborn. However, circumstances conspired to prevent that from happening, and so we are here, entrusting her remains to the earth at last. No one now living knew Gertrude personally, but based on a document written by her cousin, Lillian, I can tell you that Trudy was a vibrant, fun-loving young woman and a generous and understanding friend. Her death was tragic, and her loss made the world a poorer place. May her soul now rest in the peace it so greatly deserves."

Spontaneously and in unison, everyone present said, "Amen," just as the coffin touched bottom and the sun slid out of sight below the rooftops of the town.

Twenty-Eight

Curt watched Gertrude's ghost unfold, like a flower bud opening to receive the light and warmth of a summer morning. As the box descended past ground level, she stepped forward, seeming to stand on top of it. She turned a circle, gazing at the beings around her, and for a moment her expression radiated pure joy. Then the edges of the greyscale figure dissolved, spilling its contents in whorls and tendrils into the air, where they finally dissipated like smoke, leaving not a trace of Gertrude McFadyen's spirit behind.

Apparently, all she had wanted was to be found and remembered. Now she would be.

Curt let out the breath he'd been holding and glanced at Prue and Selena. They'd felt her emotion too—both women were wiping away tears.

"That was beautiful, Mr. Wakefield," Lillian said. *"It was just what she needed. Thank you."*

"How many shovels did you bring, Andrew?" Larry called to the gravedigger, a husky fellow who appeared to be in his late teens or early twenties.

The kid grinned at him. "I brought three, sir. It's standard policy, for in case."

"Hand one over here, then, and let's finish this job before we lose the light entirely."

As the two men set to work filling in the grave, Prue stared expectantly at Ben, who pointedly ignored her. After a couple of moments, she let out a huff and stepped forward herself to pitch in.

To his credit, Andrew didn't blink or hesitate, just passed her his shovel and went to get another from his truck.

"She's a Friendly, all right," Lillian commented. *"She knows what's right and is stubborn as hell about seeing it done."*

Afterwards, they made their way back to their cars in the deepening gloom. The hearse driver had left immediately after delivering the casket. The Davidsons returned to their hotel room, to have a long talk, most likely. Selena and Larry had carpooled, so they would be heading back to Sara's place. And Curt had a couple of excited and talkative ghosts to drop off at the museum before he went home to sleep.

It had been a very long and busy day. With luck, the rest of the weekend would be much more peaceful. But he wouldn't bet on it.

There were text messages on his phone when Curt woke up Saturday morning. As always, they had to take their place in the queue, following his morning routine and the drive to the museum. So, it came as something of a surprise to find Selena's baby blue Buick sitting in the parking lot and herself sitting inside it when he arrived.

As he pulled into his accustomed spot near the boarding platform, she left her car and hurried to meet him. "I texted you last night," she said.

"Did you? I was going to check my inbox once I got into the office." He fished his keys out of his pocket and unlocked the door, and she followed him inside, fairly vibrating with curiosity.

"Did what I think happened yesterday really happen?" she demanded. "Is Gertrude—"

"—gone? Yes," he told her as he relocked the door behind them. "We've exorcised the castle, so you can probably go ahead and make an offer on it, if you're still that way inclined."

"Actually, I'm leaning more toward another place, one that won't be a heritage property for quite some time."

"Ah! Can't say I blame you. Which one is it?"

"It's…" She gave him a hopeful smile. "…the former gift shop." As he opened his mouth to reply, she rushed ahead and cut him off. "Listen, I know it's haunted, but in every other way it's perfect for me. And I know you had a long conversation with the ghost in that building because you want to help him the same way we helped Gertrude. I realize it's a lot to ask on top of everything else that's going on right now, but—"

"Stop!"

She froze in mid-gesture, with a pleading expression in her eyes.

"I'll do it," he told her, "on one condition."

"That I never ask you for another favour again?" Her voice held a note of resignation.

"No, that you help me to make another one happen," he corrected her gently. "When I came back to the museum last night, I found a parcel on my desk, delivered that afternoon by a jeweller friend of mine. Let me show you."

Curt led the way to the tower. Noting that the handle of his office door was room temperature, he checked for ghosts as he entered and saw none. Of course. Lillian had to be happy that her cousin was finally at peace. Now she could focus entirely on her relationship with Barbara.

What would make Lillian even happier, he suspected, was having her tether switched away from the letter to something else. His plan to achieve this was risky with a capital 'R'. Just contemplating the havoc Barbara could wreak if it went sideways and he ended up exorcising her lover instead was enough to make Curt's teeth chatter. Nonetheless, like his earlier visit to the morgue, it was something he felt obligated to try.

"I've taken the liberty of having this modified," he told Selena as he set the brooch down on the desktop between them.

She turned querying eyes on him and he nodded, giving her permission to handle the piece.

"I don't see anything different about it," she said after a moment's inspection. "No, wait. This looks like—a plug…?"

"The base of the brooch now contains a hidden compartment, just large enough to conceal a folded slip of paper."

She frowned. "A slip? Not a full page?"

"Obsidian is relatively soft, and the brooch isn't that thick. My theory is that a piece of the letter will be sufficient to act as a tether. I need you to help me prove it—once Barbara and Lillian have both consented to the experiment, of course. There's a fair amount of danger involved."

"Hold on. You're planning to cut up the letter?" she said, her voice rising in disbelief. "What about the Historical Society? Won't they have something to say about this?"

"Probably, but it's not as serious as you think. The document won't be lost. Most of it will survive. And even if it doesn't, they've already scanned the original into their computer and printed out a true copy for their files."

She shot him a dubious look—not deceived for one second, he realized. Of *course* he would have to destroy what was left of the letter once they were sure Lillian was tethered to the brooch. Ruth had given him three options and, for better or for worse, Curt had made his choice.

After Selena left, promising to return after the ghosts had been consulted, he read his incoming text messages.

From Selena: *What the hell just happened tonight?! Did it work? Get back to me. Please!*

From Staff Sergeant Brassard: *Meet me in my office 9 a.m. Monday re the Ryan case. New developments.*

From Nena: *Not available next three days. Lucien has my museum keys. Glad things seem to have gone smoothly today. Grandfather sends regards. See you Tuesday.*

From Tricia Vickery: *Will set up a third showing of gift shop property Monday p.m., as you requested.*

From Prue: *Forgot to thank you for all your help. Headed back to city first thing Saturday a.m. and will return to Groverton on Monday. Lunch?*

From Sara: *Dinner Saturday, my place. 6:00 sharp. Bring good news.*

Curt sent his replies.

To Brassard and Sara: *I'll be there. Thank you.*

To Tricia: *Text me the time and I'll be there, with a couple of friends.*

To Prue: *Sure thing. Text me when you get to town.*

Lillian glowered down at the brooch as though challenging its innocent appearance on Curt's desktop.

"How certain are you that this will work?" she asked.

"To be honest, I'm not certain at all," Curt told her. "That's why I'm calling it an experiment. And I promise you, I won't do anything to the rest of the letter until you are both quite sure the result will be what you want."

Lillian and Barbara exchanged meaningful looks.

"All right, then, Mr. Wakefield. Let's give it a try," Lillian said.

Curt opened the file folder and turned to the final page of the letter, his pulse loud in his ears. He was about to deliberately mutilate a piece of local history, in clear violation of the Society's rules. Rule breakers were to be shunned, according to his mother. Not even Nena might be able to save his job this time. And yet, deep down, he knew he was doing the right thing.

Huh! Maybe there was some Friendly in his DNA as well.

Scissors in hand, Curt paused to advise the ghosts, "The second either one of you can feel what I'm doing to this paper, tell me, and I'll stop immediately. Okay?"

"*Okay,*" they replied in unison.

The letter had been written on sheets of six-by-nine-inch stationery paper and folded in thirds to fit inside the envelope. Curt cut carefully along one of the creases, hedging his bet by ensuring that he captured Lillian's signature on the piece he was removing. Then, even more carefully, he folded the paper until it was small enough to fit through the opening in the brooch, slipped it inside, and reinserted the plug.

To ensure they had privacy, Curt waited until closing time. He saw everyone out and locked the door. Then he contacted Selena and asked her to come to the museum. Ten minutes later, she arrived. He handed her the brooch and told her what he needed her to do.

"That's it?" she said. "You want me to take this out to the edge of the parking lot and stand there for a while?"

"Well, you can put it in your car and drive it around the block if you like, but the point will already be made. Normally, the boarding platform is as far as any of the tethered ghosts in the museum can go. If Lillian is able to follow you beyond that boundary, it will be because some part of her is attached to the brooch."

"Some part? Not all?"

"That's the next stage of the experiment," he told her.

"Let's take this one step at a time and not get ahead of ourselves."

"All right. How long do you want me to stand there?"

"Until I signal you to come back inside."

They went as a group to the front entrance of the building. Curt and Barbara stopped just outside the door and stood watching as Selena and Lillian proceeded across the paved lot, toward the grassy area in front of the fence. Curt strained to keep them in focus, then cursed under his breath. He wasn't imagining this: with each additional couple of steps that she took away from the building, Lillian lost a shade of grey.

Clearly, a ghost couldn't be tethered to two things at once, even if they were parts of the same object. Curt had suspected this might be a problem. He'd even prepared for it.

He raced back to his office and found the metal wastebasket under his desk. Emptying it onto the floor, he threw the file folder and a box of wooden matches into it, then grabbed the pendant from his desk drawer and headed back outside.

"Do you know what you're doing, Mr. Wakefield?" Barbara demanded, her voice rising in panic.

"Absolutely!" he replied, putting the pendant around his neck. "Get as close as you can to Lillian and watch her. If she doesn't grow darker and firmer with each additional page that I burn, give me a two-handed wave and I'll stop."

There was only a slight breeze on this side of the building. He blocked it with his body, then dropped the first page of the letter into the wastebasket, along with a lighted match. The old paper caught fire immediately and was rapidly consumed.

Curt glanced up and saw Barbara standing motionless, facing Lillian across several metres of pavement and grass. No wave-off? He fed the wastebasket a second page and struck a second match, and the flames leaped back to life. Then he raised his gaze to the greyscale figure in the parking lot, took a breath, and held it.

Barbara still hadn't turned around, but something was wrong. Her head was drooping and her shoulders sagging, almost as if—

Oh, no! No, no, no…!

Curt dropped the file folder and hurried across the pavement toward her, shouting as he ran. "I've stopped, Barbara. Go to her! Go! Selena, catch!"

He slipped the pendant off and tossed it to her. It fell short. Selena bent to pick it up off the grass, a puzzled expression on her face.

Meanwhile, Lillian was even paler and less substantial than before. "*NO!*" she bellowed hoarsely. "*Keep going, Mr. Wakefield. It's working. I can feel it.*"

"Lillian, you're fading away," he protested. "Is this really what you want? Are you sure?"

She turned pitying eyes on him. "*Oh, yes. Barbara and I have talked about it. You can see us, Mr. Wakefield, and you can hear us, but you are trapped in a prison of flesh that insulates you from what we feel. When Trudy was released from her tether and tasted true freedom for the first time, she couldn't contain her joy. Rapture poured out of her and into me, and I realized that this was all I wanted, all I ever wanted, for her and for myself. So, yes, I am sure. I've done everything I set out to do in this mortal world. Now— please!—burn the rest of the paper that keeps me chained here. Let my spirit be free so my soul can rest in peace.*"

"I promised you would both have a say," he reminded her. "Barbara?"

She drew herself up and replied sadly, "*I felt it too, and wanted it more than you can imagine, but it's not my time yet. I love her too much to make her wait. So, give her what she wants, Mr. Wakefield, and I'll join her as soon as I'm able.*"

"That settles it, then. I'm going to miss you, Lillian Friendly," he said, his voice thickened by emotion.

"Good," she replied. *"Remember me well, and think of me often, because eventually we will meet again."*

Barbara turned toward him. *"I want to stay with her until she's—you know."*

That did it—the tears that had been welling up in his eyes began sliding down his cheeks.

Selena looked about to cry as well. "How can I help, Curt?"

She couldn't. Nobody could. That was the thing he'd grown to hate most about death—the unavoidable pain it inflicted on those who were left behind.

"Just stay here while I finish up. I'll let you know when it's over."

So saying, he returned to the wastebasket and the matches and proceeded to burn the rest of the letter to ashes. And when that was done and all that remained of Lillian was a faint outline sketched on a sheet of late afternoon sunshine, he pulled the final remnant of paper out of the brooch and lit that on fire as well.

And then, at last, Lillian Friendly was gone.

After handing him back the pendant, Selena tried to persuade him to accompany her to Sara's place. However, Curt didn't have much appetite for dinner, or for the discussion that he knew would follow the meal, and he told her so.

Not good enough! She insisted that he shouldn't be alone at a time like this.

Alone? He nearly laughed. Those who lived completely on the mortal plane didn't—couldn't—understand what a rare and precious commodity privacy was for someone like him. Outside of his apartment, Curt Wakefield was never alone.

When Selena had finally given up and departed, he texted Sara his regrets. Then he and Barbara sat on the boarding platform with Ruth and Clara, comforting one another, until darkness swallowed up the day and he couldn't see them anymore.

Sunday happened. Curt didn't stand in its way. In fact, he spent most of it sitting at his desk, reading light fiction—humorous stories with happy endings to boost his spirits. Sara had dropped off half a dozen rom-com novels at the museum that morning, unbidden, after Selena had shared with her the reason for his absence from her dinner table the evening before. They helped to pass the time, if nothing else.

Shortly before lunch, Lucien Burton, a senior Society member, had popped his head through the doorway of Curt's office. He was wondering whether the museum's curator/manager knew anything about a certain letter that had disappeared from its file folder upstairs…?

Feeling reckless, Curt had told him the truth: he'd burned the letter to exorcise the spirit of its author, at her own request.

"Ah! Uh-huh." And, evidently finding nothing more to say, Lucien had withdrawn from Curt's space and not intruded again.

It would be interesting to see whether Nena could smooth *that* one over with the Historical Society.

Monday was rainy. Of *course* it was. As Curt raced across the PPS parking lot, he was hoping that the "new developments" Brassard wanted to share included the contents of the safe deposit box Brenda Ryan had rented earlier at the Dominion Bank of Canada.

Text messages had been arriving on his phone pretty much nonstop for the past half-hour. They would have to wait until he got to the museum and could give them his full attention.

"Mr. Wakefield," Brassard greeted him, getting to her feet behind her desk and gesturing him toward a guest chair. "And you are right on time, as usual. Excellent!"

As he settled onto his seat, Curt met the gaze of the third being in the room—Brenda Ryan's smiling ghost—and nodded to acknowledge her presence. Clearly, the officer had good news to share. She was also in possession of the key they'd found in the castle on Friday.

Brassard cleared her throat. "Since you are consulting with us on Ms. Ryan's case, I felt it would be reasonable to bring you up to date on the progress of our investigation."

"I appreciate that. Thank you, Staff Sergeant."

"And I have a privilege to accord you."

"Oh?"

"The 'insurance policy' Ms. Ryan was keeping in that safe deposit box has been taken into evidence. It has given us a most valuable lead as we continue to investigate. Normally, we would now return the client's key to the bank. However, a special request has been made regarding the disposition of this particular key, and I have decided to let you carry it out."

Brenda's smile was widening. Apparently, she was the source of the request. Curt wasn't sure how she'd managed to convey it, but he could guess what she wanted done; and just thinking about how perfectly it would fit with his plans for the rest of the day was putting an answering grin on his own face.

"I would be honoured, Ma'am," he responded.

"I thought as much. The bank has been told that the key has been misplaced in our evidence storage warehouse and may never turn up again, so your hands are free."

"And what about the investigation?" he reminded her. "Were you able to take a statement from—?" He stopped himself just in time.

She frowned a warning at him. "I was. Your 'yes and no'

technique proved to be quite useful. We now believe we have identified her killer and we are working to locate and apprehend this individual. Unfortunately, that is all I can tell you for now. However, I will keep you in the loop, as they say." Placing a familiar small brown envelope on the desktop in front of him, she added, "Thank you for coming in, Mr. Wakefield. Have a good day."

"*What a relief!*" Brenda exclaimed as they exited the building. "*If I had to spend one more day in there, I was going to lose it.*"

Once they were inside his car, Curt turned to face her and asked, "So, was it Tommy?"

"*Yes, but I don't think he meant to kill me. Like I told Sergeant Brassard, he was beating me up, and when I tried to get away I fell down the stairs. Hit my head pretty hard. I couldn't see straight, could hardly stand up. Made it outside, then I fell down again, and... that was it. But it wasn't Tommy's idea to come after me. Somebody else ordered him to find me and take back what I'd stolen from them. Somebody who scared the crap out of Tommy. That's who the police are going after now. It's why they're being so close-mouthed about the investigation.*"

"Can you tell me what was in the safe deposit box?"

"*I'm not supposed to. But even if I could, are you sure you want to know?*"

And land in the middle of yet another PPS matter? Good grief, no!

Curt changed the subject. "How would you like to help me free another ghost from a building they're stuck in?"

"*Sure! What do I have to do?*"

"Nothing, really. Just get married."

"*You're joking!*"

"To Rachel Vickery."

Her grey eyes gleamed in his rear-view mirror. "*Count me*

in, Mr. Wakefield. "

They arrived at the museum shortly before ten o'clock. Amy was behind her counter, bent forward and dusting the shelves of the display case, while Orville sat on his invisible stool, gazing admiringly at her backside.

"*Whoa!*" Brenda murmured. "*There are other ghosts in here?*"

"Yep," Curt muttered back, adding in response to Amy's welcoming wave, "Good morning. I'll be right back. Just have to put something in my office."

She made the OK sign with her thumb and forefinger.

As he'd been hoping, Barbara was sitting cross-legged in the middle of his desktop when he walked in. "I believe you two ladies are acquainted with each other?" he said.

Curt unlocked the drawer with the pendant inside it and added the brown envelope before closing it again. When he looked up, the two ghosts were chatting away in a corner of the room.

He smiled to himself and left them there alone.

Tricia's text suggested that they meet at the former gift shop at three o'clock, and Curt replied to agree to the time. Then he called Prue, who was on the road and already halfway to Groverton, to confirm their lunch date at noon. The schedule was looking a little tight, so he also contacted Selena and invited her to join them at the restaurant.

Promising to return and pick up Barbara and Brenda, he pocketed the brooch and left Lucien in charge of things at the museum.

By now, the rain had stopped and the sky was clearing. As before, Selena and Prue were waiting for him in a booth with padded seats, against the wall farthest from the windows.

"This is yours now," he said, pushing the brooch across the table to Prue. "My experiment failed, but I ended up giving

Lillian what she wanted, which was to reunite with her cousin Gertrude."

"So she's gone now? For good?" Prue sounded disappointed.

"How is Barbara dealing with this?" Selena asked.

"Pretty well, actually, since she's made a new friend." He told them about Brenda and the safe deposit box key.

"It sounds as if they've got a lot in common," Prue observed, finally picking up the brooch and dropping it into her purse.

"Getting justice for a murder can take years. I don't think either one of them will be going up in smoke anytime soon," Curt agreed.

After their server—Jean-Paul this time—had taken their orders, Curt leaned across the table and lowered his voice. "I've enlisted Barbara and Brenda to help me liberate another ghost—the Reverend Upworthy—and I'm hoping the two of you will agree to participate as well."

"By doing what?" Selena asked.

"How serious are you about wanting that property?" he countered. "If it weren't haunted, would you put an offer down on it today?"

"Yes, I think I would," she replied. "But what does that have to do with—?"

"Remember how you distracted Tricia so I could talk to Upworthy earlier? I need you to do it again. But this is the third time she's shown us this place, so her patience may be wearing thin."

Selena's face lit up with comprehension. "You want me to make it worth her while by talking about conditions and dates and financing and so on. I can do that. And how do the other ghosts figure in?"

He gave her a grin. "They're going to get married."

*   *   *

At three o'clock sharp, three ghosts and three living humans gathered at the front entrance of the vacant property that had once been a gift shop. Brenda and Rachel spied each other immediately. Squealing with delight, they rushed to hug, then remained side by side in animated conversation. Curt could tell when it turned to a discussion of his wedding plan. Rachel's eyes widened and her mouth formed an O.

She could scupper this project with a single shake of her head. Was she in?

Both ghosts turned to smile at him, and Brenda gave him a thumbs-up.

Excellent!

They waited while Tricia unlocked the door and let them in. Then they reassembled in front of the long glass display case. Fortunately, Rachel had already met Upworthy, and Curt had warned Barbara and Brenda what to expect, so there were no shocked cries or nervous laughter when he appeared, flapping and fulminating. For this to work, the Reverend had to believe that he was being taken seriously… which, of course, he was.

"What unholy nonsense is this?" came Upworthy's thundering voice. *"More of Satan's harem, come to give sinful pleasure? You're all going to burn in hell!"*

"Tricia, could we talk for a moment?" said Selena. "I've made up my mind to put an offer down on this place, and I want to clarify some details with you. Some conditions, dates, that sort of thing."

The realtor's expression morphed from polite to genuinely pleased, and then to cautious. "That's wonderful, Selena, but couldn't we have discussed this privately at my office?" Curt could practically hear her mentally adding, *and why did Mr. Wakefield make the appointment instead of you?*

He tensed, waiting to hear how Selena would reply.

"It was a last-minute decision, and since Curt had already arranged this meeting, I thought you wouldn't mind if I piggybacked onto it. I also wanted to take a last look around the place in case something had changed. I hope that's okay."

"Of course it is. I'll be down here with Mr. Wakefield. Call out to me if you have any questions."

"Actually… could we talk while I'm checking the upstairs? It would save a lot of time."

The realtor tossed Curt an inquiring look. Would he mind waiting? Not at all. He smiled and waved dismissively at them, and the two women set off across the hall.

This was Rachel's cue.

"Deacon O'Donnell, we need your help," came her voice inside Curt's head. He nodded his approval of her tone, which was somewhere between inviting and commanding. The last thing they wanted was for Upworthy to think these spirits were trying to seduce him.

Instantly attentive, the Reverend broke off his road-to-hell tirade and demanded, *"To save your souls?"*

"To join us in matrimony," said Brenda. *"You're ordained. You can do that."*

"Two women married to each other? Never!" he declaimed, his face a portrait of righteous horror. *"There was only one Eve in the Garden of Eden. This was the will of our Lord the Creator. One man, one woman. Anything else would be a blasphemy!"*

"Not anymore, Deacon," Rachel told him. *"Time has passed. Society has changed."*

"The Church has not! The Church is immutable! Its teachings are immutable! And you are sinners, damned for eternity!"

"What about the teachings of Jesus? He preached love, remember?" said Brenda. *"Well, we are two people who love each other, and love is not a sin."*

"And would you have me marry you to a beloved pet? Or a favourite tree? There are rules for a reason, and the rules of the Church do not change with the seasons, nor with the shifting of the wind."

Standing atop the display case, he loomed over them, like an angry parent laying down the law to a pair of wayward children. However, Rachel was not intimidated.

She stepped forward and declared defiantly, *"But they do change with the times, because the Church is a living thing, and life goes on. It moves forward, and the Church moves forward with it, accepting new ideas, growing in understanding. You've been dead and out of the loop for a hundred years, Deacon. That means you have some catching up to do."*

Barbara had been silent to this point. Feeling a warning drop in room temperature, Curt swung his gaze in her direction, saw the strained expression on her face, and wondered belatedly whether it had been wise to bring her here so soon after Lillian's... what? Demise? Departure? Before he could decide how to complete that thought, she sprang to her feet as though launched by a catapult and blurted, *"Love isn't just for certain kinds of people, you foolish old man! It's for all people. That's why Jesus lived, and it's what he taught. And if these two want their love to be sanctified, who in the* hell *are you to deny them that?"* Then, her anger spent, she subsided back onto her chair.

Meanwhile, taken completely aback, Upworthy had lost several shades of grey. *"I'm... in Hell...?"* he said in a faltering voice.

This was the opening they needed. Without missing a beat, Rachel changed tack, taking Brenda with her.

"Of course not. You're on the mortal plane, in the twenty-first century," Rachel replied, in the soothing tone Curt had heard used by hospital staff to reassure people waking up from

unconsciousness. *"You're Deacon Joshua O'Donnell, ordained by the Anglican Church of Canada, and we are asking you for the sacrament of marriage."*

"No! This is a test," Upworthy said hoarsely, casting wild-eyed glances around the room. *"You're here to tempt me into sin. But I will not succumb! I have a calling, and you shall not deter me from doing God's work!"*

The longer this scene played out, the lower Curt's heart sank. What was Upworthy seeing? And who did he think he was talking to? If it was a pair of whores in the brothel…!

"Yes! You did *have a calling once,"* Brenda reminded him sternly. *"You had a calling, and you spent your life trying to answer it. The synod wouldn't let you have a parish, so you found another way. But it wasn't enough, was it? Your mission was unfulfilled when you died. It was a tragic, shameful death. But you can still redeem yourself, with love. Show us the love that Jesus showed to Mary Magdalene. Recognize the love that we have for each other. Marry us, Deacon. Please!"*

As Curt watched, O'Donnell's spirit seemed to sag and deflate. *"I can't. Even if I believe it is the right and holy thing to do, a deacon cannot perform the sacrament of marriage without prior consent from an ordained minister."*

They had him on the ropes and they knew it.

"That may be true among the living," Rachel pointed out. *"But we are not the living. In the afterlife, people can marry whomever they love, and deacons can officiate at their weddings. You know you want to do this. You've always wanted to do this, to perform the holy sacraments. It's been your dream. And now you can, and there's no synod to stand in the way of you finally answering your calling and claiming your reward in Heaven."*

That did it. *"I'm… Yes. You're right. I can earn my way to Heaven."* He drew himself up, fairly glowing with righteous zeal. *"Yes! I can do this. We have the marriage partners. Are there witnesses?"*

"*Yes!*" said Barbara, raising her hand.

And "Here!" said Curt, unable to contain his elation.

Tricia leaned through the doorway. "Did you call me, Mr. Wakefield?"

Oops!

Heat rose in his cheeks. "No, sorry, I was… thinking about something and it just popped out."

She nodded and smiled, then withdrew.

"In the sight of God, whose love is all-encompassing, let us begin. Dearly beloved…"

The deacon had probably rehearsed this many times while living. He'd been like an understudy, learning the part in the vain hope of getting a chance to go onstage and perform it. The words rolled out of him without pause or hesitation, even when he substituted "for all eternity" instead of "for as long as you both shall live". Briefed ahead of time, Prue stood respectfully silent throughout the ceremony. And when O'Donnell reached the end and pronounced Rachel and Brenda a married couple, it was with an utterly rapturous smile on his face.

Curt took a breath and held it, praying that his theory about this ghost had been correct. And…

There!

Before his eyes, Deacon Joshua O'Donnell was fading, his outline dissolving as the chain of regret binding him to the mortal plane slipped away. In a matter of seconds, his unformed essence spilled out, then rarefied until it was indistinguishable from the air around him. His spirit was finally free.

Barbara had retreated to a corner of the room, sobbing. As Rachel and Brenda rushed to comfort her, Curt turned to Prue and gave her a single, emphatic nod. Then he strode into the hall to speak with Tricia.

If the happy couple were to stay together, there was one last thing to do. The safe deposit key had been too large and awkward a shape to add to a charm bracelet, so Curt had taken Barbara and Brenda on a field trip right after lunch, to visit his jeweller friend and see what he could do with it in a limited amount of time. The result had been much better than Curt could have imagined.

"I have something for you," he told Tricia. "It's a bequest from Brenda. Hold out your hand."

With a frown of puzzlement, the realtor did as he asked, and he poured onto her palm the contents of the brown envelope—two charms linked by a single delicate gold circle, one shaped like the letter B and the other like a T. Brenda and Tricia, together.

She raised tear-filled eyes to his face. "What—How—?"

Glancing at Brenda, who had come to stand nearby, he replied, "Apparently, she'd been saving it to give you for some future occasion."

"I'll treasure this forever," Tricia blubbered. "Thank you so much!"

"Here," he said, producing from his pocket the needle-nosed pliers that he'd borrowed from the jeweller for just this purpose. "Let's attach it to the bracelet now so it can't possibly get lost."

When he was finished, Selena sidled up to him and asked quietly, "So, it's done?"

"The Reverend has been freed, and as far as I can tell, he was the only ghost haunting the property. You can go ahead and make your offer," he told her.

"Thank you!" she said with a grin. "I will."

Twenty-Nine

Sara's kitchen was redolent with the aromas of pot roast and apple pie.

"So, who gets the pendant?" she asked between sips of chai tea.

Curt and Selena exchanged looks across the table.

"I was thinking we ought to leave that up to Barbara," Selena told her.

"She's always welcome at the museum… assuming that I'm still working there after Lucien informs the Society about what I did on Saturday," said Curt.

"Nena won't let them fire you," Sara assured him. "She's a believer, and she's come through for you before. And Staff Sergeant Brassard will want to keep you nearby—she needs you to help her solve crimes."

"Besides, the ghosts will revolt and put everyone in the deep freeze if you're forced to leave town," Selena told him. "You're like the genie in the lamp, granting them their dearest wishes. Thanks to you, Brenda gets to keep showing houses, and the Reverend Upworthy is finally in Heaven."

"Is Larry joining us tonight?" Curt asked.

Sara shook her head. "He's got something going on at the firehouse. And the boys may be eating separately as well. They came home hyper from their first day at camp, so I sent them to their rooms to calm down before dinner. We'll have to see how well that's worked out."

As if on cue, Eric's voice floated down from the second-floor landing.

"Mom!" he shouted. "Donnie's doing it again and I can't get him to stop! Can I go down to the rec room instead?"

She rolled her eyes. "Yes," she called back to him, drawing the word out in a sigh.

"Doing it?" Curt repeated.

"He has an imaginary friend. They have conversations in his bedroom. Loud ones, sometimes. Never outside the house, thank goodness."

"Does this friend have a name?"

"I asked him that once, and he answered yes, but that he'd promised to keep it a secret."

Curt heard a clatter of footsteps and turned just in time to catch a glimpse of Eric disappearing through the basement door.

"Are you sure he isn't just talking on the phone or something?" Selena suggested.

"I'm certain. I've peeked in on him when I hear him laughing, and he's all alone in there, chattering away."

"That must be troubling. Have you consulted a professional about it?" Curt wondered.

"Yes. I took Donnie to a pediatric psychologist a couple of years ago. The doctor assured me that my son was normal in every respect, but apparently feeling lonely. She explained that children who lack real friends will often create imaginary ones to compensate, and that it's nothing to worry about."

A shiver of recognition trickled across Curt's shoulders. "If I may ask, how long has he been talking to himself?"

"Ever since he was a toddler." As their eyes locked, Sara gasped. "You don't suppose...?"

He shrugged. "It's unlikely. But would you mind if I look in on him, just to make sure?"

"Not at all. One way or the other, I would like to know. So go ahead. Please."

The boys' bedroom doors had been identified with their names on novelty licence plates. Curt stood just outside Donnie's room and listened carefully for a minute, debating how he ought to feel about the fact that he could hear two different voices speaking on the other side of the door. One of them was Donnie's. The other was deep, belonging to an adult male.

A parade of possibilities marched across Curt's mind. Some of them were unpleasant to contemplate. But he knew what he was hoping to find.

As quietly as he could, he turned the knob and pushed, just enough to give him a view of the greyscale figure sitting beside Donnie on the bed. Sara had shown Curt photos of her late husband. When the figure turned its head and smiled at him, the truth was undeniable.

"Don't just stand there, Wakefield. Come inside," Doug Traynor's ghost commanded him heartily. *"I've been hearing stories about you, and I figure it's time you and I had a man-to-man talk. What exactly are your intentions regarding my wife?"*

Curt swallowed hard. So, he'd been crushing on a married woman?

Wait until Ruth and Clara learned about *this!*

Like Stephen Leacock's Mariposa, Groverton is a fictional Ontario town, inspired by a real one. That said, there are many Grovertons across Canada, each with its own history and ghostly population. If you live in one of these places, count yourself fortunate, for you'll never run out of stories to discover and share. Otherwise, make a point of visiting—*really* visiting—a small town from time to time. I promise, you won't regret it.

Arlene F. Marks began writing at the age of 6, and she has no plans to stop. A veteran teacher of the craft, she has authored two popular literacy programs for the classroom in addition to conducting numerous workshops. Her short stories have appeared online and in print, notably in an anthology of reimagined fairy tales, *Grimmer Tales Volume One*. She is also the creator/author of the Sic Transit Terra space opera series (from Edge Publishing) and *Adventures in Godhood*, her first of a growing number of books from Brain Lag Publishing. Sic Transit Stragon, a continuation of Sic Transit Terra, launched in January 2025 with *The Stragori Deception*. Arlene lives with her husband on the shore of beautiful Nottawasaga Bay, where she spends an inordinate amount of time exploring imaginary worlds, collecting interesting-looking owls, and helping to bring literary events such as CollingWord and The Word on the Bay to the reading and writing community.

http://thewritersnest.ca/

If you enjoyed *Remains to be Seen*, try:

When Glasgow's only practicing Curse-Breaker is hired to find a missing girl, answers may lie in the wilds of Scotland.

Something's tipped the balance of magic and it's up to tattooed witch AJ to find out what.

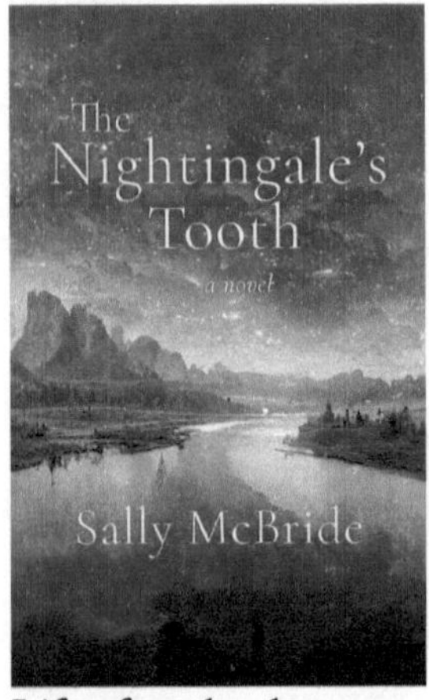

Life after death, uncanny powers born of dust and wind—a dangerous gift for a young woman in medieval France.

AIs maintain the Toronto of the future. But when technology fails, people with extrasensory gifts may be the city's only hope.

See all 50+ titles at brain-lag.com